31.99   1/3/13   31490101

LIONEL ASBO

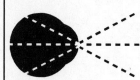

LIONEL ASBO

STATE OF ENGLAND

MARTIN AMIS

THORNDIKE PRESS

A part of Gale, Cengage Learning

GALE
CENGAGE Learning

Detroit • New York • San Francisco • New Haven, Conn • Waterville, Maine • London

GALE
CENGAGE Learning®

LIBRARY OF CONGRESS CATALOGING-IN-PUBLICATION DATA

Amis, Martin.
    Lionel Asbo : state of England / by Martin Amis. — Large print ed.
        p. cm. — (Thorndike Press large print reviewers' choice)
    ISBN-13: 978-1-4104-5359-4 (hardcover)
    ISBN-10: 1-4104-5359-6 (hardcover)
    1. Guardian and ward—Fiction. 2. Hoodlums—Fiction. 3. Lottery winners—Fiction. 4. Great Britain—Social life and customs—Fiction. 5. Satire. I. Title.
    PR6051.M5L56 2012b
    823'.914—dc23   2012034840

Published in 2012 by arrangement with Alfred A. Knopf, Inc., a division of Random House, Inc.

Printed in the United States of America
1 2 3 4 5 6 7 16 15 14 13 12

To Christopher Hitchens

CONTENTS

■ ■ ■ ■

Part I

■ ■ ■ ■

Who let the dogs in?
   . . . This, we fear, is going to be the
   question.
   Who let the dogs in?

Who let the dogs in?
   Who?
   Who?

2006 DESMOND PEPPERDINE, RENAISSANCE BOY

1

Dear Jennaveieve,

I'm having an affair with an older woman. Shes' a lady of some sophistication, and makes a refreshing change from the teen agers I know (like Alektra for example, or Chanel.) The sex is fantastic and I think I'm in love. But ther'es one very serious complication and i'ts this; shes' my Gran!

Desmond Pepperdine (Desmond, Des, Desi), the author of this document, was fifteen and a half. And his handwriting, nowadays, was self-consciously elegant; the letters used to slope backward, but he patiently trained them to slope forward; and when everything was smoothly conjoined he started adding little flourishes (his *e* was positively ornate — like a *w* turned on its side). Using the computer he now shared with his uncle, Des had given himself a course on calligraphy, among several other courses.

On the plus-side, the age-difference is sur-prisingly

He crossed that bit out, and resumed.

It started a fort-night ago when she rang up and said its the plumbing again love. And I said nan? I'll be right over. She lives in a granny flat under a house about a mile away and theres allways some thing wrong with it's plumbing. Now I'm no plumber but I learnd a bit from my Uncle George whose in the trade. I sorted it out for her and she said why not stay for a few drink's? ___

Calligraphy (and sociology, and anthropology, and psychology), but not yet punctuation. He was a good little speller, Des, but he knew how weak his punctuation was because he had just begun a course on it. And punctuation, he (quite rightly) intuited, was something of an art.

So we had a few Dubonnet's which I'm not used to, and she was giving me these funny look's. She's all ways got the Beatles' on and she was playing all the slow one's like Golden Slumber's, Yester-day, and Sh'es Leaving Home. Then gran says its so hot I'll just slip in to my night-dress. And she came back in a babydoll!

He was trying to give himself an education — not at Squeers Free, recently singled out, he read in the *Diston Gazette,* as the worst school in England. But his understanding of the planet and the universe had inconceivable voids in it. He was repeatedly amazed by the tonnage of what he didn't know.

So we had a few more drink's, and I was noticing how well preserved she is. She's taken good care of herself and shes really fit considering the life shes' led. So after a few more drink's she says are'nt you frying alive in that blazer? Come over here handsome, and give us a cuddle! Well what could I do. She put her hand on my thigh and slid it up my short's. Well I'm only human aren't I? The stereo was playing I Should Of Known Better — but one thing lead to another, and it was mind blowing!

For instance, the only national newspaper Des had ever read was the *Morning Lark.* And Jennaveieve, his addressee, was its agony aunt — or better say its ecstasy aunt. The page she presided over consisted of detailed accounts of perhaps wholly imaginary liaisons, and her replies consisted of a lewd pun followed by an exclamation mark. Desmond's tale was not imaginary.

Now you must believe me that this is all very "out of character." It was never mean't to be! Okay we live in Diston, where that sort of thing isnt much frownd up on. And, okay my Gran had a mischivous youth. But she's a respectable woman. The thing is shes got a big birthday coming up and I reckon its turnd her head. As for myself, my background is strict christian at least on my fathers side (Pentecostalist.) And you see Jennaveieve, I've been very unhappy since my Mum, Cilla passed away three year's ago. I can't find the word's. I needed gentleness. And when gran touched me like that. Well.

Des had no intention of actually mailing his letter to Jennaveieve (whose partly naked body also adorned the page headed, not Ecstasy Aunt, but Agony Angel). He was writing it simply to ease his own mind. He imagined Jennaveieve's dependably non-judgemental reply. Something like: *At least you're having a Gran old time!* Des wrote on.

Apart from the legal question which is worrying me sick, theres another huge problem. Her son, Lionel is my uncle, and hes' like a father to me when he's not in prison. See hes an extremely violent criminal and if he find's out I'm giving his Mum one, hell fucking kill me. Litrally!

It might be argued that this was a grave underestimation of Lionel's views on trespass and reprisal . . . The immediate goal, for Des, was to master the apostrophe. After

14

that, the arcana of the colon and the semi-colon, the hyphen, the dash, the slash.

On the plus-side, the age-gap is not that big. See Granny Grace was an early starter, and fell pregnant when she was 12, just like my M

He heard the thick clunks of the locks, he looked with horror at his watch, he tried to stand upright on deadened legs — and suddenly Lionel was there.

2

Lionel was there, a great white shape, leaning on the open door with his brow pressed to his raised wrist, panting huskily, and giving off a faint grey steam in his purple singlet (the lift was misbehaving, and the flat was on the thirty-third floor — but then again Lionel could give off steam while dozing in bed on a quiet afternoon). Under his other arm he was carrying a consignment of lager. Two dozen, covered in polythene. Brand: Cobra.

"You're back early, Uncle Li."

He held up a callused palm. They waited. In his outward appearance Lionel was brutally generic — the slablike body, the full lump of the face, the tight-shaved crown with its tawny stubble. Out in the great world city, there were hundreds of thousands of young men who looked pretty much like Lionel Asbo. In certain lights and settings he resembled, some said, the England and Manchester United prodigy, striker Wayne Rooney: not exceptionally tall, and not fat, but exceptionally broad and exceptionally *deep* (Des saw his uncle every day — and Lionel was always one size bigger than expected). He even had Rooney's gap-toothed smile. Well, the upper incisors were widely spaced, yet Lionel very seldom smiled. You only saw them when he sneered.

". . . What you doing there with that *pen?* What's that you writing? Guiss it."

Des thought fast. "Uh, it's about poetry, Uncle Li."

"*Poetry?*" said Lionel and started back.

"Yeah. Poem called *The Faerie Queene.*"

"The *what? . . .* I despair of you sometimes, Des. Why aren't you out smashing windows? It's not healthy. Oh yeah, listen to this. You know that bloke I bashed up in the pub the other Friday? Mr. 'Ross Knowles,' if you please? He's only pressing charges. Grassed me. Would you credit it."

Desmond knew how Lionel was likely to feel about such a move. One night last year Lionel came home to find Des on the black leatherette sofa, innocently slumped in front of *Crimewatch.* The result was one of the

16

longest and noisiest slappings he had ever received at his uncle's hands. *They asking members of the public,* said Lionel, standing in front of the giant screen with his arms akimbo, *to fink on they own neighbours.* Crimewatch, *it's like a . . . like a programme for* paedophiles, *that is. It disgusts me.* Now Des said,

"He went to the law? Aw, that's . . . That's . . . the lowest of the low, that is. What you going to do, Uncle Li?"

"Well I've been asking around and it turns out he's a loner. Lives in a bedsit. So there's no one I can go and terrify. Except him."

"But he's still in hospital."

"So? I'll take him a bunch of grapes. You feed the dogs?"

"Yeah. Only we're out of Tabasco."

The dogs, Joe and Jeff, were Lionel's psychopathic pitbulls. Their domain was the narrow balcony off the kitchen, where, all day, the two of them snarled, paced, and swivelled — and prosecuted their barking war with the pack of Rottweilers that lived on the roof of the next high-rise along.

"Don't lie to me, Desmond," said Lionel quietly. "Don't ever lie to me."

"I'm not!"

"You told me you fed them. And you never give them they Tabasco!"

17

"Uncle Li, I didn't have the cash! They've only got the big bottles and they're five ninety-five!"

"That's no excuse. You should've nicked one. You spent thirty quid, *thirty quid*, on a fucking dictionary, and you can't spare a couple of bob for the dogs."

"I never spent thirty quid! . . . Gran give it me. She won it on the crossword. The prize crossword."

"Joe and Jeff — they not *pets*, Desmond Pepperdine. They tools of me trade."

Lionel's trade was still something of a mystery to Des. He knew that part of it had to do with the very hairiest end of debt collection; and he knew that part of it involved "selling on" (Lionel's word for selling on was *reset*). Des knew this by simple logic, because Extortion With Menaces and Receiving Stolen Property were what Lionel most often went to prison for . . . He stood there, Lionel, doing something he was very good at: disseminating tension. Des loved him deeply and more or less unquestioningly (*I wouldn't be here today without Uncle Li*, he often said to himself). But he always felt slightly ill in his presence. Not ill at ease. Ill.

". . . You're back early, Uncle Li," he

repeated as airily as he could. "Where you been?"

"Cynthia. I don't know why I bestir meself. Gaa, the *state* of that Cynthia."

The spectral blonde called Cynthia, or *Cymfia*, as he pronounced it, was the nearest thing Lionel had to a childhood sweetheart, in that he started sleeping with her when she was ten (and Lionel was nine). She was also the nearest thing he had to a regular girlfriend, in that he saw her regularly — once every four or five months. Of women in general, Lionel sometimes had this to say: *More trouble than they worth, if you ask me. Women? I'm not bothered. I'm not bothered about women.* Des thought that this was probably just as well: women, in general, should be very pleased that Lionel wasn't bothered about them. One woman bothered him — yes, but she bothered everyone. She was a promiscuous beauty named Gina Drago . . .

"Des. That Cynthia," said Lionel with a surfeited leer. "Christ. Even uh, during the uh, you know, during the other, I was thinking, Lionel, you wasting you youth. Lionel, go home. Go home, boy. Go home and watch some decent porn."

Des picked up the Mac and got smartly to his feet. "Here. I'm off out anyway."

"Yeah? Where? Seeing that Alektra?"

"Nah. Meet up with me mates."

"Well do something useful. Steal a car. Eh, guess what. You Uncle Ringo won the Lottery."

"He never. How much?"

"Twelve pounds fifty. It's a mug's game, the Lottery, if you ask me. Oy. I've been meaning to ask you something. When you creep off at night . . ."

Des was standing there holding the Mac in both hands, like a waiter with a tray. Lionel was standing there with the Cobras in both hands, like a drayman with a load.

"When you creep off at night, you carry a blade?"

"Uncle Li! You know me."

"Well you should. For you own security. And you peace of mind. You going to get youself striped. Or worse. There's no fist-fights any more, not in Diston. There's only knife fights. To the death. Or guns. Well," he relented, "I suppose they can't see you in the fucking dark."

And Des just smiled with his clean white teeth.

"Take a knife from the drawer on you way out. One of them black ones."

Des didn't meet up with his mates. (He

20

didn't have any mates. And he didn't want any mates.) He crept off to his gran's.

As we know, Desmond Pepperdine was fifteen. Grace Pepperdine, who had led a very demanding life and borne many, many children, was a reasonably presentable thirty-nine. Lionel Asbo was a heavily weathered twenty-one.

. . . In dusty Diston (also known as Diston Town or, more simply, Town), nothing — and no one — was over sixty years old. On an international chart for life expectancy, Diston would appear between Benin and Djibouti (fifty-four for men and fifty-seven for women). And that wasn't all. On an international chart for fertility rates, Diston would appear between Malawi and Yemen (six children per couple — or per single mother). Thus the age structure in Diston was strangely shaped. But still: Town would not be thinning out.

Des was fifteen. Lionel was twenty-one. Grace was thirty-nine . . .

He bent to unlatch the gate, he skipped down the seven stone steps, he knocked the knocker. He listened. Here came the shuffle of her fluffy slippers, and in the background (as ever) the melodic purity of a Beatles song. Her all-time favourite: "When I'm Sixty-Four."

3

Dawn simmered over the incredible edifice — the stacked immensity of Avalon Tower.

On the curtained balcony (the size of a tight parking space), Joe lay dreaming of other dogs, enemy dogs, jewel-eyed hellhounds. He barked in his sleep. Jeff rolled over with a blissful sigh.

In bedroom number one (the size of a low-ceilinged squash court, with considerable distances between things, between the door and the bed, between the bed and the wardrobe, between the wardrobe and the free-standing swing mirror), Lionel lay dreaming of prison and his five brothers. They were all in the commissary, queuing for Mars Bars.

And in bedroom number two (the size of a generous four-poster), Des lay dreaming of a ladder that rose up to heaven.

Day came. Lionel left early with Joe and Jeff (business). Des dreamed on.

For six or seven months now he had been sensing it: the pangs and quickenings of intelligence within his being. Cilla, Des's mother, died when he was twelve, and for three years he entered a kind of trance, a leaden sleep; all was numb and Mumless . . . Then he woke up.

He started keeping a diary — and a notebook. There was a voice in his head, and he listened to it and he talked to it. No, he communed with it, he communed with the whispers of his intelligence. Did everybody have one, an inner voice? An inner voice that was cleverer than they were? He thought probably not. Then where did it come from?

Des looked to his family tree — to his personal Tree of Knowledge.

Well, Grace Pepperdine, Granny Grace, had not attended all that closely to her education, for obvious reasons: she was the mother of seven children by the age of nineteen. Cilla came first. All the rest were boys: John (now a plasterer), Paul (a foreman), George (a plumber), Ringo (unemployed), and Stuart (a seedy registrar). Having run out of Beatles (including the "forgotten" Beatle, Stuart Sutcliffe), Grace exasperatedly christened her seventh child Lionel (after a much lesser hero, the choreographer Lionel Blair). Lionel Asbo, as he would later become, was the youngest of a very large family superintended by a single parent who was barely old enough to vote.

Although she did the *Telegraph* crossword (not the Kwik but the Cryptic — she had a weird knack for it), Grace wasn't otherwise a sharp thinker. Cilla, on the other hand, *was as bright as a barrelful of monkeys*, according to Lionel. *"Gifted," they said. Top of her class without even trying. Then she got knocked up with you. She was six months gone when she sat her Eleven Plus. Still passed. But after that, after you come, Des, it was all off.* Cilla Pepperdine didn't bear any more children, but she went on to have as riotous a youth as was humanly possible with a baby in the house — a baby, then a toddler, and then a little boy.

What did he know about his dad? Very little. And it was an ignorance that Cilla largely shared. But everyone knew this about him: he was black. Hence Desmond's resinous colour, *café crème*, with the shadow of something darker in it. Rosewood, perhaps: close-grained, and giving off a distinctive fragrance. He was a sweet-smelling youth, and delicately put together, with regular mint-white teeth and mournful eyes. When he smiled in the mirror, he smiled sadly at the ghost of his father — at the ghost of the lost begetter. But in the waking world he only saw him once.

They were walking up Steep Slope, hand in hand, Des (seven) and Cilla (nineteen), after a spree at the funfair in Happy Valley, when she said suddenly,

"It's *him!*"

"Who?"

"Your father! . . . Look. He's you! . . . Mouth. Nose. Christ!"

Very poorly dressed, and shockingly shod, Des's father was on a metal bench, sitting between a soiled yellow rucksack and five empty flagons of Strongbow. For several minutes Cilla tried to rouse him, with violent shakes and nails-only pinches and, towards the end, alarmingly loud wallops delivered with the flat of her hand.

"D'you think he's *dead?*" Cilla leaned down and put an ear to his chest. "This sometimes works," she said — and intently, lingeringly, kissed his eyes . . . "Hopeless." She straightened up and gave Des's father one last deafening clout. "Oh well. Come on, darling."

She took his hand and walked off fast and Des stumbled along beside her with his head still veering wildly round.

"You sure it's him, Mum?"

"Course I'm sure. Don't be cheeky!"

"Mum, stop! He's waking up. Go and kiss his eyes again. He's stirring."

"No. It's just the wind, love. And I wanted to ask him something. I wanted to ask him his name."

"You said his name was Edwin!"

"That was a guess. You know me. I can remember a face — but I can't remember a name. Ah, Crybaby. Don't . . ." She crouched down beside him. "Listen. I'm sorry, sweetheart. But what can I say? He came and went in an afternoon!"

"You said it lasted a whole week!"

"Ah, don't. Don't, darling. It breaks my heart . . . Listen. He was nice. He was gentle. That's where you get your religion from."

"I'm not religious," he said, and blew into the tissue she was pressing to his nose. "I hate church. I just like the stories. The miracles."

"Well it's where you get your gentleness from, my love. You don't get it from me."

So Des only saw him once (and Cilla, apparently, only saw him twice). And neither of them could possibly know how excruciating this encounter would become in Desmond's memory. For he too, in five years' time, would try very hard to wake someone up — to wake someone up, to bring someone back . . .

It was just a slip, it was just a little slip, just a little slip on the supermarket floor.

■ ■ ■ ■

So Des (now rising from his bed, in the great citadel) — Des thought it would be rash to attribute any great acuity, any great nous, to his father. Who, then, was the source of these rustlings, these delightful expansions, like solar flares, that were going about their work in his mind? Dominic Oldman — that's who.

Grandpa Dom was barely out of primary school when he knocked up Granny Grace with Cilla. But by the time he returned (and stuck around long enough to knock her up with Lionel), he was at the University of Manchester, studying Economics. *University*: it would be hard to exaggerate the reverence and the frequency with which Des murmured this word. His personal translation of it was *the one poem*. For him it meant something like the harmony of the cosmos . . . And he wanted it. He wanted *university* — he wanted the one poem.

And here was the funny thing. Cilla and Lionel were known in the family as "the twins," because they were the only children who had the same father. And Des believed that Lionel (despite his dreadful CV) secretly partook of the Oldman acumen. The difference, it seemed, was one of attitude. Des loved it, his intelligence; and Lionel hated it. Hated it? Well, it was plain as day that he had always fought it, and took pride in being stupid on purpose.

When Des went to his gran's, was he being stupid on purpose? And was she doing it too — when she let him in? After the fateful night came the fateful morning . . .

Got you some milk, he said at the door.

She turned. He followed. Grace took up position on the armchair by the window, in her granny glasses (the circular metal rims), with her powderless face bent penitently over the *Telegraph* crossword. After a while she said,

Frequently arrested, I'm heading east at the last minute. Two, three, four, two, four . . . In the nick of time.

In the nick of time. *How d'you work that one out?*

Frequently arrested — in the nick oft. I'm — i, m. Heading east — e. At the last minute. In the nick of time. *Des. You and I. We're going to go to Hell.*

Ten minutes later, on the low divan, she said, *As long as no one knows. Ever. Where's the harm?*

Yeah. And round here, I mean, it's not

considered that bad.

No, it's not. Uncles and nieces. Fathers and daughters all over the place.

And at the Tower there's that pair of twins living in sin . . . But you and me. Gran, d'you think it's legal?

Don't call me Gran! . . . Maybe a misdemeanour. Because you're not sixteen.

What, like a fine? Yeah, you're probably right. Grace. Still.

Still. Try and stay away, Des. Even if I ask . . . Try and stay away.

And he did try. But when she asked, he went, as if magnetised. He went back — back to the free-fall pantomime of doom.

"The main role of the semicolon," he read in his *Concise Oxford Dictionary*, "is to mark a grammatical separation that is stronger in effect than a comma but less strong than a full stop."

Des had the weight of the book on his lap. It was his prize possession. Its paper jacket was *royal* blue ("deep, vivid").

"You can also use a semicolon as a stronger division in a sentence that already contains commas:

What has crippled me? Was it my grandmother, frowning on my childish affection and turning it to formality and cold courtesy; or was it my pious mother, with her pathological caution; or was it my spineless uncle, who, despite numerous affronts and wrongs, proved incapable of even . . ."

Des heard the dogs. They weren't barking, he realised, not exactly: they were swearing (and the rooftop Rottweilers, faintly and almost plaintively, at this distance, were swearing back).

Fuckoff! yelled Joe (or Jeff). It was almost a monosyllable. *Fuckoff! . . . Fuck! . . . Fuck! . . . Fuckoff!*

Fuckoff! yelled Jeff (or Joe). *Fuckoff! . . . Fuck! . . . Fuck! . . . Fuckoff!*

4

"Dogs," said Lionel, "they descended from wolves. That's they heritage. Now *wolves*," he went on, "they not man's natural enemy. Oh no. You wolf won't attack a human. That's a myth, that is, Des. A total myth."

Des listened. Lionel pronounced "myth" *miff*. Full possessive pronouns — *your, their, my* — still made guest appearances in his English, and he didn't invariably defy grammatical number (*they was*, and so on). But his verbal prose and his accent were in steep decline. Until a couple of years ago Lionel pronounced "Lionel" *Lionel*. But these days he pronounced "Lionel" *Loyonel*, or even *Loyonoo*.

"Now I know you reckon I'm harsh with Jeff and Joe. But that's for why. To make them attack humans — at me own bidding . . . It's about time I got them pissed again."

Every couple of weeks Lionel got the dogs pissed on Special Brews. Interesting, that, thought Des. In America, evidently, *pissed* meant angered, or pissed off; in England, *pissed* just meant drunk. After six cans each of potent malt lager, Jeff and Joe were pissed in both senses. *Course, they useless when they actually pissed*, said Lionel. *They come on tough but they can't hardly walk. It's the next morning — ooh. That's when they tasty* . . . That *ooh* sounded more like *où*. Nor was this the only example of Lionel's inadvertent French. He also used *un* — as a modest expletive, denoting frustration, effort, or even mild physical pain. Now Des said,

"You got them pissed Saturday before last."

"Did I? What for?"

"You had that meet with the shark from Redbridge. Sunday morning."

31

Lionel said, "So I did, Des. So I did."

They were enjoying their usual breakfast of sweet milky tea and Pop-Tarts (there were also a few tins of Cobra close to hand). Like Lionel's room, the kitchen was spacious, but it was dominated by two items of furniture that made it feel cramped. First, the wall-wide TV, impressive in itself but almost impossible to watch. You couldn't get far enough away from it, and the colours swam and everyone wore a wraithlike nimbus of white. Whatever was actually showing, Des always felt he was watching a documentary about the Ku Klux Klan. Item number two, known as *the tank*, was a cuboid gunmetal rubbish bin, its dimensions corresponding to those of an average dishwasher. *It not only looks smart*, said Lionel, as with Des's help he dragged it out of the lift. *It's a fine piece of machine-tooled workmanship. German. Christ. Weighs enough.* But this item, too, had its flaw.

Lionel now lit a cigarette and said, "You been sitting on it."

"I never."

"Then why won't it open?"

"It hardly ever opened, Uncle Li," said Des. "Right from the start." They had been through this many times before. "And when it does open, you can't get it shut."

32

"It sometimes opens. It's no fucking use to man or beast, is it. Shut."

"I lost half a nail trying to open it."

Lionel leaned over and gave the lid a tug. "*Un* . . . You been sitting on it."

They ate and drank in silence.

"Ross Knowles."

There followed a grave debate, or a grave disquisition, on the difference between ABH and GBH — between Actual Bodily Harm and its sterner older brother, Grievous. Like many career delinquents, Lionel was almost up to PhD level on questions of criminal law. Criminal law, after all, was the third element in his vocational trinity, the other two being villainy and prison. When Lionel talked about the law (reaching for a kind of high style), Des always paid close attention. Criminal law was in any case much on his mind.

"In a nutshell, Des, in a nutshell, it's the difference between the first-aid kit and the casualty ward."

"And this Ross Knowles, Uncle Li. How long's he been in Diston General?" asked Des (referring to the worst hospital in England).

"Oy. Objection. That's prejudicial."

Panting and drooling, Jeff and Joe stared

in through the glass door: brickfaced, with thuggish foreheads, and their little ears trying to point towards each other.

"Why prejudicial?"

"Hypothesis." *Hypoffesis*. "I give Ross Knowles a little tap in a fair fight, he comes out of the Hobgoblin — and walks under a truck." Truck: pronounced *truc-kuh* (with a glottal stop on the terminal plosive). "See? Prejudicial."

Des nodded. It was in fact strongly rumoured that Ross Knowles came out of the Hobgoblin on a stretcher.

"According to the Offences Against the Person Act," Lionel went on, "there's Common Assault, ABH, and G. It's decided, Des, by you level of intent and the seriousness of the injury. Offensive weapon, offensive weapon of any kind, you know, something like a beer glass — that's G. If he needs a blood transfusion — that's G. If you kick him in the bonce — that's G."

"What did you use on him, Uncle Li?"

"A beer glass."

"Did he need a blood transfusion?"

"So they say."

"And did you kick him in the bonce?"

"No. I jumped on it. In me trainers, mind . . . Uh, visible disfigurement or

34

permanent disability — that's the clincher, Des."

"And in this case, Uncle Li?"

"Well I don't know, do I. I don't know what sort of nick he was in before."

". . . Why d'you smash him up?"

"Didn't like the smile on his face." Lionel gave his laugh — a series of visceral grunts. "No. I'm not *that* thick." (*Thic-kuh.*) "I had two reasons, Des. Ross Knowles — I heard Ross Knowles saying something about buying a banger off Jayden Drago. And he's got the same moustache as Marlon. Ross has. So I smashed him up."

"Hang on." Des tried to work it out (he went in search of the sequitur). Jayden Drago, the renowned used-car salesman, was Gina Drago's father. And Marlon, Marlon Welkway, was Lionel's first cousin (and closest associate). "I still don't get it."

"Jesus. Haven't you heard? Marlon's pulled Gina! Yeah. Marlon's pulled Gina . . . So all that come together in me mind. And it put me in a mood." For a while Lionel gnawed on his thumb. He looked up and said neutrally, "I'm still hoping for Common Assault. But me brief said the injuries were uh, *more consistent with Attempted Manslaughter.* So we'll see. Are you going to school today?"

"Yeah, I thought I might look in."

"Ah, you such a little angel. Come on."

They refilled the water bowls. Then man and boy filed down the thirty-three floors. Lionel, as usual, went to the corner shop for his smokes and his *Morning Lark* while Des waited out on the street.

". . . Fruit, Uncle Li? Not like you. You don't eat fruit."

"Yeah I do. What you think a Pop-Tart is? Look. Nice bunch of grapes. See, I got a friend who's uh, indisposed. Thought I'd go and cheer him up. Put this in you satchel."

He handed over the bottle of Tabasco. Plus an apple.

"A nice Granny Smith. For you teacher."

To evoke the London borough of Diston, we turn to the poetry of Chaos:

Each thing hostile
To every other thing: at every point
Hot fought cold, moist dry, soft hard, and
   the weightless
Resisted weight.

So Des lived his life in tunnels. The tunnel from flat to school, the tunnel (not the same tunnel) from school to flat. And all the warrens that took him to Grace, and brought him back again. He lived his life in tunnels . . . And yet for the sensitive soul, in Diston Town, there was really only one place to look. Where did the eyes go? They went up, up.

School — Squeers Free, under a sky of white: the weakling headmaster, the demoralised chalkies in their rayon tracksuits, the ramshackle little gym with its tripwires and booby traps, the Lifestyle Consultants (Every Child Matters), and the Special Needs Coordinators (who dealt with all the "non-readers"). In addition, Squeers Free set the standard for the most police call-outs, the least GCSE passes, and the highest truancy rates. It also led the pack in suspensions, expulsions, and PRU "offrolls"; such an offroll — a transfer to a Pupil Referral Unit — was usually the doorway to a Youth Custody Centre and then a Young Offender Institution. Lionel, who had followed this route, always spoke of his five and a half years (on and off) in a Young Offender Institution (or *Yoi*, as he called it) with rueful fondness, like one recalling a rite of passage — inevitable, bittersweet. *I was out for a month*, he would typically reminisce. *Then I was back up north. Doing me Yoi.*

■ ■ ■ ■

On the other hand, Squeers Free had in its
staff room an exceptional Learning Mentor
— a Mr. Vincent Tigg.

*What's going on with you, Desmond? You
were always an idle little sod. Now you can't
get enough of it. Well, what next?*

*I fancy modern languages, sir. And history.
And sociology. And astronomy. And —*

You can't study everything, you know.

Yes I can. Renaissance boy, innit.

*. . . You want to watch that smile, lad. All
right. We'll see about you. Now off you go.*

And in the schoolyard? On the face of it,
Des was a prime candidate for persecution.
He seldom bunked off, he never slept in
class, he didn't assault the teachers or shoot
up in the toilets — and he preferred the
company of the gentler sex (the gentler sex,
at Squeers Free, being quite rough enough).
So in the normal course of things Des
would have been savagely bullied, as all the
other misfits (swats, wimps, four-eyes,
sweating fatties) were savagely bullied — to
the brink of suicide and beyond. They called
him Skiprope and Hopscotch, but Des
wasn't bullied. How to explain this? To use
Uncle Ringo's favourite expression, it was *a*

no-brainer. Desmond Pepperdine was inviolable. He was the nephew, and ward, of Lionel Asbo.

It was different on the street. Once a term, true, Lionel escorted him to Squeers Free, and escorted him back again the same day (restraining, with exaggerated difficulty, the two frothing pitbulls on their thick steel chains). But it would be foolish to suppose that each and every gangbanger and posse-artist (and every Yardie and jihadi) in the entire manor had heard tell of the great asocial. And it was different at night, because different people, different shapes, levered themselves upward after dark . . . Des was fleet of foot, but he was otherwise unsuited to life in Diston Town. Second or even first nature to Lionel (who was pronounced "uncontrollable" at the age of eighteen months), violence was alien to Des, who always felt that violence — extreme and ubiquitous though it certainly seemed to be — came from another dimension.

So, this day, he went down the tunnel and attended school. But on his way home he feinted sideways and took a detour. With hesitation, and with deafening self-consciousness, he entered the Public Library on Blimber Road. Squeers Free had a library, of course, a distant Portakabin with a few primers and ripped paperbacks scattered across its floor . . . But this: rank upon rank of proud-chested bookcases, like lavishly decorated generals. By what right or title could you claim any share of it? He entered the Reading Room, where the newspapers, firmly clamped to long wooden struts, were apparently available for scrutiny. No one stopped him as he approached.

He had of course *seen* the dailies before, in the corner shop and so on, and there were Gran's *Telegraph*s, but his experience of actual newsprint was confined to the *Morning Lark*s that Lionel left around the flat, all scrumpled up, like origami tumbleweeds (there was also the occasional *Diston Gazette*). Respectfully averting his eyes from the *Times*, the *Independent*, and the *Guardian*, Des reached for the *Sun*, which at least *looked* like a *Lark*, with its crimson logo and the footballer's fiancée on the cover staggering out of a nightclub with blood running down her neck. And, sure enough, on page three (News in Briefs) there was a hefty redhead wearing knickers and a sombrero.

But then all resemblances ceased. You got scandal and gossip, and more girls, but also international news, parliamentary reports,

40

comment, analysis . . . Until now he had accepted the *Morning Lark* as an accurate reflection of reality. Indeed, he sometimes thought it was a local paper (a light-hearted adjunct to the *Gazette*), such was its fidelity to the customs and mores of his borough. Now, though, as he stood there with the *Sun* quivering in his hands, the *Lark* stood revealed for what it was — a daily lads' mag, perfunctorily posing as a journal of record.

The *Sun*, additionally to recommend it, had an agony column presided over not by the feckless Jennaveieve, but by a wise-looking old dear called Daphne, who dealt sympathetically, that day, with a number of quite serious problems and dilemmas, and suggested leaflets and helplines, and seemed genuinely . . .

"Dear Daphne," whispered Desmond.

5

Turn the clock back to January and the eve of his fifteenth birthday.

Uncle Lionel was out on the balcony, chivvying the dogs. Des, in a white apron (at that time he had done no wrong and knew no guile), was washing up.

Come out here, Des. Forget you housework . . . Listen. You forbidden to go to school tomorrow.

41

Why's this, Uncle Li?

Tell you in the morning . . . Des. Girls. Have you done it? No, don't answer. I don't want to know. Look at you in you white pinny. Fourteen.

Des was woken by a gust of cigarette smoke. He squinted up with his unfallen eyes. Lionel, in a black mesh T-shirt, boded over him.

Shove up, he said, and sat. *Okay. You a young man now. You fifteen. And an orphan. So you got to listen to you Uncle Li.*

Yeah. Course.

Right. From this day forth, son, you can borrow me Mac. When I'm out.

Smiling, Des said thanks, and he meant it. He also had that familiar sense of Lionel as a kind of anti-dad or counterfather.

But listen. Lionel raised a stubby forefinger. *It's not just for messing around with. I want you to concentrate you efforts.*

On what?

Porn.

In common with every other Distonite old enough to walk, Des knew about the existence of pornography on the Web. He had never gone looking for it. *Porn, Uncle Li?*

Porn. You see, Des, this is it. You don't actually need *girls. Girls? They more trouble than*

42

they worth if you ask me. With the Mac, you can have three new bunk-ups every day — just by using you imagination! And it doesn't cost you fuck all. Okay. Lecture over. So endeth the first lesson. Just promise you'll ponder me words. And here's an extra fiver for yuh.

Lionel got to his feet. He grinned (a rare occurrence) and said,

Go on, fill you boots . . . When I come back tonight, you'll be holding a white stick. In you hairy palm. His grin deepened. *I just hope Jeff and Joe hit it off with you guide dog. And here's a tip*: Fucked-up Facials. *Start you off on the right foot. Well, son. Happy birthday. I'm glad we had this talk. It's cleared the air.*

Des did, in fact, have a quick look at *Fucked-up Facials*. And the site, he found, was accurately so called: he had never seen anything half so fucked-up in all his life. After gaping his way through thirty seconds of that, he clicked on History. There was no doubt about it. The pornography Lionel watched was in highly questionable taste. So for an hour Des randomly surfed, or foundered, in the Pacific of filth. This surfing or foundering, he realised with a kind of terror, was a way of finding out who you were, sexually, by finding out what you liked

43

— whether you liked what you liked or not.

And what did he like, Des Pepperdine? Well, his soul instantly and reassuringly recoiled from anything weird. Or anything rough. In churning and interminable close-up, even straightfoward copulation looked horrific (this is what happens, he suddenly thought, when a zoo rapes an aquarium). And all these stripped blokes, with biker or convict faces, and their third-degree tattoos . . . The lez stuff was okay, but what he liked, it turned out, was this: a pretty girl acting alone, slowly undressing (it was never slowly enough), and indulging, perhaps, in a discreet self-caress — with the lighting all misty and vague. Practically everything else seemed gladiatorial. I'm a romantic! he thought. I knew it . . . And after a pensive interlude, under the auspices of *Strictly Solo Tease* and more particularly a wandlike blonde called Cadence Meadowbrook, Des put the Web aside, reached for the Cloud, and started learning about calligraphy.

The Cloud, the Web: it was the fruit of the Tree of Knowledge — the Knowledge of Good and Evil. It was the modern Fall. And there was no going back.

You're doing that funny face again, he said during his next session with Alektra.

What funny face?

44

*Like you're looking in a mirror. Or at a
camera . . . Ow. That hurts.*

Chanel was the same — and Joslinne, and
Jade. What did you expect? They had started
learning about the birds and the bees (in
high definition) when they were three.

*. . . Why're you always spitting and saying
how* nasty *you are?*

Boys expect it.

He said, *Not me. You see, love, I'm a
romantic. It's just the way I'm made.*

And it was all so very different with Grace.

That first time, when she was giving him
the funny looks, he was paralysed by the
unreality of it all, what with the Dubonnets
— and then the babydoll! *Come over here,
handsome, and give us a cuddle.* This was
the unalterable premise: he couldn't hurt
her, he couldn't spurn her, it wasn't in him,
it wasn't the way he was made. So he
walked across the room. And what a long
walk that was — fifteen feet, across the
granny flat, from grace to Grace. He walked
across the room because of the clear impos-
sibility of doing otherwise, and entered the
heedless world of the deaf. Then he lay back
and succumbed to an experiment — an
experiment in gentleness. And the texture
of her flesh to the touch, with that strange

give in it, and the depth of all that lived life, now brought languidly to bear on him and his body.

Oh, you're so beautiful, Desi my dearest. It hurts my heart you're so beautiful.

And his heart, in its turn, flared up on him, like an inner climax running through his chest to his throat. He kissed her neck. She touched his brow. On the table was a jar of strawberry jam with a spoon in it. The stereo, with its tiny but furious red eye, was playing "If I Fell."

That was in March, and now it was April. It was April, with its drip drip drip . . .

"Des, there's something I never told you."

They were getting dressed. It was all behind them for the moment — the sound-proofed laboratory of sin.

"What's that, Gran? Sorry. What's that, Grace?"

"Remember — remember when I used to have gentlemen friends? Remember Toby?"

"Toby. I remember. And Kevin."

"And Kevin. Guess why I stopped."

"Why?"

"Because of Lionel . . . Remember the summer your grandad died?"

Dominic Oldman was out fishing with his boy Mark (the one child of his twelve-year

46

marriage to a pharmacist named Eileen). And suddenly nature became too big and too loud, and Mark slipped down the bank and into the headstrong River Avon, and Dominic went in after him. Only Mark came back — only Mark came back from under the thick nets of the mists.

"They let Lionel out of Yoi for the cremation. You were there, Des. After it was over, he sees me home, he comes in here, and he takes the Bible down from the shelf. And he jams my hand on it and makes me swear. *No more of your bleeding geezers, Mum*, he says. *No more of your nonsense, woman. You're past it anyway. It's all over.*"

Des pictured himself — that day in Golders Green, wearing white shirt, blue tie, black longs. He was ten. Gran would have been thirty-four.

"And he scared me. He really did." She held her wrist and rotated it. "Time goes by and Toby pops in for a cup of tea. He's been here half an hour and the doorbell rings. Lionel. He drags poor Toby out by his hair and gives him a right mauling there on the steps. For a cup of tea! Ooh. Mean Mr. Mustard. See, he's got *spies* . . . Don't look so stricken, Des! It's all right with you — you're in and out all the time anyway. And I'm your gran."

47

She gave her strange new spiralling laugh, reached for the crossword, and sat down with a bounce on the windowside armchair.

"Eight letters . . . It's an anagram. Got it. *Features*."

"Yeah? What's the clue?"

"Mug smashed after use."

As he walked through the spangles of an April shower (he was going to the sub-post office for an envelope and a first-class stamp), Des was thinking of things his mother told him — about Lionel as a child.

The nickname Mean Mr. Mustard was derived from the Beatles song, and referred not just to Lionel's spite but also to his stinginess (*Sleeps in a hole in the road . . . Keeps a ten-bob note up his nose. Such a* mean *old man*). He earned the nickname during his toddler period — he was an implacable hoarder and non-sharer. If any of the brothers played with his toys (even when he wasn't there), they lived to wish they hadn't. John, Paul, George, Ringo and Stuart were all very afraid of their little brother. John, who was then aged seven, told Cilla, who was then aged eight, that he was very afraid of Lionel, who was then aged two.

Last thing at night little Lionel would seal

the lid of his toybox with a moistened strand of hair plucked from his own scalp. So he could tell if anyone took a liberty while he was asleep . . . Then he made his enquiries (it was nearly always Ringo); and the next time *Ringo* was asleep, Lionel would steal up on him wielding his heaviest Transformer.

He was served his first Restraining Directive when he was three. Three years and two days: a national record (though disputed by other claimants). This was for smashing car windscreens with paving stones; the authorities also noted his habit, when out shopping with his mother, of booting over display pyramids of bottles and tin cans; a childish interest in cruelty to animals was perhaps only to be expected, but Lionel went further, and one night made a serious attempt to torch a pet shop. Had he come along half a generation later, Lionel's first Restraining Directive would have been called a BASBO, or Baby ASBO . . . ASBO, which (as all the kingdom now knew) stood for Anti-Social Behaviour Order.

What was the matter with him? Why did he *work* at being stupid? I mean (thought Des), if you spend about a third of your waking life in court, isn't it a bit bloody daft to change your name, by deed poll, on your eighteenth birthday, from Lionel Pepperdine to Lionel Asbo? All his uncle would say was that *Pepperdine's a crap name anyhow. And Asbo has a nice ring to it.* This was literally the case: Lionel would flaunt his electronic loop (it looked like an ankle strap with a battery attached), even as he took the stand at the Old Bailey (*Ah yes. Mr. . . . "Asbo." Mr. Asbo, this is not the first time you have . . .*). You could only do that if you gave being stupid a lot of very intelligent thought.

Dear Daphne, wrote Desmond in the Library Reading Room.

I'm a young Liverpudlian (15) and I'm having an affair with my grandmother. Obviously, it's not an ideal situation. We both live in Kensington, which sounds posh but is in fact the poorest area in the city (we call it "Kenny"). I'm on a charity trip to London to watch "the Reds" play West Ham, which explains the postmark.

Could you fill me in on the legal side of it? This is worrying me to distraction. And when that point is cleared up, I'll write again (if that's alright) about my uncle and the other problem I face. You see, Daphne, I'm very <u>confused</u>.

Maybe I should come clean about living in Diston, he thought. Then she'd under-

50

stand. I mean it's a different demographic . . . Des shrugged. No, it was okay. "Kenny" must surely be almost as bad.

A chat on one of your HelpLines might be a good idea. And do you have any pamphlets you think I should read?

6

In Diston there were many thousands of pylons, and they all sizzled. The worst stretch of Cuttle Canal was as active as a geyser: it spat and splatted, blowing thick-lipped kisses to the hastening passers-by. Beyond Jupes Lanes sprawled Stung Meanchey (so christened by its inhabitants, who were Korean), a twelve-acre dump of house-high electronic waste, old computers, televisions, phones and fridges: lead, mercury, beryllium, aluminium. Diston hummed. Background radiation, background music for a half-life of fifty-five years.

He heard Lionel attacking the locks. The snaps and rattles dispersed his soothing daydream. In this daydream, diligent Daphne was applying herself to a tall stack of mail. She unsheathed Desmond's letter; her frown melted into a lenient twinkle; and she started to type her reply. *You poor dear, you must have been worried out of your wits. And all for no reason! Happily, following an amendment to the law in 1979, it is no longer . . .* But now Lionel stomped in. Lionel stomped in, with two unlabelled quart bottles of liquor (one of them half empty), plus a takeaway mutton vindaloo — for the dogs.

"I tasted success," he said, "with Ross Knowles. At the tenth attempt. But here. Summon up all you courage, Des, and have a look at this."

Lionel seemed stirred, stimulated, if not downright drunk (and, as always, one size bigger than expected). Yet Des could tell that something was wrong, and he sensed danger . . . Lionel wasn't drunk — he never got drunk. He put away suicidal quantities of alcohol; and he never got drunk. It was the same with dope, blow, crack, aitch, e, and methamphetamine. Nothing had any effect on him (there was no intoxication, and no repercussion). In this sphere at least, Lionel was steady-state. But tonight he had a look of lit purpose in him, and something was wrong.

Lionel now upended the quart bottle and took six swallows, seven, eight. He wiped his mouth on his wrist and said, "This is what this country's come to, Des. A national newspaper printing *this*." With finger and thumb, and with some show of fastidiousness, Lionel took from his back pocket a rolled copy of the *Morning Lark*. "Second page of Classifieds. They calling them *GILFs*."

"Jesus . . . That one's seventy-eight!"

"GILFs, Des. Topless at seventy-eight. What's she doing still *living* at seventy-eight? Leave alone topless! And that's a uh, a contradiction in terms, that is, Des. GILFs. Grans I'd Like to . . . Nobody'd *like* to fuck a gran. Now would they. Contradiction in terms." Lionel added vaguely, "Suppose you could call them NILFs."

"NILFs?"

"NILFs. Nans I'd Like to . . . And that's England, Des. A once-proud nation. Look. *Beefy Bedmate Sought by Bonking Biddy*. That's England."

It was a clear night in early May with a tang of chill in it. Des wiped the sweat from his upper lip.

". . . What's up with you, Des? You got a funny look on you face."

"No, I'm fine, Uncle Li. So uh, so you got a result today. With Ross Knowles."

"What? Oh. Change of subject, is it." He yawned and went on blandly, "Yeah, I'm outside the Watch Ward with me grapes.

And here I've had a bit of luck. The copper's there — but he's on a stretcher. With blood coming out of his ears. One of them uh, superbugs, I don't know."

Des shrugged and said, "Diston General."

"Yeah. Diston General . . . So now I'm stood over the bed and he opens his eyes. I never raised me voice above a whisper. I said uh, *Remember me, Mr. Knowles? Or may I call you Ross? I sincerely apologise, Ross, for any distress caused. See, that night, I wasn't meself. I was suffering for* love. *For love, Ross. How would you feel, how would you feel, Ross, if the girl of you dreams got porked by you best mate?*"

"He say anything, Uncle Li?"

"No. His jaws're wired shut. Then I go, *You got to understand, Ross, that I'm a very unbalanced young man. Now if you proceed with this matter, I'll be inside for — what? Eight months? A year? But when I come out, Ross, I'll do you again. Only worse. And go straight back inside. Because I'm* stupid, *I am. I'm* stupid . . . So he had a think and we settled out of court."

"What you give him?"

"I give him a bunch of grapes." Lionel stood up and said, "I call it the moron theory, Des. You can't go wrong with it. Okay. Where's they Tabasco?"

■ ■ ■ ■

The dogs were tonguing the glass door. Lionel stood at the counter by the fridge, shaking out jets of chilli over the fuming meat. With the two bowls under the span of his palms, he slid and then kicked his way out on to the balcony. Des readied the rogan josh.

"Ah, rogan josh," said Lionel. "You know where you are with a rogan josh."

As they poked at their food (Lionel was in any case an erratic eater, and Des felt full to his craw), a heavy silence began to fuse and climb. A muscular, pumped-up, steroidal silence, a Lionel silence, shrill enough to smother the parched whimpers of Jeff and Joe . . .

"It's too hot for them," mouthed Des drily.

Now Lionel flung his irons aside. He turned and stiffly extended his legs, and folded his arms with a grunt. Minutes passed. He stood, and took several turns round the room, staring critically at his shoes. Minutes passed.

"You know, I'm ever so slightly concerned," he said, "about you gran."

"Yeah?" Des swallowed. "Why's that?"

"Her morals."

"Her morals?"

"Yeah, you know old Dudley."

"Dudley. Yeah." Dudley was the cheerful racist in the next granny flat along.

"Dudley. Old Dud. He reckons he hears *noises.*"

". . . What sort of noises?"

"Groans." Lionel looked ceilingward. "As if, God forbid, someone's giving her one . . ."

Des managed to say, "Uh, that's prejudicial, that is, Uncle Li. Could be groaning from something else. Pain."

"You know, Des, that's exactly what *I* thought. That's exactly what *I* thought. In fact, I give old Dud a thump for the uh, for the insinuation. She'd never do that to me, Mum. Not Mum, mate! Not my mum!"

For a moment Des believed that Lionel was about to start crying; but his face cleared and he said conversationally,

"I know she used to see the odd bloke. Toby and that. But when Dominic passed away she had a change of heart. Turned over a new leaf. She said to me, *Lionel? When you dad died, he give up his life for his little boy. He'd've done the same for you. Or for Cilla. And I'm going to respect that, Lionel. Respect Dom's memory. So no more of me blokes.* And she has a little laugh and says,

And look at me. I'm well past it anyway! . . .
But now — but now there's these *groans.*"

Des said, "I'm in and out all the time. And
I never see anything."

"Mm. Well keep you eyes peeled, Des.
Look in the bathroom. Razor. Extra tooth-
brush. Anything uh, untoward."

"Course I will."

"Mm . . . The groaning granny. It's pain.
That's all it is. It's her time of life. Gaa,
Des, you wouldn't believe what they suffer.
During the Change. It's they insides. You
creeping off again tonight?"

Des had a date with Gran. He scratched
his chest and said, "Nah. I'll stop home.
Watch the football. Might take the dogs out.
In a bit."

". . . It's they insides. There's all this stuff
down there *raring* to go wrong . . . *My* mum
some GILF? No. *My* mum some bonking
biddy? No."

Minutes later Des reeled down the infinite
staircase with Jeff and Joe. Now this really
did do his head in — because Gran *never*
groaned. Not with pain, not with passion.
He brought his fingertips to his temples and
searched the windtunnels and the echo
chambers of his aural memory. He heard
her laughter (the long-ago laughter), he

57

heard her sing scraps of Beatles songs, and again he heard her laughter (the more recent laughter, abandoned, and with an unnerving edge to it). But Gran never groaned. It was Jade and Alektra who kicked up a racket (at least when their mums weren't indoors) — not Gran. Gran groan? Never . . .

In the forecourt he ducked into the sketchily vandalised phonebox.

Does Gran groan because she's got some wasting disease she never told me about? Or does she groan because she — !

The thought stopped dead.

He made the call and postponed their meeting for twenty-four hours. He didn't tell Gran anything, yet, about Dudley and the groans.

7

Day came. He heard a snatch, a twist, of weak birdsong; slowly the city heaved into life; and by eight o'clock the whole Tower was a foundry of DIY — hammers, grinders, the gnawing whine of power sanders . . . Des took a shower and drank a cup of tea. Lionel was sleeping in; he had gone out late and stayed out late (boisterously returning just after five). His door was open, and for a moment Des paused in the passage. This was once his mother's room. That tall swing mirror: she used to appraise herself in front of it, with a palm flat on her midriff, full face, in profile, once again full face; and then she'd be gone. Now Lionel rolled on to his back — the heaving chest, the dredging snore.

Outside it was bright and dry — and drunkenly stormy. Gates flapped and banged, dustbins tumbled, shutters clattered. And Des, today, felt that he would give his eyesight for a minute's peace, a minute's quiet. Just to get his head straight. But his thoughts wandered, and he wandered after them, under a swift and hectic sky. Women, mothers, noticed it, the density of trouble in the childish roundness of his face. Long-legged in shorts and blazer, carrying a satchel, and stopping every ten yards to run tremulous fingers through the close files of his hair.

. . . On the streets of Cairo the ambient noise, scientifically averaged out, was ninety decibels, or the equivalent of a freight train passing by at a distance of fourteen feet (the ambient noise caused partial deafness, neuroses, heart attacks, miscarriages). Town wasn't quite as noisy as Cairo, but it was famous for its auto-repair yards, sawmills, and tanneries, and for its lawless traffic; it seemed also to get more than its fair share of demolitions, roadworks, municipal tree-prunings and leaf-hooverings, and more than its fair share of car alarms, burglar alarms, and fire alarms (the caff hates the van! the bike hates the shop! the pub hates the bus!), and, of course, more than its fair share of sirens.

In this sector of the world city, compact technology had not yet fully supplanted the blaring trannies and boom boxes and windowsill hi-fi speakers. People yelled at each other anyway, but now they yelled all the louder. Nor were Jeff and Joe the only neighbourhood dogs who suffered from canine Tourette's. The foul-mouthed pit-bulls, the screeching cats, the grimily milling pigeons; only the fugitive foxes observed their code of silence.

Diston, with its burping, magmatic canal, its fizzy low-rise pylons, its buzzing waste. Diston — a world of italics and exclamation marks.

On his way to school Des slipped into the Public Library on Blimber Road. This was a place where you could actually hear yourself cough, sigh, breathe — where you could hear the points and junctions of your own sinuses. He made straight for the radiant Reading Room with its silvery motes of dust.

First, naturally, he wrenched open the *Sun*, and thrashed his way to "Dear Daphne." Worries about getting an erection, worries about keeping an erection, the many girls whose married boyfriends wouldn't leave their wives, the many boys who loved the feel of women's clothing: all this, but nothing about a fifteen-year-old and his nan. Eleven days had passed since he posted his letter. Why hadn't Daphne printed it? Was it too terrible? No (or so a part of him still wanly hoped): it was too trivial.

Des closed his eyes and saw himself in the granny flat at the age of thirteen. He was, as usual, weeping into his sleeve — while Gran stroked his hair and softly hummed along with that emollient melody, "Hey Jude." *Hey Jude, don't make it bad, Take a sad song And make it better.* The hugs, the hand-clasps, the vast and trackless silences. Gran said that grief was like the sea; you had to ride the tides (*So let it out and let it in, hey Jude, begin*), and then, after months, after years . . .

Now in the sidestreet two hammer drills revved up, atomising his thoughts. And just then an old janitor (the one with the pony-tail and the dented cheeks) stuck his head

61

round the door.

"Why you not in school?"

"Got a project," said Des. And reapplied himself to his *Sun*.

International news. Slaughter in Darfur. N. Korea's breakout N-test? Dozens slain in Mex drug clash . . . After a look over his shoulder, he reached out an unsteady hand for the *Independent* (which was at least recognisably tabloidal in size). He expected the spidery print to exclude him. But it didn't; it let him in . . . Des read all the international news in the *Independent*, and then moved on to the *Times*. When he looked at his watch it was half past four (and he was keenly hungry).

He had spent eight hours in the place called World.

"I've been reading the papers."

"What papers?"

"The proper ones. The *Guardian* and that."

"You don't want to read the papers, Des," said Lionel, turning the page of his *Morning Lark* and smoothly realigning its wings: Hubbie Nabbed Over Wheelie Bin Corpse Find. With a look of the sharpest disapproval, he added, "All that's none of you concern."

"So you don't follow it — all that . . .

Uncle Li, why are we in Iraq?" Lionel turned the page: Noreen's Lezbo Boob Romp Shock. "Or don't you know about Iraq?"

"Course I know about Iraq," he said without looking up. "9/11, mate. See, Des, on 9/11, these blokes with J-cloths on they heads went and —"

"But Iraq had nothing to do with 9/11!"

"So? . . . Des, you being very naïve. See, America's top boy. He's the Daddy. And after a fucking liberty like 9/11, well, it's all off, and the Daddy lashes out."

"Yeah, but who at?"

"Doesn't matter who at. Anyone'll do. Like me and Ross Knowles. It's the moron theory. Keeps them all honest."

Lionel turned the page: Knife Yobs Dodge Nick, Proves Probe. Des sat back and said wonderingly,

"When it started, Uncle Li. I mean don't we have allies in the region? They can't've been too happy about it. The instability. Our allies in the region."

"Allies?" said Lionel wearily. "What allies?"

"Uh, Saudi Arabia. Turkey . . . Egypt. I bet they weren't too pleased."

"*So?* Jesus Christ, Des, you can't half bang on."

"They're our allies. What did we tell them?"

Lionel dropped his head. "What you think we told them? We told them, *Listen. We doing Iraq, all right? And if you fucking want some, you can fucking have some and all.*" He levelled his shoulders. "Now shut it. I'm reading this."

And Des entertained the image of a planet-sized Hobgoblin at twelve o'clock on a Friday night. This was the place called World.

"Gaa. Look, Des. More GILFs."

The cat was there again. The cat was there again — at the end of the tunnel that led to Grace. Hairless and whiskerless, as bald as a white hotwater bottle, with its soft, ancient, ear-hurting cry . . . He pressed the bell, and heard the fluffy pink slippers padding towards the mat (as the tape played "Dear Prudence").

"Gran," he was almost immediately saying. "The groans."

"Groans? What are you talking about?"

He told her. "And you *don't* groan, do you," he said. "Do you?"

". . . I *do* groan," she said carefully. "Now and then. You just don't notice. Ah, old *Dud*, what would he know?"

"Stop laughing like that! How many Dubonnets've you had?"

"Now you stay just where you are, young sir."

"No, Grace . . . Well get a pillow then. In case you groan. And put the Beatles up!"

Later, as she smoked a thickly appreciated Silk Cut, Grace said mysteriously (and she would not enlarge on it), "Oh, Des, you're gorgeous. But the trouble is . . . The trouble is, love, you've been giving me ideas!"

8

Another week passed. Then it all came to a head — on a day of three-ply horror for Desmond Pepperdine.

Another week passed, and by now Des had more or less given up on Daphne, on Daphne and her counsel. And yet there it was, in the *Sun* on Saturday (on Saturdays Daphne commanded a two-page spread). All the other letters bore headlines (I Feel Like a Tart As I Can't Stop Bedding Strangers, Trapped in a Man's Body, I Want to Wed My Dead Hubbie's Dad, Heartbreak at Text Cheat, Grief Over Mum Won't Lift); but Des's plea was untitled, and appeared in the bottom left-hand corner against a funereal background of dark grey.

Dear Daphne, I'm a young man from Ken-

sington in Liverpool, and I've been having
sexual relations with my grandmother. Could
you explain the legal situation?

DAPHNE SAYS: This must end at once! You
are both committing statutory rape, and could
face a custodial sentence. Write again ur-
gently with a PO address, and I will send you
my leaflet, Intrafamilial Sexual Abuse and
the Law.

Des spent the rest of the day on Steep
Slope, stumbling from bench to bench. He
could hear the brittle fairground music
swirling up from Happy Valley; and the air
was dotted with spores of moisture that
couldn't quite become rain. Something dark
seemed to be growing bigger on the other
side of the rise.

At seven o'clock Lionel shouldered his way
into the kitchen with a great load of dog
gear in his arms. He halted and his head
jerked back.

". . . The tank's open."

"Yeah, I tried it," said Des quietly, "and
the lid just came up. But now it won't shut."

"There you are then." With a crash Lionel
dropped the tangled mass onto the counter
— lunge poles, break sticks, and four thick
leather collars with pyramidal steel spikes.
"You been sitting on it."

Des's brow never rippled when he frowned, but tonight his eyes felt (and looked) very close together, like a levelled figure eight. He now saw that Lionel had a newspaper in his sweatpants pocket: not the *Morning Lark*, not the *Diston Gazette* (also a red-top tabloid) — but the *Sun*!

Lionel uncapped a Cobra three inches from Des's left ear, saying,

"Dire news about you gran."

His voice cracked as he whispered, "Oh yeah, Uncle Li?"

"The plot thickens . . . I had another talk with old Dud. It's not only groans, Des."

"Uh, what else?"

"Giggles. Giggles. So it's not *pain*, is it. It's not *pain*. And you know what else?"

Des was scratching his chest with both sets of fingernails.

"She's started turning the music up loud! . . . Tuesday night Dud said he heard giggles. Then the music went up. And that ain't the clincher." He stuck his tongue out and removed a hair from it. "You won't believe this, Des, but the old . . ."

Lionel fell silent. He went to the glass door, pulled back the curtain, and gazed down at Jeff and Joe; they lay there side by side, humped in sleep.

"I placed a bet today," he said in a sur-

67

prised voice. "See for youself." And with a flourish he produced his newspaper and fanned it out on the table.

"Reading the *Sun* now are we?"

"Yeah. Gone uh, gone boffin for the day." A new beer can sneezed. "No, Des, Page Three Playoffs. And I've put money on Julietta. See, she reminds me of someone . . . I'm not a gambler, Des. Never was. I leave that to fucking Marlon."

The odds on the gypsyish Julietta were duly noted and briefly discussed. Lionel turned the page, moving on to the *Sun*'s TV Guide. Again he turned the page: Dear Daphne!

"*I Feel Like a Tart As I Can't Stop Bedding Strangers.*" Lionel read on (with his lips slowly shaping the words). "Well you *are* a tart, darling. Get on with it . . . Here, Des. Daphne reckons — Daphne reckons that a bloke dressing up as a bird is uh, is *an attempt to create a marriage of one* . . . Can a widow get hitched to her father-in-law? . . . Here. Here Des. There's this lad from Liverpool . . ."

And Des gave thanks to the half-forgotten dream or dread that had prompted the stuff about Liverpool and Kensington. How was it he knew about Kensington and "Kenny"?

"Gaw. This dirty little Scouse git's been

68

giving his *nan* one! His own nan . . . Funny old world, eh Des?"

Des nodded and coughed.

". . . Yeah, too right, Daph. Custodial sentence. Definitely. *Où*, they'll love him inside. You know what they'll do to him, Des? When he goes away?"

"No. What'll they do?"

"Well. First they'll fuck his arse off. Then they'll slash his throat in the showers. They got nans too mate! . . . Kensington. 'Kenny' — that's where I did me Yoi!"

The room quietened and stilled as a passing cloud lent it the colour of slate.

"Mum's visitor, Des. He comes in, he goes out. Just as he pleases. He comes in, he goes out."

And Des felt obscurely moved to say, "Half the time it's probably just me, Uncle Li. I'm always in and out."

Lionel detonated another Cobra. "You? Oh, sure. Listen. When you go calling on Grace, Des, is it you habit . . . Is it you habit to come in whistling at half past midnight? And go out whistling at ten? After another quickie and you English breakfast?"

She came hurrying down Crimple Way, quicker, busier, head tipped forward but chin outthrust, she'd had her hair shaped and trimmed and tinted, she wore a red sweater and a tight trouser suit of metallic grey. The gripped thinness of her mouth and the scissors of her legs were asserting something — asserting her determination to thrive. And she looked younger, he thought (he was leaning on her gate); but now, as she crossed the road, every six feet she got six years older.

"Des," said Grace quietly as she moved past him. "Well come in, love, but you won't want to stay."

She laid out the shopping on the kitchenette counter: bread, eggs, tomatoes, a packet of bacon, a tin of baked beans (and her Silk Cut and a fresh bottle of Dubonnet). She was eyeing his reflection in the window above the sink.

"What's going on, Grace?"

"Don't say another word, dear. Everything's as it should be."

"No, Grace," he said with his pleading frown, "everything's changed. Lionel — he's got old Dud with his ear jammed up against the wall!"

"Lionel? *Bugger* Lionel. Listen. I'll be forty any minute and all right I'm past it — yeah, past caring! . . . Ah, Des. I've got something to tell you, dear. I've got something to tell you."

Outside, it had rained and grown dark under a lilac sky, and a film of water swam on the flagstones. Orange blotches of mirrored streetlight kept pace with him as he walked down Crimple Way. The awe of his relief was sumptuous, hallucinatory . . . Des Pepperdine was fifteen years old. And he supposed it was a good thing to get this learned early on. Now he bowed and threw his head back and almost laughed as he consented to the Distonic logic of it.

It's better this way, Des. You can start calling me Gran again. You and me, we'll just go back to how we were before. And no one'll be any the wiser. It's better this way.

It is. It is. But Gran. *Think. He's on to you and your new friend. Uncle Li knows!*

Oh yeah? He doesn't give a monkey's about his mum. I haven't seen him this century! And what's he going to do about it? If this gets out, who'll suffer more? Him! *What's he going to do? What's he going to do?*

9

Lionel had a lock-up or godown on Skinthrift Close. You approached it crunching on a snowfield of shattered glass, and

71

skirting your way past scorched or smouldering mattresses and swamps and copses of outlandish junk and clutter, including a wide variety of abandoned vehicles. Scooter, camper, tractor; there was even a dodgem, clog-shaped, its electric pole like a withered shank; and a lifesize rocking horse, with the eyes of an ageing barmaid . . . Des was summoned to this address by mobile phone: his sixteenth-birthday present had been brought forward, in response to the general emergency (and issued to him like a piece of military equipment).

"I'm in here!"

The shop, as Lionel called it, was not looking its best — partly because Lionel had just finished smashing the place up. It comprised a double garage (housing the sooty Ford Transit), a congested office, and a chilly cubicle containing a deep sink and a cracked toilet. Des heard the jerk of the chain; and now a singleted Lionel emerged, mopping himself down with a length of kitchen towel. He said equably,

"I'm over it now." He pointed to his left: a broken chair, splintered racks and brackets, stoved-in tea chests. "Because this isn't a time for anger, Des. It's a time for clear thought. Come in here."

Lionel's office: heaps of jumbled drawers

full of watches, cameras, power tools, game consoles; a low bookcase full of bottled drugs (for bodybuilders — synthetic hormones and the like); a fruit crate full of knuckledusters and machetes. All of it swiped, blagged, hoisted . . . How intelligent was Uncle Li? Even the most generous answer to this question — which had bedevilled Des since the age of five or six — would have to include a firm entry on the debit side: there was no evidence whatever that Lionel was any good at his job. He was a subsistence criminal who spent half his life in jail.

"Gran. Christ. I know it's Town," he said, "but this is ridiculous."

They faced each other across a raw table strewn with knocked-off jewellery and sold-on credit cards. Without warning Lionel gave one of his tight little sneezes: it sounded like a bullet fired through a silencer. He wiped his nose and said,

"There's been a sighting. It's a schoolboy, Des. Purple blazer. The Squeers blazer. She's doing it with a schoolboy."

Des tried to look surprised. Because he wasn't surprised. This was the Distonic logic of it: he was fifteen years old — and Gran had passed him over for a younger man. Lionel said,

"Dud saw him. Purple blazer. Dud saw him taking his leave."

Feeling an unfamiliar latitude, Des asked, "Sure it wasn't me?"

"He *said* it wasn't you. He said, *And* not *you spearchucker nephew, neither.* Squeers Free. So, Des, you'll be lending a hand with me enquiries."

"What d'you reckon you'll do, Uncle Li?"

"With such a matter as this, Des, you got to consider you objectives." He sat back. "Which are. One. Put an end to the nonsense with the sexual relations. Obviously. Two. Keep it quiet. Fucking hell, I'd have to *emigrate*. The States, I suppose. Or Australia. A paedo for a mum? A *nonce* for a mum. Nice . . . Three. Ensure, beyond doubt, that nothing of this nature happens again. Ever . . . It's like — like a puzzle. A labyrinth. You consider you objectives. Then you turn to you options."

From experience Des half-subliminally sensed that something fairly bad was on its way. Lionel's linear style, his show of rationality, even the modest improvements in his vocabulary and enunciation ("labyrinth," for instance, came out as *labyrinf*, rather than the expected *labyrimf*): whenever Lionel talked like this, you could be pretty certain that something fairly bad was on its way.

Now he reached for a torn pack of Marlboro
Hundreds, on which a clump of capital letters had been grimly scored.

"Long black hair. Wears a lip ring. And
cowboy boots. And *shorts*. Who is he?"

"Uh, let me think."

"Ah *come* on. How many kids wear cowboy boots with they shorts? I ask again. Who
is he?"

Des had no doubt: it was Rory Nightingale. It could only be Rory Nightingale . . .
Rory was a chronic truant (and just
fourteen), but everyone at Squeers Free was
aware of Rory Nightingale. Shapely-faced,
and sidlingly self-sufficient, and far more
than averagely wised up. He always reminded Des of the youths you saw behind
the scenes at funfairs and circuses — in
their own sphere, with their own secrets,
and with that carny, peepshow knowledge
in the thin smile of their eyes.

"Yeah, I know him."

"Name?"

"Name?" The window of latitude — of air
and freedom — was already closing. "Uh.
Uh, put it down to your influence, Uncle
Li. But this is like grassing someone up. You
know. Playing Judas."

Lionel arched his eyebrows as his gaze

rolled slowly ceilingward, and he joined his hands round the back of his neck (revealing two vulpine armpits). "Fine words, Des. Fine words. But you know, son, life's not as uh, straightforward as that. Sometimes, sometimes you high ideals have to . . . Okay. How often's he go to school? Cowboy boots and shorts. Lip ring. I can pick him out meself."

"About once a fortnight."

". . . Well I'm not going to stand there at the gates for a fucking fortnight, am I. Think of the effect that'd have on me temper . . . Listen, Des. I want to put you mind at rest. I'm going to do this *neat*. Clean. And I won't lay a finger on him. All right? So next time he shows up, you give me a call on you nice new phone. Will you do that at least for yer own uncle? Bloody hell, boy. She's *you* fucking nan."

A rough-edged wind frisked him down as he made his way back up Skinthrift Close. The dumped rocking horse, the dumped dodgem. And now, in just the last half-hour, a consignment of dumped kiddies' dolls, heat-damaged, in a gummy pink mass.

The new development entailed a new perplexity. Although Des very seldom engaged with Rory Nightingale, he happened

to be on friendly terms with his parents —
with Ernest and Joy. It was nothing out of
the way: Mr. and Mrs. Nightingale used the
corner shop, under the shadow of Avalon
Tower, and they first hailed Des simply on
the strength of his Squeers blazer. And so it
went on — greetings, small talk, encouraging words . . .

Rory himself was on the very tideline of
the modern, but his parents seemed to have
waddled out of the 1950s. Both about forty-
five, both about five foot four, and both un-
prosperously but contentedly tublike in
shape. You never saw them singly; and on
the streets they always walked in step, and
hand in hand. Once, as he ate an apple that
Joy had just given him, Des watched the
Nightingales negotiate the zebra crossing.
Halfway over, a dropped handkerchief and
a passing truck contrived to separate them;
Ernest waited attentively on the far curb-
side, and then off they went again, in step,
and hand in hand. And Rory (Des knew)
was their only child.

How's it going to go? he wondered as he
approached the main road. Ahead of him a
succession of white vans flashed past. There
were many white vans in Diston, and many
white-van men — and they were white
white-van men, too, because Diston was

predominantly white, as white as Belgravia (and no one really knew why). Lionel had a white van, the Ford Transit. Amazing, thought Des, how all the white vans wore the same thickness of soot, just enough to coat them in a shadow of grey. *Clean Me*, a wistful finger had written on the Transit's smudged breast.

"I left the door open — just a crack. Half an inch. First Jeff has a go, then Joe has a go. They're mashing their noses in the gap. And ten minutes later they're inside!"

"There. You condemning youself out of you own mouth. Would they do that if *I* was in here? It's wide open now and are they coming in? You too soft on them, Des. You like a *girl* when it comes to the dogs. And *don't* change the subject."

The subject. Night after night Des faced moody and repetitive interrogation on the subject of Rory Nightingale. Tensions glided under the fluorescent tubes at the same speed as the shifting silks of Lionel's cigarette smoke. With a Marlboro Hundred in one hand and a fork in the other, he broodingly consumed great quantities of the only dish he ever consented to cook (or at least heat up): Sweeney Todd Meat Pies. And these pies, these quantities, were not without significance. Des was too close in to see the pattern clearly, but Lionel's appetite always climbed sharply when he was readying himself for something fairly bad.

"So he's clever," Lionel would say. And Des would say, "Yeah. Mr. Tigg reckons he'd be very clever if he tried. But he's never there."

"So he's always after everyone for money," Lionel would say. And Des would say, "Yeah. He's always after everyone for a couple of quid. Trying it on."

"So he's a chancer. Like Ringo," Lionel would say. And Des would say, "Yeah. He's a bit like Uncle Ring. In that respect at least."

". . . Tell me, Des. Do girls like him? Or just old boilers? . . . Come on, Des, you hiding something. I can tell. I can always tell."

"Well, yeah, Alektra says they're all mad for him. But he likes them older. He says when it comes to sex, kids are crap."

"Continue, Des. Let's have it."

"He — he's always saying he's bi. I'm adventurous, he says. I'm a sexy boy."

After an intermission (chewing, smoking, nodding), Lionel said, "Nah. I won't lay a finger on him. Wouldn't demean meself. I wouldn't demean meself, Desmond."

". . . What'll it be then, Uncle Li? Warn him off?"

"Warn him off? Warn him off what? He's already done it! Round there *again* last night. Gran must think I've gone soft in me old age." He licked his lips. "Sexy boy, is it. I'll give him sexy."

This was on the Thursday. On the Friday, who should show up at Squeers Free but Rory Nightingale.

10

It was the kind of morning that the citizens of this island kingdom very rarely saw: an established and adamant clarity, with the sun pinned into place, as firm as a gilt tack; and the sky, seemingly embarrassed by such exalted pressure, kept blushing an even deeper blue . . . Dark and gaunt, like his shadow, Desmond (to whom lovely skies always whispered of loss and grief) stood on the patch of sandy astroturf beyond the gym. Rory Nightingale was here. And Des made the call. He failed to see what else he could do.

Three fifty-five. Crisply dressed, with his face half-obscured by a copy of the *Diston Gazette*, Lionel sat waiting in the open-fronted bus shelter across the street. Des approached.

"He's in detention. Got an hour's detention."

Lionel gazed out from his solarium of dust-stippled glass. "Better," he quickly decided as he took out his phone and thumbed in a message (it consisted of one digit). "We'll get this rubbish out of the way a bit quicker than we thought."

"Well I'll be off home then. You can't miss him."

"No, Des. You sit by here."

The school emptied, the blazered figures unenergetically dispersed, the thin traffic grew thinner and thinner . . .

"There he is."

"Get to you feet. Call him over — call him."

Lionel flung an arm round his shoulder and Des felt a prehensile tightening at the back of his neck.

"Here, Rory! Ror!"

With a kind of lolling wariness the boy crossed the road. For an instant his lip ring gave off a molten gleam.

"Let you out in the end, did they?" said Lionel. "And on an afternoon like this. Teachers, they a load of losers. Now you know me — I'm Des here's uncle. And listen. I got a pal, I got a pal, he's a uh, an amateur photographer. Fashion. With more

81

money than sense, eh Des? Named Rhett. And he . . . Hang on. Here he is now."

A sleek and muscular saloon pulled up, and out climbed Marlon Welkway. Marlon Welkway — his glistening quiff, his ironical squint, his matinee smile.

Des felt himself dismissed with a push, and off he started, trying not to hurry. A minute later, as he made for the first side-street, he turned his head — and it was all right, it was all right, the boy was walking away in the other direction, the two men were poised to duck under the car's glossy carapace, and the three of them were waving airily, and Marlon's pink shirt pulsated in the breeze.

The weekend passed quietly.

"Be gone all night," said Lionel, with resignation (it was Saturday evening). "Cynthia. It's her birthday. And I hardly ever miss her birthdays. Well. Never two in a row."

On Sunday Lionel again took his leave at dusk, stern and silent (all business), and again wasn't seen until morning. So the weekend passed quietly — indeed for Des almost inaudibly. He couldn't say why, quite, but he seemed to have re-entered the plugged world of the deaf.

"Ah, Des. Little Des. How's the lad this morning?"

They had collided on the landing of the twenty-first floor, Des going down, Lionel coming up. At Avalon Tower, the lift was now terminating on the twenty-first floor.

"Oh, you know," said Des. "Not so bad."

"Mm. Well this'll put a spring in you step. That matter with the boy. Problem solved."

"What you go and do?" said Des sullenly. "Smash him up?"

"Desmond! No. No. Nothing of that nature. You can't smash up a *kid* . . . Des. You say you friendly with his mum and dad. Well. They need never know. Need never know how he come to bring this on hisself. There . . . We're due a celebration, Des. Tonight — let's have one of our usuals. Deal?"

Beyond, through the pillbox window, you could see the tallowy sky of London, like thin snow on a field of ash. Turning, Lionel gave out a soft snort and said,

"I thought you told me he was *clever* . . ."

The word hung there, as Lionel went on up, and Des went on down.

"Kay Yeff *Cee*. Kay Yeff *Cee*. Kay Yeff *Cee*. Kay Yeff *Cee*." Lionel's voice wasn't that loud, but it had the defiant, white-lipped

83

force of a football chant. "Kay Yeff *Cee*. Kay Yeff *Cee*. Kay Yeff *Cee*."

They lowered their trays, and sat facing each other over a ledge of zebra-patterned laminate, unzipping little sachets of ketchup, mustard, sweet relish; they sampled their Sprites through the fat straws, and started on the chips and the Kentucky-fried chicken.

"Don't say I don't look after yer."

"I'd never say that, Uncle Li."

". . . I reckon you doing all right, Des. Since I took you under me wing. Gaa, the state you were in when I come to you rescue. Crying youself to sleep at night. You was . . . you were always brushing up against me for a hug, like a cat. And I'd say, *Get off, you little fairy. Get off, you little poof.* I'd say, *If you want to ponce a cuddle you can go round to you gran's.* But now," he said, "you doing all right."

". . . Yeah, I'm okay."

"Oy. You not eating you dinner. *Eat* you dinner. *Eat* you dinner."

Desmond ate. Ate the chicken, fried just as he liked it, Kentucky-style, the way Colonel Sanders himself prepared it, and normally so answeringly luscious to his taste. But now . . . He thought of the only time he had ever a tooth filled, four or five years ago, and afterwards, as promised, Cilla took him to the caff for his favourite, mushrooms on toast, and his mouth was full of novocaine and he couldn't distinguish anything more than a presence on his frozen tongue — his tongue, which he then caught in his jaws without even feeling it, and there was blood on his chin but no tears on his cheeks . . .

"You know, Des," said Lionel, with unusual thoughtfulness (with unusual difficulty in his worked brow), "Sunday morning. I'm lying there Sunday morning. I'd just had this dream about Gina Drago. And she was all dark and uh, *glowing*. Beautiful. Then I open my eyes and what do I see? Cynthia. Like a dairy product. Like a fucking yoghurt. And she says, *What's the matter with you? You had a nightmare?* And I said, *No, love. It's just me guts playing up.* Because they all got feelings, haven't they, Des. All got feelings. God bless them." He swiped a hand across his mouth. "Kay Yeff *Cee*, Kay Yeff *Cee*, Kay Yeff *Cee*."

From KFC they went on to the Lady Godiva.

"*Get* yuh tits fixed, *Get* yuh tits fixed, Get yuh tits-fixed-for-the-boys!" sang Lionel. "*Get* yuh tits fixed *For the boys — OOH* . . .

Attend to the performance, Desmond. I paid a fiver at the door for yer, and you not watching. Attend to the performance."

A visit to KFC traditionally entailed a visit to the Lady Godiva. The boozy hues of amber and mahogany, the hangings of mirrored cigarette smoke. The shallow stage, and the listlessly undulating dancer. Des's whole being hated it here (the worst bit, for him, was when the girls went round with their collection bags for the tips, and the customers felt them up for an extra fifty pee). But tonight he was hardly aware of the Lady Godiva — just as, earlier on, he was hardly aware of KFC, with its bank of illustrated edibles above the service counter (each plateful, it seemed to him, in a different stage of garish putrefaction), and the presiding icon of Colonel Sanders himself, like a blind seer.

"Ten years I been with her — Cynthia. Ten years. More. And I don't even . . . I reckon something must've put me off skirt. Something in me childhood. Everyone else is at it. Why aren't I? Eh?"

". . . You're too busy, maybe," said Des with a gulp. "And you're away a lot."

"That's true. *Anyhow.* Let's not spoil the celebration. The scales of justice, son. The scales of justice. She's had it coming for

86

years. Grace has. Now, Des. I know you slightly concerned about uh, young Rory. But it doesn't matter what happens to Rory. That's immaterial. Totally immaterial. What matters is putting the right fucking wind up you gran. Besides," he said with a grunt and a smile, "Rory's adventurous. He'll try anything . . . Hang on darling, here's a quid for yer. All right? I won't touch! *Get* yuh tits fixed, *Get* yuh tits fixed. *GET* yuh tits fixed *For the boys — OOH*."

Now all this began to take on shape and form in the world of the manifest.

As early as Wednesday morning Des passed the corner shop and saw a familiar face staring helplessly out at him through the sweating glass: Have You Seen This Boy? The same sign was tacked to the door of the sub-post office. At school, a greatcoated police officer stood at the gates and, within, there were eager rumours about the two plainclothesmen who were questioning everyone in year ten. Des sat bent at his desk beneath his personal thunderhead; but nothing happened, and Wednesday passed. On Thursday there were stickers gummed to every other lamp post in Carker Square — plus a filler in the *Sun* (Another Diston Lad Missing). And in Friday's *Gazette* there was a report, on page twelve, entitled "We Are At Our Wits' End." *Already on Tuesday morning*, Joy Nightingale was quoted as saying, *I knew something terrible had happened. I felt it here in my throat. Because he always calls in, without fail. No matter wherever he is, he always calls in.* Two photographs: Rory between his parents on a park bench at Happy Valley, smiling over a cloud of candyfloss; and Joy and Ernest at home, on a low settee, and hand in hand. *If anyone knows anything, then please, please, please . . .*

"He's standing there at the door. I hadn't seen him in five years. Five years. Not since he smashed up poor Toby. And he says, *Hello Mum. Here. Hold this.* And he's put this *sticker* on my face, this thing *sticking* to my face . . . And my knees went and I sank down. I sank down, dear."

Entirely unadorned, entirely undisguised, Grace was sitting by the window in her usual chair. But no music played, no folded *Telegraph* rested on her lap, no teacup steamed on the little round table, no Silk Cut twined its spirals in the saucer ashtray.

"Look at me, Des."

He looked. The fluffy pink slippers

huddled together, the arms leanly and stiffly folded, the notched mouth, the sepia ringlets, the weak grey stare. And he imagined the blank grid of a crossword, with no answers and no clues.

"Oh, it's all up with me now, love," she said, and hugged herself tighter. "I can't close my eyes. The boy. I can't close my eyes for fear of what I'll see."

11

Lionel was on the balcony with Joe and Jeff. With Joe, Jeff, the break stick, the lunge pole, the plastic bucket, the twelve-pack of Special Brew, the sagging cardboard box. Beyond him, the usual London sky. The white-van sky of London.

Des dropped his satchel and went on out.

"Seize. And hold," said Lionel. "Seize. And hold."

". . . You giving them a drink tonight?"

"Yeah. I'm doing a deep-eye in the morning. For Marlon. There's a nasty nip in the air over in Rotherhithe. And I'm going to go and sort him out. See the new doll?"

Lionel's sagging cardboard box contained half a dozen joke-shop rubber effigies, a black, a brown, a tan, a pale. The new doll was Fu Manchu-ish, with tendril moustache.

"Why?" said Des, with an edge in his voice. "What for?"

"*I* don't know. I didn't ask." He shrugged. "We cousins. We help each other out. You don't ask *what for.*"

Des went back inside and sat down hard on a kitchen chair. He had just seen Joy Nightingale on Creakle Street — Mrs. Nightingale, alone. With his heart thudding in his ears he watched her plod by, eerily and wrongly alone; no Ernest matched her step, no Ernest held her hand . . . *Clutch. And clench*, said Lionel, wielding the lunge pole, with the drool-soaked Chinaman speared on its pointed end . . . Now Des closed his eyes — and what did he see? Rory. But Rory wasn't dead; he was death-less; the immortal boy kept disappearing and reappearing — kept being plucked apart, and put together again, and plucked apart again . . . *Straddle, grab, sunder*, said Lionel, wielding the break stick. The break stick was a kind of hardwood chisel. In it went between the dog's back teeth. Then came the vicious twist.

One by one the twelve tall cans of Special Brew were primed like grenades and up-ended over the plastic bucket.

"Here. Ringo won the Lottery again. Guess

how much."

". . . How much?"

"A tenner. The Lottery's a mug's game if you ask me." Lionel was leafing with quiet satisfaction through the *Diston Gazette* (the *Diston Gazette* had had time to fill up again, like a sump). Behind him, their tails high, Joe and Jeff licked and lapped with clopping sounds. "It's funny. A missing girl — that'll hold they attention for a bit. But a missing boy? It's as if he's never been . . . See this, Des? Jesus. That's *senseless*, that is. That's *senseless*."

Des now had before him the front page and a headline saying THE LOOK OF GUILT and the dismally mesmerised faces of six young men, all of them black.

"Six of them. Gangers," Lionel went on. "So six London Fields Boys come down here. They come down here to put they-selves about. And they go and top this fifteen-year-old. All six of them! That's *senseless*, that is. And he wasn't even white!"

On page four there was a photograph of the mother, Venus, and a photograph of the boy, Dashiel. *A parent never expects their child to die before them*, said Venus in her statement at the Old Bailey, *especially when they are taken away so suddenly, the victim of the violent brutality of others.* The mother, in the photograph, still young, elegantly ear-ringed, lawyerly in a woollen coat with what looked like a thick velvet ruff. And the boy, Dashiel, his skin the colour of rosewood . . .

"Now they going down for fifteen years. Six of them. That's what? *Ninety* years for one little kid!"

All he would do was look at you with those big eyes and your heart just melted. Everyone loved his eyes. The boy, against a green set-ting, with his hair in tight rows, his spear-mint teeth, his eyes, flirtatiously sunlit.

"That goes against all reason. Violates all reason."

Dashiel was a "free spirit" who enjoyed the sun, the sea and Mother Nature on summer holidays in Jamaica with his grandmother . . .

"All right. Say uh, Dashiel was being a bit annoying. Needs to be taught a lesson. Fair enough. But you don't *all* go and do it. You turn to you mates and say, *Any volunteers?* You say, *Whose turn is it?* But oh no. All *six* of them get life! That's *senseless*, that is."

"Did you kill him, Uncle Li?"

"Come again?"

"Did you kill him?"

"Who? *Rory?* Now Desmond," he said soberly. "Why would I do that? I mean he's nothing to me is he."

92

"Yeah. Nothing."

"All he is is some little slag who goes to you school. What am I, a ganger? Out boying? Like a wild animal? . . . No, Des. I just fixed him up with a uh — with a circle of new friends. I didn't kill him. I *sold* him."

And Des had a vision of another grainy gallery, in the *Gazette* or the *Sun* or the *Daily Telegraph*, with six faces on it, all white this time, but not otherwise similar (a beard, a shining pate, a pair of rimless spectacles) — no, with nothing else in common except pallor, unreadable eyes, and a fixity of sullen purpose in the thinness of the lips. Lionel said,

"Reset. I didn't kill him. I sold him. Ooh. *Où* — I gave him sexy."

Left alone, Des gazed out at the pissed dogs. They reeled in circles, worrying one another's tails, and listing sideways as if on sloping ground. Joe turned, and they both reared up in a ragged clinch, and then, with their claws scraping for purchase, collapsed in an entanglement of haunch and crotch and snout. Finding his feet, Jeff began to make moan, a song or dirge addressed to the evening gloom.

Now Lionel filled the doorway in shell top and baseball cap. "Off out," he said. "And be reasonable, Des. What you expect? He gave my mum one. And if you *fuck my mum*, there's going to be consequences. Obviously. Here. Catch."

As he moved off Lionel lobbed something in the air. Des caught it: tiny, gluey, heavy. He straightened his fingers — and the trinket seemed to leap from his palm. Warily he crouched to pick it up. A metal loop smeared with dried blood and an additional gout of pink tissue. Rory's lip ring.

For those who harmed him, one day they will understand the meaning of love and the pain that you feel when you lose a loved one.

A knot is in our hearts that will not undo. A light has been dimmed and put out of our lives.

We never had a chance to say goodbye to Dashiel. We know he is resting, he is safe and he is at peace. I heard once that grief is the price we pay for love.

Desmond's head wagged back . . . When Cilla fell that time — it was just a little slip, just a little slip on the supermarket floor. Down she went on her elbows and shoulder blades, and her head wagged back. But she was laughing when she got to her feet. And then the next day she wouldn't wake up. He smoothed her, he pinched her, he shook her. He kissed her eyes. She was breathing, but she wouldn't wake up.

. . . Minutes later, as he stood wiping his cheeks and chin and throat with a kitchen towel, he looked out through the glass of the sliding door. The dogs: their sloppy faces, their tongues hanging from the corners of their jaws like something half-eaten, their blind eyes and staring nostrils, their forelimbs planted stupidly far apart. They thickly barked. And they weren't barking out — they were barking in.

Fuckoff, said Joe.

Fuckoff, said Jeff.

XII

Nothing really out of the ordinary happened between 2006 and 2009.

Lionel Asbo served five prison terms, two months for Receiving Stolen Property, two months for Extortion With Menaces, two months for Receiving Stolen Property, two months for Extortion With Menaces, and two months for Receiving Stolen Property. There was also, in the spring of 2009, his arrest and incarceration on the rare charge of Grievous Affray (plus Criminal Damage) — but that's another story.

When Des turned seventeen (by that time he had found a way of coexisting with his conscience), Lionel gave him a course of driving lessons in the Ford Transit. Quietly discounting Lionel's general advice (overtake whenever you can, use the horn as often as possible, never stop at zebra crossings, amber always means go), Des saved up for the Test, memorised the Highway Code, and conducted himself, on the day, with elderly sanctimony — and passed first time! . . . It was the way they'd always seemed to manage it. The anti-dad, the counterfather. Lionel spoke; Des listened, and did otherwise.

During these years Grace Pepperdine's life became a monothematic saga of anxiety, weight loss, heart palpitations, insomnia, depression, chronic fatigue, and osteoporosis. In addition, she kept mislaying things. Her phone would find its way into her bathroom cabinet; her doorkeys would hide behind the frozen peas in her fridge. Someone went round there every day — almost invariably Des, but often Paul, and frequently John, George, and Stuart (though seldom Ringo, and never Lionel).

Joe was shot dead by an Armed Response marksman in the summer of 2008. Out for a stroll with Cynthia (Lionel was away), Joe attacked a police horse, with a policewoman on it, in Carker Square. He was under its clattering hooves for the entire length of Diston High Street and for seven and a half miles up on the London Orbital, with the heavy chain slithering and scintillating in his wake. With Joe gone, Jeff inconsolably pined and sickened. And when he was next out of prison Lionel decided to make a fresh start. He sold Jeff for a token sum to one of Marlon's brothers (Troy), and purchased two pedigree pitbull pups — Joel and Jon.

There were no further developments in the Rory Nightingale case (which, all the same, was not yet officially closed) . . . Des started calling on Rory's parents, Joy and Ernest; he drank a mug of tea with them every couple of weeks, and ran errands; they said they found comfort, and not anguish, in his youth, his purple blazer, the space he filled. During his visits he thought many things, most often this: what an hourly mockery and misery it could be — the name Joy.

Meanwhile, Des had set about astonishing Squeers Free. In 2006 he sat his GCSEs — and got eleven A's! He was transferred, on the Gifted Programme, to Blifil Hall, where, in 2007, he sat his A-levels — and picked up four distinctions! He was sixteen. Next, he was offered a provisional place (he would have to survive the interview) at Queen Anne's College! Queen Anne's College — of the University of London . . . It took him a long time to break the news to Lionel. Lionel was bitterly opposed to higher education.

Des continued, off and on, to see a fair bit of Alektra, then a fair bit of Jade, then a fair bit of Chanel (who was Irish). *Try being gentle, Chanel,* he said to her late one night. *All soft and romantic. Go on. You're adventurous. Try being gentle. See what you think.* A week later she said, *I like it with you, Des. All romantic. All soft and dreamy. I don't know why, but it's just a better ride.*

And then, in 2008, when he went for his interview at Queen Anne's College, Des met Dawn Sheringham, and everything changed.

For a while it seemed that a similar transformation had already surprised Uncle Lionel. What happened was this. In the Indian summer of 2008, Gina Drago broke up with Marlon Welkway. The problem was as always Marlon's gambling (and rumour spoke of a tooth-and-claw catfight between Gina and a croupier named Antoinette — one of Marlon's exes — in a Jupes Lanes spieler). Anyway, the next thing everyone knew, Gina had homed in on Lionel Asbo!

Now what? A faithful reader of Dear Daphne and other forums, Des prepared himself for the expected benefits. How would Daphne put it? *Although your uncle is obviously a late developer, there should presently be a steady easing of tension as he adopts a more* . . . It wasn't like that. *No, Daphne, it isn't like that*, he muttered (Des often had these dialogues with Daphne, in the hours between waking and rising).

He's more nerve-racking than ever! He comes on all cool and masterful, but his hands tremble and his eyes are all over the place. I don't understand Gina either. Indoors, she treats him like he isn't there, and they never touch or kiss or smile. But on the street she's all over him. I saw them once on a bench outside the Hobgoblin. Gina was up on his lap, straddling his thighs in her catsuit and tutu! What's her game? Personally speaking, mind, it has to be said that I . . .

It had to be said, personally speaking, that Des was riveted by Gina. Always in the highest good humour, she was a dark mass of roundnesses with vivid eyes and silky cheeks (her colouring further beautified, somehow, by the pale traces of adolescent acne on the hinges of her jaw). At any moment she'd jump to her feet and do a whole scene from (say) a Sicilian operetta, with all the choruses, the voices, the dances . . . Lionel watched these displays with an expression Des had never seen before. A false smile, and a remarkably talentless false smile: he simply hooked his upper lip over his front teeth, and that was that (Lionel's front teeth were white and square, but so broadly spaced that you thought of a cutout pumpkin on Halloween). She never spent the night. They went off to her maisonette in Doyce Grove. For Gina wasn't just Miss Diston; she was also Lady Town — the favourite daughter of the controversial coin-op king and used-car czar, Jayden Drago.

Gina passed many an hour helping Des with his Italian, his Spanish, and his French (and she knew Basque too — and even Mallorquin!). *So Daphne, what do you think? Why would a girl who can speak six languages go around with a bloke who can barely speak English? Plus she's a famous sexpot — and he's almost a virgin! What's Jezebel doing with Joseph? What's the princess see in the frog? What's Gina's game?*

■ ■ ■ ■

One half-term morning in the chill fall of 2008 he looked in on Gran and found her frowning over the *Daily Telegraph* with a biro in her hand. He said encouragingly, *Back on the crosswords, are we?*

There was a silence, and without looking up she said, *One clue. For a week I've been staring at it. One clue.*

. . . But Gran, some are more difficult than others. You always said. Depends on the setters. They vary.

She handed it over. And the crossword, it wasn't the Cryptic — it was the Kwik! The single clue that Grace had solved, or at least filled in, was 22 down. It went, *Garden of – – – – (4).* And in the bottom righthand corner of the grid she had written, *ENED.*

And even that's not quite right, is it.

No, not quite.

. . . So I'm going daft now am I?

Their eyes met.

Des. What happens when I don't know what I'm saying?

It'll pass, Gran.

. . . I won't be able to open my eyes. I won't be able to close my mouth.

No, Gran. The other way round.

And he felt he was preparing for a long voyage on a dark sea where, one by one, all the stars would be going out.

Why was Gina Drago seeing Lionel Asbo? Because she wanted to spite and goad — and thus reactivate — Marlon Welkway. Des tried always to be elsewhere; but anyone could tell how it was shaping. Gina's pink cellphone, with its lip-prints and snowdrop spangles, took on terrible powers: every chirrup had the rousting force of a siren. She would answer it, saying, *Well you should've thought of that*, or *Eff off*, or, simply, Fuera! But sometimes she would get to her feet and laughingly leave the room with the instrument nestling in the cusp of her throat. Des kept his eyes on the floor . . . Whether Lionel had words with Marlon was not known; but nothing changed, nothing happened, until November, when destiny ponderously intervened in the form of RSP: Lionel received some stolen property, and was arrested for it.

He got two months in Wormwood Scrubs in west London. Des went to visit him on Boxing Day. The interminable bus ride, the blasted heath. Lionel, in his wrinkly dark-blue overalls, stood at the counter of the

102

commissary snackbar. They ordered, and went to the square table with their hot chocolates and their bags of Maltesers. Over the years Des had visited his uncle in a great variety of prisons (and borstals and Yois), and Lionel, even when settling in for a much longer stay, never seemed more than mildly inconvenienced (*Prison's not too bad*, he often said. *You know where you are in prison*). But today he sat in a propulsive crouch on the very brink of the tin chair. *RSP*, he kept direly saying, and shaking his head. *RSP!* . . . Des couldn't understand why this should seem so staggering in itself, because Lionel was arrested for RSP two or three times a year. But as dusk fell (and as the wardens wordlessly impended with their keys), Lionel said,

You know what, Des? He *put me here. Marlon. He done me! For Gina!*

Des left him there, the tense slope of the back, the chainlit Marlboro Hundred . . . And even before Lionel regained his freedom the *Diston Gazette* announced that Mr. Jayden Drago's firstborn child, Gina Maria, was officially engaged — to Marlon Welkway! The day was already named. It was to be a Whitsun wedding . . .

As he continued on his journey, his journey from boy to man, Des found that the thoughts that stayed with him about his uncle were getting a little bit harder to file away. For instance. Lionel, sitting in prison, and hating it as thoroughgoingly as any sane and innocent man would hate it (but for completely different reasons). Or again. The unexpected element in his response to the defection of Gina Drago. Together with the hurt, the rage, the humiliation, and the tearing need for vengeance, there was the furtive glimmer of relief.

Things were at least much simpler now. On the day he came out Lionel challenged Marlon to what was called *a garage meet* (bare-knuckle, stripped to the waist, with paying spectators, no ref, no rules, and no limit) and Marlon of course accepted — but that's another story.

On his seventeenth birthday (in January 2008) Des threw a little party all for himself. The only guests were the pups, Jon and Joel (who were given a fresh bone each). Well, they were hardly pups any longer. On the move they were like missiles of muscle . . . He bought two flagons of Strongbow, and sprinkled a pinch of keef into a rolled cigarette. Des only knew a handful of things about his father. Edwin (as he continued to think of him) was a Trinidadian, and a Pentecostalist; he refrained — earlier on, anyway — from harmful liquors; as against that, though, he didn't deny the clarifying effects of a pensive burn of keef. So Des sipped his cider, and smoked the sparkling grass; and he felt the spirit of Edwin darn its way through him: the smell of thick damp foliage, a vast church on a village hilltop, a fat moon sliced and swallowed by the sharp horizon. He knew another thing about his father — that he referred to babies as *youths*. Des knew too that Edwin was gentle. Cilla said.

It was just a little slip. Her legs shot out in front of her, her head twanged back and then twanged up again — but she was laughing when she got to her feet. As they walked home arm in arm the sun hit the thin rain, turning each drop into a gout of solder, and a fabulous rainbow of blue and violet bandily straddled the roofscapes of Diston Town . . . It was just a little slip. The autopsy report spoke of *blunt impact to the head* and *epidural haematoma*. But the phrase that held him was *massive insult to the brain*. And it was unfair, he felt, to say such a thing about Mum — because, this time, it was just a little slip.

As he rinsed the glass and cleaned the ashtray (and put the dogs out) and vaguely dreamed about Queen Anne's College (the one poem, the cosmos of the University), something struck him as suddenly as the sun struck the rain on that last day with his mother: It will take a whole new person to make *me* whole. A whole new person. It can't come from anything within. I'll just have to . . . I'll just have to wait. I'll wait.

Where is she?

I'll wait.

She was sitting next to him on a hardbacked chair. There were about twenty young people in the room (down from about thirty-five), and she was the only one present who was doing something sensible: she was reading (he stole a glance — *The Golden Bough*) . . . The rest of them, Des included, were merely helplessly and dumbly waiting, like patients waiting for the doctor's nod. Every fifteen minutes or so a name was called . . . The setting was a panelled antechamber in Queen Anne's College, London. A fat bee kept bluntly knocking against the window pane, as if seriously expecting the viny garden to open up and let it in. What was *that* doing here? It was early February. Des's mind was clogged and wordless; the vertical ribs of the radiators, he felt, were giving off the acrid tang of a dry-cleaner's. He wiped the sweat off his upper lip, and reached with both sets of fingers for his brow.

Are you nervous? she said, tilting her head an inch or two, but without looking up. *I don't mean in general. I mean at the minute.*

Nervous? he said. *I'm giving birth!*

Oh don't be . . .

Now he saw her face, under its weight of golden hair — the gold of sunlight and lions. And her exorbitant eyes, fairy-tale blue, and ideally round.

Well you know, she said, *I was in a terrible condition this morning. Then I had a thought whilst I made my tea. I thought: What'll they be looking for in myself? And I felt all calm. I'm Dawn.*

I'm Desmond. They shook hands. Her voice was high and musical, but her diction, her choice of words, put him in mind of a category he could not yet name: the minutely declassed. *And what was that thought? Dawn.*

It suddenly came to me. Well, we've all got the grades, haven't we. So what is it they'll be looking for in ourselves? And it suddenly came to me. Eagerness to learn. *Simple. I've got that. And I don't doubt you've got it too.*

Yeah, he said. *I've got that.*

Well then. Desmond.

She shrugged or shivered; her body sighed and realigned. And he saw her crossing the road, crossing one of the many roads of the future, and quite differently dressed, with her jeans tucked into knee-high boots, and in a tightish top — crossing the road, strongly stepping up to the island and then stepping down from it and walking on . . . He experienced a gravitational desire, just then (as his blood eased and altered), to reach out and touch her. But all that happened was that his face gave her its clearest possible smile.

Desmond Pepperdine, said a voice.

So it was his turn first, and when he came out, twenty minutes later, they bent their heads and winced at each other . . .

Dawn Sheringham, said a voice (a different voice).

As she gathered her things he said, "I'll wait. If you like. I'll wait and we'll go for some tea."

"Ooh, I'd love a cup," she called out. "I'll be needing one!"

He watched her walk off. He hesitated, and said, ". . . I'll wait!"

As a result of a further steepening of Ernest's depression, the Nightingales moved to Joy's mother's place in Hull. Des looked up Hull on the Cloud. Its sister city was called Grimsby. The fog that came in at night smelled of fish.

It seemed to Des that now would be the moment to get shot of Rory's lip ring. But it stayed where it was. He opened his desk drawer: the sealed white envelope with the circular indentation, and the evil little heaviness at the bottom of it.

In September 2006, there was a much-studied but in the end unfathomable traffic jam which enchained West Diston — all the way from Sillery Circle to the Malencey Tunnel — for five days and five nights (it was relieved only by hundreds of grapple-hoists from RAF helicopters). In April 2007, there was an outbreak among local schoolchildren (all morbidly obese) of deficiency diseases not seen for generations (pellagra, beriberi, rickets). In October 2008, there was a weeklong nine-acre blaze in Stung Meanchey, enveloping the site in a layer of diaphanous smoke like the sloughed skin of a gigantic dragon (it was said to be very beautiful from the air).

The winters were unsmilingly cold.

■ ■ ■ ■

PART II

■ ■ ■ ■

Who let the dogs in? That was going to be
the question. Who let the dogs in?
Who let the dogs in — who? Who?

2009 LIONEL ASBO, LOTTO LOUT

1

It was as he was *mucking out* — which is to say, it was as he was passing his spoutless kettle of shit to the aproned orderly — that Lionel Asbo first got wind of the fact that he had just won very slightly less than a hundred and forty million pounds.

"Yeah, you've had a bit of luck. Apparently. Don't know what," said Officer Fips (who wasn't such a bad bloke). "The Light wants a word. You'll be sent for."

"The who?"

"The Light. You know, light of your love. Guv. Love. That's rhyming slang."

". . . Jesus, you need you head seen to, you do. And rhyming slang's all crap."

Officer Fips continued to go about his tasks. "According to him, you've had a bit of good fortune. And he was well fucked off about it and all."

"Yeah? What's this then?"

"You'll be sent for."

Lionel turned to his cellmate, Pete New, and said, "Dropped charges. Looks like they've seen reason and dropped charges."

"Yes, Lionel. Could very well be."

Stallwort was a remand prison — for those awaiting trial or sentence — and its inmates were banged up on a colourful array of charges. Banged up for non-payment of alimony, banged up for serial rape, banged up for possession of marijuana, banged up for knifing a family of six.

"Well, let's hope so," said Pete New.

Pete New was banged up for having a fat dog.

Banged up for having a fat dog? said Lionel on his first day there.

I know, said New. *Sounds stupid. Yes, well. Twelve Reprimands and five Final Warnings. From the Social.*

Tinkerbell, New's basset hound, was fourteen stone. She could only sleep and eat; she lay there on the mattress with her limbs splayed out flat.

She has to be turned, see, Tinkerbell. Or you try. And she creates. She makes a right old racket. And then the neighbours . . .

Lionel said, *What you have a fucking dog for if you let it get into that state? You ought to give it a uh, an appropriate diet.*

New shrugged humbly and limped back to his bunk. He had his left leg in a light cast: Pete New had managed to snap a ligament while watching TV. Eleven hours in the same position, and when he readied himself to get to his feet, he said, he heard it pop.

You snapped a ligament watching TV?

I know. Doesn't sound too clever either.

You want to brush up you ideas, mate.

Well you know how it is, Mr. Asbo.

Call me Lionel.

It was June.

Pete New was banged up for having a fat dog.

And what was Lionel banged up for, along with four Pepperdines, eleven Welkways, and twenty-seven Dragos (including Gina)?

Why were they all in prison — prison, with its zinc trays and iron trolleys, its tame spiders, and its brickwork the colour of beef tea?

Ah, but to answer that question we must go back in time — back to May, and to Whitsun.

2

"It's a family reunion, as well as a wedding. You know, Dawnie, I'm going to change

115

subjects. I can't stand German."

". . . Des, at this do, are they *all* going to be bent?"

"*No*," he said with some show of indignation. "Mm. Well . . . *No*. Not quite. Uncle Paul's straight. Uncle Stuart's straight. But yeah. I suppose they're all up to something or other. The men anyway. They're all doing a bit of this and a bit of that."

"And the bother with Marlon?"

"It's sorted out. I told you. Uncle Li's best man. He's best man."

"Here," she said. "Kiss."

Des was almost eighteen and a half; he stood just over six foot tall; his face had lengthened and narrowed, but he still had a smile whose hooded brightness of eye made others smile. And here on his arm was Dawn Sheringham — her slender shape in the white print dress, her dandelion hair.

"Mum says you're too thin."

"Well she's right. It's the late hours. And the customers."

"Mm. It's Goodcars. And it's all my fault."

"It's nothing, Dawnie. Everyone our age worries about money."

Money had certainly become very tight — what with Lionel being so often away. Lionel was currently at large, but when he was away Des got no weekly tenners (for doing all the housework), no chicken tikkas or rogan joshes, no KFCs. And no rent (he was obliged to apply to the Assistance). He also had to feed Joel and Jon: when he was away, Lionel's only contribution to their upkeep was the odd pint of Tabasco and the odd plastic bagful of Special Brews that Cynthia sometimes hauled round. More pressingly and mysteriously, there was Dawn's credit card and the logarithmic debt now clinging to it. Six nights a week, therefore, from seven to midnight (and all day Sunday), Des minicabbed for Goodcars. *Goodcars*, their poster said: *You Drink, We Drive* . . .

"I never liked Marlon," he went on. "His nickname's Rhett Butler. And he's handsome. But there's something . . . There's a phrase in that book of short stories. It really sums him up. Uh, *a vague velvety vileness.* That's Marlon."

"And they used to be such great mates, him and Lionel. Since they were little."

"Oh, yeah. They were like twin brothers."

"Until Gina."

"Mm. Then it was all off."

"That can happen."

At King's Cross they changed from the Piccadilly line to the Metropolitan. They continued west, holding hands, with books on their laps. Dawn was reading Jessie Hunter. Des was reading Emile Durkheim.

He said, "Modern History. Or Sociology. Criminology."

"Des, they don't like it if you change. And it costs. Means you do another year."

"Not necessarily. And lots of people change . . . I can't *stand* German."

"What's wrong with it?"

"Well. Okay. In French, Wednesday is *mercredi*. In Spanish, it's *miércoles*. In Italian, it's *mercoledi*. And in *German*, it's *Mittwoch!* Midweek. What kind of language do you call that?"

Holding hands. Books on their laps. Kisses. Civilisation, thought Des Pepperdine.

It was to be a Whitsun wedding. People got married at Whitsun — the maypole, the fertility rites of spring. Whitsun: white Sunday. And today was Whitsun Eve. Des stretched and loosened his shoulders. It was Saturday: meaning Dawn would be spending the night. And no minicabbing till Sunday.

"Young women dancing round the maypole," he said. "Is that the origin of pole dancing?"

"Yeah, but nowadays you get lessons in it.

Empowerment."

Suddenly the train unsheathed itself from the black tunnel and soared out into the light of the May noon. And the weather — the air — was so fresh and bright, so swift and busy. Dawn said,

"Look, Des." She meant Metroland. The orderly villas, the innocent back gardens, all aflutter in the swerving wind. "I once came this way at night," she said. "And you look and you think, Every light out there stands for something. A hope. An ambition . . ."

The carriage was thinning out, and their kisses were growing more frequent, and lasting longer . . . *Dear Daphne*, he said to himself. *How are things? Me, I'm still having an affair with an older woman — I'm eighteen, and she's twenty! And it's not even an affair — not yet! I've been with Dawn for fourteen months, but we're slightly holding back — on the physical side. You see, Daph, Dawn's "unawakened." And we want to be "ready."* I'm *ready. She says she's* nearly *ready. And the foreplay's out of this world. But there's a real problem with her parents. Her mum, Prunella, is a darling, but her dad, Horace, is a right old —*

"Des? What was that fight they had? That garage meet."

"Well hang on. It'll sound a bit . . . See,

119

Uncle Li reckoned Marlon finked on him. Got him jugged — to put him out of the frame with Gina. But why would he? Gina only went with Uncle Li to make Marlon jealous. Nah. He just cooked that up, Uncle Li. To soothe his own pride."

"His pride? This is over my head, this is. This is Criminology."

"To soothe his own pride. And to give him someone to hurt when he got out. So they had the garage meet. Bare-knuckle. Stripped to the waist. With a paying audience." It must have been like the Lady Godiva — but all-male. "Lasted an hour."

"Who won?"

"Uncle Li. On a technicality. He was in hospital for a week. But Marlon was in hospital for a month. I heard they were still going at it in the ambulance."

"Bit stupid, isn't it?"

"Yeah."

"But now it's all patched up."

"Supposedly. Daggers drawn, but they buried the hatchet."

"Smoked the pipe of peace."

"They had a rendezvous. All very stiff to start with. Then they shook on it. Then they hugged. All weepy. And the next thing you know — Uncle Li's agreed to be best man!"

Dawn said, "Then why're you so worried

about it all?"

"I'm not!" he said, and kissed her. "It's just that . . . Burying the hatchet — I can't see him doing that, Uncle Li. That's not his way."

"Look outside. Oh Des," she said, and kissed him back. "Des, imagine *we* were getting married today."

"Yeah. Imagine. And jetting off to Malta for our honeymoon."

". . . You know those candles Mum gave us? I'll make a cottage pie when we get back. Let's have dinner by candlelight. And let's go mad and get a little packet of *vin de table*."

Three pound ninety-five! he thought.

With a stern look she kissed him again, on the lips, the cheeks, the brow, the eyes . . . "Tonight," she said. "Tonight. I'm ready. I'm ready, Desmond my love."

His head lolled on to her shoulder, and he gasped and smiled and closed his eyes.

"Yeah, that's it, darling. Have a little drowse. That's it. Lie down. There. On my lap. There you are. There."

He closed his eyes and was immediately encircled by the familiar moods and memories that came to him whenever he neared sleep — the time he touched tongues after

Sunday school with the girl in the white beret, the time Cilla cut her hand on the prised lid of the tin of soup (her fingers under the cold tap with their gaping mouths of red and white), the time he stole that fiver from Uncle George and made himself sick on sherbet lemons, the ruby wine and his fairy grandmother in her pink babydoll, the sticky sweets and sticky drinks, and the lord of his world of half-dreams, a hooded shape (always one size bigger than expected, broader, deeper), and the panting dogs . . .

"Come on. Come on, Des. End of the line!"

"We here?" He sat up straight and rubbed his eyes with both sets of knuckles.

"Who made the first move?" Dawn was asking as she rummaged in her straw bag. "Did Lionel reach out to Marlon? Or the other way around?"

"Uh, back channel." He got to his feet and straightened his tie. "Ringo. Uncle Ring. And Troy. Troy Welkway. They brokered it."

"But you said Ringo hates Marlon."

"Yeah. He does. And Troy hates him too."

". . . Ooh, Des, will it be all right?"

"Course it will. It's a wedding party. Uncle Li's been working on his speech. The best man's speech. You know. The eulogy."

122

3

It was easy to find — the Imperial Palace, a broad low-rise hotel set back from the road beyond a strip of lawn and a crammed car park. Doormen dressed like town criers were guiding the guests through the foyer, past the Beefeater Bar, and into an L-shaped anteroom where you could already hear a wall of sound, like the clamour of a schoolyard but on a lowered register — the contraltos of the women, the baritones of the men, in festive concord. Springtime, amatory union, massed revelry . . . With due allowance made for the imperfections of all those present, this wall of sound was a wall of love.

Dawn at once hurried off to the ladies' room, and Des was at once confronted by a cream-jacketed waiter with a silver tray: prosecco! The bubbles sizzled in his nose and romped and swarmed round his brain and after a second sip he was already feeling tremendously happy and proud. Dawn joined him, and together they advanced through the tall doorway.

Now, Des had never been in a hotel before, and he was a little overawed, perhaps, by the way the place seemed to set itself the task of pampering his senses — the smiling, dipping waiters, the limitless refreshments, the soft music, the padded chairs in lines against the walls, the thick rayon drapes, the twinkling plastic chandeliers, the fitted nylon carpet (orange, with attractive sprinklings of yellow), and the brilliant company, all around, in their Whitsun best.

"They're not so bad, Dawnie," he said, reaching for a second glass. "They're all right, I reckon. They'll do. Look at them."

Of the ninety-odd souls gathered in that lofty ballroom, the most august, probably, was Brian "Skanker" Fitzwilliam (Uncle John's father-in-law), his compact head adorned by a scythe of snow-white hair, together with his lady wife, Minnie, spryly wielding her black crutches. Next in seniority was Jayden "One Mile" Drago, father of the bride, in all his immovable girth, together with his current partner, Britt, half his age, with her miniskirt, her freckled poitrine. Then, too, there was Dennis "Mumper" Welkway, and Mrs. Mercy Welkway (née Pepperdine), and her younger sister Grace, with her walking-frame and her hairnet and her . . .

"You look lovely, dear. Lovely. Doesn't she, Des."

"Yeah, she does. Eh, what's that, Gran? Orange juice?"

"No. Buck's Fizz!"

"Prosecco, me! Gaw, all this. Must be costing a —"

"Oops," said Gran, turning away. "Here comes summer. And I can tell. He's got that look in his eye."

Lionel Asbo moved smoothly through the crush, patting a back here, giving a wrist-clasp there, embracing Uncle John, Uncle Paul, Uncle George, Uncle Ringo, and Uncle Stuart, slapping hands with Marlon's brothers, Charlton, Rod, Yul, Burt, Troy, and Rock, bowing in solemn introduction to Gina's innumerable siblings (bowing to Dejan, to Shakira, to Namru, to Aaliyah, to Vassallo, to Yasmine, to Oreste, to little Foozaloo) . . . And Des thought: Could it be possible? Could it be possible that Lionel Asbo, the great asocial, was in certain settings a social being?

Dawn said, "And over there, Des. Ooh. There's posh."

A waistcoated string quartet, up on the stage, rose as one and began playing the theme of *The Godfather.* Yes, there would be dancing, after the formalities, and then a great array of traditional Maltese dishes, artichoke hearts, beans with parsley, vegetable medleys, ricotta pie, nougat. But for

now the fingerfood was reassuringly English
— honest tavern fare — and Des said,

"You'd better eat your fill now, Dawnie.
You won't be wanting that foreign muck.
Horace wouldn't like it. Here. Have a nice
ham bap."

"Oh, *get* off . . . What are you smiling at?"

"I'm just thinking. I'm thinking about tonight."

"Mm. So am I."

They kissed.

"Oy!"

And here he was (in his one good suit, his
white shirt, his cord-thin blue tie), scrubbed
and shaven, with a stubborn tin of Cobra in
his meaty hand.

"Lionel, can I ask you something?"

"Course you can, girl," he said, leaning
over the table. He speared a rollmop and
reached out, with impatient fingers, for two
bite-sized pork pies.

"Why's Mr. Drago called 'One Mile'?"

Crunching his way through a mouthful of
pickled onions, Lionel explained. Jayden
Drago's cars were very cheap; but "One
Mile" was as far as anyone ever got in them
before they broke down.

"Sorry — but how's he stay in business?"

"Ah you see, Dawn, one mile's a uh, an
exaggeration. It's more like five miles. Or

126

even ten," he said through the gingery crumbs of a Scotch egg. "I bought one off him once. It's worth it if you going all the way across town. Same as a cab."

"Your speech, Uncle Li. You were going to dictate it to me. But you never."

His head tipped back, Lionel negotiated a ziggurat of salt-and-vinegar crisps, dusted his palms, and gave his brow a sharp knock with his knuckle. "It's all up here, son. It's all up here . . . Beautiful ceremony this morning. No, it was," he went on, looking lost and wistful. "The little bridesmaids with they bouquets. The stained glass . . . Gina. Gina, she took me aside in the garden. All in white, with them little white ribbons in her hair. And she said, *Lionel? Thank you, Lionel*, she said, *thank you for helping to make this the most perfect day of me life*. And her smile was like a little ray of sunshine. I tell you, it warmed me heart. It warmed my heart."

The string quartet withdrew. After a skirling volley of whoops and yells, and then a gurgling hush, the groom, the bride, and the best man approached and mounted the low stage. Lionel and Marlon embraced; Lionel and Gina embraced, and, as she too lingeringly stepped back and to the side, he kissed her hand (a nice touch).

And Lionel Asbo began.

"Can you all hear me, my friends?" A mutter of assent. ". . . Marl and me? What can I tell you. We been best mates," he said scathingly (as if settling the hash of anyone who claimed otherwise), "since we was *babies*." The womenfolk led a soft chuckle. "Sometimes, for a hoot, our mums'd take it in turns to feed us both at once. Didn't you, Grace. Didn't you, Auntie Mercy. *That's* how close we were, me and Marl — he was the bloke on the next tit along." More maternal mirth. "So the months passed. Then, when we stopped brawling over the next bottle of formula, well, we started putting ourselves about like normal little boys. All right. We was so-and-sos. There's no other word for it. We were right so-and-sos. Scallywags, if you like."

And Des thought, He's found a style, Uncle Li. There'll be some rough edges, but he's found a style. Dawn was watching with her arms intently crossed.

"Bunking off day care and sneaking into X-films through the fire escapes." Male laughter. "Ringing all the neighbours' doorbells and giving them the finger. Aged two." Female laughter. "And, when we was

taller, pissing through they letterboxes."
General laughter. "We had a specialty, me
and Marl. It started one Bonfire Night,
when we was three, but soon we were doing
it all year round. What you looked out for
was a big heap of wet dogshit near a nice
smart car. You'd ease a fat cherry bomb in
under the slime, light the fuse, then nip
round the corner." Affectionate tut-tutting.
"Bang! You come back, and it's all over the
paintwork. Every inch. Beautiful. Not so
popular with the uh, the passers-by." More
affectionate tut-tutting.

"Nicking trikes, then bikes, then mopeds,
then scooters. This is how you grow. Then
proper motors, then vans, then lorries. We
had the odd scrap, I don't mind telling you,
about whose turn it was to steer. See, we
was only six or seven when we started." A
deep hum of admiration. "So one of us did
the pedals and the other sat on his chest
and did the wheel. If you were on top you'd
go *brake* or *power*. And if you was under-
neath, and it was a pantechnicon, and Marl
was all *power power power power power*,
well, you just closed you eyes and hoped for
the best."

He had them. File upon file of beaming
moist-eyed faces. When this bit's over,
thought Des, I'll ask Granny Grace for a

dance. Just a gentle shuffle on the edge of the floor, if she's game.

"Then comes uh, adolescence. Shoplifting, credit cards, mug jobs, smash and grab. At school — suspension, expulsion, PRU offroll. Youth Court, Youth Custody, and the odd spot of Yoi. Then came maturity. Which in my case meant prison." Some muffled snorts, a single guffaw. "Marl was craftier, and quicker on his toes. I was more headstrong. I wouldn't learn. For me, for me that's a point of principle. *Never learn.*

"So. We had our careers to make. I was drawn to *reset* — you know, selling on — and to debt work. Marlon here was a natural thruster. B and E. Otherwise known as burgling. And ooh was he useful. It's why he's called *the Floater*. Marl, he could ransack a barracks in broad daylight and no one'd turn a hair. What a talent. What a gift. So him with his thrusting, and me with me reset. Plus, you know, there was always uh, a bit of this, that, and the other.

"Okay. Okay. What we was doing was not in uh, strict accordance with the law. But we make no apologies, Marl and me." An intensely interested quiescence. "For why? Because the law's there to protect the *rich man's shilling.*" A hot murmur of agreement. "And no bloke worth the name's going to

130

bend over for *that*." Prolonged and stormy applause.

Which Lionel now quelled, with raised palms and lowered head. "And all the way along, of course, there was skirt. Birds, birds, birds. And Jesus, with Rhett Butler here, tall, dark and handsome with his lovely scar, it was like he'd entered the Olympics. Which event? The Legover!" Reluctant amusement. "Like how many can he do in one day. Or one hour. His bedroom — he fit it with a revolving door!" Unreluctant amusement. "As for me, with my ugly mug, I just held his coat and warmed his dunkers." Quiet male laughter. "Sorry, ladies. I mean his johnnies — his uh, family planning." Quiet female laughter. "Well, I wasn't that bothered. But him? With the minge? He was styling his hair with it. That's the Floater. That's Marlon Welkway."

Lionel half turned. The bride was smiling at the groom in coquettish reproach; Marlon's wet eyes were shut and his shoulders were shaking. Des, too, half turned, and noticed Ringo slipping out through the tall double doors.

"Now I always thought, Marl? Marlon Welkway? He's not the marrying kind. Marl? No danger. Ladies' man. Confirmed bachelor if you like . . . Ah, but then he goes and falls under the spell . . . of the gorgeous Gina." Cheers, whoops, and ear-stinging whistles. "Gina Drago. Look at her. Pretty as a sunset on a waterfall. Yes, there'll be gloom in the pubs of Diston tonight. As it sinks in with all the blokes that the jewel of the manor, Gina Drago, has now become Gina Welkway."

Lionel solemnly clapped his hands, and was joined by the entire company. This went on for a minute and a half.

"There's been a lot of talk about the so-called *garage meet*." An affirmatory murmur. "Didn't mean a thing. See, we *always* rucked. As babies, toddlers, kids, youths, grown-ups — always rucked. Long fights, serious fights. Why? Out of *respect*. To keep ourselves honest. Yeah, we fought, Marl and me. Well," he said, with a comparatively lenient sneer, "no one *else* was any good at it." Deferential clearing of throats.

"Now I've gone on long enough. Without further ado — let the celebrations begin! . . . Oh yeah — before I forget. You know, friends, half an hour ago I happened to pop up to the first floor. And there was a queue of uh, hotel staff on the stairs. Not them handsome young waiters in they cream jackets. No. Kitchen skivvies. Horrible bloody old geezers from the boiler rooms and the compost heap. With flies buzzing round they heads. And they all undoing they belts." Silence. Lionel frowned. "I said, *What's happening, gents?* And one of them points down the corridor. And what do I see? Gina." Extreme silence. "With her *fucking trousseau up round her waist and her fucking knickers down round her shins and her great big fat arse in the air and her — !*"

. . . So, no. No, Marlon and Gina did not spend the evening hours drinking Girgentina and eating *bebbux* on the poolside veranda of their rented villa on the Maltese islet of Gozo.

And, no, Desmond and Dawn did not spend the evening hours drinking *vin de table* and eating cottage pie, by candlelight, on the thirty-third floor of Avalon Tower.

No. Each and every one of those present, even the bridesmaids, even the grandmothers, spent the night in the copshops (and clinics) of Metroland, on preliminary charges of Criminal Damage and Affray.

The cost of the repairs to the Imperial Palace would eventually run to six hundred and fifty thousand pounds.

Dawn was released the next morning, and Des the next afternoon. It was made clear to them that they would have to testify in court. Four days later, Dawn's body stopped shaking.

And Des remembered his last glimpse of the Imperial Palace (he had his bleeding face crushed up against the back window of the Black Maria). He saw a sign saying *Eats. Drinks. Beds. Decent Rooms At Decent Prices*. And he saw the white-ribboned Austin Princess, with its starred and cratered windscreen and the brick still lying on its bonnet — Ringo's contribution to the Whitsun wedding.

4

At two in the afternoon Officer Fips came to fetch him.

"Best of luck, Lionel," said Pete New from his bunk.

Asbo sauntered freely down the stone passage. He was led up four flights of steps, then through a hall bracingly redolent of vomit and carbolic, and then out on to the colonnade with its dripping arches. The Governor's door stood wide open.

Slight, bald, with frizzled eyebrows and a bulging forehead, Governor Wolf did not at all resemble the bearer of good news as he said drily,

"Ah. Here he is. The estimable Mr.

Asbo . . . I suppose you just plug away at it, don't you, Lionel. Month after month. With your brain hurting. And your tongue sticking out of the corner of your mouth. Plugging away at the Lottery."

"The Lottery? Course I don't. Think I'm stupid? And what about it?"

"What *about* it?"

Lionel barely remembered; he had only filched the coupon to give a certain old lag a niggle (and it was all a load of bollocks anyway). He stood there with his hands in his pockets. Governor Wolf — who had long ago stopped trying to make Lionel call him *sir* — said again,

"What *about* it?"

Sighing, Lionel said, "Okay. You got me up here because I won fifteen quid. It's a mug's game, the Lottery. If you ask me."

Governor Wolf threw his pencil on to the desk and said, "Well. I suppose this proves that God's got a sense of humour."

Lionel grew alert.

"It's more than fifteen pounds, Asbo. It's a substantial sum."

Like a soldier Lionel went from the at-ease posture to full attention.

"How substantial? Sir!"

Owing to an earlier infraction, Lionel was

confined to his cell. But the next morning Pete New was carted off to the san for an hour of physiotherapy, and when he came back he said,

"You're on the front page of the *Sun*."

A recumbent Lionel was examining his fingernails. He said, "Headline?"

"Lionel Asbo, Lotto Lout."

"Photo?"

"You outside the Bailey. Being led away and giving the finger."

Lionel merely shrugged, and New ventured to say,

"Wasn't there a box you could tick, Lionel? You should've ticked it. *Confidential* or whatever. Now you'll never get a moment's peace."

"I'm not bothered. By the publicity. I can handle it . . . You know, Pete, the funny thing is, I never done the Lottery in all me life! Fucking mug's game, if you ask me."

That afternoon Lionel received an official visitor: Dallen Mahon, the lawyer assigned to him by Legal Aid. They sat at a square table in the commissary, Dallen with her briefcase and her mineral water, Lionel, in his navy overalls, drinking coffee and eating Toblerone.

"It's simple," she said. "Pay off the civil

suit, and they'll prosecute you on a lesser charge. Say Drunk and Disorderly. A fine and a caution. And you walk."

"What, I pay *all* of it?"

"Well no one *else* has got any money, have they. Mr. Drago's willing to make a modest contribution. I mean Gina's still inside. Not to mention" — she took out her notebook — "Dejan, Namru, Oreste, and Vassallo. And all the uncles and cousins."

Lionel's face assumed a fond expression. Gina, after it went off at the Imperial Palace, had certainly caught the eye. With a chair leg in one hand and half a violin in the other. "She's a spirited girl, that Gina . . . Listen. I'm prepared to pay me share. I worked it out. Eight thousand. And that's it."

"Lionel. You're a millionaire a hundred and forty times over."

"Yeah, but seven hundred k!"

"Nine hundred. Lost custom."

"Jesus Christ. Some people . . ."

"Lionel, your financial situation has changed. Has this sunk in?"

"Wait. If I stump up, does Marlon walk?"

"Marlon walks. And so do . . . and so do Charlton, Rod, Yul, Burt, Troy, and Rock."

"Well I'm not having that, am I. It was Marlon started it. And now he *walks?* On my hard-earned . . . Marlon poncing off my success? Enjoy you daydream, Dallen."

"You all walk. John, Paul, George, and Stuart. Sleep on it. In your cell."

"I'll do that."

"And tomorrow morning, when you and your colleague are mucking out," she said, "you might have second thoughts."

"I might. Now where's this uh, adviser?"

Dallen made a come-nearer gesture to the guard, who went off and shortly returned with a suntanned forty-year-old in a pin-stripe suit.

"Lionel Asbo? Jack Firth-Heatherington."

"Excuse us, would you, Dallen? We going to have a little chat. About cash streams. And uh, me portfolio."

Des was in the kitchen, with Jon on his lap. Dawn sat opposite, with Joel on her lap. That day's *Sun* lay between them, open at pages four and five: a bullet-point retrospective of the whole career, with more photographs, including two mugshots (full face and profile) of Lionel at the age of three. Dawn said,

"Ring rang. Again. He's all on pins. He said, *How much d'you reckon he'll be giving away? How much should I ask for?*"

"Ask for? Ask Lionel for? Ringo's off his

138

nut. You never *ask* Uncle Li for money. He's been that way since he was a nipper. You ask him for money and he'll smash your face in."

". . . Ooh, Mean Mr. Mustard. And you say you love him. He's a truly dreadful person. And you love him."

"Dawn, he's worse than you know. But I can't help it. It's like you and Horace. He's a truly dreadful person too — and you love him. You can't help it either."

"Yeah, and I wish I could. Help it."

"Look on the bright side. No more of them bleeding dinners up Jorliss."

Horace Sheringham?

It's nothing personal, Desmond, he would typically begin as he settled down to his bowl of Heinz tomato soup (to be followed, invariably, by Birds Eye fish fingers), *but you see, you and Dawn have different brains.*

Oh come on Dad, groaned his daughter.

Please love, don't start, groaned his wife.

Different how, Mr. Sheringham?

And Horace, who was an unemployed traffic warden (in Diston — where traffic wardens were in any case unknown), would patiently proceed. *Well. Your brain's smaller and a different shape. Whilst hers is normal, yours is closer to a primate's. Nothing per-*

139

sonal, lad . . . Oh, I *see. I can't even state a scientific fact. In my own home.*

Horace's home was a low-ceilinged flatlet above an electrics shop on Jorliss Parkway. After a few months of this Des started saying,

What about your brain, Mr. Sheringham? Is yours bigger than mine too?

Course it is. Stands to reason. It's why you've got such a childish face.

Horace's face was dark red, and twisted and seized, a crustacean face (with nose and chin shaped like a claw), and tiny black eyes.

You see, Dawn, he's different from you and I.

You and me, said Des.

Pardon?

You and me. You wouldn't say, He's different from I, *would you?*

Of course not. But you and me's rude.

It's not rude. It's right. How's your French, Mr. Sheringham?

My French?

Oui. Ton français, c'est bien? *How's your Italian?* Puedes hablar español?

Whatever is he going on about? No more of your mumbo-jumbo, Desmond my lad . . . Well then. Thank you. Thank you very much indeed. There's my dinner ruined.

So after the business in Metroland, it was all very simple. Des was not a witness to that climactic scene — Horace scrawnily gasping and coughing and falling over as he bundled great armfuls of Dawn's clothes and books out of the first-floor window, Prunella Sheringham weeping on her knees . . .

Off! I'm disowning you, my girl. Go and live with your darkie. In jail! That's where you both belong. Go on. Off with you. Out!

Des sipped his tea and said, "He'll look more kindly on me now. Now there's a millionaire in the family."

"Seriously, Des. We've got our pride, and we're not coming cap in hand. But seriously. He's *got* to give you something. He wouldn't have won a penny piece if it wasn't for you! . . . Look at this. Okay. He can keep the hundred and thirty-nine million. He can keep the nine hundred and ninety-nine thousand. What about the nine hundred and ninety-nine pounds fifty! . . . It's only right, Des. *You* filled in the numbers."

This was true enough. On one of his prison visits, a month or so earlier, Lionel said, *Hang on to this for us, Des. Load of bollocks. I've signed me name and that.* And Des, looking at it, said, *It's the new one,*

141

Uncle Li. You got to fill out the numbers and post it in. After an affronted moment Lionel said, *Well fill it out youself, Des. Yeah. Nah, wouldn't soil me hands. You fill it out. It's a fucking mug's game, the Lottery. If you ask me.*

"Well you never know with Uncle Li. And I'm still in his bad books."

"Whatever for?"

"Eh. You don't say *whatever*. You just say *what*. It's like *while* and *whilst*. Sorry."

"No. No, Des, keep doing it."

". . . He didn't like my statement in court."

"Your statement was better than *his* statement. *I solemnly swear, under oaf . . .*"

"You don't understand the criminal mind, Dawnie . . . And the other matter. The dogs."

"Mm. The dogs."

"Dawn, never mind the money. It's . . . we shouldn't think about the money. Just look at it this way. We've got a whole extra room."

"We could take in a lodger!"

". . . No. No. We'll make it a nice study for the two of us. Like a library."

"Yeah . . . It's not right to think about the money."

"And one day, Dawnie — maybe a nursery

and all."

"Oh, Desi. The things you say."

"A whole extra room. He's got no use for it now. He won't be coming back here. Will he."

5

After agonising about it for a couple of weeks (and after many grave discussions with Pete New), Lionel undertook to cover the eight hundred and eighty-five k (Jayden Drago making up the difference). Then progress was swift.

The hideous envelope (windowed, dun-coloured, and spitefully undersized) came by second-class post, in late June. It contained by far the longest literary effort that Des had ever seen from his uncle's pen (MILK and TOILITPAPER and TU-BASKO — this was the kind of thing he was used to). Lionel's letter was in block capitals and unpunctuated, like a telegram without the stops. Des and Dawn took another look at it on the bus on the way to Queen Anne's:

DES BE AT NORF GATE ON SATDEE JULY 11 TWELVEFIRTY BRING ME DRIVE-IN LISENSE ME BIRF STATIFICAT ME BLAK

SELL FONE AND ME CUMPEW UH [the last four words were crossed out] AND THE DOGS PEDDYGREES BE THERE SO NO MINNIE CABIN FOR YOU THAT SAT-DEE TELL SIMFEA ALRIGHT LIONEL

"Jesus," said Des. "He's winding me up. *Simfea!* Why didn't he sign it *Loyonoo?*"

"He's taking the piss. Simfea."

"Simfea. You know Simfea's mum and — Christ, you know Cynthia's mum and dad both call her Simfea? Amazing, that. You give your daughter a name of — seven letters. And you can only pronounce four of them!"

"They can't pronounce it," said Dawn. "But I bet they can spell it!"

"And the only bit *he* got right was the *a!* Computer — look at that glottal stop. He's taking the piss."

But the letter had an atmosphere: Lionel had hated writing it, and the words themselves had hated being written. Even the paper had hated the pen. With a frown Des said,

"I can't work him out, Dawnie. Never could. I mean, he's clever when he wants to be. Last time I was there he said something really good. Very acute, I thought."

"Go on then."

144

"Well there was this bloke in the prison caff. Who was obviously off his chump. Dribbling and gibbering away to himself. And Uncle Li said the bloke'd get off light. Diminished responsibility. And Uncle Li said it was all crap, diminished responsibility. They get these experts in, and ask them, *Did the defendant know what he was doing, and did he know what he was doing was wrong?* Uncle Li says that's all crap."

"How's he work that one out?"

"Well he's right. There's only one question the law needs to ask. And Li goes, *Oy, nutcase!* To the psycho. *Oy! Mental! Would you have done that old lady if a copper'd been watching?* And the psycho shakes his head . . . Uncle Li's right. Would you do it if a copper was watching? That's the question, and never mind all the other stuff. I thought that was very acute."

". . . Just a few hundred would be brilliant," said Dawn. "He wouldn't even notice it. Don't worry, love. *You* filled in the numbers. Lionel'll do the right thing."

"Yeah," said Des.

Outside the north gates of Stallwort Prison, at noon, on Saturday, July 11, Desmond hung back, taking note of the thirty-odd reporters and photographers, the TV crew,

145

and the white limousine with the two men leaning on it — the chauffeur in his serge uniform and peaked cap, and the city gent in pinstripes and a bowler hat. Saturday was sunless but intensely humid, and the red-brick building dankly gleamed in its sweat, looking like a terrible school for very old men.

At half past twelve Lionel was punctually escorted from the inner gate to the outer, wearing the clothes he'd had on when he went inside — the mauled grey suit, the ripped and bloodied white shirt, and the slender rag of his dark-blue tie. He signed a form on a clipboard while the guard busied himself with the locks.

In the course of his thoughtful reply to Lionel's prison letter, Des offered the following advice (*of course, I wouldn't know, but this seems to make sense*): try to establish a cheerful and (*even though it might go against the grain*) respectful relationship with the media crowd, because (*like it or not, Uncle Li*) they're going to play a part in your immediate future. *And remember — they're just doing their job. A bit of common courtesy, that's the thing. What would it cost you, after all?* And Des recurrently imagined his uncle, frowning in his cell as he pondered

146

these words . . .

"Some questions, Mr. Asbo!"

"*Fuck* off out of it," said Lionel with a convulsive shrug as he pushed himself through.

"Mr. Asbo! How will you —"

"*Fuck* off out of it. You know what you are? You the fucking *scum of the earth*. Here, Des. Away from these fucking slags. Come on, boy."

"Desmond! One question!"

"Goo on. I *told* yuh. *Fuck* off out of it!"

The chauffeur opened the rear door. Lionel paused. Then, while the cameras flashed and mewed, he unleashed a surprisingly cosmopolitan flurry of obscene gestures: the V-sign, the middle finger, the pinkie and index, the tensed five digits, the thumbnail flicked against the upper teeth; and then he smacked his left hand down on the biceps of his right arm — whose fist shot skyward. Finally, as he bent to enter the car, Lionel reached for his anal cleft and lingeringly freed his underpants.

"Des?" he said as he settled, and took a can of Cobra from the ice bucket. "Don't *never* talk to the press. See, Des, they'll *distort* it. You say one thing — and they go and print another! Uh, excuse me uh, Mr. Firth-Heatherington." *Mr. Firf-Hevrington.*

"Hello!"

"Yes, sir?"

"You don't mind, do you?" And, with the stolidity of a man who had never in his life travelled by other means, Lionel pressed the necessary button, and a glass partition slowly surged towards the roof. "Want a quiet word with me nephew."

"Of course, Mr. Asbo."

Des drew in a chestful of breath and said, "Well, congratulations, Uncle Li. It's like a fairy tale. Magic."

"Yeah, and tomorrow it'll all disappear. The market's gone and wanked itself out, Des. The banks've sploshed it all away and they *kiping* on us now! What can you trust?"

They rode on. After a while, to fill the silence (it was a new kind of silence), Des said mildly, "Gold. I was reading that it never drops in value. Gold."

". . . Oh, you was reading, was you. You brought me stuff?"

"Course." And Des handed him the plastic bag.

"No computer!"

"You crossed that bit out, Uncle Li. I thought you crossed that bit out."

Now the whirring white machine was up on the London Orbital. A motorbike drew level, fell back, drew level. A goggled face peered in.

"What's this?"

"The glass, it's tinted, Uncle Li. He can't see you. He's just a snapper. A pap."

"I'll give him fucking pap!"

Lionel lowered the window with one hand and reached for a full can of Cobra with the other, but before he could fling it Des yelled out — "*No! No*, Uncle Li! They're provoking you. Don't! Don't give them the satisfaction . . ."

Over the next two minutes Lionel's eyes calmed and cleared.

"You got to be careful, Uncle Li. Make allowances. You've had a shock to your system."

"Shock?" *Shoc-kuh?*

"Yeah. Your whole life's changed. Make allowances. You're a public figure. With a hundred and forty million quid."

"Mm. Huh. More like thirty-nine. After them bloodsuckers been at it."

"Uncle Li, you're not going to be yourself for a week or two. You got to be cool."

"I *am* cool."

Then silence. The new silence.

"Where you off to now then?"

"The Pantheon Grand." *The Pamfeon Grand.* "Till I sort meself out. Christ, there's

149

no end to it. Sign this, sign that. Sign *this*, sign *that*. Sign *this*, sign *that*." For a while Lionel railed against red tape — and bent MPs. After another silence Des said,

"Dawn's moved into the flat. Bit tight in the single but we manage. You aren't bothered, are you Uncle Li? See, her —"

"Gaw, don't tell me." And for the first time Lionel smiled. "Don't tell me. What's he called, the old arsehole? Horace. Don't tell me. Horace found out about her night in the nick. *And if you ever darken me door* . . . So she's in. You got you Uncle Li to thank for that, Des Pepperdine."

In the private street off St. James's that served as the driveway to the Pantheon Grand Hotel there were more reporters, and more obscene gestures, and more choice anathemas (plus a momentary flurry of raised fists). Lionel shouldered his way through the revolving doors — and into the ancient hangar of the atrium. With his head down he followed Firth-Heatherington to the check-in bay, and rocked to a halt, breathing harshly and wiping his upper lip on his cuff. Round about, small groups of sleek metallic seniors murmured and milled.

"The items you requested are in your suite, sir. The toiletries and so on."

Lionel grimly nodded.

"And the outfitters and whatnot, they'll be coming to you at three. If that's convenient."

Lionel grimly nodded.

"Will you be dining with us tonight, Mr. Asbo?"

". . . Yeah, girl. It's booked. Seven-thirty. Table for six."

"Ah, so it is. And may I take an impression of your credit card?"

"Course you can." Lionel nodded his head sideways. Firth-Heatherington snapped open his valise. "There. Take you pick."

"And would you like a newspaper tomorrow morning, sir?"

"Yeah. Guiss a *Lark.*"

"I'm sorry, sir?"

"Jesus. Guiss a *Sun.*"

"I hope you have a nice stay with us, sir." They stepped back.

"I was just thinking, Mr. Asbo, that you —"

"Call me Lionel. Jack."

"I was just wondering, Lionel, if you wouldn't be happier elsewhere. There's a far more —"

"What's that mean?" said Lionel with abrupt and inordinate menace. "What's that mean? Is this, or is this *not*, the dearest hotel in London?"

"Well yes it is. But it's slightly fuddy-duddy here. And there's a place near Sloane Square, a new place called the South Central, where I think you'd feel . . . more at home."

"More at home? More at home? What, it's council flats, is it? I've had enough *home*. Okay? I've had enough fucking *home*."

Des looked on as Lionel's face began to swell (he had seen this before). It was the size of a carnival balloon when he said, in a froth of fricatives,

"I'll be thoroughly at me ease in the Pantheon Grand thanks very much Mr. Firth-Heatherington."

Heads turned — then dropped . . . Everyone waited for the break, this fissure in the order of things, to close and heal.

"Well," came the whisper as Firth-Heatherington backed away. "Please ring me at any time, Lionel."

"Call me *sir*. Jack." He loosened his tie with a gasp and a violent hoist of the chin. "*You* can run along and all, Des. Oh and listen."

"Yes, Uncle Li."

"I'll be round in a day or two. Uh, Desmond, I intend to relieve you financial situation. And that's a promise. On me mother's

152

life." He smiled and said, "Oh yeah. How is the old . . . ?"

"Poorly, Uncle Li."

"Mm. Well. I'll take care of Grace. Once and for all. On you way, boy."

"Uncle Li, seriously. *That* lot," he said, jerking a thumb towards the forecourt, "they want you back inside! It's envy, Uncle Li, that's what it is. Don't let them work you up. All right?"

"Ah, but you fears are unfounded. I'm in full control."

And Des left him there on the other side of the glass at the Pantheon Grand. The shorn crown with its twinkling studs of sweat. The ripped suit, the bloodstained shirt, the thin blue tie. The new silence. The eyes.

"Just out of interest. Has your dad got an actual grudge against black people? Or was he just born that way?"

"Well," she said cautiously. "He does sometimes go on about how they ruined his profession."

"His profession? Ha — that's a good one! Since when's being a *parking* warden a . . . No. That's unkind. Forget I ever said that, Dawnie."

She was lying on the bed with Joel and

Jon (while Des climbed into his minicabbing gear — old trainers and sweats). What she liked to do was — she'd slide the dogs' ears between her toes. Said it felt like silk. *Mmm.* And whenever they got the chance Joel and Jon would give her feet a furtive, reverential lick.

"I'm tense. About Uncle Li."

"I'm not. Not any more. If he does something for us, that'd be nice. If he doesn't. Well."

Dawn worked four nights a week — teaching English to foreign students. And the minicabbing? What Des minded, in the end, was the inanition. He kept asking himself: Is there *anything* stupider than sitting and staring at a red light?

"When I was little," she said, "I wanted a pup so much. Or a kitten. I kept a pet *ant*. I had an ant bar on my windowsill. I fed it jam . . . And now I've got these two fine fellas. And I've got you. And we'll have a whole new room. We'll have twice the space, Des. Just think."

He checked his keys and his money.

"His eyes. His eyes've gone . . . I just hope there's a copper watching. He won't do anything if there's a copper watching. I just hope there's a copper watching."

6

In the silver cube Lionel Asbo rode up to his suite on the eleventh floor. Bedroom, lounge, office area, bathroom with two sinks (and an extra shitter in a little closet of its own). The leading segment of the toilet roll was shaped in a V: a thoughtful touch. He stripped, and stood for ten minutes under a shower head the size of an umbrella — sluicing off all that Stallwort. He shaved, wielding the heavy brush and the heavy razor. The heaviness of the brush, the heaviness of the razor: these weights had a meaning that Lionel could not yet parse.

Next door he climbed into the new clothes Firth-Heatherington had laid on for him: white shirt, dark slacks, tasselled loafers, sports jacket. But he'd put on a few, what with the stodge they give you inside, and he couldn't quite get the trousers joined up at the waist. So he used the fluffy white belt off the complimentary robe. Looked a bit stupid but there it was. Half past one. Now what?

Having hosed himself down and all that, Lionel expected to feel twice the price. But he had to admit that he was still coming over slightly queer. Not himself. In fact, he was coming over very peculiar indeed. The air seemed glazed and two-dimensional:

filmic. James Bond or what have you. Except James Bond never . . . There was a solid pressure in Lionel's loins, like a stuck crank, and his left pillock ached. Once again he tried to move his bowels. With no joy. Come to think of it, he hadn't had a proper stint since that day with the Governor. And usually he was as regular as time itself . . . Mind you, he was looking forward to his dinner. Seven-thirty, table for six: John, Paul, George, Ringo, and Stuart. Lionel gave a grin, with scrolled upper lip. It was going to be a good one, this. He had it all worked out.

Now Lionel betook himself to the Bolingbroke Bar on the ground floor. Straddling a tall stool, he had a couple of bottles of champagne and cleared a few trays of Bombay Mix. The *whole hotel* was nonsmoking; but as against that, there was a garden beyond the open doors and he stepped outside, every fifteen or twenty minutes, for a quiet Hundred. Milk-white statues. And the drugging scents of roses and hyacinths. Also a fountain and the placid patter of its shimmering droplets. He believed for a moment (not a long moment) that he was feeling somewhat improved.

With a copy of *Country Life* on his lap, he

sat by the dormant fireplace in the Lancaster Lounge. Two burnished old gents were chatting away on the adjacent settee. Lionel unthinkingly assumed they were in their late forties; but then he began to decode the static of their talk — and they were reminiscing about Normandy and D-Day! Now Lionel, as a boy, had been dead keen on the bloodbaths of World War II, so it only took him a minute. 1944 — that made them well over eighty! . . . Gazing ceilingward, Lionel had a little think about the vale of years. There was that doddering tycoon who married some tart a fifth his age, and there was the Queen, of course — but they were bound to keep *her* walking, weren't they, what with the . . . Or could this mean that, among the rich, it was maybe even halfway *normal* to live that long? And then the two gents leapt to their feet and strode forward to hail and hug their wives!

After a little accident in the Lancaster Lounge, and after a lively exchange of views with certain fellow guests in the shopping arcade, Lionel found himself in the foyer. Looking out. He supposed that, if he'd been feeling better, he would've taken a stroll — buy a *Lark*, see how the local pubs compared . . . Nine or ten representatives of the Fourth Estate: still out there. He registered the urge to go and give them a piece of his mind; but an unfamiliar qualm restrained him (what? It was something like an unexamined fear of derision). He went on standing there, leaning against the pillar, looking out. Gilded cage, if you like. He went on standing there, leaning there, looking out.

Then it was three o'clock and he had the outfitters to deal with back upstairs. The couturier, the hatmaker, the bespoke cobbler, the hosier, the mercer, the jeweller, and the furrier. Bolts of cloth were glowingly unfurled. He stood there like a felon about to be frisked as the tailors whispered round him with their pins and tapes. In such circumstances, where was the mannequin's mind supposed to go? He started the hour with his chin up but after twenty minutes it dropped and slewed. A beast at the altar — his martyred, his crucified form. When this lot pack up, he kept mechanically thinking, I'll avail myself of the hotel facilities . . . Just then a whippet in a waistcoat with needles for teeth veered close and chalked a cross on the waxwork's smarting breast.

First the gym: on the bench with the weights. He'd maintained his regime, as you always do inside, and his arms were soon

158

shunting away like hairy pistons. Then something struck him. *What do I need me strength for?* he said out loud. *Now?* Still, he worked up a fair sweat and then went for a dip in the pool and a long rubdown (after a slight misunderstanding) from the Danish bird in the pink smock. Next he got his nails trimmed and glazed, and his prison toejam sorted out. As an afterthought he had his nut tightened in the barber's.

Upstairs again he was surprised by a need for human company. He considered summoning Cynthia. *Cynthia?* he said out loud. *Cynthia in the Pantheon Grand? Nah. Cynthia in the Pantheon Grand? Nah. Gina, though. Gina wouldn't give a toss. She'd love it. Walking around swinging her arse and . . .* He suddenly realised what he was doing: he was talking to himself. *Oy. Steady on, mate. You losing you . . .* The heavy furnishings, the heavy room, the heavy hotel on its unfathomable foundations, gripping it to the earth.

. . . So he watched some (crap) porn on the TV (get the computer back off Des), put on his new red tie (it was almost six-thirty), and spent the last hour in the business centre on the ground floor (causing a bit of bother). All day he'd been an astronaut, weightless, without connection, swimming in air . . .

But dinner, at least: this would be perfect Asbo.

"How d'you get an upper-class cunt to burn his face?"

"Go on then."

"Phone him when he's doing the ironing! . . . An upper-class cunt goes into a pub with a —"

"Excuse me, sir, are you ready to order?" said the bearded waiter for the seventh or eighth time (and the bearded waiter, though young, was as Lionel saw it an upper-class cunt).

"Hang *on* . . . An upper-class cunt goes into a pub with a heap of wet dogshit in his hand. He says to the barman, *Look what I nearly stepped in!* . . . How many upper-class cunts does it take to . . . ? Wait up. Wait up. Uh, concentrate, lads."

They were dining in the Grosvenor Grill. It was now just after ten.

"Well, it stares you in the face, doesn't it. Steak and chips."

"Plain as day," said John.

"Open-and-shut," said Paul.

"Common sense," said George.

"No-brainer," said Ringo.

Stuart, on this occasion, was silent; but then Stuart (the seedy registrar) hardly ever

160

said anything anyway.

"That one'll do," said Lionel, pointing to the filet mignon.

And did these young men — evenly spaced round the glistening ellipse of the white tabletop — did they resemble a band of brothers? No. They shared a mother, true, but Grace Pepperdine's genetic footprint was vanishingly light, and the boys were all duplicates of their fathers. So John, twenty-nine, looked Nordic, Paul, twenty-eight, looked Hispanic, George, twenty-seven, looked Belgic (or Afrikaans), and Ringo, also twenty-seven, looked East Asiatic; only Stuart, twenty-six, and of course Lionel, looked English (though Stuart was in fact half-Silesian). John, Paul, George, and Ringo, at any rate, wore the same threadbare zootsuits and had the same hairstyle — slashbacks, with long sideburns that tapered to a point.

"How would you like that cooked, sir?"

"Cooked?" said Lionel. "Just take its horns off, wipe its arse, and sling it on the plate. And bring all you jams and pickles and mustards . . . Us against the world, eh, lads?"

It did not escape Lionel's notice that when he went out for his trihourly smokes he always returned to five strained faces and a sudden, stoppered hush. And he knew all about their difficulties, John, Paul, and George with their bad debts and cramped flats (their shattered wives, their rioting toddlers), Ringo with his decade on the dole, and Stuart (who alone could probably look forward to some kind of pension) sharing a bedsit with a bus conductor in SE24. Now Lionel invited the company to raise their glasses. He thought that everything was coming along quite nicely.

"Why did the upper-class cunt cross the road?" he resumed.

"Go on then."

The brothers had had, between them, forty-eight gin and tonics.

"Lionel."

"Ring, mate."

Ringo coughed. He wiped a hand across his mouth and lowered his head.

". . . I spent twelve grand today," said Lionel, "on guess what."

"What."

"Socks. Us against the world, eh lads?"

So after a bit John starts having a go at Ringo, and Ringo starts having a go at George, and George starts having a go at Paul, and Paul starts having a go at John, and Lionel, not to be left out, starts having a go at Stuart (for never saying anything). That bit soon quietened down.

"Lionel."

"John, mate."

John coughed. He wiped a hand across his mouth and lowered his head.

Then the food came, and all the beers, and all the wines.

"See that?" said Lionel, tapping the label of the Château Latour Pauillac. "That's the vintage — the date. And guess what. Give or take a tenner, it's the same as the price! We'll have one each. Us against the world, eh lads?"

So John starts having a go at Paul, and Paul starts having a go at George, and George starts having a go at Ringo, and Ringo starts having a go at John (and Lionel starts having a go at Stuart). That bit took much longer to quieten down.

It was close to midnight when Lionel called for the bill.

"There's tension in the air, lads," he said as he followed the fairy lights up the garden path with his brandy balloon and his cigar. "Bound to be. I mean, look around. This ain't Diston. This ain't KFC. Everything's different now."

Lionel heard the gulp of five Adam's

apples in five shrivelled throats.

"Tension. It's only natural. You kid brother's been tipped the wink by Lady Luck. And you asking youself, What's he going to do for his own?"

Lionel heard the soft seethe of five intakes of breath.

"John. Paul. George. Ringo. Stuart. You lives are about to be transformed."

Lionel turned. Five pairs of feet staggered back.

"You number-one headache — from now on, completely taken care of. You needn't give it another thought. Ever. That shadow that never goes away? That nagging concern that wakes you up in the middle of the night? A thing of the past. *Over*."

Lionel looked forgivingly from face to face.

"And what's that worry? Well. Come on, let's not be shy. Begins with an *em*. Say it. *Em*. Mm. Mmuh . . ."

Lionel lifted his gaze to the night sky.

"Mum," he said.

The brothers. As pale, still, and silent as the statues.

"Mum. *Mum*. 'Mum.' Our mum, in her declining years — what's going to become of Mum? . . . They not having our mum mate!" Lionel dipped his head and wiped

164

his eyes. He sniffed richly. "Ah, look. I can see the lovely glow in you faces. You feeling better already. Knowing I'll take care of Mum. Our mum. Us against the world, eh lads? Us for Mum!"

. . . So. Stunned hugs in the foyer. Then, one after the other, the five Pepperdines shot out through the revolving doors, ran a brief sprint, and stumbled to a halt.

Sharply watched by Lionel Asbo. Whose head abruptly jerked forward as something interesting seemed to develop with the skeleton staff of press — but it was just Stuart rebounding off a lamp post and falling over backwards, and John and George kneeling down to be sick.

7

"They chucked him out on Sunday morning. He set fire to his suite. But apparently they're only using that as an excuse!"

"Jesus," said Des. "What else did he do?"

"Well he . . . Jesus. Hang on."

Des lay on the couch in the kitchen, wrapped in a white sheet. He was having one of his neurasthenic episodes (for half a day at a time, the world seemed too much for him, too many for him, too full, too rich, too strong). Dawn's wide eyes were staring at the *Sun*.

"He was groaning his head off in the Bolingbroke Bar. And releasing wind from both ends . . . He swam in the pool in his Y-fronts . . . And he asked the masseuse for 'relief' . . . He watched a film in his room called *MILFs Gone Mad*. Then he went and watched more filth in the business centre!"

"The business centre?"

"Where they have the computers. And Lionel was watching it with the sound up!"

"With the sound up?"

"That's what it says. He was sitting there with all these bankers and diplomats and sheiks. Watching something they can't print about *facials*. Facials? Des, what's *that* all about?"

"Uh, I'm not sure. With the sound up?"

"The manager came and . . . There were *two* fights at dinner. The first just a bit of face-slapping. But the second one . . . Ringo, they think it was, crashed into the dessert trolley . . . John and George vomited in the street. And Stuart fell and smashed his head open. And then Lionel goes and dozes off with a fag in his hand. All the sprinklers came on . . . Drink your cocoa!"

"I am!"

"Ooh. They say the hotel's suing him. Not for the physical damage. *The untold detri-*

ment to our reputation and goodwill. That was yesterday. And listen. On Saturday . . . On Saturday there were these two elderly couples standing in the foyer. Minding their own business. And Lionel goes up and says . . . See it? Lionel goes up and says, *What are you lot still doing here? Why don't you all just f*** off and die!*"

It was a while before Lionel looked in at Avalon Tower. But in the meantime they always knew exactly what he was up to. They stayed abreast of his remarkably unvarying activities (fights, expenditures, admissions, ejections), hour by hour, in the tabloids (and in the *Daily Telegraph*).

Sunday. 10:00. Lotto Lout Lionel Asbo chucked out of the Pantheon Grand. *11:15.* Asbo checks into the Castle on the Arch. *12:45.* Asbo caught up in a brief brawl in a pub called the Happy Man in Leicester Square. *15:15.* Asbo enters La Cage d'Or in Dover Street and spends £1,900 on lunch for one. *18:40.* Asbo becomes a provisional member of the Sunset Strip Lounge on Old Compton Street. *21:50.* Asbo becomes a provisional member of the Soho Sporting Club (where his losses at craps and black-jack are said to be prodigious).

"I can't stand it, Dawnie," said Des.

"What's going on? Uncle Li — he's disappeared into the front page!"

Monday. 2:05. Lotto Lout Lionel Asbo becomes a provisional member of the Taboo in Garrick Street. *4:15.* Asbo returns to Soho Sporting Club. *7:50.* Asbo chucked out of the Castle on the Arch. *9:35.* Asbo checks into the Launceston in Berkeley Square. *11:15* Asbo caught up in a brief brawl in a pub called the Surprise in Shepherd Market. *13:00.* Asbo orders a Bentley "Aurora" at the Piers Edwards Showrooms on Park Lane (£377,990). *15:20.* Asbo chucked out of the Launceston. *16:10.* Accompanied by his financial adviser, Jack Firth-Heatherington, Asbo checks into the South Central Hotel in Pimlico. *17:30.* Asbo takes delivery of a consignment of merchandise, mostly clothing, valued at —

Then the story went cold.

"Hello?"

"Dawn. Lionel. I'll be round in fifteen minutes. Get Des."

It was teatime on Saturday. Des was out cabbing (the medium-late shift) and was expected back in good time for *Match of the Day*. With a hot face Dawn rang the pointman at Goodcars, and waited. The dogs smiled up at her. They, too, always seemed gripped by *Match of the Day*, and sat side by side in front of the screen, lightly panting, like a pair of old-fashioned hooligans thirsting for the final whistle and the post-match maul . . .

Lionel used his own keys.

"That you, Lionel?"

He approached, he appeared, he gave a slow nod, and stood there with his head dropped and his arms folded. Three different organisms — one human, two canine — stared out at him.

To Dawn he looked like one of the huge but semi-retired or injured or (more likely) suspended footballers who occasionally deigned to contribute to the analyses on TV: a squarely powerful, low-slung, much-punished body, now swathed in a suit of truly presidential costliness (as if cut from some liturgical material used for hassocks or surplices). He raised his chin and she saw his sky-blue silk tie and the lavish equilateral of its Windsor.

"Well welcome. Settle down, boys!"

To Jon and Joel . . . Jon and Joel were affectionate and intelligent animals — and how could these qualities be combined and brought to bear on Lionel Asbo? Their glossy backsides keenly shimmied but their foreheads were creased with apology and strain. Dawn said,

"They don't know whether to . . ."

After a moment the dogs seemed to wither into themselves, and they turned away.

"Yeah. Turn away. I hate yuh. I'm disgusted with yer. Yer . . ."

Dawn tried to say it brightly. "Lovely suit, Lionel."

"Where's Des?"

Des was taking the stairs three at a time.

". . . Ah. The traveller returns. Tears hisself away from carting pissers round Diston. To keep his meet with his Uncle Li . . . I want a serious talk with you, Master Pepperdine. Dawn, girl. Why don't you take the uh, 'the dogs' for a bit of fresh air."

"Yeah, might as well, Dawnie. It's nice out."

She picked up her keys and reached for the leads on their hook. "I shall," she said. Joel and Jon were already milling at the door. As Des saw them off, Dawn confusedly whispered,

"Ask him to clear his room."

"Well not *yet*," he whispered back.

Des used the toilet and splashed his face with cold water. Behind him the kitchen waited and glared.

"Peace at last. Relax. I'll be chewing you

arse off, Des, in due course. But for now you can just uh . . . kick off you shoes. After you hard day's toil." He was leaning on the fridge with his hands in his trouser pockets. "It's different round here. A woman's touch, if you like."

Dawn's touch: cushions of eye-pleasing colours, framed reproductions on the walls, a spray of scarlet poppies in the glass vase, and, in general, a different standard of order and cleanliness and with something like the promise of confectionery in the air. Lionel took a cigar from its gunmetal tube and lit it with a kitchen match, saying,

"Oy. Where's me TV?"

"Uh, we traded it in. The picture got even hazier. To make anything out, you had to go and sit halfway up the passage . . . This one's still your property, Uncle Li."

"Well put the kettle on. I don't read that rubbish."

He was referring to Saturday's *Daily Mirror* (page five), where Lionel was to be seen signing autographs outside the South Central Hotel.

"I run me eye over it. See, Des, I've hired me own PR team. Megan Jones Associates. Of Acme Talent. Bit steep, but I don't mind paying for the uh, for the expertise. Sounds funny, Des, but what you got to do is — I

171

know this sounds mad, but with the press what you got to do is, you got to show them a bit of *respect*. You know, be friendly! And when you think about it, what's that cost you? *Listen, lads. You got you living to earn. I got me life to live. Fair do's. All right?* They good as gold now. Get on me nerves and that, but . . . See, Des, they was trying to *provoke*. They wanted me back inside!"

Des said, "And why was that, Uncle Li?"

"Envy! Would you credit it. Anyway. Pressure's off. I found meself a decent hotel at last. Not like them other dumps. In this place they know how to let a man breathe."

The Lotto Lout coverage was in any case easing off. Lionel was safely installed in the South Central, and never went out except on business. So. A photograph of the Westminster townhouse Lionel had made an offer on; a photograph of the yacht Lionel was supposedly thinking of buying; a photograph of the Threadneedle Street boardroom where Lionel was introduced to his investment team. And there was occasional stuff from the past. A jocular piece about John, Paul, George, and Ringo (but not Stuart); references to (and photos of) Marlon and Gina Welkway (on the day of their wedding), to Des himself, and to the precocious matriarch Grace Pepperdine . . .

"Oh yeah. Be sure to pop in and say good-bye to you gran."

"What you mean?"

"I'm slinging her in a home," he said. "Just been round there. I told her, *Mum? Pack you nightie.* They coming for her in the morning. Two nice male nurses."

Des had seen Gran as recently as Friday afternoon. It was a visit well caught, he felt, by the musical accompaniment — the jaunty, wonky rhymes and chimes of "Maxwell's Silver Hammer." She was in her chair by the window, with a Silk Cut in one hand and the Kwik crossword in the other — and with a kitten on her lap (a gift from old Dudley's granddaughter). The kitten, tiny Goldie, was so young it could hardly open its eyes. *Isn't she gorgeous, Des? Mwa.* The crossword, he ascertained, was all filled in; but the answers were just alphabet soup.

"A home, Uncle Li? Where?"

"Up a bit. North."

"How far north?"

"Scotland."

"Scotland?"

"Cape Wrath."

Cape Roff. Des happened to know that Cape Wrath, a famously desolate spot, lay on the kingdom's topmost left-hand tip. "How'd she take it?"

"Oh, you know. On come the waterworks. *I'll miss me sister!* All this. I said, *Woman — you forty-two. You can't fight the march of time!* . . . She'll love it once she's there." Lionel went on expansively, "See, Des, there's something new in my life. A new uh, *dimension.* And it's — what? What?"

"The money?"

"No. The future! The future, Des. See, before, it was just day by day. The proverbial wing and a prayer. If you like. No thought of the morrow. The future? *What* fucking future." (Whoff *fucking future.*) "Nothing weighed anything. Everything just uh . . . So Gran — Gran, she ain't that bad *now.* But what'll she be like in a year or two? Eh? Eh?"

"Worse."

"Worse. Let's face it, Des. Her bonce is going. And when you bonce goes . . . I had a long talk with the bloke who runs the home. He's a uh, specialist. Specialist in old people. And he reckons she could be coming down with that *German* disease."

"Alzheimer's?"

"Yeah. That German lurgy that rots you brain. And if she's got that, then it's *all* off. They start *babbling,* see. And we can't have Gran babbling, can we Des. Can't have her babbling. Might say . . . something she'll regret."

Lionel turned and strolled out on to the balcony. Des joined him. Diston, in the gritty shimmer of late July, with its slopes and tiers.

"But Uncle Li, she won't have anyone to talk to up there."

"That's the point."

"You had a look at the place?"

"Why waste me time? The prices tell they own story. She needs skilled care, Des." Lionel rinsed his mouth with saliva before saying, "It's . . . pathetic." *Puffeh ic-cuh.* "She repeats herself. Says one thing. Says it again. *You repeating youself, woman!* . . . This home, Des, it's like a five-star hotel — but with doctors. Okay, four-star. She'll be as happy as a pig in shit up there. Mum. Where's me tea?"

As Des warmed the pot Lionel's eyes settled on the burnished metal tank. "As for *that,*" he said wearily, "open now, is it?"

"Yeah. Shut for weeks. Then it opened . . . Better open than shut. Once it shuts, you can't open it."

"You been sitting —"

"No I *never.*"

". . . Oh. Oh. So this is the way he talks to his own uncle now, is it? His own uncle.

175

Who raised him. Take a seat there. There."
He reached out for the yawning lid
(serrated, like the upper jaw of some black-
gummed deep-sea fish) and smacked it shut.

"There," he said. "On the *tank*."

8

Before making its drop over the shoulder of
the next block along, the sun took a last
look at 33F Avalon Tower — the balcony
with its litter tray and water bowls, the sliding glass door, the kitchen and the two silent
silhouettes . . .

Lionel stood; he tasted his tea; with an
unusually graceful movement he slipped off
his jacket; he reversed his chair, and sat. He
placed a thick-fingered hand on his nephew's nape. He spoke softly.

"You tense, Des. I can feel you tension.
Crouched behind that wheel. Diston traffic.
That's a killing job, that is. Even for a young
man. You do that and you be dead by thirty.
You shouldn't be out there, boy. Should be
studying. With you books. Jesus. You shoulder's like rock. You neck — there's no give
in it . . . The dogs, Desmond. The dogs.
They never had a chance. You fucked them
up when they was just *pups*."

Des could feel Lionel's newly metallic
breath on his cheek.

176

"I go away for a while. I return. And they both lying on they backs and wagging they tails! They like *poodles* . . . I only asked you to do three things. One, two, three. One. Two. Three."

Tabasco. Special Brew. Harsh and regular use of the training tools.

"Uncle Li, I tried. But it's not — it's not in my nature."

". . . *Your* nature? What about *they* nature? They meant to be hard. That's why they were *born.*"

His fierce gaze never wavering, Lionel reached to his right and swung open the cupboard door. There for all to see: the untouched case of red-pepper sauce, the untouched six-packs of malt lager, the untouched training tools — break stick, lunge pole, the ethnic mannequins.

"You was saying?"

". . . You don't *need* them hard any more. You're not going to be out collecting debts *now*, are you."

"Ah, but that's to be wise after the event. You flash little cunt. And I'll always be needing hard dogs. For why? For me security."

"All right. I'm very sorry, Uncle Li."

"All right. You sorry about that. Try being very sorry about this. You statement in court. I died a thousand deaths as those words left you lips. A thousand deaths."

"Which bit?"

. . . I have known Lionel Asbo all my life. And after my mother passed away, when I was twelve, he became more like a father than an uncle. He has always treated me with kindness, understanding, and generosity. I took my mother's death very hard, and I think it's fair to say that I wouldn't have got through it without Uncle Lionel's love and care . . . Everyone knows that Uncle Lionel has a dry sense of humour. And all right, his speech at the wedding reception could be regarded as contentious. But I confirm, under oath, that Lionel Asbo did not *land the first blow.*

Then who did *land the first blow? Is that man in court today?*

. . . "Which *bit?*" said Lionel. "When you pointed you finger! When you *named* him."

Des gave a silent sigh. His statement did no more than corroborate the testimony of eleven waiters, four hired musicians, three Dragos (Dejan, Oreste, and Vassallo), and two of Marlon's own brothers (Troy and Yul).

"What should I have said?"

"Same as John, Paul, and George! That you never saw nothing! You was looking the other way!"

". . . Marlon grassed *you* up. For Gina."

"No he didn't. All in me own head, that was. See, this is what girls do to you, Des. They make you mad."

Lionel lit a fresh cigar (and proceeded to smoke it as he would a Marlboro Hundred, with long drags and emphatic inhalations). The room darkened another shade. With a wistful smile Lionel asked quietly,

"Remember Rory Nightingale, Des? Course you do, course you do. He said something, Rory. Before they uh . . . He said something. Something about you . . . *Des did . . . did it and all!* Stressful moment for the boy, of course," Lionel conceded (and momentarily raised his chin). "They was gagging him. About to take him off. *Des — Des did it and all.* Now why's that stuck in me mind? That's what I want to know. Why's that stuck in me mind? Look at me, Des . . ."

For one minute, two minutes, three, Des laid himself open to those small mobile eyes. And so, perhaps, it might have gone on, and on, for ever and ever . . . But at last he heard the jolts of the locks, the jink and scuffle of the dogs.

"Up you get, boy. We got work to do."

As Des slid to his feet the tank gaped open.

". . . You been sitting on it."

Lionel changed into sweatpants, trainers, and mesh vest. Then the two of them spent three and a half hours ferrying packing cases, tea chests, and cardboard boxes from Lionel's lock-up in Skinthrift Close to Lionel's bedroom at Avalon Tower — which, by the time they were done, was an impenetrable mass of stolen property. They couldn't even get the door shut.

"You be all right," said Lionel. "Just squeeze round it."

"*I* can. But what about you? How'll you get out?"

Fuming, glowing, throbbing (they had relied on the Ford Transit and the stunted lift), Lionel surged into the kitchen and toppled on to the couch.

"You look downhearted, girl. Now why's that? Here, Des. Seen the brothers at all?"

Sitting at the table with Dawn's hand on his shoulder, Des looked up as he wiped his face with a paper towel. "They're ill. All five of them. I saw Uncle Paul."

"Yeah?"

"Yeah. Uncle John's been served with an Order of Distraint. They've seized his flat.

And they've gone and repossessed Uncle George's —"

"Yeah. Well I made me contribution." He gave one of his masterful sniffs. "If it wasn't for me they'd still be inside."

"They wouldn't've been inside in the first place," said Dawn, "if it wasn't for you."

"Dawnie . . ."

"Don't worry, Des, I won't take offence. I'm uh, immune. See, that's what happens when you win a hundred-odd million quid. You go numb. Not happy. Not sad. *Numb*. . . . Here. Jon and Joel. Cost a fair bit to feed."

"Well yeah. They do."

"Okay. I told you I'd relieve you financial situation. And I'll be as good as my word," he said, rising. "I'm taking the dogs off yer."

"But Dawn loves the dogs!"

This weak cry, with its leapt octave, came from Des (who of course loved them too). Dawn sat down suddenly and said,

"What you going to do with them?"

"Cut me losses. I got a buyer. Four hundred quid. Think youself lucky, Des. No more shelling out for they Tabasco."

Now Lionel bathed (causing a not very serious flood in the passage). Ten minutes later, they heard a mighty uprush and downflow of water; and then with a towel round his waist he squelched into the kitchen.

"I don't understand how you can live in these conditions. And there's *nowhere to change*. Go on. Get the dogs in."

Dawn gave Des a meaning nod and he said, "We'll match it, Uncle Li. We'll match the four hundred."

Lionel squelched out again. "Get them in."

Jon and Joel were coiled up under the table. They were painfully aware that they were the cause of a dreadful misunderstanding — which, surely, would very soon be resolved. Leaning forward, Dawn was stroking them with purposeful fingers, as if kneading hope into their harrowed brows.

When Lionel re-entered he was knotting his tie. He said,

"Fair enough. How can any reasonable man refuse?"

Dawn said, "Oh thank you, Lionel. Thank you, thank you."

"You welcome. Let's have it then. Four hundred . . . Oh. You haven't got it on you?" he said. "Oh dear. How unfortunate. See, Des, I need the cash tonight." He threw on his jacket and held out his hand. "The leads. Come on, yer . . . Come on, yer fucking little wankers. Come on, yer fucking little slags."

The dogs lay on their sides with their forepaws bent as Lionel hooked them to the steel hawsers. They rose and their leg muscles stiffened; and there was a terrible minute while they cowered and wheeled. Des half turned away from their beseeching smiles.

"Go with Uncle Li," he said unsteadily. "Good boys." He felt, just now, that if Lionel hit the dogs in front of her then Dawn might give up utterly. "Go with Uncle Li."

Lionel shortened his grip with a sudden tug and the dogs, leaning backward, skidded from the room. There came the sounds of wrenching and rending, the giddy-up of the steel reins, the slammed front door.

". . . Maybe I should've stood up to him."

"Don't talk bloody stupid," said Dawn. "D'you see his eyes?"

"Yeah. What's happened to his eyes?"

"He's stopped blinking! . . . They're murderer's eyes."

Des and Dawn went and looked: the bedroom door torn off its hinges, the room itself stacked deep from floor to ceiling, Lionel's sweats and mesh vest in a loose knot in the passage . . .

"There goes our nursery," said Dawn.

"No. No. I want a youth. And he's not stopping us."

"Oh, Des, you're mad. The things you say."

"I want a youth," he said. "And he's not stopping us. I want a youth."

Just before midnight Des spent a largely speechless half-hour with his gran. Grace sat facing the window, and when he spoke to her she just waved him away . . . There were no pets allowed — in the old people's home singled out by her son. And so Des returned to Dawn with the kitten Goldie zipped up and purring in his windbreaker.

9

"That's absolutely fine, Mr. Asbo. Don't give it another thought, sir. And have a fantastic day."

It wasn't hard to see why Lionel was so very much happier in the South Central — the asymmetric ninety-suite high-rise that loomed like a whimsical robot over the stubby bohemia of north Pimlico. As fancily priced as the Pantheon Grand (and the Castle on the Arch and the Launceston), the South Central described itself, in its publicity material, as *the heavy-metal hotel.*

It catered to rock stars, and not just to heavy-metal rock stars. And not just to rock stars: in its candyishly bright and airy public rooms you might glimpse a recently imprisoned bratpack actor, an incensed fashion model, a woman-beating Premiership footballer — and so on. In brief, the core clientele was rich and famous; and none of them got that way by work of mind. Lionel, at last, had happened upon his peers.

There were never fewer than three plasma TV sets at the bottom of the swimming pool on the back terrace, plus a selection of iPod docks, camcorders, laptops, and minibars. Day-Glo crime-scene tape frequently adorned the entrance to this or that forbidden passageway — illegal firearms, assaults, investigations of rape (statutory and otherwise). There were often fire engines snorting and sneezing in the forecourt — but no ambulances: the hotel deployed its own medical teams to cope with all the pharmaceutical misadventures and the more serious self-mutilations. Similarly, the floodings, the wreckings, the sometimes storey-wide devastations were taken care of by squads of discreet and cheerful young men in sky-blue jumpsuits.

Thrown out of the Pantheon Grand, thrown out of the Castle on the Arch, and thrown out of the Launceston, Lionel was intrigued to learn that nobody had ever been thrown out of the South Central. *Zero Ejections*, it said in his desktop brochure. Anti-social behaviour, among the guests at least, was considered a civic virtue; and the incorrigible monotony of Lionel's criminal record (often reinventoried in the press) was widely admired. His prestige, here, was boundless, his legitimacy beyond challenge. But it hadn't gone away — the internal question mark, like a rusty hook, snagged in his innards.

He made several good mates during his short time there. Scott Ronson, the arthritic, lantern-jawed rhythm guitarist of a band called the Pretty Faces. Eamon O'Nolan, the two-time World Snooker Champion (who was always doing community service for various unambitious misdemeanours — roughing up referees, relieving himself in pot plants, and the like). Lorne Brown, the winner of a huge reality telethon (a month in the South Central was one of his prizes). Brent Medwin, the (teenage) cokehead Manchester City midfielder, both of whose parents were in jail (the mum for living off immoral earnings, the dad for manslaughter). Hereabouts, Lionel Asbo could just relax and be himself, freely mingling with his fellow superstars.

Lionel sounded fine. For instance,

"You watch. We'll do you at Upton Park. Then we'll come to your place and nick a point," he might say to Brent Medwin (*we* being West Ham United).

"The important thing about fame? Don't let it change you personality," he might say to Lorne Brown.

"So that's how you do it. You pick the bird you like and send one of you deaf roadies to go and bring her in," he might say to Scott Ronson.

"I can get stun. I can get screw. But I can't get *deep* screw. The white always jumps off the table!" he might say to Eamon O'Nolan.

Or else Lionel was in the Los Feliz Lounge with Megan Jones, going through the interview requests (and the assorted business proposals) over a cup of cappuccino. Megan had a *strategy* for her client. *Now Lionel. No one wants to see a multimillionaire with a scowl on his face. You've got a lovely sense of humour. Just let it shine through! And we'll turn you into a national treasure.* Lionel nodded absently; he was gazing, as he often gazed, at the plasma screen above Megan's head. *Uh, yeah. Okay,* he said, and wiped the froth off his upper lip. They were oc-

187

casionally joined by Megan's number two, Sebastian Drinker. Drinker noticed the peculiar way Lionel reacted to the sound of nearby laughter: his head jerked round like a weathervane in a crosswind.

Every suite had a balcony, which took pressure off the smokers (and gave all the parasuicides somewhere conspicuous to threaten to jump from). And anyway, there was the Sepulveda Cigar Saloon in the basement. It featured video games and pinball machines, a snooker table (the swerve Eamon could put on the cue ball: defied the laws of physics!), and a full bar (twenty-four-hour and self-service). The food was good, the waiters prompt, the pornography decent, the gym ever-empty. And though he continued to inspect certain properties (a Canary Wharf penthouse, a fourteen-room mansion flat in Chelsea), Lionel had no plans to move.

There were large screens in all the public rooms at the South Central — a soundless succession of clips and images, newsreels, silent movies, Miss World, Sputnik, *101 Dalmatians*, chorus line, death camp, Bela Lugosi, Victoria's Secret, goosestep, wet T-shirt, moonshot, *Dumbo*, what the butler saw, grassy knoll, catwalk bikini, Bikini Atoll . . .

■ ■ ■ ■

"Yeah, but I don't use those girls," said Scott Ronson (he meant the frilly little half-clad fans who gathered daily in the roped-off area just to the left of the forecourt). "They're too young, half of them. I use the uh, the in-house amenity. We all do."

"Eh?" queried Lionel. The two of them were enjoying a few midmorning Bloody Marys in the Beverley Bar. "What amenity's this?"

"On your phone there's a button marked Companionship. Press that."

"Then what?"

"They put you through to this chummy bloke at the escort agency. Then you give your specifications . . . You know. Blonde. Big tits. Whatever. Dead confidential. And bingo. It's addictive, mind."

Lionel said, "I'm not bothered."

A day or two later he took his lunch in the Watts Diner — with Brent Medwin and Eamon O'Nolan.

"Give it a go," suggested Brent. "I told the bloke, I want a woman with a bit of class. No tattoos. Next thing I know, I got fucking Snow White stood over the bed. For a flat grand!"

"You give a tip?" asked Eamon.

"Service included. Goes on your bill. No questions asked."

Lionel said, "I'm not bothered."

A day or two later he finally admitted it. He *was* bothered. Well. How else do you get through all the hours before seven-thirty (when the casino opened)?

This, at any rate, was how Lionel put it to himself. Thereby evading a recurrent question, and one of enormous size. Why, with the exceptions of Cynthia and Gina (both, for different reasons, exceptional girls), had he steered so abnormally clear of the opposite sex?

Too busy with me career, he murmured. *Workaholic, if you like. Earning a crust and keeping the old wolf from the door . . . But now?* Resentfully Lionel twisted round in his chair. *Load of bollocks, all that. Never paid for it in me life. More trouble than they worth. Stick to porn, mate. You know where you are with the porn. No, you can't go far wrong with the . . .*

A day later Lionel pressed Companionship and gave the bloke a reasonably unsalacious description of Gina Drago. An hour later he heard a tactful knock . . . She was called Dylis, she was twenty-seven, she was from Cardiff, she was dark and round.

Very soon it became clear, even to Lionel, that he was the wrong kind of man to consort with prostitutes. Dylis took her leave twenty minutes later, trying to hurry but swaying about quite a bit and bumping into things . . .

That's a turn-up, he said into the silence. *Christ. Frighten meself sometimes. No, mate. No. Anyway, look at the time!* A quick shower. Then off to the penthouse floor (have a steak sandwich around ten), the green baize, the little white ball gliding and then hopping up and down in the twirl of the spun wheel.

Lionel was shaving — he relied on the plastic razor provided by the South Central (and faithfully replaced every day). Becalmed for a moment in front of the mirror, he weighed the toylike implement in the palm of his hand . . . Hollow. Hardly there. Not like the bloody great spanner provided by Mr. Firth-Heatherington (which Lionel had lost in the Castle on the Arch or the Launceston). They called the South Central the heavy-metal hotel, but everything was light, the cutlery, the glassware, the furniture, even the bedclothes (his white duvet caressed him like a mist) . . . Without warning the flow of water hesitated, paused for a mesmeric minute, gave a polite cough, and coolly resumed. Amazing how fast they patched things up and got them working again. That afternoon, a well-known vocalist on the floor above had dropped a kind of hand grenade into his toilet bowl . . .

That's what I need, said Lionel. *A fucking hand grenade in me toilet bowl.* His insides had loosened, somewhat; but his crouched vigils bore little resemblance to the thoughtless evacuations of old. All the same he felt light, light, insubstantial, hardly there. Every time he went to the casino and the lift came to a halt on the penthouse floor, Lionel expected to keep on surging upward, past the helipad and the Century City Eyrie and out into the summer blue . . . The weightless world, the light limbo, of the South Central, where nothing weighed, nothing counted, and everything was allowed.

He peered into the mirror; it peered back at him; he raised thumb and forefinger to part his sticky lids . . . A process was under way within Lionel Asbo, within his head and breast. He was twenty-four — and he suddenly had time to think. Money, *money* (his sole and devouring preoccupation since infancy), was now meaningless to him. *Lionel,* a voice would say. *Yeah? What you want?* Then silence. Then, *Lionel, mate.* And he'd go, *Jesus. What? What you want?* Then they'd talk. Lionel was no longer merely thinking out loud. He was having a conversation with what seemed to be a higher intelligence. The voice was cleverer than he was. It even had a better accent.

Lionel dressed with slow care. He was going out to dinner. Table for one. Just him and his thoughts. Before he left he popped up to see Scott Ronson: they were going to have a little smoke on his balcony. That feeling again in the elevator. He stepped out and paused. Right floor — but what was the number? Lionel barged around for a bit. Ah, there he was. Scott had just sawn off the top half of the door to his suite, and he was standing there waiting like a horse in a stable.

At 7:45 p.m. Lionel had a few words with the girl at the desk, and extended his stay for another three weeks.

In fact he wouldn't be returning to the South Central — not for another three years.

10

"Off to a function, are we, Lionel?"

"What, no Megan, Lionel?"

"Any truth in the rumours, Lionel?"

"Rumours? Me and Megan? No, footloose

and fancy-free. That's Lionel Asbo. More trouble than they worth if you ask me."

". . . Off to a function, are we, Lionel?"

This was a second reference to Lionel's oufit, which of course had raised no eyebrows in the hotel. In the hotel there were loads of people dressed up as pirates and nuns and Nazis. But now Lionel was out and about — strolling across Sloane Square and down Sloane Street, in flawless weather. The traffic, seeming to shrug something off, rolled forward into the ease and freedom, the innocuous proficiency, of a London summer, beneath a flattering sky. Lionel said buoyantly,

"No, lads, I'm off to me new job. Bouncing in a bingo parlour. But tonight I'm calling the numbers!"

There was laughter from the three representatives of the Fourth Estate. This laughter went on for longer than usual — because Lionel did in fact quite closely resemble a bingo caller. His tuxedo, true, and his vast trousers were impeccably and superaccurately cut; his buxom bow tie was no elasticated clip-on but a fine length of schmutter (Eamon, who earned his living in a bow tie, showed him how you looped it); and the shoes, at ten thousand pounds apiece, performed as expected — two padded floats of glistening ebony. On the other hand, only an unusually confident and sexually secure bingo caller would have consented to wear Lionel's shirt and waistcoat. The waistcoat was of canary-yellow suede, with turquoise buttons. And the white shirt was an impossible orgy of vents and flounces (his hands were only just visible beneath the ruches of its cuffs). He slowed as he lit a cigar, saying,

"Here, lads, I got one for yer. What's got lots of balls and screws old ladies? . . . A bingo machine!"

"You won't win a hundred and forty mil on the bingo, Lionel."

"You know, lads, back in Diston, me mum used to take me to the bingo. Every Friday. Friday. Reno Night. Can do all the numbers, me. Legs eleven. Sweet sixteen. Thirty — dirty Gertie. Ninety — top of the shop."

"Where's the function then, Lionel?" persisted the man from the *Sun*.

"*What* fucking function? . . . No, seriously, lads. Remember the uh, remember that bistro I popped into for a minute this afternoon? Down that little alley behind Harrods? Well I booked a table."

"For two, Lionel?" said the man from the *Daily Telegraph*.

"You deaf? I'm on me tod tonight. Get a

bit of peace. And read me paper."

"Which paper, Lionel? Where's your trademark *Lark?*" said the man from the *Lark*.

"It's all in hand, son," said Lionel, patting his trouser pocket. "It's all in hand."

To a relay of encouraging cheers he climbed the seven steps to the restaurant (which was called Mount's). Obligingly he paused and posed — but soon drew back beneath the awning, his head and shoulders lost in shadow, and the three men turned away, leaving him in quiet communion with his cigar . . . It should at this point be revealed that Lionel had just smoked two nine-paper joints on Scott Ronson's balcony: Swaziland skunkweed marijuana. Now, in normal times the fiercest possible intoxicants made no mark on Lionel Asbo. Tonight would be different. And the difference had to do with the recent activation of his subliminal mind. For the time being, though, Lionel was in excellent fettle, and imagined that a nice little treat lay ahead of him. A quiet dinner, and a thoughtful read of the *Morning Lark*.

"Good evening, sir," said a resonant and resolute voice. "Welcome. Your table."

"Ah. Lovely."

"If you don't mind my asking, sir, are you going on somewhere after your meal? To the amateur boxing at the Queensbury perhaps?"

"Amateur boxing?"

"Yes, sir. I hear Prince Philip's going to be there. You know — for the Duke of Edinburgh Awards."

"The Duke of Edinburgh? . . . Yeah well I follow the boxing. That's a proper sport, boxing. Not like all the other rubbish. What's you name, mate?"

". . . Well, here they call me Mr. Mount."

"No." Lionel looked him up and down: a tall and mournful figure in lounge suit and tie, with an icecap of thick white hair. "What's you first name?"

". . . Cuthbert, sir."

And Lionel said simply, "Cuthbert."

Mr. Mount took a step backwards. He hadn't heard *Cuthbert* pronounced quite like that for thirty years. Not since 1979, when he stopped going to Billingsgate Market (at five o'clock on Monday mornings, to assess the catch). He now said,

"Yes. Cuthbert Mount."

"Well I'll tell you what, Cuthbert. I'm starting me new job! Bouncing in a bingo parlour! And tonight I'm calling the numbers!"

For some reason all this came out much, much louder than Lionel intended — as if through a stadium bullhorn. He grew aware that thirty or forty faces, crowned with wisps of hoar and rime, were staring his way.

He thought, Must be cold, getting old. Old, cold: like poetry. "Evening all!" he found himself hollering as he lowered himself into his chair.

". . . Would you like a drink before your meal, sir?"

"Yeah. Guiss a uh, give us a —"

But Mr. Mount stepped aside, and was instantly supplanted by a knowing youth in a white dinner jacket.

"What's up with you?"

"Sorry, sir?"

"You amused," said Lionel.

"Amused, sir? No, not at all, sir."

"You look too light on you feet, mate . . ." Lionel sniffed and said, "Okay. Fuck it. Guiss a pint of . . ." In the South Central you could get champagne by the pint (and by the half-pint — very popular with the ladies); and Lionel had in any case come to regard champagne as rich man's beer. "Bubbles, son. What kind you got?"

A ribboned wine list was opened and handed over. Lionel pointed to the most prohibitive of the vintages, and the waiter bowed and withdrew.

The restaurant was something of a surprise. Earlier that day, when he poked his head round the door, his sunstruck stare registered a grotto of pulsing shadow, and he imagined a kind of family brasserie. But Mount's . . . The furnishings were plump and plush, the walls practically panelled with paintings, with haywains and cloudscapes and cavaliers. Yeah, the place was like some fat old cavalier, buttoned up far too tight. Lionel hefted but did not yet open the crested redleather menu. *England's Oldest Restaurant. Established by Clarence Fitzmaurice Mount. 1797.* And Lionel thought: 1797!

"Your champagne's on its way, sir."

Lionel had intended to make a start on the *Morning Lark* while enjoying his aperitif. Catch up on current events. But now he was having his doubts. He already knew that the cover was devoted to a truly mountainous blonde; and it might look a bit . . . The *Lark*, that day, appeared for the first time in two editions, tabloid and broadsheet, and Lionel had succumbed to the novelty of the larger format. Anyway, he slipped the thing out of his trouser pocket, unfolded it under the table, and awkwardly searched for a page that didn't have a topless model on it.

Page two usually contained the day's news, but today the day's news was about a topless model (bust-up with childhood sweetheart) . . . Looks a bit like Gina, he thought — and Lionel was abruptly transfixed by an unpleasant memory.

As he was finishing off with Dylis, he happened to glance sideways at the closet mirror. And there it was, his body, all hammer and tongs, like the driving mechanism of a runaway train. The expression on his face. Teeth bared, and furious eyes, and his —

The champagne arrived in its steel bucket. Lionel calmly compressed the *Morning Lark* between his knees, and said,

"Got a bigger glass? You know, like a beer mug." Lionel grimly monitored the waiter's movements. ". . . Yeah, that'll do. Fill her up, boy."

Then it started happening. For just half a minute or so, Lionel's mind became a vertiginous succession of false bottoms, of snapping trapdoors . . .

Champagne in a beer mug? he fiercely subvocalised. *Are you a cunt? They staring now! No they ain't! They thinking you off to the boxing with the Duke of Edinburgh! No they ain't! They laughing at yer — they pissing theyselves! Why'd you say that about the bingo? They thinking you some cunt of a bingo caller!*

200

No they ain't! They see they Daily Telegraph!
*They know you the Lotto Lout! They know you
a cunt anyway! They — they* . . .

Lionel looked up. The diners were dining,
hypernormally. The soft echoes and vibra-
tions, the pings and chimes, of tableware,
the drones and murmurs of polite conversation . . .

"May I take your order, sir?" said his
waiter.

"Hang on . . . Hang on. I don't see no
meat."

"This is a fish restaurant, sir."

"What, *just* fish? . . . Oh well. So be it."
He chose the most expensive starter
(caviar), to be followed by the most expensive entrée (lobster). "Fresh, is it?"

"Oh yes, sir. Alive and kicking. Flown in
today from Helsinki."

Helsinki! thought Lionel.

"And how would you like it dressed?"

"Uh," said Lionel. He'd only ever had
lobster in cocktail form, when Gina made it
for him in traditional Maltese style: with
lashings of ketchup. "As it comes," he said
from under half-open eyes . . .

"Shall we shell it for you, sir?"

"Shell it?" said Lionel with sudden and
inscrutable venom. "I'm not helpless, son.
Do I look helpless? I'm not helpless. Do I

201

look helpless? . . . Ah, don't cry. Here, do me napkin." That's what they did in decent restaurants — smoothed it over your lap. "*Où,*" said Lionel.

He finished his pint and ordered another. The caviar came. He'd had caviar before, because it was often the most expensive starter, and caviar, he found, was tasty enough so long as you seasoned it with Tabasco and plenty of . . . Not that he was feeling weak or giddy or anything, but he noticed that the salt cellar was heavy, was implausibly heavy. The knife in his hand was implausibly heavy. That was when you . . . The rich world was heavy, rooted to the ground. It had the weight of the past securing it. Whereas his world, as was, Diston, things were . . .

"May we serve your lobster with some melted butter, sir?" said Mr. Mount.

"Go on then. And some tomato uh, some tomato sauce, Cuthbert. Of you own preparation. On the side."

Mr. Mount seemed to be frowning at Lionel's suit, and he said, "That's a truly remarkable cloth, sir, if you don't mind my saying. And I do know something about cloth. Is it . . . pashmina wool? Is it — my God, is it shah*toosh?* Why, I've never heard of such a thing. Must have cost you an absolute —"

"Wasn't cheap."

"May I?"

"Course you can." Lionel held up his right arm. "Take you time, Cuthbert," he said. "Don't stint youself."

Mr. Mount bent, straightened, bowed and said, "So extraordinarily *fine* . . . I hope you enjoy your meal with us tonight, sir."

After much cramped contortion Lionel found a page without a topless model on it, page forty-eight, up near the classifieds. He carefully flattened the paper out on the table. He settled. He drank . . . And with miming lips he started on a report about a *two*-year-old who was already in trouble with the law! . . . This little minx, this little . . . This little monkey — she was striping all the cars with a doorkey . . . She was stealing cash and smashing windows . . . And she got pissed on her mum's vodka and when the woman from the Social come round she bit her one on the . . .

Lionel's frown deepened.

This little terror was being served an *ASBO* . . . There goes me record!

"There goes me record!" he shouted out, and hunched himself forward.

Let's see: two years and three hundred

and sixty days. Pips me by a week! . . . Well, fair's fair. No, come on, you got to give her credit. Yet to celebrate her third birthday, and this little bleeder's already . . .

Lionel became aware of a silence, a silence of considerable purity, no voices, no background tittle-tattle of tumblers and tines. He peered up and out. It seemed he had the undivided attention of every pair of eyes in the room. Whitely shining spectacles. Raised lorgnettes. Even two sets of opera glasses. *What's all this then?* And Lionel now realised that in his innocent absorption he was holding the *Morning Lark* at shoulder height. Savagely he yanked it round.

11

And saw what? A *whole page* of GILFs!

He took it all in with his frozen eyes . . . The sheet was dominated by a huge small ad — and even the most hardened readers of the *Morning Lark* were seldom expected to contemplate anything quite as dreadful as this. A blubbery, curly-haired old woman, wearing nothing but gumboots, pictured from the rear, on all fours, her lower haunches half-obscured, her rustic features contorted in a snarl of agony. HORNY HILDA, 74. TEXT HER NOW AT —

With a single galvanic convulsion Lionel

wrestled and scrunched the *Lark* to his lap. Then he blushed. And it was as if all his blushes, all the blushes of a lifetime, had come to him at once. Like flames they plumed and hummed, wave after wave . . . Indeed, for the next five minutes or so, Lionel bore certain affinities with what was soon to be his fateful supper — the brick-red lobster boiling to death in its pot. Another fistfight, another riot of thought; and then at last (in that way he had) Lionel calmed and cooled.

Come on now, son, he told himself — steady. The *Lark* ain't *illegal* or anything. On sale everywhere — great big stack of them in you corner shop. The *Lark*'s just a bit of fun. Everyone knows that. No harm in it. Just a bit of fun. Everyone knows that . . .

He sternly regrouped. He finished his caviar and, with some show of insouciance, ordered another pot. And another round of toast: soldiers, if you like. And another pint of champagne. Lionel steadied again. He ate all that and he drank all that. He rose.

"Uh, Cuthbert," he said, making a tremendous effort to control the volume of his voice. "Uh, Cuthbert," he croaked. "I'm just going out for a quick burn, okay? Back in a minute, Cuthbert. Back in a minute."

■ ■ ■ ■

The photojournalists from the *Morning Lark*, the *Sun*, and the *Daily Telegraph*, Lionel saw with a pang, had disappeared. *Gone for a bite theyselves, most likely*, he mused out loud. *Be along later*. And this was good anyway: he wanted to tackle that massive spliff Scott'd rolled up for him. The alley dead-ended to his left, under the frosty sheen of the coach-house lantern. Perfect: no passers-by. He stuffed his *Lark* into a rubbish bin, tamping it down. Might even dash off in a minute and get a *Sun* (or even a *Daily Telegraph!*) to have a read of with me lobster. *No. They'll think you doing a runner. Or fled in shame! . . . Nah. You being uh, oversensitive mate. The* Lark's *just a laugh — they all know that. Just a lark. Even* calls *itself as much. A laugh won't hurt yer. What's wrong with a laugh? . . .* There came another memory of Dylis. When he flipped her over, to give her a lovepat or two, how suddenly the spank became a clout, became a wallop. *Managed to exercise restraint*, he whispered. And, throughout, that whining noise in his ears — and in his chest too, somehow. *That's what happens when you up and pay for it. Gives you funny notions. Master–slave, you*

206

could say. She's like a pet animal you got it in for . . . Frighten meself sometimes. So he just got on with his joint (seemed to be tastier than the other two). He took a last inch-long drag . . . the crackling buds, the sizzling Rizlas . . . and held it in as long as he could before exhaling through his nose. And then he went back inside to confront the scarlet fortress of the crustacean.

Now the creature lay in front of him on its oval dish. There were two skewers (one with a curved tip) and a nutcracker. He picked up the gangly device: like the bottom half of a chorus girl made of steel . . . *Fucking ugly-looking bugger, this fish. The shrunken, horror-comic face. And the monstrous hydraulics of the forearms. Was that the lobster's mitt or its — its pincer?* Bending low over the table, he positioned the jagged limb in the instrument's clench; then he applied maximum force — and caught a jet of hot butter right in the eye!

"*UN!*" he cried, and jerked back . . . But as he dabbed his cheek, well, Lionel had to smile. He had to smile. He thought of Pete New, his cellmate at Stallwort. Bloke seemed to specialise in unlikely accidents. He said he once poached an egg in the microwave, took it out, went to sniff it —

and the whole mess exploded in his face! Said it fucking near blinded him! . . . So Lionel had a good old laugh about Pete New. A very good old laugh (him breaking a leg from watching TV!). And then he drained his glass, chewed on a couple of boiled potatoes, and smiled again with a little twist of the head.

"More bubbles, son."

His dinner, so far, felt a bit like a practical joke — the beer mug, the GILFs, the hot butter. Nothing serious, mind. In the South Central they were always playing practical jokes. More money than sense, half of them. Practical jokes with superglue and cling film. Whoopee cushions. Squirting HP sauce and mustard. Setting off the fire alarm. High jinks, if you like. Being stupid on purpose. More money than sense, the lot of them. Sometimes it's like they playing practical jokes on *theyselves* . . .

Lionel reapplied himself to his meal. Using the silvery tools, plus his fork.

The key moment came ten minutes later, when he threw down his weapons and reached for the enemy with his bare hands.

"I'm sorry you seemed to have such trouble with your entrée, sir."

". . . Well, you know how it is, Cuthbert.

You win some, you lose some."

"Do take the napkin, sir. Take a clean one. Here . . . That looks really quite nasty. Might need a stitch or two."

"Look at this one!"

"Dear oh dear."

Lionel's yttrium credit card was slotted into the gadget and he did the rigmarole with the PIN. He added a startling tip and said,

"They'll patch me together at the hotel."

"May I ask where you're putting up, sir?" Mr. Mount's eyes widened and he said, "Well they have a very advanced valet service at the South Central. They might, they just *might*, have some luck with those . . ." Mr. Mount seemed to submit to a gust of anguish. "Those *stains*."

"Yeah?"

"My God. It's rather more serious than I thought." Mr. Mount was no longer calling Lionel *sir*, because he knew that his customer would be taking his leave in fairly good order. This had not looked probable during Lionel's endlessly self-regenerating fit of laughter; and it had looked even less probable during his climactic struggle with his main course — when Lionel was crashing around and visibly giving off a faint grey

209

steam. "What can one say? Bad luck, old chap."

"Yeah cheers, Cuthbert. An unfortunate choice." Lionel was still short of breath, and there were still tears in his eyes; but he was in complete control. "Next time I'll have the haddock."

". . . Why, thank you very much indeed, sir."

He swung himself down the steps and out into the alley, his tie half off, his jacket, shirt, and waistcoat colourfully impasted with butter and blood. He felt very hungry.

"The bingo get a bit rough, Lionel?" said the man from the *Sun*.

"Just stand there a minute, Lionel," said the man from the *Lark* as he raised his camera. "Ooh, this is priceless, this is."

"The old ladies take their revenge on you, Lionel?" said the man from the *Daily Telegraph*.

Lionel glanced right. At the far end of the alley there was a policeman, standing stock still, and staring his way.

"Copper watching. That settles the matter," said Lionel Asbo succinctly.

He moved to his left.

"Come on then," he said wearily. "Gaa, Christ, let's have it. Go on — get you laughing done with. Yeah, I will. I will. I'll do five years for the three of yer."

XII

Nothing really out of the ordinary happened between 2009 and 2012.

"He'll get ten, they reckon, and do five. And serve him bloody well right."

"Come on, Dawn. Think. He won't be out till 2014!"

It was Sunday. They were having what they called *breakfast on bed* (it was a single bed), and rereading Saturday's *Mirror* (their new tabloid of choice).

"He *fancied* prison," said Des dazedly. "He did. He *fancied* prison."

"Three counts of GBH. Plus Assaulting a Police Officer."

On their laps (and on facing pages) were the iconic Before and After shots from the dead-ended alley off Brompton Road. Before: Lionel posing on the steps of the restaurant, Pickwickian, vaudevillian, aglow with combustible bonhomie. The After photograph (not taken immediately after, because the journalists' cameras had all been smashed): this was more interestingly composed. The malefactor, like a city scarecrow, his lolling head, his arms up around

211

the shoulders of the two policemen, with all the stuffing coming out of him (the ripped and twisted suit, the frothy white shirt); and then, to the right, just behind and beyond, the wheeled ambulance trolley with its own fixed light and the lumpy body lying on it (this was the man from the *Daily Telegraph*).

"Tsuh-tsuh," said Dawn. "Tsuh-tsuh." She was addressing the cat. "Here, Goldie. Here, love . . . The restaurant bloke says he had a fight to the death with his lobster."

"Mm. The QC's preparing his defence. Lord Barcleigh."

"The fat one . . . *Diminished responsibility*. Oh yeah. It was the lobster, your honour."

"I can't understand him, Dawnie. He did it when a copper was watching!"

"Mm. And not even nutters do that. Here, Goldie. Here, girl."

In early 2010, incidentally, they traded in their single bed — not for a double bed (because the room itself was the size of a double bed), but for what was called a Bachelor's Occasional.

Minicabbing, clambering over speed bumps, forever staring into the unlanced boil of the red light (and then the lurid matter of the amber). Diston traffic was obedient to the hierarchy of size: the Smart car feared the Mini, the Mini feared the Golf, the Golf feared the Jeep, the Jeep feared the . . . Des, driving, impatiently aware of the frail flustered presence of the bicycle on his inner flank, but himself obedient to the great swung mass of the bus.

Here's a tale of the unexpected, said Lionel in August 2009, on his first day back in Stallwort (awaiting trial). *I had a shit this morning. Hey. Go up and see you gran.*
  I am, Uncle Li.
  I want a report. And oy. While I'm away — don't you dare go near me stuff.

The first-class train fare to the North West Highlands and back, by sleeper, ran well into four figures. But Des went on the Cloud and got a bargain-berth "apex" split-ticket — for eighteen quid! . . . You rose before first light (Inverness, then motor-coach via Lairg), and you returned in the next day's early darkness: the grey hours. Des did his Christian duty, and his Christian penance, about every six weeks, and sometimes Dawn came too.

The home was a townhouse, five floors high and unusually deep, with a great many internal partitions of hardboard (and cardboard). The atmosphere of the place frightened Des right from the start, and every time he went up there it seemed measurably slacker, shabbier, more demoralised. Souness itself (fifteen miles east of Cape Wrath): there were prettier enclaves further back and up on the cliffs, but the township, the port, where Grace dwelt, was a maze of dark flint, populated by taupe genies of sopping mist. It was never not raining. A spittling, hair-frizzing drizzle was your absolute basic — what the locals called *smirr;* and it was smirr that kept guard between downpours.

Grace was in a conical attic — the hospital bed, the chair beside it, and a cavernous sink with thick rubber tubing attached to the spouts. *Des, dear,* she said, clearly enough. But thereafter she spoke in random clauses that made no sense. Some stuck in his mind for a moment, and he thought he'd remember them later, but he never did. So he started writing them down.

Nine owls out where it's high and cold: that was one.

Partial to gains I stake claim: that was another.

No-no disturbs sin, etc: that was yet another.

The chief physician, furtive Dr. Ardagh in his shaggy marmalade suit, used the phrase *early onset degenerative brain disease.* He mumbled something Des didn't quite catch.

Sorry? A few more good years?

Uh, no. A good few more years. Is what I said.

He returned to the conical attic.

Unresisting, even so, moaned Gran as he eventually kissed her goodbye. *Fifteen!*

Des remembered that one. Was it a reference to the things that took place between them in 2006 — when he was fifteen, and hadn't resisted? Neither Des nor Grace had said a word about it all since the disappearance of Rory Nightingale.

At his trial at the Old Bailey, Lionel, for the first time in his life, pleaded guilty.

Diminished responsibility was Lord Barcleigh's theme: he asked the jury to consider *the massive senselessness of the offence, committed, after all, in plain view of an officer of the law. Medical science calls it an* ictus — *a spasm of the brain.*

Lionel himself, dressed for the occasion in the pathetic shreds of his shahtoosh dinner jacket (woven from the wool of the chiru, an endangered Tibetan antelope), was archaically humble: *I deeply regret all distress caused,* he said. *I'm just a boy from Diston who got out of his depth . . . I'll do me time*

215

with no complaints, and I swear I'll never again be a threat to uh, to society like. I've done it the hard way, You Honour, but I've come to see the error of me ways.

One character witness turned out to be disproportionately influential: Fiona King, the co-manager of the South Central Hotel. *He was a model guest. If all our clients comported themselves like Mr. Asbo, I can assure you that my life would be very much simpler. Ask anybody. Lionel Asbo behaved like a true English gentleman.*

Even more tellingly, Police Constable George Hands (*Yeah*, Lionel would later admit, *he was dearer than Lord Barcleigh*) informed the court (through splintered teeth) that Lionel's conduct, in the Knightsbridge alleyway, had in fact been more consistent with the lesser charge of Resisting Arrest.

He got six years — a light sentence, many felt (and wrote). Five months were already served, and Lord Barcleigh, making due allowance for Lionel's good behaviour, predicted that he would be a free man by the spring or early summer of 2012.

Des switched subjects: from Modern Languages to Sociology, with a special emphasis on crime and punishment. Lionel, when told of this, simply shrugged and turned away. As usual he had his cellphone on loudspeaker — a conference call with his investment team (he was accumulating dead equity). This was in the prison outside Exeter: its name was Silent Green.

You can't go far wrong in prison, Lionel might say, between calls . . . And Des came to a tentative conclusion: the career criminal *didn't really mind* being in prison. Being in prison didn't ceaselessly strike him as an unendurable outrage on his dignity. Des resolved to ask Lionel why this was — but not today.

Prison, said Lionel. *Good place to get you head sorted out. You know where you are in prison.*

Well yeah, thought Des. You're in prison.

Go on then. Off you hop, said Lionel as he leaned into another call.

And Des would eat a cheese roll at the station, and head back to London on his day return.

The next time he went down there Lionel was busy buying half a dozen forests' worth of Uruguayan timber.

The next time he went down there Lionel was busy attacking the yen.

A word, therefore, about Lionel's finances.

In his three weeks of freedom Lionel Asbo spent nine million pounds, nearly all of it on craps, blackjack, and roulette (there was also the unused Bentley "Aurora," and a seven-figure clothes bill). But his investments prospered almost uncontrollably right from the start. He instructed his young squad of free-market idealists to be as aggressive as possible. *Don't fuck about on five per cent*, he told them. *Go for it.*

Right, said Lionel, as he sauntered round the exercise yard. *Take sixty out of the one-thirty and have a punt.*

Depressed bank stock? he said, while watching TV in the rec room. *Yeah, give it a crack. Fifty. No. Sixty.*

Vend, he said, activating the flush toilet in the privacy of his cell. *Now take ninety and have another punt. I fancy oil. And get me eight per cent on the principal.*

Good effort, boys and girls, he said as he ate chocolates in the commissary (Quality Street and Black Magic). *Me gains'll be reflected in you bonuses.*

On August 2, 2011, Des and Dawn were informed that they'd both got Two Ones!

"Well, after all that graft, we'd've looked like bloody fools if we'd got Thirds."

"Yeah, or even *Desmonds*," said Desmond (a *Desmond* was a Two Two — after Desmond Tutu). "Complete bloody fools."

"And you'd've got a First if you'd had the three years. Easy."

Dawn took a teaching job at an enormous girls' school in Pentonville called St. Swithin's.

Des wrote to every newspaper in London, enclosing a sample of his work (it was an eyewitness description of two simultaneous but unrelated incidents — a non-fatal stabbing and an acid-attack blinding — in a local takeout). And he was summoned to two interviews, one at the *Diston Gazette* — and one at the *Daily Mirror!*

Grace Pepperdine had a minor stroke on Guy Fawkes Night of that year. Her mouth seemed to be torqued round on its axis — and yet she was now lucid. That is to say, she could explore little air pockets of her very distant past. Her childhood — before the days of Cilla, and John and Paul and George . . .

"She can't stay in this place, Des," said Dawn (who hadn't been up there for over a year). They were taking a breather in the street. "Look at it. Smell it."

He looked at it. The home had let itself go

— it was like a tea trolley rattling down a hillside. And he smelled it. In 2009 it smelled of deodorant and cabbage; by 2011 it smelled of urine and mice.

As dusk was falling, in the early afternoon, Grace took Des's hand and met his eye and whispered: *I smell something . . . I scent tangled crime. Six, six, six.*

Lionel was whiling away the last months of his sentence at Wormwood Scrubs — the desolate rain-steeped stronghold that presided over a huge stretch of common land (brush and stunted forest growth) in Hammersmith, west London. It was his first prison and, as he sometimes said, probably his favourite.

When Des next went to see him (in January 2012), he was led not to the commissary but to an administrative office evidently dedicated to Lionel's use (there were warm beers, damp sandwiches, and silent pretzels). Pale Cynthia sat at his side. Dressed in the usual navy overalls, Lionel was reviewing country properties — properties thought worthy of a whole brochure each.

An extensive paddock? he was saying (with the full plosive on the terminal *k*). *Why would I want a fucking paddock?*

*. . . Uncle Li. Gran's Home. She can't —
Jesus.*

It's you *I'm thinking of. Partly. What if the —*

*Oy! Des, give you face a rest, all right? You
depressing me . . . Here, Cynth, look at this
one. A bit over the top? Des — what's a
ha-ha?*

In January Dawn Sheringham fell pregnant! . . . *Fell pregnant*: how awful and
beautiful that phrase sounded: *fell pregnant*.
Beautiful, but full of awe. Over and above
everything else, though, it meant that Des
would now have to tell Dawn about Grace.

He sat her down in the kitchen, and
began. Ten minutes later he was saying,

"I can't excuse it, I can't even explain it."
He sniffed and wiped his cheeks. ". . . Will
you still have me, Dawnie?"

Slowly her eyes narrowed and her mouth
broadened, and she said, "But nothing actually happened. All right, you got dependent
on the cuddles. You might've . . . But nothing actually *happened*."

He sank back in his chair. It was, at least,
immediately clear that this avenue would
remain forever closed. "Don't be silly," he
said. "Course not. Nothing *happened*. Just
got dependent on the cuddles. That's all."
There was a silence, a silence that only he

had the power to break. "Knock knock," he heard himself say.

"Who's there?"

"Little old lady."

"Little old lady who?"

"Didn't know you could yodel."

And somehow that got them to the other side.

Later he went out and walked as far as the canal . . . Was this a version of what they called *cognitive dissonance?* Because Dawn had only ever known Grace as a thoroughgoing little old lady (a *viejita*, as the Spanish so economically put it). And today, almost six years on, he himself found it close to inconceivable that he had ever kissed those eyes, those lips. That mouth, which now looked as though there was a toy boomerang wedged into it . . . Des turned on his heel and started back. And imagine! He had planned to tell Dawn about Rory Nightingale too, and about what Lionel did to him. No. His head shuddered in negation as he walked. All that — the whole bad dream. All that was his to hold.

With Vincent Tigg as best man, and with Prunella Sheringham in proud attendance, Des and Dawn were married on Valentine's Day in Carker Square Registry Office. And then Uncle John, Uncle George, and Uncle Stuart whisked them off for a surprise slap-up Chinese — hosted and paid for by Uncle Paul!

The baby, at this stage, was a fifth the size of a full stop.

"Now the blastocyst," said Des the next morning (he was reading a huge baby book in the Bachelor's Occasional), "has completed its journey from Fallopian tube to uterus."

"Don't call it that! . . . I don't *feel* pregnant. And anyway. Who wants a blastocyst?"

That same day he was hired as a trainee reporter on the *Diston Gazette!*

De-leverage, said Lionel into his phone, and snapped it shut. *No, tell them this*, he went on coldly. *Tell them I'll be on the same money as me namesake, Lionel Messi. European Footballer of the Year. Tell them that.*

They were in Lionel's office in Wormwood Scrubs, wondering what, if anything, to say to the world about the true dimensions of the Asbo fortune — Lionel, Megan Jones, and Sebastian Drinker.

And tell them that's just the interest. *On me principal. Lionel Messi gets paid for running round a fucking football pitch. I get paid for sitting on me arse. Tell them that.*

We shouldn't stir them up, Lionel, said Megan. *It's nobody's business but yours.* She laughed and went on, *As it is you've got every gold-digger in England after you!*

More fanmail? Go on then, sling it over. Lionel's fanmail consisted of letters of introduction from young women, with photographs enclosed. *No, the fanmail's — it's all right. It's good. See, it's like a brothel. It's you privilege to choose. It's you uh, prerogative. You know. Like in a brothel.* Lionel raised a finger. *Except I won't be paying for it. You don't want to pay for it, Megan. Starts you off on the wrong foot.*

The first time he said *brothel* he pronounced it *broffle,* and the second time he said *brothel* he pronounced it *brovvle.* But that wasn't why Megan Jones and Sebastian Drinker were glancing at each other from under their brows.

I'll make a pile of the ones I might fancy. You can drop them a note, Megan. Say I look forward to making they acquaintance, Lionel specified, *upon me release.*

One warm May Saturday (the baby, in recent weeks, had grown from olive-size to prune-size to plum-size to peach-size), Des and Dawn went boating on the Serpentine in Hyde Park. And guess who they ran into.

224

Jon and Joel!

It had been three years — but the dogs went completely berserk. And they had a brilliant half-hour with them out on the green. And when the new owners (a dad and his daughter) took them off again, it was murder watching them disappear, Jon and Joel, with their crestfallen ears, their brimming eyes . . .

After they were gone Des dropped to his knees and rolled on to his side. It wasn't the dogs, not really; but the air was so fast and free, and he felt he was being roughly tickled from within, by his own heart, his own blood . . . That afternoon the lake was minutely runnelled by the wind, like corduroy; Dawn sat and soothed him, and they both stared out at the corded water.

Later that week Des was summoned to Canary Wharf. For a second interview at the *Daily Mirror!*

Old Dud died. Brian "Skanker" Fitzwilliam died. Yul Welkway was left paralysed after a fistfight behind the Hobgoblin. Grace Pepperdine had another minor stroke. Uncle Ringo (a southpaw) was run over by the moped of a trainee taxi driver (who was out acquiring the Knowledge) and lost the use of his left arm. Pete New was again sent to prison for having a fat dog. Uncle Stuart suffered a stress-induced nervous breakdown. Troy Welkway was blinded by an oxyacetylene burner in a worksite accident. Uncle John's wife left him, taking four of the five kids. Horace Sheringham was hospitalised with violent pains in his abdomen (it was by now quite widely known that Horace was a secret drinker). Jayden Drago died. Ernest Nightingale died. This was the loose, the floating world of Diston Town.

The winters were medievally cold.

■ ■ ■ ■

PART III

■ ■ ■ ■

Who let the dogs in? Oh, who let the dogs
  in?
Who let the dogs in? Who, who?

2012 CILLA DAWN PEPPERDINE, BABE IN ARMS

1

" 'Elizabeth Sheringham-Pepperdine.' What d'you think? . . . Des, he'll call you when he calls you. Don't feel hurt. He's busy with his birds."

"Yeah. Funny, isn't it. Not that bothered before. Now it's a new one every night."

"The Lotto Libertine. The Lotto Lecher."

"The Lotto Lothario. The *Mirror* called him that. They even called him the Lotto Lancelot!"

"The Lotto Ladykiller. Ah, but now he's moved on. And found *true love* . . ."

"You know I'm a feminist, Dawn," he resumed. "And all that. But it just won't work. 'Elizabeth Sheringham-Pepperdine'? That's — ten syllables. No."

"Mm. And we're only delaying the problem, aren't we. What if she grows up and marries someone whose parents did the same thing?"

229

"Yeah. She'd be uh, 'Elizabeth Sheringham-Pepperdine-Avalon-Fitzwilliam.' That goes right across the page!"

"All right. 'Elizabeth *Dawn* Pepperdine.' No hyphen. Just a middle name."

"Ooh. I like it. Wait. What if it's a . . . Hang on. 'Desmond Dawn Pepperdine.' I wouldn't mind that. I'd be proud. Yeah. Good, Dawnie."

" 'Robert Dawn Pepperdine.' Nothing wrong with it."

" 'Georgia Dawn Pepperdine.' 'Sybil.' 'Maria.' 'Thea.' I like 'Thea.' But then Uncle Li'll call her 'Fea.' "

"We can live with that, surely to God . . . Des, go and tell him our news. And say we need the space. For the baby."

Des sighed. And the flat itself, roosting atop Avalon Tower, endeavoured to go on seeming stoical: the tidy kitchen with its balcony, the windowless bathroom, the smaller bedroom — and Lionel's commodious lair, still crammed with contraband (though long since sealed by a new plywood door).

"And admit it," said Dawn. "You're upset. You're pining. He's been out a month and you haven't heard a single word."

"Yes I have. He sent his change-of-address card."

"Yeah. Change of address. From Wormwood Scrubs to 'Wormwood Scrubs.' "

"You know, I ought to go up. Tell him our news. I ought to. Now that you're showing."

"I'm *not!* Why is it, Des? I still don't *feel* I'm expecting. Even when he flutters."

"She. How's your dad?"

It was true. Dawn's pregnancy was so far asymptomatic. And it was Des who had the dry skin and the migraines, Des who had the heartburn and the mood swings, Des who had the torrents of drool, and the sense, day in, day out, that he was sucking on a pocketful of loose change.

". . . Go and see him. Go on, Des. There's Grace. And that's urgent."

"There's Grace. Yeah, I will."

Sitting on the table, Goldie (now a ladylike three-year-old) held up a forepaw, as if to receive a courtly kiss; then she kissed it herself, and tongued it, and rolled over on to the *Daily Mirror*.

"Funny, isn't it, Dawnie. They're back to going on about how stupid he is. After three years of him just being vicious. Now he's stupid again. Why's that?"

"Because his new bird claims he's clever."

"Does she?"

"All the time. Says he got his head sorted out while he was away. Says he read a whole dictionary."

"Which dictionary?"

"Pocket Cassell's, but still. Says he's secretly very clever. And they're not having that, the papers. Oh no."

". . . I'll give him a ring. Ask if I can look in on him one Saturday. I'm curious. I want to see how he's getting on."

Propped up on silken pillows, Lionel Asbo sat in the great barge of the four-ton four-poster with the gilt breakfast tray resting on his keglike thighs.

"Photo op," he said, and tossed aside his phone. "Oy! 'Threnody'!"

"What!"

"Photo op!"

"When? And what's it in aid of?" Naked but for her black high heels, "Threnody" came clicking out of her bathroom (they had a bathroom each) and on to the solid silence of the rugs.

"For a uh, an in-depth profile." Lionel scratched one of the dents in his crown. "Eight-page pull-out. Photo op's Saturday."

"That's not a photo op. That's a photo shoot. Isn't your cousin coming Saturday?"

"Not me cousin." Lionel reached for the

squat cigarette lighter on the bedside table. "Me nephew . . . Now what's *he* after?"

"I'll give you three guesses. Gimme gimme gimme." "Threnody" was noisily brushing her hair. "Lesson number one. See, with the press, Lionel, you got to practise the art of manipulation. *You* call the tune. Not them. You. One step ahead. Like Danube does. See, *Danube*, she —"

"Stop going on about Danube! You always going on about Danube!"

"Yeah yeah yeah."

"*Yeah* yeah yeah yeah."

"*Yeah* yeah yeah yeah yeah. Photo shoot who for? What paper?"

He told her. "Eight-page pull-out. A fresh approach. Megan reckons it'll do wonders for me image."

"Threnody" started getting dressed . . . The vast bay-windowed bedchamber was doing its best to think well of the new occupants; now it looked on with a polite smile at "Threnody" 's satin thong and spangled garter belt, at Lionel's cigar ash in the untouched bowl of muesli and yoghurt . . .

"You know, 'Threnody,' they can write what they want about Lionel Asbo. I don't give a fuck."

"You say that, Lionel, but you do. Go on,

233

you do."

"It's when they . . . It's when they uh, when they suggest I'm not quite right in the head. You know, that I'm not the full quid up here," he said, tapping another concavity in his scalp. "Or I'm supposed to be thick. Okay, I talk bad, but that don't mean —"

"Things'll be different, Lionel. You'll get your recognition. I guarantee it."

"It's when they uh, impugn me intelligence. That's what gives me the right raging hump. You know. When they imply I'm a cunt."

"I'll make them respect you, Lionel. Trust me. I'll make you loved."

2

Lotto Lummox, Raffle Rattlepate, Numbers Numbskull, Pick Six P***brain, Sweepstake Psycho, Bingo Bozo, Tombola Tom o' Bedlam — the Lotto Lout's been called the lot.

But does the Diston Dipstick have hidden depths? His new heart-throb, thrusting "Threnody," real name Sue Ryan, 29, claims he's an Einstein — and how can we doubt "Threnody"? She's a "poetess." And she's got a whole O-level!

Our nationally famous Agony Aunt, Daphne, went to Loopy Lionel's country seat, in the *once-sleepy Essex village of Short Crendon, to offer her counsel to the Chav S***head.*

"The first thing you notice about 'Wormwood Scrubs,' Lionel Asbo's thirty-room Gothic mansion, is the little picket line of villagers standing guard at the wrought-iron gates. A smattering of ordinary folk. A shopkeeper, a housewife, a man of the cloth.

"I am early for the midday interview, so, whilst I wait, I talk to them about their grievances. Which aren't what you'd expect for a lotto lout! No wild parties, no demolition derbies or souped-up quad bikes ripping through the countryside. It's a bit more subtle than that.

"True, Asbo is hardly a pillar of the community. That the hamlet's premier residence, formerly Crendon Court (where Henry VIII once spent the night), is now named after a blighted Acton prison — this rankles.

"So do the 30-foot steel walls which now gird the 10-acre garden. And the local children are said to be terrified of the two furious pitbulls, Jek and Jak, who are taken on daily tours, or aggressive inspections, of the village.

"Who, after all, would welcome the influx of the usual rabble that bob along in the slipstream of fame and money? Parasites and predators, and all the 'Threnody' stalkers and lookalikes.

"Local rumour has it, by the way, that 'Jek' refers to Jekyll and Hyde, whilst 'Jak' alludes to Jack the Ripper. But this sounds a bit too 'erudite' for the East End 'eejit.' More likely, 'Jek' and 'Jak' are garbled versions of 'Juke' and 'Jyke,' the names fished out of a hat by Asbo's companion, 'Threnody,' for the orphaned Somalian twins she long ago stopped sponsoring.

"What you sense, in the end, is a feeling of general hurt and dismay. A sense that these orderly rural lives are somehow travestied by the intrusion of the jackpot jailbird, Lionel Asbo."

"My photographer, the *Sun*'s Chris Large (one of the three journalists brutalised by Asbo in August 2009), asks the picketers for leave to ring the buzzer and announce our arrival.

"Wearing a blue silk dressing gown and, of all things, mid-calf snakeskin boots, Asbo walks briskly up the drive. He welcomes Chris and myself most cordially, then endures a brief heckling from the petitioners at the gates.

" 'You know what I got, Daph?' he says.

'Neighbours from hell.'

"This remark intrigues me. I have come here with an 'open mind' — after all, you can't believe everything you read in the papers! And I ask him, as we walk down the drive, passing the famous Bentley 'Aurora,' 'Weren't *you* a neighbour from hell, Lionel? Back in Diston?'

" 'Me? Never. Except when I was a kid. You don't want to be a neighbour from hell, Daph,' he confides. 'That's lower class.'

"Built in 1350, rebuilt in 1800, and completely refurbished in 1999, the house, I admit, is magnificent. Asbo gives me a brief tour: the semicircular drawing room with its nine bay windows, the library with its billiard table and recessed bookcases, the baronial dining hall. Of course, the cultured fixtures and furnishings are those of the previous occupant, antiques mogul Sir Vaughan Ashley, 73, who now resides in Monaco.

" 'I'm going to rip it all out,' says Asbo, and summarises the questionable renovations he has in mind. 'Everything's got to be new. I had my fill of f***ing antiques when I was growing up in Diston.'

"Then Asbo turns thoughtful. 'Or d'you think it suits me, Daph, all this old gear? Trouble is, it aggravates me class hatred,' he says in his inimitable Diston brogue. He turns briefly to Chris. 'How's your jawbone?' he asks without meeting his eye. 'You get me cheque?'

"Carmody, the butler, brings us drinks by the pool — orange juice for me, the signature Dom Perignon for Asbo. But first the photographs! Lionel yells for 'Threnody' (we all know how particular she is about those inverted commas! And whatever you do, don't mention Danube!)

" 'Threnody,' tearing herself away from her odes and her elegies, busily appears, in pink sarong and spike heels. Her dark red hair is tightly drawn back, and bunned — the hairstyle known as the 'council-house facelift.' But in the case of 'Threnody,' of course, the surgeons have been busy elsewhere.

"It's an unseasonably torrid noon, and the sarong is soon removed to reveal a 'teardrop' bikini, three dots of yellow against the perennial bronze of her flesh. The young couple strike loving poses. In his blue swimsuit, with the unzipped snakeskin boots, and with 'Threnody' at his side, Asbo (not muscular but very solid) resembles a superhero, or supervillain, in a risqué cartoon.

" 'Pop the top off for us, love,' murmurs

Chris. 'Threnody' isn't slow to oblige. And there are the famous boobs (first unveiled last year) — more like pottery than flesh, and pointing *upward*.

" 'They weren't cheap,' says Asbo. 'She told me what they cost. And that's f*** all,' he adds, 'to what she's blown on her a***.'

" 'Threnody' lingers for a glass or three, and talks about the new line of fragrances she hopes to launch. There is also a new line of what she calls 'intimate garmenture.' And of course there's the next 'slim volume' of verse!

"She gets up and minces about, whilst Chris clicks away. Her boobs and her 'a***' (as Asbo so gallantly calls it) provide vivid testimony to the cosmeticist's skill. But her 18-inch waist is all her own (and how does she find *room* for such a curvaceous midriff?). What with that face, those strangely noble bones and that wide, intriguingly thin-lipped mouth, well, it isn't hard to see why Asbo has fallen under her spell.

"Chris and 'Threnody' slip off for their 'session' (*see pages 3–6*). Lionel calls for Carmody and more champagne. And in a moment of weakness I consent to enjoy a small Buck's Fizz. I consult my notes, reload my tape recorder, and we proceed.

" 'Women, Lionel.' "

" 'Yeah? What about them?' asks Asbo with a wary look.

" 'Well. You played the field for a while, following your release. And now you're settling down here with your new partner. But it's true, isn't it Lionel, that in the past you were never a great ladies' man?'

" 'That's correct, Daph. That's correct. There was Cynthia. My childhood sweetheart, if you like. And then Gina.'

"This would be Mrs. Marlon Welkway (née Drago), the cause of the massive 'nuptial rumble' that put 90 wedding guests behind bars in the spring of 2009.

" 'Of course, Gina, she's happily married now, God bless her,' he says a little huskily. 'See, Marlon's my cousin. So Gina's my cousin too. And I wish them both all the luck in the world. I respect their bond. True love. It's a beautiful thing.'

"For a moment I sense that we're about to move on to his feelings for 'Threnody.' But I'm a trifle premature.

" 'You're not wrong, Daph. I never had much time for the other. Before. Wasn't bothered. Perfectly happy with the porn.'

"This is casually said. As if for all the world adult videos were a traditional alternative to adult relationships.

" 'You can't go far wrong with the porn. It's like prison. You know where you are with the porn.'

"I'm beginning to find this *very* weird, so I quickly ask, 'Er, how did you and "Threnody" meet?'

" 'Ah, you see, Daph, all these birds wrote me letters when I was away. And when I come out, I had them over. One at a time to my place in London.' (In London, Asbo now maintains a penthouse apartment at the infamous South Central Hotel.) 'And they were all glamour girls on the make!'

"Asbo seems to find this scandalous. Yes, what a contrast to 'Threnody,' that shrinking violet, with her well-known vow of poverty! (Remember Fernando, the Argie beef baron? Remember Azwat, the Bollywood billionaire?)

" 'Lads' mag types. All tits and teeth. Grasping slags, basically, Daph.'

" 'And "Threnody"?' I ask, suppressing a titter.

" 'See, I'm in this nightclub. And her bodyguard slips me her number in the gents. So we had a few drinks. And I knew. I knew. "Threnody"? She's got it *up here*,' he says, tapping not his chest but his poor old brainbox. 'Excellent head for *careers*.'

"*Careers? A career* for Lionel Asbo? Doing what? Giving lessons in filling out lotto tickets? Or perhaps a new 'line' in bingo shirts?

" 'And see, Daph,' Asbo goes on, 'she's an established celebrity. In her own right. She can handle herself. A woman of er, true sophistication.'

"At this point 'Threnody' bustles out, wearing a turquoise rubber catsuit, retrieves her sunglasses, and bustles back in again.

"There's a silence.

" 'Them other birds,' says Asbo, 'they were all up for a porking on the very first night! Not "Threnody." She's not that kind of girl. "Lionel," she says, "you're like a little boy lost. Trust me. I'll be your . . . shepherdess. And guide you through the er, celebrity circuit. Give me your hand." We shake on it. And she gazes into me eyes and she whispers, "Let's seal our pledge," she says, "with a swift 'jobbie' in the stretch." You know, the limo. There. Dead discreet.'

"Another silence (and I hope he doesn't hear me gulp). 'She knows how to deal with the er, the media spotlight. From her I'll learn to cope with the pressures of me new lifestyle.'

"I struggle on as best I can. 'What about that notorious temper, Lionel? You're having anger-management therapy, isn't that right?'

" 'Tommy Trum,' he says with satisfaction. (Tom Trumble, UK Light Heavyweight Champion, 1971–3.) 'Tommy lives near and he comes over twice a week. Teaching me the art of boxing.' He alertly moves his head from side to side. 'To channel me aggression.'

" 'But you've got a serious problem there, Lionel. Surely you need psychiatric help?'

" 'What, lying on some f***ing couch all afternoon moaning on about me childhood?' Asbo pauses. 'Listen, you can talk to all the so-called experts. But it's down to you, isn't it, in the end, Daph? It's down to you. See, when you're away, Daph, you get a lot of time to think. I went over it in me mind, over and over. And now I've got me head right.'

"Mm, well we'll be the judge of that!

"He folds his hands round the back of his neck and looks out over the rolling lawns. The rough spud of his face cracks into a gap-toothed smile, and he says, 'You know, Daph, one day I reckon I'll write the story of me life.'

"Now I feel a definite urge to tiptoe off into the afternoon. But I listen, as Asbo struggles on.

" 'I wouldn't do the typing, mind,' he says with disdain. 'I'd *dictate* it, like they do. A lad from Diston. Scraping out a living with this and that. Sticks at it, and by sheer . . Makes something of himself. Achieves something in this life. Comes good. Yeah. He comes good.' "

"I am still struggling to contain a fit of laughter when — thank God — we are graced by a pleasant interruption: the arrival of Lionel's 21-year-old nephew.

"Desmond Pepperdine has *not* changed his name to Desmond Asbo. This tall, slender, well spoken and delightfully assured young man, a graduate of Queen Anne's College, London, is now a cub reporter on the *Diston Gazette*.

"More than once Des has claimed (in court) that Lionel was 'like a father' to him after he was orphaned at the age of 12. But there is nothing paternal about his greeting.

" 'Ah, here comes the soap-dodger,' says Lionel (for Des is of mixed race).

" 'How are you, Uncle Li?' Des replies, no whit abashed.

"Lionel fans himself and yawns aggressively whilst Des and myself exchange pleasantries. Touchingly impressed, even slightly overwhelmed, Des says, 'Not *the*

Daphne? I used to read you first thing every day!'

" 'Go and put your bathers on,' says Uncle Lionel, and gives brief directions to the changing rooms. He then looks pointedly at his watch. My hour is up.

" 'A real pleasure to meet you,' says Des, and gives a graceful little bow. With his gorgeous smile and the light of true intelligence in his hazel eyes — what a radiant contrast to the pathetic gropings of his poor old uncle!

"I say, 'You must be very proud of him.'

" 'No comment,' quoth Asbo.

" 'One last question. Tell me, Lionel,' I ask him. 'What *was* it you learned — when you were "away"?'

"He seems to think for a very long time. Then, with much vigorous frowning, he haltingly 'explains.' Later, when I played this through, I thought my tape recorder was on the blink — but no. These are Asbo's very words.

" 'See Daph, the rich world . . is heavy. Everything weighs. Because it's here for the duration. It's here to stay . . And *my* old world, Diston as was, it's . . it's light! Nothing weighs an ounce! People die! It, things — fly away!' He does some more frowning and says, 'So that's me challenge. To go from the floating world . . to the heavy. That's me challenge. And I can handle it.' "

"I smile. Well, honestly — have you ever heard such a load of self-serving twaddle in all your life? And really, the truth is almost too sad for words, isn't it? Lionel Asbo is now a very wealthy man (*see sidebar*). And for what? The rewards have been huge, whilst the endeavour, and the talent, have always been non-existent. Thus, the trappings of wealth, in Asbo's case, are just a constant reminder of his basic worthlessness. His self-esteem is no higher than his IQ (which barely aspires to double figures). This — combined with severe emotional disorders, and an alarming shakiness in the sexual domain — has produced a terrible stew of violent insecurity and hollow pride.

" 'So that's me challenge.' Indeed . . . Chris and myself slip away, leaving Asbo to his dosh, his drivel, and his doxy. And I'm thinking, of course, that it's young Des Pepperdine who's faced a challenge and surmounted it. It's young Des Pepperdine who's achieved something in this life. It's young Des Pepperdine who's 'come good.'

"Not Lionel Asbo."

No, not the Hog Heaven Headcase. Not the Megabucks Moron. Hidden depths? Don't *make us weep. Put it on your tombstone, mate. If you can spell it. LIONEL ASBO: FAT-CAT F***WIT. RIP.*

Rape? Murder? What'll it be next, you brain-less BERK? Remember your rhyming slang, Lionel? Berk? From Berkeley Hunt? Four let-ters? Begins with a C?

Don't worry, folks. Give him long enough, and he'll work it out — one of these years. Back at the Scrubs they're already warming his toilet seat. And repadding his cell.

Go easy, lad, and take it nice and slow. You'll have all the TIME in the world . . .

4

In the planetarium of Lionel's glass-domed spa, as he slid into the trunks he'd been told to bring along, Des took it all in, the plunge pool, the lap pool, the saunas of various ferocities, the gargling jacuzzis, and the orderly forest of potted plants and gleaming pine. Then he went out through the wrong door — and found himself, barefoot, in a large and luxurious library . . . On the near-est coffee table (he saw with a pang) there was a roughly splayed *Morning Lark*, plus a roughly splayed *Diston Gazette*, plus two cans of Cobra with a crushed Marlboro Hundred on either lid, like a tableau of earlier times . . .

With the white towel across his shoulders he stepped out on to the deck. Daphne had gone (and with a blush he imagined her reading it, all those years ago: *Dear Daphne, I'm having an affair with an older . . .*). Poolside, Lionel lay chewing on a cigar while Carmody replenished his ice bucket. Des stood there, hands on hips . . . The village nestled on a rise over a shallow valley, and Lionel's vast garden was arranged on three levels, three graded distances, eventually subsiding into a pasture of paler green where two tiny horses nuzzled and browsed. The uppermost lawn was tyrannised by a sky-filling cedar, caught in mid-flail, ancient, grand, and haggard, and half-supported, now, by tripods made from its own wood. Dropped branches, fashioned into crutches.

"Get wet then," urged Lionel.

In Des dived, and the tepid water streamed past him, seeming to clog his pores and filling his head with memories of school trips, chlorine, foot troughs, pimpled white chests. He surfaced, saying,

"It's a bit warm, isn't it?"

"Yeah. I know. Blood-heat. That's 'Threnody.' She insists."

Out of politeness Des swam a few laps . . . You could count on Lionel (he thought) to have a girlfriend whose name he couldn't pronounce. And didn't *threnody* mean a lament or a dirge? . . . Up he climbed, feeling as though he was covered in sweat; he retrieved his towel and went and sat on the white wicker chair next to Lionel's plumply padded lounger. He said,

"Ah. Nice."

"Yeah. Most refreshing. Like a bath you just pissed in . . . Suppose you want a drop of this. Go on then. Nah, fill you glass. I already had a couple of pints with Daph. You know, she's right, 'Threnody.' There's nothing to it."

"Nothing to what?"

"Shaping you image in the press. It's easy. You just let you personality come out. And then they putty in you hands."

"Cheers, Uncle Li."

"It's not even like *beer*, champagne. It's like *pop*. This is more like it — Macallan's." He hoisted the heavy glass. "It's older than me, this is. And as for that fucking tree, it's been there, it's been there for a thousand years. A thousand years. They brought it back from Lebanon. On they crusades."

The two of them were looking out and away.

". . . You know, Des, I've had every ponce and mumper in England come knocking on me door. Ringo. Ringo shows up. Says he can't find work because of his arm. I said, *You couldn't find a fucking job, Ring, even before you was crippled.* You Uncle John, he shows up and all." Lionel ruefully but in the end quite indulgently shook his head. "They'll try anything! Oh yeah — and guess who else come calling. Guess what else crept out from under its fucking stone. Ross Knowles!"

Des remembered Ross Knowles. The unexceptionable drinker Lionel smashed up that time in the Hobgoblin, on account of the news about Marlon and Gina Drago.

"Ross Knowles, if you please. Ross Knowles come hobbling up me drive. Yeah — on you way, brother. What am I, a fucking *bank*?"

Ban-kuh. After a silence Des said, "Dawn's expecting." The silence resumed.

"Is she now. Expecting what? . . . Come on, let's have it, son. Why're you here?"

Des said, "Just some family business. That's all."

"What business?"

"You know. The flat. Gran."

"Oh yeah. Gran. You been up there? How is the old . . . ?"

"And I came to tell you our news, Uncle Li," said Des, rerousing himself. "I'm chuffed. Dawn's in the family way and we're

250

both dead chuffed."

Breathing in, Lionel resettled himself. "You too young, Des," he said quietly. "You twenty-one."

"Well. Dawn's twenty-three. We aren't kids."

"Okay. You not like *Grace*. Or you mum. You not *twelve* . . . But you should be putting youself about," he went on. "With the birds. Applying youself."

"I don't seem to be the type . . . I'm like you, Uncle Li. Back then. Not bothered."

"Yeah, well I'm bothered now, by Christ. Obsessed. And when that happens, Des, it's all off. You at they mercy!"

Des leaned back and closed his eyes and said dreamily, "I fancy a girl."

"Oh yeah? Who?"

Was Lionel being sarcastic — or just stupid on purpose? "No. I fancy *having* a girl."

"Yeah? Who?"

"*No*, Uncle Li. I fancy *fathering* a girl."

"Oh. Oh. Well that's you own business . . . Sorry, Des, me mind's elsewhere. I'm due a treat this afternoon." He winced three times, four, as if in pain, and then his mouth broke into a lavish sneer. "Gaw. Birds. The way they . . . And then you . . ."

Des closed his eyes again. "Well I'm

chuffed. Just think. What if it's twins?"

". . . Forget it."

"Forget what?"

"You after me room. And you *can't have it*."

Des sat forward. "Ah come on, Uncle Li. Come on. What you need it for?"

"All me stuff!"

"All *what* stuff? Crates of dodgy old mobile phones. Old bottles of North Korean steroids all stuck together. And a load of old videos off the Adult Channel!"

". . . Oh. So you saying you been sniffing round in there."

"Yeah." And Des told him how he had gained entry (on all fours), and spent a week restacking the merchandise. "So we could put a new door back on the hinges and get it shut. This was years ago. I *told* you, Uncle Li."

"You never!"

"I can prove it!"

"Go on then!"

"Okay. Am I married?"

". . . How would I know?"

"See? I told you *that* and all! Silent Green. You were on the phone with your people. Attacking the yen. I said, *We're engaged*. But you weren't listening, Uncle Li. You were too busy attacking the yen! . . . We

252

need the space. It's my mother's room. And I want it back."

"Oh, boo-hoo. Where's you violin."

"Listen. The minute you're earning they stop the Assistance. So we're paying the rent."

Now something happened to Lionel's eyes: their blues glowed and swelled, like a pair of headlights going from dipped to full. "Ah but Des!" he cried. "That room's me — me only . . . It's my only . . ."

"Your only what? Your only — your only link?"

"Yeah, I suppose. Something like that . . . Okay, Desmond. You win."

And then and there Lionel undertook, in future, to pay a half — no, a third — of all the outgoings that pertained to Avalon Tower.

"We'd rather have the room."

"Jesus. There's no pleasing yer, is there. Okay," he said, "I'll pay the *lot*. The whole whack . . . Come on, Des. Humour me. It's just for a month or two. Till I'm settled."

He held out a hand, and Des took it.

"Well. You got what you come for. Mission accomplished. *Now* are you happy? . . . Ooh, it's hot, isn't it, Des. D'you know how dear it is, Dom Perignon?"

"No, I don't."

With a grunt Lionel got to his feet. He hoisted the bottle out of the ice bucket: it was five-sixths full. With a hooked thumb he tugged out his waistband, and poured.

"Ooh, that's better. *Où*. Nice little tingle and all. Well. It deserves it! . . . Who you grinning at?"

"No one, Uncle Li!"

Rolling the spent bottle on to the tabletop, Lionel threw himself raggedly into the water and pounded down to the shallow end.

5

It was half past one.

His bare legs cooled by sprinklers, his bare feet on the feathery and succulent grass, and his mobile phone in his hand (he was awaiting Lionel's summons), Des took a turn round the grounds. They were landscaped, he assumed — giant hands had taken them and moulded them. The three lawns were girt on either side by tall thicknesses of electrified steel grilling, but the view of the valley and beyond was uninterrupted — maybe a hidden barrier, he thought. While he made his way down there, motion-sensitive CCTV cameras, on branches, in bushes, indignantly craned their necks to watch him pass; and he was also politely accosted by three different security men (all of them early middle-aged, with capped teeth and fresh suntans: they looked like minor filmstars, or their stand-ins or body doubles). As the land flattened out towards the pasture, and as the horses now nobly loomed, he came to a deep trench perhaps twenty feet across. Within was a thrill ride of twirling razor wire; it squirmed like a barber's pole, and faintly crackled.

His phone gave its pulse. *Des?* said Lionel briskly. *Have a word with Mrs. Lucy in the kitchen. She'll give you a turnip for you lunch. And then come to me office. You can say hello to "Threnody." Have a little chat about you future. Three. There.* As he pocketed his phone Des noticed the twin searchlights on the gabled roof (the mansion's staring antennae), and he thought he heard the muffled or subterranean shouts of dogs . . . But for now he was far from Diston — distant Diston and its savage rhythms. Look how gently the ancient tree decayed, losing its green needles, its slow fall broken by its own struts and stays. All was quiet, except for birdsong and the subliminal murmur of heat and fertility; and all was still, except for the shoals of frantic white butterflies.

Having done what he could with an old-style ploughman's lunch (root vegetables, lightly steamed), he went from the kitchen to the library. It was two forty-five . . . The books: some of them might have been bought by the yard (fifty-odd leather-clad volumes of Bulwer-Lytton), but there were many treasures — Macaulay, Gibbon, the Churchill–Roosevelt letters, Trotsky's *History of the Russian Revolution* . . . At the far end of the room, gazing at one another across the length of the billiard table, were two gilt-framed paintings — the current master, the current mistress. In a cream singlet against a rich blue sky (and strenuously idealised), Lionel resembled a Young Pioneer of early Soviet propaganda, the humped shoulder muscles, the corded forearms, the sheen of honest exertion on his open brow. As for "Threnody," seen against the same background, she could have been a survivor from the Old Regime — a high-born harpist, say, now tempered by a year or two of forced labour.

"Mr. Pepperdine?"

He took one last look around. Yes, the luxury of the garden was the luxury of space and silence; and the luxury of the library was the luxury of thought and time.

Carmody led him through the entrance hall and down a wide stone-flagged passage

and came to a halt in front of a wall of mir-
rors.

"You just push the door, sir, and it opens outward."

Des pushed, and went on through the looking glass.

He entered a long, low room, parched of all natural light, and with treated air (cooled, humidified) — the scene, he immediately sensed, of a grim and singular preoccupation. Lionel sat on a square-shouldered swivel chair in the far corner, wanly illumined by a bank of TV screens. And now it was Des's turn to think of James Bond — of Bond, James Bond, and his licence to kill. Of course, Lionel would not be the secret agent, would not be 007; he would be the talented maniac bent on world domination. Where was his moat full of shark or piranha? Where was his bushy white cat, his chessboard, his monorail? And, having achieved world domination, what would Lionel do with it? . . . The burgundy smoking-jacket, the stout cigar, and the brandy balloon were all of a piece; on the other hand, the likes of Mr. Big and Dr. No, with their planetary ambitions, would not normally be seen frowning down at a tousled copy of the *Diston Gazette*. This Lionel now put aside.

"Sit there, would you?" He nodded at a low couch of studded red leather. ". . . How could you do it, Des?" he asked. "Something so sick. So *twisted*."

Fear, like a terrible old friend, took Des Pepperdine and hugged him close.

"Look at you eyes. Says it all." He ran a thumbnail across his brow, from temple to temple. "The eyes of guilt. Tell me why, Des. You know what I'm talking about. Why, Des, why?"

With his face tipped back (and wearing its smile of pain), Lionel described a full circle in his swivel chair.

"See, I'm a man in a predicament. I got this nephew. After his mum sadly died, I raised him meself. As best I could. Not a bad lad, I thought. Here and there he let me down. Loose tongue. Such is youth . . . Then what's he do? Turns *bent* on me. Goes to the university, gets his head full of ideas. Studies uh, Criminology. And now he's finking for a *living* . . ."

It took Des a moment to work out that Lionel did in fact mean *finking* (and not *thinking*). His tension seeped away — to be replaced by a kind of sumptuous boredom. All this would be nothing new.

"D'you remember, Des, years and years ago, when I come home and caught you red-handed in front of *Crimewatch?* And I give you a smack? Well, I thought you'd learned you lesson. Apparently not."

"What're you driving at, Uncle Li?"

"What am I driving at? I open me *Diston Gazette*," he said, opening his *Diston Gazette* — "and you on the crime desk!"

"Yeah. Sort of."

"Look at this. Gutsy Grandma Thwarts Ganger Getaway. *By Desmond Pepperdine.* Look at this. Brave Bank Guard Frees Trapped Raid Blonde . . . No. No. You got to walk away from that, Des. Forthwith," he said (with difficulty). "You betraying *you own class!* And I can't have it, son. I can't have it."

"You can't have it. So what should I do?"

"No need to ask. It's simple. You tender you resignation."

". . . Yeah. That makes a lot of sense. These days there's loads of jobs."

"Oh. Sarcastic. All right," said Lionel, with the air of someone perhaps already prepared to seek a compromise. "All right. Ask to be transferred to other duties. Away from the uh, the crime desk."

"Uncle Li, *every* desk at the *Gazette*'s a crime desk. It's Diston."

"Crap. There's sport."

"Sport?"

"Yeah. Look at this. At the back. They got football. Snooker. Bit of darts . . ." Lionel turned boldly to the centre pages. "Or the Xtra Section. Look . . . TV Guide . . . Do It Youself . . . Signs of the Zodiac . . . You Problems Solved . . . Or there's the small ads."

"Yeah, there's the small ads. Sorry, Uncle Li, I'm happy where I am."

"Are you now. Well you lost to shame. You lost to shame. And *I ain't* . . . Okay. Okay." Lionel's face now took on a leer of naked cunning — cunning undisguised, cunning entirely uncontained. So much cunning — even Lionel didn't know what to do with it all. "Uh. Now Des. Obviously I been meaning to put something aside for you and uh, little Dawnie. Obviously. All that's stayed me hand," he said, staring at that hand (its scarred knuckles, its bitten tips), "is the best way to go about it. You know. Lump sum. A uh, an annuity. Shares. I'm a wealthy man and it's a worthy cause." *Welfy, wervy.* "But there's no chance, no chance, if you go on doing what you doing at the *Diston Gazette*."

Des smiled and said, "Forget it, Uncle Li. You know me — I'm a socialist. Don't hold with unearned income. Anyway. I'm going up in the world. I'm being taken on by the *Daily Mirror!*"

". . . The *Mirror?* Well now. The *Mirror*'s a bit different. The *Mirror*'s —"

With an electric flurry the overhead lights came on.

"Ah, 'Threnody'!"

6

She said from the doorway, "Does he want a lift in? I wouldn't mind the company. I'll give him a lift in. I'm driving."

"Driving? Where's Mal?"

"His kid's sick. So I sent him home . . . Does he want a lift in?"

"Him? No. He'll have his ticket, 'Threnody.' He's eaten. Mrs. Lucy give him a nice slice of peat for his lunch. No, he's going in a minute but he's got his cheap ticket, 'Threnody.' He doesn't believe in free rides. He's got his cheap return."

"Well I'm off."

She stood quite still; then, as if released, she strode forward. In a sharply waisted black jacket, a tight hoop-striped black-and-yellow skirt, and yellow stockings, she reminded Des of a thought that had once or twice surprised him: the unlooked-for prettiness of young wasps . . . Lionel angled his cheek to receive her kiss, and she remained there fragrantly murmuring over him and smoothing the stubble of his hair.

There were more kisses, more murmurs. Des took this in with approval. *They seem to be making a real go of it*, he could already hear himself telling Dawn. *You know. Mutually supportive. Really caring and . . .*

"Threnody" straightened up and said, "I'll give them three per cent. For the credit line. And the exposure."

"Sounds about right."

"They can reapply."

"Go on then. Oy. Are you seeing that bloke tonight?"

"What bloke?"

"The yacht salesman. The J-cloth. Where's he from?"

"Raoul? Beirut. And he's a Christian if you must know. You bet I'm seeing him. I'm gasping for a shag."

"I know the feeling."

"Well don't look at me."

"I won't."

"*Yeah* yeah yeah yeah."

"*Yeah* yeah yeah yeah yeah yeah."

"*Yeah* yeah yeah yeah yeah yeah yeah yeah."

After this (at least) numerical victory, "Threnody" turned to Des and said,

"Here. Les. You're young. You work for the papers. How come they don't go on about me like they go on about Danube?

It's always Danube. Danube Danube Danube."

"Jesus," said Lionel with a passionate groan. "*Danube*."

"Danube. Yeah, Danube. Why'm I the wannabe Danube, Les? Why isn't Danube the wannabe 'Threnody'? Why? Why?"

"All them foreign blokes," said Lionel. "It's because you been out with all them foreign blokes. No Englishmen."

"What about *you? You're* an Englishman and no fucking mistake."

"Yeah. You first one."

"Yeah yeah yeah yeah. *Come* on, Les. Tell me. Why's it always Danube? Go on. Why?"

"Uh," said Des, "you've put me on the spot here. I don't know, maybe it's because she's a mum. Celebrity Mum of the Year, wasn't she? She's got children. Whatever else she is, she's a mum."

"Threnody" narrowed her eyes at him. And with that mouth, like the zip on a lady's purse: for a moment she looked like a rock-hard oil-rigger recalling some murderous offshore blaze. "Hear that, Lionel? I got to have a fucking *baby* now!"

And away she scissored with her swift, fussy stride — and Des thought of Gran, coming back from the shops that time, with egg and bacon for Rory Nightingale. That same determination, and yet with something precarious in it. That same determination to thrive.

"Love you," snapped "Threnody" over her shoulder as she pushed on the door.

Mournfully Lionel called out after her, "Not the 'Aurora,' 'Threnody.' Take a Merc." *A Mer-cuh.* "Or a BM! . . . Ooh Des," he said, with decided admiration, "remember that bird in that prison in Iraq? Lynndie England? That's what I call 'Threnody.' Lynndie England. She's *torture.* It'll take about a year, she says. Then we'll both have what we want . . . Okay, any other business?" Not for the first time he looked intently at his watch. "Jesus, it's always later than I think. Tick-tock goes the clock. You better be on you way, boy."

"There's all these barebacked plugs and the fire doors are all jammed. She's got rope burns on her wrists. And frozen joints and pressure sores. And I saw a tin of Whiskas on her bedside table."

"Whiskas?"

"She needs better care, Uncle Li."

"Well it's not for fairies, is it. Old age."

"She's just turned forty-five."

"Then what she expect? Comes to us all. And anyway, why bother moving her? It's all one to Grace. She's past caring."

They were now in the domed entrance hall — the size of a quarry, with its sluggish echoes, and the chutes of sunlight coming through the fleur-de-lis windows up above the orbital gallery. Des said,

"I see Ringo — I see Uncle Ring'll be in the *People*. Next Sunday."

"Yeah, Megan told me they was flagging it. Who cares. Let him spill his guts for fifty pee."

"Still, that might get picked up on, Uncle Li. All over again. You and the five brothers. They might want something on Grace. And they could make it look bad. You here — and her there. Picture it." Des pictured it: a Shock Issue of the *Daily Mirror*, on Gran's home. "You on your lounger by the pool. Grace strapped to her mattress in the attic. Could make it look bad."

". . . They could and all. Yeah. They'd distort it and make it look bad. That's what they do, Des. Consistently. Distort it and make it look bad . . . Christ, how come Megan never thought of that? She costs enough. Or Seb fucking Drinker."

"There's a better place, Uncle Li. I went up there. Couple of miles out of Souness. On the promontory. Called the Northern Lights. It's dearer, mind."

"How much dearer? Jesus, you a one-man Black Monday, you are."

"It's up on Clo Mor Bluff. There." He reached into his shoulder bag and handed over the sleek brochure. "Looking down on Lochinvar Strand."

". . . All right. All right, I'll have it taken care of. Well. I can't be angry today, Des. No I can't be angry today."

"And why's that?"

"It's not often, Des, it's not often you get you chance to right a wrong. To strike a blow for justice. And to do it *nice*, Des. With a bit of style."

". . . Uncle Li, is that dogs I can hear?"

"In the cellar. Jak and Jek. They good boys, but they pining for me now." From deep in its alcove a grandfather clock struck four. "Okay. Off with yer. Back to you crime desk. On you cheap return."

"Got some news for you. From the crime desk," he said boldly as they headed off towards the vestibule. "About Rory Nightingale."

"Oh yeah?" said Lionel, his breeziness in no way compromised by this turn. "What about him?"

"They found a body in an allotment in Southend. Uncovered by the rains. It wasn't Rory. It was another kid. But he had Rory's

266

school ID on him. And his gold toothpick. They did the DNA. Guess what else was in there. Wigs."

"Wigs . . . You know, Des, I haven't forgotten. Rory — he said something." And here Lionel produced his rictal false smile. "*Des did it and all*, he said. What he mean by that?"

But Desmond was more or less ready for this. Careful to keep a faint smile on his lips, he said, "Probably just meant I set him up. Don't you remember? You had me finger him. Had me fink him. Remember?"

There was a moment of stillness. Then Lionel violently applied himself to all the locks and bolts, all the chains and ratchets that shackled the front doors.

"Rory Nightingale got off light. He gave my mum one. Take care, boy."

Des went forth.

"Uh, hang on." Lionel was looking at his watch. "Quick. Show you me cars."

7

In Diston — in Diston, everything hated everything else, and everything else, in return, hated everything back. Everything soft hated everything hard, and vice versa, cold fought heat, heat fought cold, everything honked and yelled and swore at everything, and all was weightless, and all hated weight.

In Short Crendon, on the other hand, everything contemplated everything else with unqualified satisfaction. As if the whole village was leaning back, hands on hips, and lightly rocking on its heels. Or so it seemed to Des Pepperdine as he made his way to the train station, feeling exotic and conspicuous among the whites and greys, the farm voices, the bicycles and hatchbacks — tea shop, greengrocer, family butcher. Two illustrated road signs caught his eye. One showed a pair of stick figures edging along, with infinite difficulty, all jagged and aquiver, as if in mid-electrocution (ELDERLY PEDESTRIANS). The other was an uncaptioned mugshot of a cow.

The idiocy of rural life. Who said that? Lenin? And is it idiocy, he asked himself (in his new editorial voice), or is it just innocence? What he sensed, in any case, was a bewildering deficit of urgency, of haste and purpose. And, somehow, a deficit of intelligence. For it was his obstinate belief that Town contained hidden force of mind — nearly all of it trapped or cross-purposed. And how will it go, he often wondered, when all the brain-dead awaken? When all the Lionels decide to be intelligent? . . . Meanwhile, here was Short Crendon and its pottering and pootering. I suppose I'm just a creature of the world city, he thought, and walked on.

Up ahead a battered blue Mini rounded the corner, shuddered and veered, and rolled to a halt with brown smoke funnelling from its hood. Traffic — and there was at least no shortage of traffic — started to accumulate in the blocked lane, and a horn or two tentatively sounded. As he passed by, Des took a look at the young couple in the front seats: they were yelling inaudibly at each other while trying to nudge the car forward with spasmodic jerks of their loins. And it was Marlon and Gina Welkway! Gina all in white, with those slender ribbons in her hair, as she was on the day of her wedding. And the little Mini (extracted, perhaps, from the forecourts of the late Jayden Drago) did in fact jolt gamely forward, and the traffic duly stirred and oozed free and eventually caught up with itself.

As he approached, and as he took in the childish scale of the station (he was used to the termini that you shared with millions upon millions), Des was struck by an unpleasant thought. A tedious thought: he had left without his bathers (now he remembered the bench by the plunge pool and the parallelogram of sunlight where he had laid them out to dry). Habits of thrift and good order made him at once turn on his heel. He now faced the minor idiocy of retracing his steps, steps that would then need to be re-retraced, for the five thirty-five.

On the way he diverted himself by going over his uncle's deeply conflicted response to the news about the *Daily Mirror*. Writing about law and order for the *Daily Mirror* was in a way much worse than writing about law and order for the *Diston Gazette*, because of the greater reach (*You be doing you narking on a national scale!*); as against that, though, Lionel argued, the *Mirror* was a traditional friend of the working class, and was therefore comparatively soft on crime.

Are you telling me the Mirror*'s pro-crime, Uncle Li?*

Don't talk stupid. They not pro-crime as such. But they not going to make a to-do about a little bit of theft. It serves equality, Des. The uh, the redistribution of wealth.

And how pro-theft are you? With your guards and your razor wire?

Ah, but that's on me own initiative, he said. They were in the echoing entrance hall, and Lionel was standing in one of the pools of three-petalled sunlight. *That's different. See, I don't use the law, Des. And I get threats all the time! They say*, Guiss ten million quid

270

or we'll fucking kill yer. *I say*, Come and get it. You welcome to try. *And if some bleeding thrusters fancy they chances, then we'll take it from there. See, Des, this is it. You don't let money change yer. You don't let money change you deepest convictions. And I* never use the law. *This is it. This is it.*

No, it couldn't have been a coincidence. The old Mini, which now had a flat back tyre, was cravenly slumped alongside the imperial contours of the "Aurora" . . . Des was silently admitted by Carmody (who soon withdrew). He advanced to the library and was halfway across the darkened room before he noticed Marlon, on a low settee, with a glass in one hand and a decanter of brown liquor in the other.

"Marlon."

"Ah. Little Des," said Marlon thickly.

And the air itself was thick. Thick and weak, as if the room was about to faint. Des recognised this atmosphere — its wrongness, its deafened, bad-dream feel.

"I, I left something next door. I'll just pop through and . . ."

"No. Don't do that, mate. Don't do that."

Marlon dragged a hand across his forehead, which was frosted in sweat, and grey-pale against the damp black blade of his

271

widow's peak. With a heavy tongue he said,

"You, you're like a canary. A little yellow canary. You fucked me in court."

"Well so did Yul and Troy."

"Yeah, and look what happened to them."

With his adapted vision Des now saw that there were items of white clothing strewn across the black carpet, white ribbons, a brassiere, a pair of knickers, a slip, a stained trousseau . . .

"Little yellow canary."

Marlon was making an attempt to suffuse his smile with menace. But then came Lionel's reverberating bawl from beyond (*Get you fat prat in that sauna!*), followed by the blast of a whistle and Gina's scandalised screech.

The wide door swung open in blinding light. And there was the stippled, mottled nudity of Lionel Asbo. Des's eyes sought what they could not but seek: and Lionel was rawly and barbarically erect . . . Beyond him, through the curved glass, greenery trembled, foxtail, flowering rush, the leaves of trees and their shadows.

Obliviously Lionel pushed past him (what after all was Des doing in this dream?).

"Marlon! You all right in the dark there, Marl? I'm not neglecting you needs?"

There was no answer. Lionel moved forward.

"Look up, son. *Meet me eye.* Meet me eye. And see this? See the lipstick on it? See it?"

Marlon looked up — then dropped his head. And Des again was gone.

8

"Nice. I hope you're proud of him. That's really nice, that is. Charming."

"Can we change the subject for a minute? I'm still in recovery."

"Okay. How about . . . Matthew?" she said. "Matthew. Mark. Luke. John."

"John," he said. "John, Paul, George, Ringo. Please. No names."

"Yeah. No names. No more names . . . I hate names."

He had just come in (train delay caused by a suicide on the sunken tracks a mile or two from Liverpool Street), and Dawn was about to serve up dinner. In the meantime he was enjoying a saucerful of pickled onions.

"Rachel. Delilah. Gaw, you should've seen his cars, Dawnie." Des listed some of the makes. "And he's got this mammoth SUV. It's called a Venganza. Spanish for *revenge*. Carbon-black — no shine. It's like an Armoured Personnel Carrier. For Special

Forces. And it's split-level! You press a button and this little steel ladder comes down. Headlights the size of dustbin lids. Does three miles to the gallon. Esther. Ruth."

"Nahum. Solomon. So you reckon he was at it with Gina in the sauna. Peter."

"Looked that way. Not Peter. Peter Pepperdine? That's like Peter Piper picked a peck of . . . Giving Gina one in the sauna. There he was. Mother-naked."

"And with a big bonk on."

"Dawnie," said Des (and he hadn't told her about the lipstick). "Yeah. Like that pissed demigod. Bacchus."

"Or Nessus," said Dawn. "The centaur. Who kidnapped the wife of Hercules."

"Yeah. Dejanira . . . Dejanira Pepperdine. Niobe. Echo. Echo Pepperdine."

Dawn said, "Bloody hell. Why'd they go along with it? And Gina giggling away in there. Jacob."

"Jacqueline. I don't know. Must be for the money. See, there's all Jayden's debts. And Marlon's a gambler. But Gina. She sounded — all keen. I don't get Gina . . . Tina. Nina. Zina."

For a moment Des tried to think like a criminal (this was in any case becoming a professional habit). And he realised that in the little encounter at "Wormwood Scrubs" he had dangerously strengthened an enmity — as a witness to the unmanning of Marlon Welkway. That would be remembered.

"And he had her strip in the library! . . . Des, remember his speech? At the wedding?"

"Oh yeah. How'd it go? *With her trousseau up round her waist and her knickers round her* . . . Must've done a sort of re-enactment. Mary. Eve. Dawn, this chicken smells funny. And the broccoli's all bitter."

". . . You love your chicken and broccoli!"

He reached for the jar of pickled onions and speared a big one with his fork. "Miriam."

". . . Mean Mr. Mustard. What'd he say about the rent? Tell me again? Hector."

"Antigone. He said he'd help out. Whatever that means. I'll believe it when I see it. Callisto."

"Mm. If it's a girl I want it to sound . . . ethereal."

"Ethereal. Okay. Let's call her Frenody."

They laughed. Despite everything, which was saying something, they were both, for the most part, irresponsibly happy.

"But what if it's a boy? Go on, Des. Let's phone Iqbal and find out."

Iqbal was the enormous Punjabi warrior

who — immaculate in his green rompers — oversaw the sonogram at the Maternity Centre. Des and Dawn loved Iqbal. They loved Mrs. Treacher, the head midwife (she looked like the Nurse in Zeffirelli's *Romeo and Juliet*: a ravenous, eager-eyed rustic — ravenous for life, life). And they loved the Maternity Centre. Unlike all the other hospitals they'd ever been in, the Maternity Centre was eerily odourless. Hospitals, in their experience, smelled of school dinners. As if pain, mortality, death, birth, all the great excruciations, subsisted on a diet of boiled carrots and semolina . . .

"Why should *Iqbal* know what sex it is when we don't?"

"*Iqbal* doesn't care. He's not sitting there gloating over it. Sniggering and rubbing his hands. To him it's just another baby!"

"Oh, let's, Des. Then we'll only spend *half* the time talking about names. Edward."

"Edwina. No, Dawnie. It's better not to know."

"Why is it?"

"Just because you *can* find out doesn't mean you should."

"Well it doesn't mean you shouldn't. Either."

Twisting in his chair, he said, "Cilla never knew. Gran never knew. And *her* mum, and

276

her gran — they never knew." Meaning what? Meaning something like: you oughtn't to separate yourself from your predecessors — your predecessors, in their countless millions. "Angelina." And there was another reason too (he was superstitiously convinced), though he hadn't yet quite fathomed it. "Some kinds of knowledge it's better not to have, Dawnie. Angeletta."

"Andrew. D'you think he'll do anything for Gran, Lionel?"

"He might. He might well. He's worried about his image. Gudrun."

"Gudrun Dawn Pepperdine . . . No. Then she'd be GDP! Gross Domestic Product. Sounds horrible. You got to keep your eye on the initials, Des . . . And Daphne?"

"Daphne? Nah. Oh. You mean *Daphne.*"

"Yeah, Daphne."

"She was . . ."

He again unscrewed the jar of pickled onions . . . For obvious reasons Des had never regaled Dawn with the story of his application to the famous agony aunt. And Daphne's reply, back then (*You are both committing statutory rape*) was so durably terrifying that Des almost fell over backwards when Lionel, looking up from his lounger, said airily, *This is you Auntie Daphne. Daphne — from the* Sun.

277

"I'd imagined an avenging angel," he said. "You know — a judger. But she seemed a nice little dear. Maybe she'll send Uncle Li one of her pamphlets."

"Mm. Dos and don'ts for lotto louts. Prostitute your best mate's wife. And make him watch."

"I reckon she'll write an honest piece. Sympathetic."

"Sympathetic? I hope she gives him a right slagging."

"Dawnie! No, don't. Don't start. Angelica."

". . . Des, I've decided. Boy or girl, let's call it Toilet."

". . . Good, Dawnie. Toilet Pepperdine. That'll do."

She got to her feet and said, "So goodbye to those bathers."

"Looks like it. We got any ice cream?"

". . . Your cravings are back!"

"It's not a craving! I just fancy some ice cream!"

"Ice cream. Strawberry ice cream, Des. And pickled onions."

"Yeah well I know."

He leaned down and stroked the cat. Goldie's arched and ribby back, her tingling tail. He wasn't going to tell Dawn about his other cravings — his cravings for ash and notepaper and laundry starch. His secret cravings, and his secret aversions too, like mental allergies, his dreads, his night-sweats. And now, unbelievably (there must be some mistake), this mess of fears — Des, Desi, Desmond — was being asked to take receipt of a whole new human being . . .

"Cats are girls."

"And dogs are boys," said Dawn Pepperdine.

On the following Tuesday, May Day, at seven in the morning, a uniformed tipstaff or beadle, with rainwater dripping from his shovel hat, delivered a forty-page document, stamped and sealed with the imprimatur of Lord Barcleigh's chambers.

It took them an hour to make any sense of it.

"What can we do? The flat's in his name . . . Here. He's going to pay a third," said Des. "By banker's order."

"A third. I bet he'll cut it to a *quarter* once Toilet's here."

"He'll *have* to clear out once Toilet's here. I'll reason with him. Wish me luck . . . Still, Dawnie. It's money coming in. Not money going out. Like with Horace."

"See that? He told you it was just for a while. See that? *In perpetuity!* And look at the penalties if we even . . ."

"He's using the law! Against *us*."

"Christ. He could buy the whole Tower. What's he want the room for anyway?"

9

Now things started speeding up.

Lionel's cellphone was switched off or otherwise deactivated, so Des called the house. He hoped to hear Carmody's emollient murmur — but no. He got "Threnody."

"Ooh," she said, "you're lucky it's me who answered."

"Why's that?"

"Have you seen the fucking *Sun*?"

The *Sun* lay open on the kitchen table. With Goldie asleep on it.

"Absolutely terrible he's been," "Threnody" went on. "This morning he wrecked the barn. And that barn's *scheduled*. And then Tommy Trumble came over. For their sparring session — you know, they sort of shadowbox each other? Anger management? And Lionel went and knocked him out! And Tommy's sixty-seven! We thought he was *dead*. And it's all your fault. According to Lionel."

"How's he work that one out?"

"Threnody" lowered her voice. "According to Mr. Mastermind, if *you* hadn't wan-

280

dered in he might've come across not that bad. But you. He reckons they're up your arse because you're black. You'd better steer clear. I'm off out of the country, me. Let him calm down . . . I tell you, he hated it like fucking poison," she said, "the way they impugned his intelligence. You know. The way they implied he's a cunt."

"Yeah. They did a bit."

"And look what the arsehole said about *me!*"

Late that night (and this would be widely covered in the press), "Threnody" boarded a plane for Kabul.

At work the following lunchtime Des received a text: *2 a clock some lads coming dont worry they movers.* He went straight home and found them already there: a team of men in sharp white overalls and mining helmets. Des looked on as with military thoroughness they stripped Lionel's bedroom of all its stolen property. When they were gone he tiptoed in. The teetering, beetle-chewed wardrobe, the chest of drawers with its missing knobs and warped runnels. In the corner lay a heap of trainers, all parched and curled in on themselves; and there on the hooks were Lionel's three or four mesh vests.

■ ■ ■ ■

On Thursday they received a postcard from Cape Wrath. An artist's impression of the great frayed tray of the North Sea, under a pouting sunset. And on the other side a short message, evidently dictated. *A nice young couple came and moved me into this lovely new home.* And there was her toiling *G.*, plus a spidery kiss.

Towards the end of that week the Pepperdines, enveloped in a faint yellow glow of unreality, were reading about the doings of "Threnody" in Afghanistan.

She had flown there on a morale-boosting mission, along with the Formula 1 Pit Pets and an all-girl glamour rock band called Shy. "Threnody" gave a poetry reading and a frank Q and A at the base in Kandahar. It was rumoured that for the signing session she would shed her burqa to reveal an offering from "Self Esteem," her new line in underwear. She didn't. There was also the visit they all made to an orphanage in Badroo, where "Threnody" had what sounded like a tantrum of compassion.

Meanwhile, in the offices of Megan Jones

and Sebastian Drinker, Lionel held a kind of press conference — attended by the *Sun*, the *Mirror*, the *Star*, the *Lark*, the *Lark on Sunday*, and the *Daily Telegraph*. Extract:

So "Threnody" has your full support, Lionel?

Lionel Asbo: *Absolutely. Anything for our boys. Okay, I don't see eye to eye with John Law. Obviously. Everyone knows that. But Her Majesty's armed forces? 100 per cent. And I know they'll look out for my "Threnody" and send her home safe and sound.*

Is it true about the Cobra, Lionel?

Megan Jones: *Mr. Asbo wanted to donate a case of Cobra to every British soldier serving in Afghanistan, all 5,182 of them. But we were advised against it.*

Lionel Asbo: *See, over there, lads, they don't touch a drop. Not even beer. Getting s***faced on heroin's okay but show them a can of —*

Sebastian Drinker: *Mr. Asbo is considering various alternatives.*

Are you going out there yourself, Lionel?

Lionel Asbo (laughing): *What, and leave England? No chance. I'll never set foot outside my motherland. Well, Scotland and that. You know, maybe Wales. But I'm not going over that water, mate. I love this f***ing country. It's England, my England, for Lionel Asbo. En-*

283

gland. England. England.

And even as he spoke, a flag of St. George (measuring over two thousand square feet) was billowing high over the searchlights at "Wormwood Scrubs" . . .

"It's improving," said Dawn. "Their image."

"Yeah. Queen and country. They can't knock that."

"And she's stopped going on about how clever he is. *Let's face it, Lionel's not the brightest of sparks* . . . It's improving."

And you couldn't deny it. The famous young couple, so recently known as (say) *the Jugjob Jezebel and the Diston Dingbat*, were now referred to, alliteratively but without capital letters, as *the courageous covergirl and her patriotic paramour*.

"Yeah," said Des. "Some thought's gone into all this. I wonder how long it'll last."

The interview with Ringo Pepperdine in Sunday's *People* sparked little controversy. Ringo's complaint — *Lionel never gave me a penny piece* — counted for nothing when set against the revelations in the text: over the course of thirteen years, Ringo had cost the taxpayer well over half a million pounds in benefits and disability allowances. And the colour photograph, with its waxwork effect, won him few admirers: a dishevelled Mongolian, with sunken red-spoked eyes, a needle-thin moustache, and a watchfully parasitic leer.

There was but a single repercussion. *All he cared about*, said Ringo unguardedly, *was Mum. No thought for anyone but Mum.* And in Tuesday's *Star* there was a half-page piece about the Northern Lights — the bijou sunset parlour on the crest of Scotland where Grace Pepperdine, thanks to her youngest boy's fond munificence (and no thanks to Ringo), now contentedly dwelt.

"Where are you off to?"

"Nowhere. Just down the shop . . . You've got that frown again."

"Well don't be long, Dawnie."

A while ago, as he was working his way through another enormous baby book, Des came across the following: *During pregnancy every woman will experience an irrational fear of isolation.*

Which is funny (he thought): because that's exactly what *I'm* experiencing — and Dawn, in his view, had never seemed more unnervingly self-sufficient. Sometimes, when he got home from work, he expected to enter a grey void of slowly shifting dust. Or else an indifferent Dawn would look up at him from the kitchen table and politely ask, *Yes? Can I help you? Have you come to the wrong flat? Can I help you?*

He knew his irrational fears were irrational, and he tried to keep quiet about them, but late one night, in the dark, he found himself saying,

You wouldn't go and do a runner on me would you Dawnie?

. . . Don't be daft.

And another night he might say in the dark,

You won't suddenly up and leave me will you Dawnie?

And she might say, *Desmond,* and roll over towards him.

. . . I worry, he said with a convulsive swallow.

No need. My love. My love. No need. And then she said (solvingly, it turned out), *Oh, Desi, don't. Stop trying not to cry. Stop. Don't. It breaks my heart.*

A weekend morning, and there they were, in their limited habitat, Dawn on the balcony, reading, Des in the passage, exercising. He was now very fit; twice a day, before and after work, he went for half-hour sprints on Steep Slope; and he could polish off forty-five press-ups in less than a minute.

Why was he doing all this? Because he was a man who was going to have a baby. And his body, at least, his physical instrument, would be perfectly primed . . .

"I'll get it," he called, and went to the phone.

"Des, it's you Uncle Li. Listen. A couple of EBs'll be over to clean me room. They'll let theyselves in. Take care."

By *EBs* Lionel meant persons from the Eastern Bloc. And that afternoon, sure enough, Danuta and Kryzstina hurried talkatively into the flat with armfuls of thick towels and glowing flax. They worked for an hour, and drank a cup of tea, and left.

Again Des ventured within, and Dawn followed. The white smile of the folded upper sheet (which was quality linen, and not the scorching polyester of earlier days), the white Turkish bathrobe plumped up at the foot of the bed. And there in the drawer were Lionel's old socks and pink-tinged Y-fronts, his sweats, his combats.

Dawn sighed and said, "I know I'm always moaning on about it. But wouldn't it be lovely if we could move in here."

"Then *our* room'd be perfect for Toilet."

"Perfect. Where's Toilet going to sleep?" Dawn was looking at herself in the free-standing swing mirror, full on and then in

287

profile (as Cilla used to do before she went out). "I'm still not showing!"

Des glanced down at his own mid-section. No: his hysterical pregnancy was not quite as hysterical as that. And in fact he felt much calmer. Dawn was always praising him, admiring him, and enthusiastically returning his embraces and caresses, and it now seemed rather unlikely, on the whole, that his beloved wife, four months pregnant, would desert her home and husband and elope with the unborn child. He said,

"You're showing a *bit*, Dawnie."

"But the other mums are out here! And I still don't *feel* pregnant."

"She hasn't stopped kicking, has she?"

"Don't look so stricken! Of course she hasn't stopped kicking. You think I wouldn't tell you? And she's a boy too. It's like a pub brawl in there. She's a boy."

"Not necessarily, Dawnie. You know, I've been looking round the stalls. And I think I've found the perfect cradle for Toilet."

"Harry."

"Lally."

"Gary."

"Sally."

". . . You know, Des, I'm getting an awful feeling."

"So am I. He's moving back in."

10

By now the lovers were being referred to, simply, as *"Threnody" and Lionel,* or as *Li and "Thren,"* or (for a week or two at least) as *Thrionel* (and even *"Thr"ionel*). England looked on with an indulgent smile as the romance spread its buds and bloomed.

Lionel and "Threnody" feeding the ducks in St. James's Park, and strolling on, hand in hand. "Threnody" and Lionel drinking champagne in the directors' box at Upton Park (where they watched West Ham lose heavily to Manchester City). Lionel top-hatted, and "Threnody" extravagantly be-frocked, enjoying a day at the races. But there were also nights out at the greyhound tracks — Walthamstow, Haringey, Ockenden — with the principals in jeans and bomber jackets . . . Des gazed for a long time at a not unendearing photo (he thought) of Lionel in earnest communion with his *Morning Lark* in the stadium cocktail bar while "Threnody" paid a visit to the ladies' room.

I've finally met a man, "Threnody" told reporters (including Desmond's new colleague at the *Daily Mirror*), *who makes me feel cherished. He makes me feel safe. He's an Englishman. He's a* real *man, not like that sad, pathetic little b*****d Fernando. And don't* *get me going on that stupid s*d Azwat.*

At "Wormwood Scrubs," when it's just Lionel and I, we generally have an interlude in our room before dinner. With the lights down low, I model him the latest creations from "Self Esteem." Starting with the bustiers and ending with the teensiest little frillies. As a prelude to the obvious!

He's a decathlete in the boudoir, my Lionel, but also so very sensitive and caring. For hour upon hour we surge and meld. However, for me, the really romantic part comes after our evening meal. We go up, we lie there in the dark. I'll say, "Love you, Lionel." He'll say, "Love you, 'Threnody.'" And we'll fall asleep in one another's arms, in an ecstasy of loving.

A source at the office of Megan Jones did not deny that the couple had ordered several catalogues of engagement rings.

"There is no mistaking 'Threnody' 's heartfelt adoration," concluded Daphne, in a follow-up think-piece in the *Sun.* "And Lionel? Oh, he looks as sunny as a dog with two tails!

"And whilst the couple are impatient to start a family of their own, they also have plans to adopt the three Afghan babies that 'Threnody' fell in love with at the orphanage in Badroo.

"So who knows? The two poor little rich

things might yet become national treasures, as they find their way to the proverbial 'dream come true.'

"And what, finally, of Lionel's adorable nephew? May I, on behalf of the Street of Shame, extend a warm welcome to Des Pepperdine. As much as it pains me to praise a rival, young Des, a fresh face on a certain venerable tabloid, has already started to impress. What a striking comprehension of the criminal mentality! Hmm. Wonder where he got *that* from!"

"She's copying Danube again," said Dawn.

The Pepperdines were en route to Cape Wrath. Activated for travel, England thrummed past them with its rainbow of greens.

"Listen to this."

On her way from an *OK!* shoot to an appearance on *T4* — and before making a PA at EZ (a new nightclub) — "Threnody" instructed Sebastian Drinker to release a statement about the forthcoming ITV documentary *"Threnody" and Lionel: Fusion.*

"She's doing a Danube," said Dawn.

"Pinch me," said Des, aghast. "She's signed him up for *I'm a Superstar, What the F*** Am I Doing Here?* No. Never."

I just want to be with Lionel 24/7, said

"Threnody" in a speech at the annual Formula 1 Pit Pets Party (like Danube, who did not attend, "Threnody" was a former Formula 1 Pit Pet). *And to think I used to obsess about my career! And about Danube! Danube. Who's so over. That's what happens when you find true love. You don't give a s*** about anything else. End of.*

Then all this changed.

But before it did that, Lionel called Avalon Tower and gave warning.

"I'm going to be fussing over you. You won't have a minute's peace."

Des's tone, now, was no longer tearful or pleading. It was pitched at the level of romantic banter, and Dawn seemed to like it. She gave her new laugh (half an octave deeper) and said, "Promise?"

"Promise."

"And remember. A promise is a promise."

The phone sounded, and as he went to pick it up he saw Goldie settling on the balcony, her tail like an undulating question mark; she sat, and listened, with independently twitching ears — one ear listening right, one ear listening left.

"Des? . . . I thought I'd pop in one of these nights."

Des said, "Course, Uncle Li. Which?"

"How would I know? All this going on. Load of bollocks," he said (and in the background you could hear many faint but festive voices). "I'm standing here in a fucking black-and-yellow *romper* suit. For why? Because Lynndie England's showing off her waist in one of her wasp outfits. Colour-coordinated, see. We're throwing a party for all her lookalikes. And you know what? Half of them's on retainer! *And* her stalkers! What's happening, Des? Me face — me face, Des, it's all distorted! From the *smiling*. I can't get it back to what it was before! . . . What's happening? Where's Lionel Asbo? Gone. I'm gone, boy, I'm gone. Jesus, load of *bollocks* all this is."

When Lionel rang off Des went on sitting there with the phone in his hand. For a moment his breast throbbed with warmth; then from another direction came a kind of arrhythmia of anxiety; and then the warmth returned.

"Ah, see him? Fairly glowing, he is. Well. Love is blind," said Dawn.

He looked up. There was a temptation to say something about (that genius) Horace Sheringham, but he didn't need to because they both understood.

And now the fairy-tale romance between

293

"Threnody" and Lionel began to lose its way.

In late June "Threnody" bolted from her seat in the VIP enclosure at the *Elle* Style Awards and went back to the South Central Hotel — early, alone, and in tears. Photos: "Threnody" with smeared mascara fleeing the Churchill Ballroom in her silk tanktop and diamanté tutu; Lionel sullenly remaining at the round table with his feet up on the empty chair . . .

In early July Lionel stormed out of the Full Throttle Motor Show, in Manchester. Photos: against a background of glass and burnished metal, the opposed figures, at various angles: Lionel like a mammoth in his mink coat, "Threnody" like an elf in her Union Jack bikini, Lionel with an imperious forefinger upraised, "Threnody" with hands and arms combatively akimbo . . .

Then came the acrimonious dinner — in some paparazzi-girt trattoria in King's Road. The dailies concentrated on the post-prandial slanging match, out on the pavement (with "Threnody" *obviously the worse for wear*). But what stayed with Des was a follow-up paragraph in the *Evening Standard*'s Londoner's Diary: a well-placed fellow diner disclosed that Lionel and "Threnody" *spent the entire meal saying "yeah yeah*

yeah" to each other. The entire meal. "Yeah yeah yeah."

At this point the couple repaired to "Wormwood Scrubs" — *they've work to do on their relationship,* admitted Sebastian Drinker. *They know this fully well.* And "Threnody," in confirmation, released these simple lines:

Talking over issues
Seeing eye to eye
Learning how to compromise
As the years go by

Trifling disagreements
We hereby cast aside
For you will be mine husband
And I will be thy bride . . .

"She said Lionel cracked up when he read her poem."

"I'm not surprised."

"No, Dawn. Listen. *Poor Lionel couldn't finish it. He was crying that hard.*"

". . . It gives you a funny feeling, all this, doesn't it."

"Yeah, it does. What was all that squabbling in aid of? Her getting pissed and them yelling in the street. To make them look human?"

"To make them look English, you mean. No, I reckon it's just indiscipline."

"The strain."

"The strain."

They were out on Steep Slope: Sunday morning — and early Sunday morning (7 a.m.), before Diston stirred and rose. Dusty chestnuts, cloth-capped flowers, bent beer cans: the natural surroundings. Only the smell of liquid waste maintained the power to astonish — the way it maddened the gums.

"Wait," he said.

Their pace slowed as they approached the little memorial to Dashiel Young. Dashiel, the Jamaican teenager beaten to death by six grown men on Steep Slope — six years ago. A lozenge of grey stone, indented, flush with the ground, and the etched words: *Always Remembered. Dashiel Young, 1991– 2006*. Des bowed his head. He always remembered. Grief is the price we pay for . . . They moved on.

"Lionel and 'Threnody.' There's something infinite in it," said Dawn, peacefully and mysteriously (as always, now).

"Infinitely what?"

"Poor. Imagine pretending to be in love."

"Mm. Imagine."

11

It was on the last Saturday of Dawn's fifth month that Lionel paid his first visit.

"He said he might look in sometime. That's all. You know Uncle Li. Predictably unpredictable. Always was."

". . . That's a useless bloody phrase, that is. Predictably unpredictable. I mean, how far's it get you? Where's the predictable bit come in? Lionel's not predictably unpredictable. He's unpredictably unpredictable."

"Yeah. He's just unpredictable."

Predictable and its opposite were becoming similarly meaningless in the half-dark of the kitchen. One of those pleasant, deep-voiced, lethargic dusks when no one turns the lights on. Why aren't the lights on? Who hasn't turned the lights on? You haven't. I haven't . . . They were wondering aloud about what to have for dinner, and such talk, at Avalon Tower (after the year of cereal, the year of baked beans on toast, the year of pasta and pesto), was a sign of high living. He said,

"I just mean he may surprise us. By not being surprising."

"Oh pack it in, Des. I'm going mad."

". . . How about a Cornish pasty?" This suggestion was teasingly made. "Or a Cheltenham lamb pasanda."

"Good idea. Or Cumberland sausages and mash."

"Or a Melton Mowbray pork pie."

Although Des still sometimes gorged himself on (for example) anchovies and chocolate fudge, it was Dawn's palate that was in the ascendant at Avalon Tower. And Des bowed to the genetic suzerainty of Horace Sheringham. Always rather limited in her tastes, Dawn now wanted everything she ate to be tamely and blandly *English*.

"I know what you'd really like for your dinner. Scones. With Cow and Gate Farmer's Wife Double Devon Cream."

Then they heard the rattle, the double-thunk, the creak, and the percussive wheeze of the slammed front door.

Des stood up and reached to his left, and the neon strips came on with a flustered whinny. "In here, Uncle Li!"

". . . Yeah, well where else?" said Lionel, whose bouldery shape now filled the doorway. Intent, unsmiling, the mink coat worn cape-like over the deep-blue suit with its churchy glisten. In one tensed fist he was holding a soft leather valise, and in the other a wicker hamper, which he now swung up on to the table. "Got me beer?"

"On its way, Uncle Li. Just in the tin?"

The valise was dropped, the coat shrugged off. Lionel took a chair and swivelled it, facing out over the colourless evening. He settled himself with his Cobra and his Marlboro Hundred. His long back was sloped and still, but the tips of his shoulders now and then lightly shuddered. Many minutes passed.

"Ah, that's better," he said without turning. "Ah, that's better. Here, Dawn. What's the uh, what's the basis of domestic bliss? I'll tell yuh. *Respect*," he said pitilessly. Up came a squat forefinger. "And empathy. Empathy. 'Threnody' reckons . . ."

After a while Dawn said, "Have you eaten, Lionel?"

"Nah, I'm off out, me." He stood and started loosening his tie. "See that? That's the Hamper Supreme. Fortnum's. Eat you fill."

They could hear him in the bathroom, copiously urinating; then a bedraggled yawn; then the passage floorboards were wincing to his tread.

". . . Maison de la Truffe Olive Oil with Black Truffles," said Des.

"Jabugo Iberico Ham with Stuffed Andalucian Gherkins."

"Spiced Nut and Satay Bean Mix. With Salsa Baguettes."

"Lime and Pomeranian Coriander Dressing. With Epicure Croutons."

"Stoneground Mustard with Elephant Garlic!"

Very soon Lionel reappeared. He hovered there for a moment, baseball-capped, tracksuited, trainered, with his laces loosened . . . And you realised something. Lionel Asbo was by now a national presence, and instantaneously recognisable — but only when defined by a plutocratic setting. Behind the wheel of the "Aurora," for instance, (or abseiling earthward from the cockpit of his Venganza) or on the arm of "Threnody" at some ball or gala, or simply patrolling the lawns of "Wormwood Scrubs." Casually dressed in Diston, Lionel would reattain generic anonymity: he would be an invisible man.

"Here, Dawn," he said again. "How far gone are you?"

She told him.

"Go ahead then. Show us you gut."

Dawn's chair juddered slowly backward and she got to her feet. She turned.

". . . You wouldn't believe this, Des. But I seen it online. There's blokes who *like* girls when they pregnant. Funny old world . . . Enjoy you meal. And you *Big Match*."

They were busying themselves with the jars and pots and punnets.

"Have some of this. See, he's nervous, Dawnie. If it's true what they say about him and her. He's nervous about starting a family. Don't take it to heart."

"Why would I? He's touched, isn't he. He can't help it . . . Imagine empathising with 'Threnody.' Do anyone's head in."

"Exactly. Here, have a drop of uh, Rich and Sustaining Merlot."

"That'd go straight through Baby, that would. All of it. As if Baby had ordered a whole glass of red wine. It's the same size *he* is!"

"*She* is. A thimbleful. Go on . . . You know, I reckon he just fancies a night out in the old neighbourhood. He won't do us any harm."

"I should bloody well hope not. Here, look at this. Choice of cheddars. Which? Strong and Sharp," she said, "or Family Mild?"

"Strong and Sharp."

"No, Des. Family Mild."

. . . Lionel returned in the small hours — the rattle and double-thunk, the thrown-on light, the Neolithic trudge down the pas-

301

sage, the pole of water drilling into the stressed tin of the sink. Not that it mattered — because Dawn and Des were wide awake anyway. They lay sighing together in the dark, giving off a swampy glow. Their stomachs conversed in a sawing Q and A, like two nests of cicadas.

"That's all you needed. A lovely lie-in."

"It wasn't a lovely lie-in, Dawnie. I just couldn't get out of bed."

"Well you're up and about now."

"At the ninth attempt. How come *you're* suddenly okay?"

"Because I only had a sip. You had going on for half a bottle!"

"Gaa, well I'm paying for it now. It was the food too. Any sign of . . . ?"

Lionel emerged at four in the afternoon. His dramatic pallor was perhaps enhanced by his black satin dressing gown and also by the bright blotches on either cheek, where the flesh looked scuffed or abraded. Not hungover (Des thought): Lionel was never hungover. But he could tell that his uncle ached.

"D'you want a cup of something, Lionel? . . . You usually like a tea."

". . . Go on then. You never know. Might have some effect." Glazed with a kind of

302

comfortable vacuity, Lionel's eyes patrolled the room. His face cleared and then immediately twisted away in helpless detestation. "Look at that. *Shut*."

Des said, "Yeah it's jammed again."

"*Shut* . . ." With an unsteady hand he reached out towards it. And the tank, in what seemed to be coy anticipation, yawned open.

The three of them reared back.

After a moment Lionel said, "What happens when you wedge it?"

"It *hates* it if you wedge it," said Dawn. "It bites down on it and then it won't move either way. For a month. It hates a wedge."

"It's no good to you when it's always open, either, is it," said Des.

"The rubbish," said Dawn. "After a bit you can smell it."

"You want something you can open and shut. And when it's open you can't shut it."

"And when it's shut you can't open it."

Lionel considered all this. "So what d'you do with it?"

"We sit on it," said Dawn. "When it's shut."

Their stares returned to the tank's black gape. Which now with a soft hiss of compressed air snapped to.

The three of them jolted in their chairs.

Lionel said, "It's fucking *haunted*, that is. Like the lift." Minutes passed. "Here, Des. When they write about you in the papers, Des. When they write about you in the papers . . . I don't know. They up you arse," said Lionel, "because you black."

He showered and changed, and called from the passage for Des to come and see him out.

The day had begun freshly, with a light scattering of cloudlets floating low enough to cast their individual shadows. But promise and colour were siphoning themselves from the sky, and a hard wind blew. Beginning his first smoke of the day (a substantial cigar), Lionel said,

"I had a call from Dr. fucking No in Cape Wrath. What's his name? The deep-eye."

"Endo. Jake Endo."

"Here. When you go up there." Lionel frowned and his mouth widened. "Does she know you you?"

"Know I'm me? Hard to tell. She remembers the old times. Her schooldays."

"Well they didn't last long. She make any sense?"

"Yeah, now and then. Talks about Dominic. And Lars." Lars: father of Uncle John. "Dom and Lars." With reluctance Des went on, "She uh, she talks a bit salty. Sex stuff."

"That's what Dr. No was telling me. The life force. Fucking disgusting."

Lionel enfolded himself in his fur. Now a silver Mercedes approached and came to a halt, keeping its distance, ticking over.

"The doc. He reckons her memory's coming back. Can't remember if she had her fucking pills five minutes ago. Can remember the past. It's coming back. In chronological order! Think. She'll do the six dads. Then, who was it, Kevin. And bleeding Toby. Then she'll do Rory! That's all we need."

He tugged on the warped door of the Ford Transit. Respectfully trailed by the Mercedes-Benz, Lionel pulled away — a white-van man in a black mink coat.

And so the pattern formed and settled. The businesslike entrances, on a Friday night, a Saturday night, sometimes a Wednesday night; the brief greeting and the submission of the house present (the house presents became increasingly bizarre); Lionel changed, went out, returned in the smoky gunmetal hour (waking both of them up), rose at teatime with his face grazed and chafed, drank some tea as he sneered at the tank and the newspapers, sighed, stood, torrentially showered . . .

Soon he started bringing one or the other of his dogs with him — now Jek, now Jak. The first time it happened (this was Jek — piebald, with his four-inch tail anxiously tucked between his thick back legs) there was a lot of clacking around till Lionel located the litter tray, which he filled from the bag he brought with him in his calf valise, and then laid out the dog's evening meal: what looked like a hunk of filet mignon clumsily stuffed with peppers of a bilious, glistening light green. The pitbull, with indifferent appetite, dined on the Avalon balcony.

"Give him a drop of water, Des — after he's done. Just a cupful, mind," said Lionel as he took his leave.

Jek was still sobbing with heartburn when (so to speak) the Pepperdines invited him in. He hesitated — and cowered at first as Dawn leaned down to give his back a stroke. They gave him water and, far more efficaciously, two saucers of milk; and pretty soon he was belly-up on the sofa, as if inanely and joyously submitting to some childish sexual charade — to some childish orgy in which he himself, moreover, was the undisputed star . . . As with Jek, so with Jak. Jak was piebald too, but like a negative

306

image of his brother. Jak, mostly white, wore a black tanktop and four black moccasins; Jek, mostly black, wore a white dicky and four white spats. One Friday it would be Jek. The next Wednesday but one it would be Jak. But never Jak and Jek at the same time.

The dogs and the Pepperdines were soon very fond of one another. This was a development that Lionel would be certain to deplore: the Pepperdines knew it — and so, uncannily, did the dogs. All four of them dissembled; they behaved with the polite reserve of experienced adulterers till the moment Lionel stamped off down the passage. As the front door slammed shut, Jak or Jek would be lying on his back with forepaws cocked and tail awhirl, or springing five feet in the air . . .

On Friday it would be Jak. The next Wednesday it would be Jek. But never Jek and Jak at the same time.

12

Over these summer weeks "Threnody" got going on a little project. She wanted to *bond* with Dawn.

A text message. A series of emails. Then daily phone calls . . .

"She just checks in. Asks how we are. She

wants to give us dinner at the South Central. Just the three of us."

"What d'you think?"

"Wants to talk about Lionel. Wants to talk about her parameters with Lionel."

". . . Are we playing along? It's all a kind of madness, Dawnie."

What people don't understand is this, said "Threnody," in the course of a ground-breaking interview in the *Daily Mail. Okay, one, we're on decent money and, two, all right, we're well known. But that doesn't mean we don't have problems! That's what people are too bloody dense to understand. We're just like any other English couple, for good-ness' sake! We're* ordinary people, *the same as everyone else. Hello? Can't they get that through their thick heads?*

You see, Melanie, there's two main issues. He's a passionate man, my Lionel, which is why I call him "Lionheart." But he's madly jeal-ous of my past. And jealous I do glamour. He's like, "All those blokes w***ing off over you!" But glamour's who I am! What's "Threnody" without glamour? Glamour and myself are virtually synonymous.

And he won't travel. He's put his foot down. He's that patriotic. He hasn't even got a passport — and he won't get one! And I need

308

my destinations. "Threnody" then went on, We'll compromise. We'll have to. Now that we're trying for a baby. And I do mean trying! I know it in my heart: everything will fall into place the minute I'm up the duff.

You see, Melanie, I haven't forgotten my roots. I've now become close to Lionel's niece, Dawn Pepperdine. She lives in a pokey council flat just like I used to. And she's in the family way. So we're always on for a good old natter. We understand each other completely. And we've so much to share . . .

On Tuesday the Pepperdines high-spiritedly met up after work at Pimlico tube station and walked in the rain to the South Central Hotel. As they approached the forecourt Des was hailed by a colleague from the *Mirror*, who told him that the press was there in force: Danube herself would be attending a function in the penthouse casino.

They sat and waited with their Cokes. Round about them the clientele sat drinking and snacking in its usual fancy dress — like the cast of an opera or a pantomime; but the most conspicuous person in the Los Feliz Lounge, it turned out, was Dawn Sheringham.

"I feel pregnant now all right," she said as she returned from her second visit to the bathroom. "See the way they all stared? Are pregnant women even *allowed* in here? . . . Where is she? She told me seven-thirty!"

At twenty to nine a bespectacled and pre-occupied Megan Jones clicked up.

"Hello there! Change of plan. 'Threnody,' " she said, "is upstairs."

"Oh, is she not coming down?"

"With Danube on the premises? You're dreaming. Dawn, love, pop in on her for me. She's feeling really shit and she needs to vent . . . There's a good girl."

Des sat on. The hotel's centre of gravity, that night, had levitated sixteen floors, and only a handful of the uninvited resentfully remained in the bar. So the whole two hours passed almost without incident. Someone laughingly stripped in front of the new shark tank, someone laughingly drowned a garden frog in an ice bucket. And the affectless TV screens — Laurel and Hardy, tsunami, Pop-eye, September 11, royal wedding, *Pinocchio*, volcano, *Mandingo*, martyrdom video, *Thriller*, Godzilla . . .

"She was in bed with an eye mask on," said Dawn as they walked in the rain to the Chelsea Kitchen on King's Road. "And she spoke in a whisper."

"Look out, puddle coming up. What did she say about Lionel?"

"She didn't say anything about Lionel."

"Then what did she talk about?"

"Danube."

They ate a mushroom pie, and took the Underground from Sloane Square to Diston North. At 33F, Avalon Tower, all the lights were on; in the kitchen they found a jeroboam of Rebel Yell bourbon (another house present) and an ecstatic Jak.

He readied the bowls of Wotsits and Fairy Toast, and checked the temperature of the "Mirage" Chardonnay. "Threnody" was due at seven-thirty.

Preceded by security guard number one (thickset, apologetic, in an ageing blue suit), and escorted by security guard number two (much younger, ponytailed, in a boxy three-piece), who positioned himself at the front door, "Threnody" arrived at twenty past nine.

Then in she disconcertingly came at speed, with her busy eye-movements taking the whole of her head and neck with them, in strict and fluttery inventory, and jarred to a halt in the full light with her hands on her hips.

"Twelve floors," she said bitterly.

"I did warn you."

"Yes, Dawn, you did — but what about

my heels? What about my heels? See?"

She slid off a shoe as she sat herself down and held it up for them. It reminded Des of something he had seen the day before: an almost O-shaped hook securing a freighter in the canal lock.

"They were fucking *killing* me. Twelve floors. Mal had to give me a piggyback up the last five! . . . Twelve floors. Where's the consideration? Stressing me out."

After a silence Dawn offered their guest a glass of "Mirage." "Threnody" proudly declined — and then very briefly burst into tears. She said,

"Oh, Dawn. It's happened. Lionel's gone and filled me with his child!"

Haltingly the Pepperdines made it clear how pleased they were by this news.

"Ah, you should've seen your uncle when I told him. The tears were streaming down his face . . . *Mums*, Dawn. That's what we're going to be. Proper mums. *Mums*." She turned to Des and said, "Would you excuse yourself for me? I want to have a mums' talk with your Dawn."

He went off to the bedroom with his book. In the passage the older security guard paced and loomed; after ten minutes (and a warning cough) he peered round the door and said,

"You can go back in there now. If you fancy it." He had a way of dropping his head, chin on chest, and looking upward from under his brows, as if over a pair of invisible spectacles. "Mal MacManaman," he said and offered his hand. "I've been doing this for fifteen years. Centrefolds. Glamour queens. Page Three. And you know uh, Desmond, it's right what they call them. They're *fantasy* girls. They live in the clouds."

When Des went on through, "Threnody" was raising a huge glass of "Mirage" and saying, "It'll be a precious bond between ourselves, Dawn love. So precious. Just between you and I — the *mums*."

She gave a signal. Mal MacManaman went down the passage and you could hear the front door give its sigh. They came in very quietly, two men, introduced as Sebastian Drinker and Chris Large (Des recognised Chris Large: Daphne's photographer from the *Sun*). Mal MacManaman leaned back against the wall with folded arms and penitently dropped his head.

"Let's sit on the sofa, Dawn," said "Threnody," "and have a little smooch. Then a few standing up. So they can see your tum."

Her face solar and leonine under the strip-light, Goldie was looking on as they cleared the table — the glasses, the Wotsits, the Fairy Toast.

"Look at that. She drank the whole bottle!" Dawn's eyes widened out into space. "And she had a go at the Rebel Yell and all. That baby's *paralytic.*"

"Yeah. If there is one."

"If there is one . . . She knows what she's going to call it. Boy or girl. Lovechild."

"Lovechild?"

"Lovechild. And she's going to do what we're doing with the middle name."

". . . Lovechild 'Threnody' Asbo?"

"Lovechild 'Threnody' Asbo. State of England."

"State of England."

"And anyway. It won't *be* a lovechild, will it. What about their dream wedding?"

So for the next few days Des faced reasonably mild ridicule at his work station in Canary Wharf, and Dawn rose from archangel to seraph in the eyes of the pupils of St. Swithin's, what with Aunt "Threnody" all over the papers — and the unbelievable poem, "Sisters" (*God's gift of generation/We hold in veneration . . .*). It was official. Sebastian Drinker: *Mr. Asbo is frankly overjoyed. He greeted the news with absolute*

314

euphoria.

. . . It doesn't sound right, does it, said Dawn. "*Euphoria.*"

No, it doesn't. As if he meant to say "eutho-ria" . . . I hate this. I mean, where's the truth? Where's the poor old truth? And what'll we say to him when he comes?

"Congratulations, Uncle Li."

"Yes, all the very best, Lionel."

Lionel halted, filling the doorway in his ambassadorial suit, holding in both hands a thick glass jar of what looked like Chinese seaweed. He said,

"What're you on about?"

"Or uh, shouldn't we believe everything we read in the news, Uncle Li?"

"What? Read about what?"

Dawn said, "The baby."

"Oh the *baby*. Oh the *baby*." Lionel gave the glass jar to his nephew and with his freed hand reached up to jerk at the vast valentine of his Windsor. "You know what she's calling it?"

". . . She told us Lovechild."

"Lovechild, my arse. She's calling it her *exit strategy*. Work that one out."

The thick glass jar — Lionel's house present — turned out to contain hydroponic marijuana. The week before he had given them a thousand cigarettes (Balkan Sobranies). It seemed that Lionel, too, had been reading the baby books. Other donations included a whole hamper of sushi, ceviche, and fish tartare.

One Sunday afternoon (this wouldn't happen again) Lionel surfaced from his room and was soon joined, at the kitchen table, by his childhood sweetheart, Cynthia. This silent Distonite was now twenty-eight. Cynthia — her face as bleached as a London sky but not quite colourless, with a faint rumour of mulberry in it, like the blue of cold.

. . . Every time Lionel crashed in at night (as if returning to an empty house) Des thought how *restful* it must be (if you could imagine such a thing) — to have no consciousness of others.

13

"Cheer up, boy. It hasn't happened yet."

"Yeah but I'm all alone."

Des was all alone: his wife wasn't there, and his baby wasn't there either.

"Where she gone then?"

"Gone to look after her dad." Des reached into the fridge for a can of Cobra. "Well, she doesn't look after her dad exactly. The old bastard still won't let her near him."

"Only natural in a way. Someone like Horace. His only daughter marrying a brother . . . No offence meant, Des."

"None taken, Uncle Li. No. So she just sits in the hospital and looks after her mum."

"Yeah? What's up with him then?"

A secret drinker, Horace Sheringham had secretly given himself acute cirrhosis — diagnosed that Saturday morning.

"He's turned yellow. His liver's packed up."

"How old is he?"

"Fifty."

"Oh, so he's getting up there. Tell you what then. We'll have one of our nights out, Des. Okay?"

"Yeah. Yeah, wicked, Uncle Li."

"Yeah. Like in the days of you youth. Back in a minute."

He finished his beer, poured himself a beaker of Rebel Yell, gave the (open) tank a kick, and went shouldering off to his room.

"Talking *KFC*. KFC. KFC. KFC. KFC . . ."

These words were spoken almost conversationally, and not with the incantatory force of earlier days. Lionel's mood appeared to be unusually bright, even festive — as he dropped his tray and attended to the little sachets of mustard and relish. Round about them, the milkshake colours, and the hamburger girths, of KFC.

"Talking *KFC. KFC*. Wealth, Des. Wealth . . . Remember when you was a kid, thinking, What'll I be when I grow up? It's like that. You think — I know, I'll be an engine driver! I'll buy a, I'll buy a fucking *train* and steam around in that. But then you think, Where to? What's the point? Then you think — I know, I'll buy one of them hot-air balloons. Or a plane. Fuck it, I'll go to Cape Canaveral and have a spin in the space shuttle."

Des said, "You'd have to go to Russia for that. These days. Or maybe India."

"Be all right. Cape Bollywood. Blast-off. Have a crafty smoke in the toilet. Weightlessness. See the globe from on high. Why not? You can do *anything*, see. So you don't — you never . . . You just think, What's the point?"

Lionel gazed incuriously at his drumsticks and reached for his chips.

"What about your boxing?"

"Ah now. Me boxing. I got quite far with that. Planned it out. Set meself goals. Like — like full ABA member in eighteen months." Lionel shrugged and went on, "I talked it over with old Tommy Trum. He

"Threnody" — massive on Mars, and then massive on Mercury; first she'd do the terrestrial planets, and then she'd surge through the asteroid belt to the gas giants, to Jupiter, to Saturn. "Threnody," massive on Pluto . . .

"She said, *I'll make you famous.* I said, *I'm already famous.* She said, *Yeah, but you famous in the wrong way. You hated. I'll work on you image and I'll make you loved!* Loved . . . Jesus. She's after me to do an *I'm a Superstar.* Now normally, Des, you'd have to go down the fucking *jungle* for that. But they seeing if they can find somewhere bad enough in England. Isle of Mull. Nailsea." Lionel paused. "Wants me to start a line of *clothes.* Chav uh, Chav *Chic.* Wants me wearing earrings and a big gold chain round me neck. And a T-shirt with *Whatever* on it. Or *Innit* on it. Now tell the truth, Des. Is that Lionel Asbo? Seriously now. What're you thoughts?"

"A T-shirt with *Innit* on it? The chavs," he said, "they're proud of being stupid." And Lionel (for professional reasons) used to be proud of being stupid. But the chav was a type. And Lionel was not a type. "I don't think that's really you, Uncle Li."

"Mm. See, that *I'm a Superstar* stuff, that reality stuff — it *ain't* reality. They just get

321

famous people to make cunts of theyselves."

"Yeah, but give her credit. It's worked. You're popular now. You're — you're loved."

". . . In the street, cabbies and that, they say, *Take care, Lionel. Watch out, Lionel.* They say, *Look after youself now Lionel . . .* Being loved. I don't know."

At Lionel's lift of the chin they stood to leave. The thonged dancer was coming round with her collection pouch. Lionel said,

"*Get* you tits fixed *for the boys* — ooh."

She slowed. Des smiled at her as unpointedly as he could (a youngish mother, he guessed, trying to make ends meet). She gave Lionel a quick but level glance and moved on.

"Wait," he said. "Hang on, darling. Here's fifty quid. I'll stick it in you sock for yer. Fifty quid . . . towards you operation. There."

On the crossroads outside they had to raise their voices.

"Where you off to now, Uncle Li?" yelled Desmond, and with his thumb he made a gesture homeward.

"Ah, don't go yet, Des!" Lionel yelled back. "Come and have a nightcap at the Sleeping Beauty! I fancy a chat! About me sexuality!"

14

The Sleeping Beauty, Diston's lone place of lodging (apart from a wide variety of flops and Marmite-dark B & Bs), was on Murdstone Road — a thirty-minute walk, due east, through Saturday night. They started forward, sliding sideways through the clenched teeth of the locked cars.

"There's certain strains in me relationship with Gina!"

"How's that, Uncle Li!"

"Well it's a fine line! Marlon — he keeps raising his prices! Soon he'll be richer than I am!!"

Forward they kept on moving, past the knots and strings of the crowds, Des on his toes, Lionel with his implacable trudge. In their ten-year duologue, Des had never had to hear in any detail about his uncle's sexuality. And it scared him. Now he felt that a damp cobweb was being dragged across his face. He looked down and saw that his hands and forearms had turned a tone deeper with moist subcutaneous warmth.

"The other, Des! You know they call it that? I always wondered why! Till now!"

But here was Carker Square, impressive in scale, certainly — the two swathes of brown grass the size of football pitches (with a stout tree-stump each) and the crazy-paved spoke-shaped walkways converging on the defunct fountain, and the whole space as densely peopled, Des imagined, as São Paulo or Bangkok, but nearly all of them white, as white as Cynthia . . . It came to the ears as a scene of celebration, the willed guffaws of the men, the abandoned cackles of the women. But if you could turn the sound down (if you could turn the volume off), then the Distonites would resemble the survivors of a titanic calamity, random wanderers in the aftermath of an earthquake, say, and the ground still lurching beneath their feet. Lionel put his face up close and thickly and hotly whispered,

"Look at them — Christ. Decks awash. Full as a fairy's phonebook. Can't hold they drink, Des. Simple as that."

The two of them reached Jupes Lanes, a quieter and naturally much more dangerous entanglement of curling alleyways that moled its way out of the far end of Carker Square.

"With Gina and Marlon," said Lionel (his voice once again at room temperature), "I'm in a uh, a delicate situation."

"Delicate in what way?"

"Yeah. See, I used to make him just listen. Now I make him watch. Question is — how much can he take? And *then* what?"

The slam of a door, the clatter of lowered grillwork, a male howl, a female shriek abruptly smothered; Des kept stepping back, allowing the transit of various speckled and shadowy scowlers and sidlers in ones and twos and threes. Lionel said,

"And that's not all I got on me plate." He rubbed his palms and gazed skyward. "You know, Des, you be amazed by what fame and money does to skirt. And I'm not just talking about the usual little bints," he said with a primly dismissive shake of the head. "The little bints at the parties. With they tattoos and they tongue studs. And if you do one of them, Des, they tell the papers! And the next thing you know, you a love rat! . . . Nah, boy. Oh no. I'm talking about rich MILFs."

"Rich MILFs, Uncle Li?"

"Yeah. Posh MILFs, Des. Toff MILFs. They unbelievable! You in a jeweller's in Mayfair or you parking the 'Aurora.' Or you at some do. And this MILF'll go, *You the one, aren't you.* She'll go, *You the one in the* Telegraph. *You the one.* And they ain't housewives, Des. They like *gentry.*" Lionel's face took on a look of gratitude and wonder. "And who'd've thought that these rich MILFs, who can speak French and play the violin . . . See, this is uh, this is the *paradox*, Des. Who'd've thought that these rich MILFs were the dirtiest fucking goers you ever come across in you . . ." Lionel's pace slowed. "Hang on. They ain't MILFs. Not exactly. They DILFs!"

"DILFs, Uncle Li?"

"Yeah. See they all — Hold up . . . Have a look at this, Des. Look at this. A uh, a cultural contrast if you like."

They had reached a circular clearing. Well lit, trash-strewn . . . Her head pillowed on a glistening rubbish bag, and with her dress up around her halter top, a large adolescent redhead was trying to climb to her feet, scraping and clawing for purchase like a supine skier with the two broken wine bottles she held in her freckled fists . . . Coming towards her down the facing slope was a file of densely veiled figures, a mother and her three, no four, no five daughters, each smaller than the next, like Russian dolls. They fanned out and stared. Lionel lingered, saying,

"Don't worry, ladies. I know it don't look too clever, but you in England now. And it's different with our birds. Our birds, they can lie around all stripped and helpless. And us blokes don't turn a hair. Why? Because they *that* rough. Come on, son."

Lionel and Desmond again fell into step.

"*DILFs*, Des. All divorcees. The lot of them! You know how they do it? First they — first they get theyselves hitched to some old banker for ten minutes. Then they independent for life! And oh, they in gorgeous nick, Des. Superb. And I said to her, I said to this DILF, *How old are you anyway?* And guess what she said."

"What."

"Thirty-seven! Which means she's probably forty-three! Think. She's almost *Gran's* age — and there's not a mark on her. Pampered all they lives, they are. Beauty treatments. Massage. Yoga. Okay. Okay. You in a smart hotel room. Now it's got this lovely sneer on its face and it's saying, *Let's —*"

"Uh, Uncle Li . . ."

Up ahead, where the lane narrowed to the width of a council-flat corridor, an enormous shape awaited them. Even for Jupes Lanes it was an exceptional sight (and people, now, had to try harder and harder to be exceptional). This alley-filling apparition was about twice Lionel's mass, grossly bloated but also dynamic, and gasping mechanically for air. As they got nearer they saw that the young man's face was like a pizza of acne or even eczema, and his loose damp smock was similarly encrusted and ensmeared, with a thick gout of blood or ketchup running from armpit to armpit. He held a bulky mallet with a nubbled head, and his free hand was rummaging around in the crotch of his khaki shorts.

". . . You going courting?" asked Lionel mildly. "Well out the way then. Out the way then. Step back and to the side. By them dustbins . . . Look, we can't get round you, mate. You too fucking fat. Jesus. *Out the way then.*"

The young man held his ground — and Lionel folded his arms, lowered his head, and exhaled . . . Now, in Desmond's considerable experience, Uncle Li, as combat neared, had three distinct styles of mobilisation. With his peers he gathered about himself a fury of self-righteousness, with his near-peers he opened and widened his mouth and brightened his eyes in quasi-sexual avidity (this was the Marlon Welkway approach), and with everyone else he just rolled up his sleeves and got on with it. But here in Jupes Lanes he just seemed tragically bored, bored to the point of psychic pain — like one eternally diverted from all fascination, all delight . . . The young man said,

"Fuck you."

"Okay," said Lionel. "Well relish the moment, mate. You not going to feel half this good — ever again . . . *So you worked that one out did yuh, you thick cunt?* Jesus. Uh, this DILF toff, Des, she's taking about forty grand's worth of togs off and she's called me a — she called me a *yoik*. What's a yoik? I mean I can tell it's not nice. But what's a yoik?"

Des hesitantly suggested that it was a conflation of *yob* and *oik*. Yoik.

"You reckon? Thought it was because of me Yoi. You know. Yoi. Yoik . . . Des, I got a feeling I'm in over me head. On the DILFs. What with me class hatred. And them saying, *Come on, you yoik, come on, slumboy* . . . That could get well out of hand, that could. That could get *well* out of hand."

Murdstone Road, Des saw, was now just a block away. "It's all beyond me, Uncle Li. I can't imagine the type."

"Well that's not surprising, living round here. They no DILFs in Diston, Des."

"Wonder what's in it for them . . . No offence meant, Uncle Li."

"None taken, Des. It's a good question." In a speculative spirit Lionel went on, "People say, *Toff birds fancy a bit of rough.* They fancy rough blokes. And I always thought, Yeah, it's only rough blokes say that. Don't flatter youself. But there's something in it. See, what they fancy's a *change*."

"A change from their own kind?"

"Yeah, they own kind, they own blokes, with they degrees and that. Now. They wouldn't normally *act* on it. Just a uh, a fantasy. But they can act on it with Lionel Asbo."

"Why's that?"

"Okay, he's rough. But he's famous. He's worth a couple of bil. He's in the public eye. He's safe. Eh, and what you make of this? *They* pay for everything, Des. Consistently. It's a uh, it's a DILF trademark. *They* pay for the room and the champagne and that . . . She's *controlling* her own little treat, see. Which is?"

"I don't know."

"The joy of messing around with someone stupid."

"You're *not* stupid, Uncle Li."

"Yes I fucking am."

"Welcome back," said the man at the glass door. "How're you tonight, Mr. Smith?"

15

In the firmament of London hotels, the Sleeping Beauty (like the Imperial Palace in Metroland) was a brown dwarf, and not a blue giant (like the Pantheon Grand) or a spasmodic "flare star" (like the South Central). But it was modern, or at least recent; and Des was somehow reassured (everyone was somehow reassured) to see all the men and women in airline uniforms, having a last few rounds of stiff drinks before proceeding by minibus to Stansted for the small-hours package flights (to the Scillies, the Balearics, the Canaries). The pilots and co-pilots in suits of martial serge, the stewardesses in orange overalls, like detainees.

After checking in (and submitting a cash deposit), Lionel procured a half-pint of cider and a whole bottle of Wild Turkey. They settled at a table in the corner of the Beanstalk Bar.

"Ever wondered, Des, how I amuse meself in Diston?"

"Yeah. Sometimes."

"Well I've run out of grudges. None left. So when you toddle off tonight I'll go and do a couple of NEETs. Go and do a couple of NEDs."

NEETs were those Not in Employment, Education or Training. NEDs were Non-Educated Delinquents.

"Nothing serious. Give them a tap or two. And then sling them in the canal. Tonight

I'll go looking for that fat cunt we seen in Jupes. Maybe that'll put me in the mood."

Desmond's frown asked the question.

"The mood to do a tart. Here. Up in me room." Lionel's features now came as close as they ever did to expressing apology or self-reproach. "See, Des, with me sexuality being what it is — there has to be *pain* . . . This is it. This is it. Don't know why. But there has to be pain." He said, "So the Gina relationship's obviously ideal. For now. You know, I'm doing her in the normal way. And with every thrust," *every frust*, "I'm causing pain . . . But you can't say I'm hurting *Gina*, can you. She likes it rough in the first place. But you can't say I'm hurting Gina."

". . . How's Gina feel about it?"

"Ah, with her it's all Marlon. Gaw, them two. Talk about love–hate — they like Kilkenny cats. With they tails tied together. Gina's spiting him, see, because Marlon's giving her kid sister one. Little Foozaloo. Well he's got to do something, hasn't he. Keep his end up. How much can he take? And it won't end there. It won't end there. He'll do her. He'll mark her. He'll *have* to."

Des swallowed and said, "What about with Cynthia? D'you hurt Cynthia?"

"Cynthia? How could you hurt Cynthia? I mean look at the state of her. Hurt what?"

Lionel poured, Lionel drank. Suddenly but glazedly he said, "With them DILFs, Des. She goes, *Come on then. Let's have it you . . . unbelievable . . . fucking* yoik. *Let's have it.* And it's got a lovely sneer on its face. And you think, Okay. Let's deal with that lovely sneer. And believe me. When you giving her one, she ain't sneering no more."

Des swallowed again and said, "It's important, is it? Dealing with the sneer?"

"Ooh *yeah,*" said Lionel. "*Ooh* yeah."

As Lionel gazed at the rolling booze in his glass, Des realised that there'd been no mention whatever, in the erotic sphere, of "Threnody" — Lionel's fiancée.

"Des. Be honest. Tell me straight. Have you ever thought that there was anything . . . not quite kosher in uh, my attitude to skirt?"

"Well we're all different. I'm a bit puritanical. Dawn says. And too needy. We're all different."

"She made me go . . . 'Threnody' made me go and see a bloke about it. About me sexuality. Cavendish Square. In a flash old flat in Cavendish Square. And you'll never guess what this geezer goes and tells me. Grace. Grace. He reckons it's all down to Grace."

"How's he work that one out?"

"He says, *Lionel, when you having inter-*

course, do you find there's a rage . . . waiting *for you? As if ready-made?* I said, *Yeah. Ready-made. You put you finger on it.* We talk it over, and he says, *Well it's obvious. You got a fucking slag for a mum, mate.* Well, not in them exact words. He says, *And the evidence was there before you eyes! From when you was a baby!*"

"Before your eyes, Uncle Li?"

"Before you eyes, Uncle Li? Use you head, Desmond Pepperdine. I'm an infant. And there's all these fucking brothers! This fucking *zoo* of brothers!"

It wasn't the first time Des had considered it from Lionel's perspective — from the perspective of someone in a highchair with a pacifier in his mouth: John like a Norse albino, swarthy and piratical Paul, George with a face as flat and square as a tablemat (and sandblasted with freckles), thick-lidded, mandarinic Ringo — and of course the seedily Silesian Stuart. Des said,

"Well there was Cilla."

"Yeah. Cilla. Me so-called *twin* . . . And five brothers — and a mum who's barely eighteen years of age. It wasn't right, Des. I mean, after that, after all that — how can a man trust minge?"

Five minutes passed in silence. Then Lionel looked at his watch and said, "Doing it with *schoolboys* . . ."

Schoolboys: it had the force of an ethnic or tribal anathema. Schoolboys, like Hutus or Uighurs.

"You okay, Desi? I'm off out."

So Des readied himself — readied himself for the six-minute dash down Murdstone Road, through Jupes Lanes, across Carker Square, and beyond. But no. Lionel made a call, and Des went back to Avalon Tower by courtesy car.

"All right, son," said Lionel on the forecourt. And they embraced.

Through the tinted windscreen you could see the purity of the lunar satellite, D-shaped in the royal-blue distance. The dark side was subtly visible — as if the Man in the Moon was wearing a watch cap of black felt.

Dawn came in at one.

"Did he see you?"

"No," she said and switched off the light. "He didn't see me . . ."

For a while he comforted her, and soon she sighed for the last time, and then she slept. But Des did not sleep. He was still awake when Lionel stomped in around seven (he could hear, over and above the hobnailed-boot effect, the subtle flinch of each and every floorboard). And the two men arose within a few minutes of each other at four o'clock on Sunday afternoon.

Dawn was back at the hospital, so uncle and nephew had a sentimental breakfast: Pop-Tarts (Des ran down).

. . . What was it that kept him awake?

During his night out with Lionel he was helplessly infused with somatic memories. His body kept remembering. The crown of his head and the tight curls of his hair remembered what it was like, as a boy of five, to feel the weight of that palm whenever his eleven-year-old uncle readied him to cross the road. His whole frame remembered what it was like, later, to walk the hissing streets of Diston with Lionel alongside him, the guarantee of his nearness, like a carapace. And as they parted at the Sleeping Beauty, and they embraced, Des's body remembered itself at twelve, thirteen, fourteen, during the time of numbness and Cillalessness: once a month or so, Lionel would look at him with unusual candour, and there'd be an unimpatient lift of the chin, and he'd say, *She's gone, Desi, and she ain't coming back*, or, *Okay, boy. I know. I know. But you can't just sit there and pine*; and he'd give him a hug (though not enough — never enough), murmuring, *There there,*

336

son. There there . . . So, in the forecourt, as Lionel said, *All right, son*, and he felt the great arms and the engulfing torso, Des (as he thought about this, lying next to Dawn with his eyes open) found that love flared up in him.

Which was one half of it.

The other half, like the dark side of the half-moon, had to do with fear . . . Cilla went, Cilla was gone, excised, leaving a monstrous void behind her; and Des looked to Grace, and together they found the wrong kind of love. There it was. And there was nothing he could do about it, then or now. *Unresisting, even so. Fifteen!* . . . Over time the fear had become manageable — it was his default condition, roiling him when nothing else was roiling him; it no longer aspired to the paroxysms of 2006 (*Dear Daphne*, Gran's groans, *Ooh, they'll love him inside*, the youth in the Squeers blazer). Still, he soberly and of course ignobly reasoned that the fear wouldn't die until Grace died — or until Lionel died.

It bestrode his sleep. And sometimes, when the nights were huge, he felt the rending need for confession — for capitulation, castigation, crucifixion . . . Then morning came, and the pieces of life once again coalesced.

Grace? When they get like that, said Lionel (and he'd been saying it for years), *they better off* dead.

Des had never wished her dead. But he had often wished her dumb.

Over the rooftops of Diston the sky lightened. Getting up for more water, around five, Des found himself becalmed in the passage; the door to Lionel's bedroom was open, as usual (for the air), and he looked within. The shadow of the window frame on the carpet made him involuntarily think of a guillotine; and — Christ — there was the moon, looking on, white as death in its executioner's hood . . . Dawn turned over in her sleep. He quietly fitted himself in beside the bend of her shape.

16

The phone message was ominously curt.

Brace youself for tragedy, Desmond Pepperdine . . .

He had just got back (with a hot chocolate and a salami hero) to the open-plan fluorescence of the *Daily Mirror*. It was early afternoon and the rhythm of the office was speeding up, as deadlines neared. He made the call (one among many), and casually asked,

"It's not Gran, is it, Uncle Li?"

"What? Nah. No such luck. Hang on."

Des could hear scuffling, snarling, clinking — echoic, subterranean.

"No. It's me betrothed. I'm uh, sworn to silence. But as I said. Prepare youself for news of a uh, of a tragic complexion. Now, Des. Did I leave a scarf — West Ham colours but cashmere — somewhere in me room?"

At five o'clock it came through on AP. A matter of hours after granting her first photo opportunity for two and a half months, and revealing her "bump" in a "Self Esteem" ensemble at "Wormwood Scrubs," "Threnody" had been helicoptered to a private clinic in Southend.

Meanwhile, at Avalon Tower, everything was as it should be. Everything was embarrassingly normal. Wise nature wisely steered her course; Baby (they called the creature Baby now, because names meant nothing to them) — Baby ably and promptly and almost contemptuously prevailed in every test, its heart throbbed, its limbs flailed; Mother remained watchful but confident, while Father presided over an epic calm. There they sat, with their paperbacks, in idling Saturday light. A month and a half to go. Baby was the background radiation — the surrounding static — of their lives.

Every few minutes one of them said something or other without looking up.

"Maybe her tits exploded."

"Dawnie."

"Well they do explode . . . On aeroplanes. Maybe her arse exploded."

"Dawnie. But you couldn't call that *tragic*, could you. Something like your arse exploding."

"Yeah. Your fake arse exploding."

". . . Hear it on the news. *'Threnody' had barely completed her photo op when her fake arse tragically exploded . . .*"

"Mm. *After the tragic explosion of her fake arse, 'Threnody' was rushed to . . .*"

"Has Danube been rushed to hospital recently? . . . Thought she might be doing another Danube."

". . . Well Lionel doesn't seem too bothered."

"Mm. To put it mildly."

"Maybe her bump's fake too. Just a sandwich baggie full of silicone. Maybe her fake *bump* exploded . . . *Oof.*"

"Not again? Not still?"

". . . Yeah," said Dawn tightly.

"Have you been suffering in silence?"

Because — because there was this one

340

little thing. Towards the end of her seventh month, Dawn started suffering from twinges in the base of her spine. They went to the Centre and consulted Mrs. Treacher — and, anyway, it was all in the books. "*During the seventh month, Dawnie, the usually stable joints of the pelvis begin to loosen up to allow easier passage for the baby at delivery*," Des read out loud to her. "*This, along with your oversize abdomen, throws your body off balance. See? To compensate, you tend to bring your shoulders back and arch your neck.* That's you, that is, Dawnie. *The result: a deeply curved lower back, strained muscles, and pain.* See?" And they followed instructions: straight-back chair, footrest, two-inch heels, nocturnal heatpad, and no leg-crossing. And at first all this seemed to work.

Des said, "Let's go and look in at the Centre. See Mrs. Treacher. Come on."

"No, Des. They'll just say the same thing."

Raising his book to chest height and gazing past it, he monitored his wife. Once a minute or so an alien presence would concentrate itself in the centre of her brow, and the blue eyes defiantly hardened. Then her chest rose and fell, and she sighed.

"Okay, Dawnie, that's it. It must be something like a trapped nerve. Come on.

341

We'll be there and back by seven."

"Leave me alone. I'm tired."

"Listen, I'd like nothing better than to do it all for you," he said. "But I can't."

"Must I? All right. No rush."

"No rush."

At six o'clock he called Goodcars.

An hour later they were still sitting side by side, in a straitjacketed madness of traffic. Dawn was sighing, now, not in pain but in solemn exasperation. All four minicab windows were open to the shiftless air of early evening. Minicabs, minicabbing: the infinity of red lights . . . Raising his voice above the horns, the revved engines, the en-caged CDs and radios, and the slammed doors (people were climbing out of their cars to stare indignantly into the overheated distance), Des passed the time in lively disparagement of Diston General — whose premises lay clustered to their left, like the low-rise terminals of an ancient airport.

"It said in the *Gazette* they found *pigeon* feathers in the salad! In A & E on a Saturday night, it's a five-hour wait. And if you've only got a machete in your head, they send you to the back of the queue! . . . We're all right, Dawnie, where we are. We're all right."

"I want to go home. It's stopped hurting.

342

I'm fine."

Denied linear progress, the jammed metal, like a human crush-crowd (with all life hating all other life), now sought lateral motion, twisting into three-point turns and climbing the curb and the central divide; and Des felt so surfeited with his own strength that he wanted to step out into the road and call order — and then clear a path for them with his bare hands . . .

"I was fine when we got in the car." And she dug her small head into his side. "Sitting here in all this has brought it back. I was fine."

"It's a slipped disc, Dawnie. That's all. Maybe Braxton Hicks. Or sciatica. They said you might need a bit of therapy. A few back rubs. That's all."

Far ahead there was a sudden easing. The column started to move, like a loose-coupled train slowly picking up speed.

He said authoritatively, "Baby can blink now. And she can dream. Just imagine. What can unborn babies dream of?"

"Hush," she said. "Hush."

Dawn found it quite difficult to straighten up as they climbed from the cab and entered the odourless whiteness of the Maternity Centre.

Mrs. Treacher, paged by the front desk,

immediately, voluminously, and all-solvingly appeared. And Des started thinking about the dinner he would eventually be having with Dawn in front of *Match of the Day*.

17

She led them down a series of corridors and through a series of flabby fire doors with graph-lined portholes and past a series of water fountains of pearly enamelware. They reached a glass partition, and here Mrs. Treacher turned and said with her ogreish smile,

"I'll just take a quick look at you, my love, while we park young Des in here."

He was shown into a trim little office — evidently Mrs. Treacher's own, with its computer screen, its single shelf of textbooks, and the flat tins of paperclips and thumbtacks. Des noticed a small gilt-framed photograph (taken some time ago): Mrs. Treacher, with husband, son, daughter, and a swaddled babe in arms. He found it strange to think that the midwife (always so hungrily available) had children of her own. But nearly everyone had children. It was normal: the most normal thing in the world.

So Des paced the floor, not with anxiety, not at all; he paced the floor with a sense of unbounded restlessness — he wanted tasks, challenges, tests of strength . . . The office window looked out on a lot-sized municipal garden, and after a while he rested his forearms flat on the ledge, and slowly surrendered himself to the dusk — the line of trees, the birdflight. With regret, he thought how little he knew about nature . . . The trees: were they, perhaps, "poplars"? The birds: were they, perhaps, "wrens"? Small, short-winged, proud-breasted, they climbed above the treeline in trembling, almost visibly pulsating surges, with such ardent, such ecstatic aspiration . . . *That* wren was a girl, Des decided, as he heard the sound of his own name.

Opening the door with a flourish he almost fell over a smocked patient in a wheelchair. It was Dawn — and Mrs. Treacher was talking rapidly to a man dressed in green.

"This is the waterfall," said Dawn. "It isn't a trapped nerve, Des. It's labour. The baby's coming."

"Not possible," he said, raising his chin. "Not grown enough." He raised his chin yet further, and shrugged. "Not possible. Not prepared."

"It's coming. It's coming tonight."

He drew in breath to speak but what came out was something like a sneeze of dissolution. He groped sideways for the hard bench and toppled back on to it. Then he raised his hands to his face and lost himself in the messiest and snottiest tears he had ever shed — within a moment they were everywhere, in his mouth, up his nose, in his ears, dripping down his throat . . .

And he was no use at all in the delivery room. "Tell her to breathe!" he kept trying to say as they forcefully steered him towards the door. "Make her breathe!"

"*Desmond*," said his wife. "Go and lie down somewhere. And wait for us. Wait! . . . I can do it. I can do it all."

Dawn woke him — no, not his wife. Eos — Eos woke him: daylight woke him. When he tried to lift his head he found that his cheek was gummed to the vinyl seatcover, and he freed it with a terrifying rasp. He raised his head and saw that he was in a broad passage where others, too, waited and dozed . . . It took a while, but he eventually worked it out: no disaster could befall him, he decided, as long as he stayed perfectly still. But when he saw Mrs. Treacher in the distance walking busily in his direction, he felt his head jerk away before there was any danger of reading the expression on her face.

"Desmond?"

He swallowed chinlessly and said, "She all right? Dawn all right?"

"Oh yes."

"Baby all right?"

"They're both all right. And it's a girl."

Her last words bewildered him. *It's a girl*: he couldn't understand why anyone would think that this was something he needed or wanted to know. Not boy, not girl, not boy. Merely baby, baby, baby . . .

"Baby all right?"

"Well she's little. But she'll get bigger." Mrs. Treacher greedily added, "Same as all the others. That's what they do."

He let himself be guided into a place called the Recovery Room, and moved down a production line of triumphant feminine flesh (white nightdresses, warm limbs, white sheets); and there was his wife, sitting up in bed with her back arched and vigorously brushing her hair.

"Oh, my poor love," she said, and smiled with a hand raised to her mouth. "Whatever's gone and happened to you?"

And again he was led, or was rolled (his feet felt like castors), to an inner sanctum, or laboratory, and he gazed down with horror at the thing-alive beneath its dome of deep glass (like an inverted fishbowl), pinkish, brownish, yellowish, its limbs waving as mindlessly as the limbs of a beetle flipped on to its back. Now Desmond again deliquesced. He kept saying something, and he didn't know what it was he was saying, but he kept on saying it, as if convinced that no one could hear.

The morning air enveloped him in a rough caress. For a while he just hung there limply. And so, it seemed, he might have indefinitely remained — but some large and complicated insect came and joyfully menaced him, and after a series of gasps and whimpers he set off. It was half past nine. His mission was to go home and fetch Dawn's things. Could he accomplish that at least? Bus, tube train. He would have to move among the strong of the city.

But before he tried anything like that he entered a tea shop on the main road and ordered mushrooms on toast. He imagined himself to be bottomlessly hungry; and yet the black fungi felt quite alien to his tongue . . . There was a discarded tabloid on the chair beside him. He picked it up and spread it out. As if over a great divide, as if through the lens of a heaven-scanning telescope, he read about his astronomical uncle in the *Sunday Mirror*.

. . . All the blinds were drawn at "Wormwood Scrubs," and the flag of St. George was flying at half mast. "Threnody," having miscarried, was under deep sedation. According to a statement issued by Megan Jones, the couple were *completely devastated by this tragedy*. And the security personnel at the house, together with other friends and advisers (Des read), had mounted a suicide watch on Lionel Asbo.

She was finishing lunch when he returned with a laundry bag containing her nighties, bathrobe, and sponge bag, together with several sinister (and tasteless) items like her nursing pads and nipple cream . . .

Dawn looked him up and down as he made for the bedside chair.

"Don't I get a kiss then?" She patted her mouth with a tissue. "Cilla's sleeping. Why not go and have a look at her? They'll show you where."

He said, "Cilla? Are we calling her Cilla?"

". . . I don't understand you, Des Pepperdine. That was all you could say! Don't you remember? *Call her Cilla. Please call her Cilla. Call her Cilla, please call her Cilla.* Don't you remember? That was all you could say!"

He stared at his shoes. "Cilla. Cilla Dawn

Pepperdine. Nothing wrong with that."

"Nothing wrong with that. Go on then. Go and have a look at her."

"I'll wait for you. Eat your afters."

She said, "Des, don't worry. You'll come to love her. I know you. You'll learn . . . D'you think," she said, reaching for her apple pie, "d'you think he'll see me now?"

"Who? Oh. Him."

And he slowly thought: Father Horace, Uncle Lionel, Grandmother Grace — these were the congenital attachments. You grew up into them, and didn't have to learn how to do it, didn't have to learn how to love. He said,

"Take your time, Dawnie. I'll wait."

18

In philoprogenitive Diston the ice-cream vans (with their sliding service panels and their voluptuous illustrations of tubs and cones and multicoloured lollipops) played crackly recordings of standard nursery rhymes as they toured the summer streets. This motorised trade in frozen refreshments was known to be very lucrative, and was regularly and publicly and violently contested (with pool cues, golf clubs, and baseball bats). And yet the vans, additionally daubed though they were with trolls and dragons and goblins, looked and sounded arcadian: hear those streaming bell-like gradations — as the ice-cream vans came curling round corners and bobbled to a halt.

This, for now, would be the music of their lives.

Dawn and Cilla spent six nights in the Centre — one night for every week of the baby's prematurity.

"She takes a little more milk in her coffee than you do, doesn't she Des."

". . . Hard to tell. She's all yellow. Takes after your dad. Sorry."

For a moment naked Cilla looked up blindly; then, once again, she drowsed.

"Even her eyes are yellow. The white bits." Des peered at her. His gaze slid up from the swollen vulva and its vertical smile — to the head: a dunce's cap of flesh and blood and bone. "Her *head*. Looks like a Ku Klux Klan."

"I told you. They suctioned her. The ventouse. You weren't there, Des."

"And there's about a million other things that might go wrong with her."

". . . Have you been at the books again? Don't. Des, you can't do it all with your mind. Just feel your way towards her."

"I'm trying."

"Don't try. Wait. She'll be *fine*. Touch her. Go on. She won't hurt you."

Why did he sense this — that the baby had the power to hurt him? He reached down and ran his fingertips over the moist, adhesive surface . . .

Cilla was five pounds one.

"Just wait," said Dawn.

So he waited.

On the third day they were moved upstairs to a cubicle or ward-let intended for just two birthing mothers, and the second bed was empty. So they had the place to themselves. Which seemed to multiply Desmond's difficulties . . . Horace Sheringham, himself just out of hospital, naturally stayed away, but Prunella was of course a good deal around; and Uncle Paul came, and John came, and George came, and even Stuart came; and Great-Aunt Mercy came. No one noticed that Des was not what he appeared to be — was not the euphoric first-time father, speechless with pride. But then Lionel came.

"Pointy-headed," Dawn was saying as she positioned the wicker cradle by her side, "means clever."

"Don't joke about it. When you do that

you're —"

Des was cut short by the sound of an outlandishly brutal honk from the street below. At once he heard an answering shout of fright from the passage and the crash of a dropped tray. The honk was followed by more honks — as if a fleet of fire engines was barging its way up Slattery Road. Six or seven babies, from various directions, started crying; but Cilla lay still.

"It's the Venganza," said Des in a stunned voice. "The Venganza . . . He gave me a demonstration. In his garage. The horn's got a sliding gauge on it. It goes from quiet to normal to loud to *that*."

"I . . . We don't want him in here, Desi." She was leaning her body over the bassinet. "We're too . . ."

"What you mean?"

"We're too *fragile*. And he's too bloody much!"

Preceded by a cellophane-wrapped thicket of red roses (and wearing a suit and tie of the same gunpowder matt as his SUV), Lionel strolled in through the open door. He paused in silent assessment, and grinned.

"Now that's refreshing." He tossed the crackling bouquet onto the spare cot, and stood there with his arms folded, taking it all in. "That's very refreshing. To see some *real* misery for a change. Des, you look sick to you stomach, son. Coming home to you now, is it? Eh? Eh?" Lionel approached. "Let's have a look then."

"She's dozing," said Dawn, and leaned back to let him see.

"Jesus. Bit little isn't it?"

Des explained.

"Gaa. What's wrong with its bonce?"

Des explained.

"Well you made you bed now, son. You got to lie in it." He glanced at his watch. "All right, Dawn? Listen I brought a visitor for yer." He turned. "Come on, Des."

Out in the passage "Threnody" stepped forward, raising her black veil.

"No more talk about *babies*," said Lionel as he summoned the lift. "Now pay attention. I got a mixed report on you gran." There was good news, Lionel explained, and there was bad news. "Which d'you want first? Here. After you."

They or their washy reflections entered the sheet-metal vault. Its doors gave a shudder, but Lionel reached for the button and kept his thumb on it. The surface beneath their feet swayed and settled, finding its balance.

"Lungs. Heart. Call it old age. She's got less than a year to live." This was the good news. "Here, how long since you been up there?"

Des told him three or four weeks. Now the lift started swaying earthward.

"What was she on about? Daddy Dom still?"

"No. She's moved on to Lars. And a bit of Tolo." Tolo, Bartolome — father of Paul. "And even a bit of Jonky." Jonky, Jonker — father of George.

"Was she still talking Greek? You know, still babbling?"

"Yeah. More or less. You could work the odd thing out."

"Yeah well that's what's happening, Des. She's started making sense!"

This was the bad news.

"Who visits her?" said Lionel as they crossed the entrance hall. "Apart from you."

"Well the uncles go up. Now and then."

"Who's she phone?"

"Mercy. Every Sunday."

"Mercy. Old Ma Mischief. You know what we're in, Des? We're in a countdown . . . Okay, now look a bit grim. Go on. It'll suit you mood."

■ ■ ■ ■

They came out on to the front steps, and into the relief of the unsanitised open air. Down on the street a loose semicircle of photographers quickly readjusted itself, and three or four smart young ladies — analysts from the women's pages (Des recognised the *Mirror*'s Carli Gray) — drew nearer. Des said quietly,

"Sorry about your loss, Uncle Li."

"Yeah. Tragic." He raised his voice. "*Keep you distance now.* Guess who the father was. Raoul. Or maybe Fernando. *Hey, back off a bit.* Or even Azwat! She give it four months, to get the bump. Then she had it out. All as planned. *Show some respect there!* Exit strategy, see. Ah. Here she is."

Veil up, sunglasses on, and with a black hankie pressed to the bridge of her nose, "Threnody" took some deep breaths for the cameras . . . But now the science-fictional Venganza surged inexorably into place; its driver plummeted to the ground and ran to the nearer of the two back-up BMs; and at length Lionel ascended, and the Asbo motorcade moved off. There was more full-blast honking at the first intersection, where Lionel found himself confronted by a slow red light.

Lingering for a moment, Des heard the mechanical melody of an ice-cream van in the distance. He mumbled along with it ("Uncle Moon"), raising his face to the snowmen and snowwomen, the snowgirls and snowboys of the cooling blue sky, and then slipped back within.

19

So they stayed on at the Centre for nearly a week, and tiny Cilla had her jaundice bleached out of her (it was the colour of the undercoat of a healing bruise), and Dawn's milk began to flow, and Des was regularly and wryly handed the fearful present of the nappy (which, with its settled dankness, seemed to be heavier than the baby), and together they gave her baths, or swims, in the square sink; and Cilla, for her part, marshalled her grip reflex, and coughed and burped, and on the fifth day produced a triumphant sneeze, and, on the sixth, managed to skid a lucky thumb into her sopping mouth . . .

In late August, two Pepperdines left Avalon Tower; in early September, three came back. Almost immediately Cilla dipped beneath her birth weight, to a pitiable four pounds fifteen, and Des, watching her evaporate, felt himself again lose ground. He was like his Uncle Li. Not happy. Not sad. Numb. And he still couldn't trust himself to hold her. *No*, he kept saying. *I'll drop her. I'll smother her. I'll* crush *her. No!* But then this changed.

The love bomb exploded on September 29, at 11:45 a.m. Des stood at ground zero.

Their health visitor (an affectionate young widow called Margaret Gentleman) was just leaving, and Des was seeing her out. *Bye-bye, Diddums*, she said, and bowed to pass him the child. He turned his head, looking for Dawn. *Go on*, she said, *I can't take her with me!* And he was left holding the baby — at arm's length. *So she's all right then?* he called out. And Margaret, hurrying, said, *Cilla? Oh she's gorgeous!* . . . He inspected the warm weight in his arms. The full complement of limbs, the woozily slewing neck (steadied by his fingertips), the vestigially misangled face — whose inquisitive eyes now focused their stare. She was looking at him, or so he felt, in the way that Dawn looked at him when confronted by his frailties and confusions. Not uncritically, but tenderly, forgivingly, and above all knowingly.

He went and entrusted his child to his

wife, made some excuse, and bounded down the thirty-three floors. He walked out into Diston with all ten digits raised to his brow, saying to himself, It's a girl, it's a girl, it's a *girl* . . .

It's a girl!

He walked on, smiling, listing, dancing within himself. People looked his way wonderingly, as if for all the world he must be *on* something, and three different Distonites sidled up and asked him if he was selling any.

"Have a girl," he earnestly told them, as he swivelled and went home for more. "It isn't difficult. Go on. Just have a girl."

After a tasteful interlude (two and a half weeks), Lionel resumed his materialisations at Avalon Tower . . . It was different now. He entered, his keys gnashing at the locks, he drank a tin of Cobra, he changed his clothes, he slipped out. He returned, not at daybreak, but at two or three in the afternoon. He drank a cup of tea, changed his clothes, and slipped out again.

And he didn't seem to see Cilla. He stood there while being told about her latest stunts and accomplishments. And he always brought her something (his presents were notable for their bulk — a customised tricycle, a lifesize teddy bear). But he didn't seem to see Cilla. And she didn't seem to see him.

On the other hand, Lionel spontaneously desisted from smoking his cigars and Marlboro Hundreds in the passage, the kitchen, and the bathroom. He repaired to the balcony for his smokes, leaning on the rail and gazing out over Diston. Lionel had a new quality: he could be ignored. His presence no longer filled the room, the flat, the floor, the tower . . . And his banker's orders, now, covered all the rent.

Still, there were times that stayed in Desmond's mind. Like that Saturday morning, early on, when Lionel was accompanied by one of his dogs (Jak). He didn't say hello. Man and animal went within, and the bedroom door remained quarter open for an utterly silent hour. Then the Pepperdines glimpsed the slab of his suit in the passage and the dog giving them a haunted glance over its shoulder.

"She's not normal, is she," he said. "She never cries. And she sleeps through the night. They're not meant to do that."

Cilla proudly slept through the night in what they called her *perch*: the hip-high trestle table with raised sides, like a clothes drawer on legs. In this flanked hollow her basket lay.

"Well of course she's not normal. She's nearly two months behind. She's a *young* baby. But you're right."

"She's not normal. Have you ever heard her cry?"

Cilla's first smile was scheduled for thirteen weeks — or so, at least, the baby books had warned. But Dawn imposed a ban on baby books (which her husband didn't fully observe). They waited.

And what was this? In the fourth week she straightened her neck, more or less, and began to take a shrewd interest in baby books of her own (principally *Mr. Man*); in the fifth, she made cooing sounds and, coached by Dawn, became near-fluent in motherese; in the sixth, she could brandish a rattle; and in the seventh . . .

That was a smile, they were always saying. *No it wasn't. That was wind. A windy smile . . .* That *was a smile. No it wasn't. That was a yawn. A yawny smile.*

And then, in the seventh week, she smiled — irrefutably. You suddenly knew what an extraordinary thing a smile was, how kaleidoscopically it transformed the eyes.

"She wasn't prem," Dawn decided. "She was ready. Her body was little but her mind was ready. She was *bored* inside. That's all."

And once she started smiling — she couldn't stop.

"It's not normal," he said.

"She's just pleased to be here."

"But she smiles at *everyone*."

This was true. On the street, in the park — Diston seemed to be incapable of coming up with anyone that she didn't immediately and passionately admire.

"Des, she's not normal."

"No."

"She's fabulous."

"She is," he said. "She's magic . . . But it's not normal for a baby to smile like that. All the time."

"There. Listen. She's crying! You say she never cries — and she's crying. *Now* are you happy?"

". . . She's not crying. She's singing!"

But it is common, it is everyday, it is normal. Hear the vans? "Hush, Little Baby," "Star Light, Star Bright," "Golden Slumbers Kiss Your Eyes," "Hark, Hark, the Dogs Do Bark," "What Are Little Girls Made Of?" . . . If it's true what they say, if it's true that happiness writes white, then decency insists that we withdraw, passing over to the three of them a quire — no, a ream — of blank pages.

XX

Nothing really out of the ordinary happened between October 2012 and July 2013.

Marlon's brother Charlton was arrested after an altercation with his mother, Mercy Welkway (in the course of which she broke her hip). That same week Ringo was given another three months for Benefits Fraud. Horace Sheringham, these days, was in and out of various clinics and hospitals (and in and out of various pubs and bars and off-licences and supermarkets). Come the New Year, fate would install him at Diston General (where, ipso facto, he only had a seventy-eight per cent chance of getting out alive). According to Prunella, Horace had *no intention whatsoever* of reconsidering his stand on Dawn.

Lionel Asbo, during this period, attracted the attention of the press on several counts — an intrusion at "Wormwood Scrubs," for example, which gave rise to lively public debate. But it was the dullest and feeblest of these stories (the idlest, the tritest) that proved to be by far the most transformative . . .

In early autumn Sebastian Drinker announced that Lionel was probably going to take a financial interest in West Ham United Football Club. The season was by then in its seventh week, and the Hammers had yet to win a point or even score a goal. From the directors' box at Upton Park (unaccompanied by "Threnody," who was still bedridden with grief) Lionel witnessed the monotonous calamities in east London; but he also witnessed the monotonous calamities in stadiums as far flung as Stoke, Bolton, Portsmouth, Sunderland . . . And the following morning you'd see, on the back page of your Sunday tabloid, a foggy photo of the dripping car park at, say, Wigan Athletic, with Lionel sorrowfully finishing his meat pie and his mug of Bovril before scaling the charcoal Venganza (or bending into his new Ferrari). By October, the credits of *Match of the Day* were closing with a clip of Lionel as he shuffled from the ground, in slow motion, to the strains of the lugubrious West Ham anthem, "I'm Forever Blowing Bubbles": *I'm forever blowing bubbles, Pretty bubbles in the air, They fly so high, nearly reach the sky, Then like my dreams they fade and die* . . . And so Lionel became a kind of national symbol of intransigence, of peculiarly English intransigence in the face of relentlessly blighted hopes.

Which was the more unexpected, because

Lionel always insisted that he didn't *give a fuck about football. Basically*, he often used to say, *only cunts give a fuck about football.* Maybe, Des thought, maybe Lionel supported West Ham just to get out of the house — or maybe he took a Lionel pleasure in drinking in the pain of thousands upon thousands . . . Anyway, the running story on Lionel Asbo and West Ham United was soon at least partly overshadowed by weightier concerns — not least the attempted burglary in Short Crendon, which became known, in the spring of 2013, as the Case of the Chav Chauffeur.

Cilla's eyes turned from blue to brown. This they had been told to expect. But then she developed another abnormality . . . Her parents stared. Des said,

"It's like the way the royal family wave. During parades."

"Yeah. As if they're unscrewing a lightbulb."

"But she's doing it *fast*. With one in each hand!"

This was Cilla's latest initiative: she'd raise her wrists to head height and wiggle them in swift rotations. She couldn't stop doing that either — while of course still smiling. Dawn said,

"Like that black-face singer. Al Jolson! . . . Oh, Des, what have we done to deserve this?"

"You know, we're duty-bound to have another. I mean not now, but . . . We're duty-bound."

"We are. It might be another Cilla."

She spent most weekdays in the vast crèche at St. Swithin's, where she hob-nobbed with the innumerable babies of the schoolmarms and the schoolgirls.

And her eyes turned imperceptibly from blue to brown.

During the winter quarter Grace Pepper-dine received three sets of visitors at Cape Wrath . . . Lionel and "Threnody" went up there first, in late November, as was duly recorded in the *Sun*, the *Star*, the *Mail*, and the *Daily Telegraph*. Lionel's physiognomy, it turned out, had a talent for the sombre. It was basically his West Ham face (post-match, soaked car park, nil–six), but in a more elevated style: the photographs showed someone taking his grief like a man while maintaining a kind of yokel hopefulness, with broadened jaw and crinkled orbits. "Threnody," for her part, was unveiled but still in the strictest black. Out on the cliffs together, with the breakers exploding steeple-high, they were an arresting study, "Threnody," a woman who knew how to suffer (and endure, and avenge), under the burly arm of a more optimistic presence, one that gazed out through the mist and the spume and trustfully awaited the white sails of the new ships.

I don't know why we go up there, said Lionel from under his baseball cap when Des passed him on the twenty-first floor of Avalon Tower (Des coming home, Lionel off out). *Why do we bother? She didn't know me from "Threnody."* Lionel spoke further about "Threnody." *Oh she loves it. Says being a tragedy queen's good for her poetry books. You know, for they sales.*

. . . Grace talking, Uncle Li?

Oh yeah. Talking to the ceiling. About Tommo. About Gunther.

Mm. Doing the dads. Tommo, or Tomorbataar: father of Ringo. Gunther: father of Stuart (pronounced *Goonter* by Stuart and *Gunter* by Gran, with Lionel settling for the no-nonsense *Gumfer*). *Be back to Dominic in a minute*, said Des. *You could follow what she said then?*

Yeah, if you bent over. Gurgling on about Tommo and bleeding Gunther. Lionel adjusted the peak of his cap. *Then she'll say something really . . . really* mad.

What, when her language goes funny?

Yeah well I'll give her funny. She said — and it stuck in me mind. She said . . . she said, Insect violation? *Like it was a question. Then she said,* Six, six, six . . . Insect violation? *Now what the fuck's* that *meant to mean?*

Search me, Uncle Li.

Here. I worked it out. Lionel gave his pumpkin grin, and explained. Unless the Hammers won their next two games (away to Chelsea, away to Manchester United), they'd be doomed to relegation by Christmas.

Me new image, Des. It's killing me with the skirt. And who can blame them? These birds want a bloke with a bit of the devil in him, not . . . Not the good son. The grieving father. The caring partner — with his empathy. Not the sad cunt who gives a fuck about West Ham. Des, it's killing me with the DILFs.

But you're uh, you're sticking it out with "Threnody," Uncle Li?

With Lynndie? Yeah. She says another four months. Four months . . . I'm forever blowing bubbles, eh Des? Jesus.

And, no, Lionel never did take that financial interest in West Ham United Football Club.

The three Pepperdines went up there in mid December (and again in mid January). Cilla was profoundly impressed by her forty-five-year-old great-grandmother; and Grace, too, seemed struck. Falling silent, she gazed at the eager figure held there at the bedside; again and again the baffled creases of her brow hesitantly rearranged themselves; and then her mouth (now bent in a tick, like the Nike logo) sought the shape of a smile. With Cilla reaching up to her.

Des believed that this was the true measure of his daughter: the way she reached up to the old (or to the old-seeming — she did it everywhere), her softly moved and forgiving look as she reached up to them.

They were leaving. Grace took Dawn's hand. *Hello, dear,* she said and averted her face as if for a kiss. *Cilla was a difficult birth. Well. She* was *my first. And I was only twelve. Cilla, difficult. John, Paul, George — easy. Ringo, a bit difficult. Stuart — easy. But Lionel. You remember those knights in the olden days? It was like having one of them. He turned me inside out, he did. Lionel came in full armour. Goodbye, dear.*

■ ■ ■ ■

In February, under a day-long downpour, John, Paul, George, Ringo, and Stuart drove to Cape Wrath for their biennial visit in Stuart's two-door VW Lupo.

In the small hours of March 2, the police were called to the Welkway residence at 44 Blagstock Road, where they dealt with a *domestic* involving Marlon and Gina and Gina's youngest sister, little Foozaloo. Gina was treated for hypothermia. It was twelve degrees below, and she had been locked out on the roof in her underwear.

The announcement came in late April. "Threnody" and Lionel Asbo had agreed on a trial separation. *They find they are unable to get past the loss of Lovechild*: this was what Dawn and Des read in the press release. *They desperately want to make it work*, Megan Jones was widely quoted as saying. *There are only the tenderest feelings on both sides.* For now, "Threnody" returned to her rented mews house off Kensington High Street. Lionel stayed on at "Wormwood Scrubs." *They remain very close*, said Sebastian Drinker. *To be honest,*

Lionel's taking it hardest. First the loss of Lovechild, now the loss of "Threnody." It's tearing him apart.

In a brief statement (prior to going on the road with her story) "Threnody" said, *I wasn't able to succour him. Nor he I. It's tragic. Because I still love the guy to death.*

Death was awake, death was going about its business (in the Northern Lights, in Diston General), but during this time there was only one proximate casualty: Joy Nightingale. Joy — Ernest's widow, Rory's mother.

Des saw the notice in the *Diston Gazette*. He was having one of his days with Cilla, so he strapped her to his chest and they took the bus to the cemetery beyond Steep Slope. Yews and apple blossom against a middle distance of breezy sportsfields and pennanted pavilions, the lay churchwarden, the little group of friends and neighbours guardedly blowing their noses and clearing their throats . . . It was the kind of funeral where a mound of sand abuts the grave and where the mourners themselves begin the work of burial, throwing in their handfuls over the sunken casket. His turn came. As Des bent forward Cilla too reached into the pyramid of orange grit, and looked stern as she released her share through splayed and stiffened fingers.

The summers of 2012 and 2013 came early, but the winter in between was petrifyingly cold.

■ ■ ■ ■

PART IV

■ ■ ■ ■

2013 WHO? WHO?

The Week Before

". . . Eh, are you all right? What's wrong with you voice?"

"No, I'm coming down with something. I just told them. I'm going home sick. I'm dropping."

"Yeah? Well hear this, Des. Half an hour ago. I'm lying in bed. The phone rings. Gina picks up — and starts having a little chat. *How are you, love?* All this. *Oh, Marlon's fine. Want a word with him? You coping with the weather?* All this. Then she hands me the phone and says, *It's you mum!*"

Des raised a hand to his brow. "Grace?"

"Grace. I felt this tingle go up me spine. Like she returned from the dead . . . *Lionel? Listen, love. The end is near. Come and see you mother, love. We need to talk. Come and see you mother.*"

"She said it like that?"

"She said it like that. Haven't heard her

talk proper English for what? Five years? *I've got something on me conscience, Lionel. And I ain't got long now. Come and see you mother, love.*"

". . . So you're going up there?"

"Well I can't get out of it, can I. What you reckon's bothering the old . . . ? Rory Nightingale? Here, who's that nurse? The boiler with the white hair and the big tits."

"Mrs. Gibbs."

"Mrs. Gibbs. I had a word with Mrs. Gibbs. Says she's seen it a thousand times. They get like that — you know, just before they pop off. Lucid. And they want — they want forgiveness."

On the stairs Des paused to catch his breath, and he looked down through the window (as he often did) at the little skulk of foxes on the corrugated tin roof in the alley beneath Avalon Tower. One was curling up into a whorl of off-white and ginger, one was slowly stretching its rigid back legs. They peered this way and that with their usual scrawny apprehensiveness. Did it ever lift, their fear? In all weathers they seemed to shiver.

"Ooh, *Des* . . . Okay, that's it. I'm not going."

"No, go. Maybe it'll pass," he said faintly.

Dawn was off to Diston General — to be with her mother. "Don't be long. And don't look so hopeful, Dawnie. What're you hoping for anyway?"

"*You* know. I want his blessing. His blessing and his goodbye."

"Horace's blessing? Well good luck, Dawnie. And give my love to Pru."

. . . Cilla was asleep in the basket on her free-standing perch. And for once he was hoping that she wouldn't wake up. His main symptom was a feeling of helpless stupefaction — and the child, the four-limbed figure in its Babygro, looked forbiddingly complicated and mysterious: how to wield her, wash her, feed her? How to do all that, above all, without smearing her with his emanations, his moist whisper, his sickening breath? . . . He sank down on the couch. Goldie prowled towards him. She was four, but she still looked liquid in movement, and as light as air when she jumped, and it always surprised you — the weight of her when she landed on your lap. He reached out.

The cat sniffed his fingernails, gave a sneezelike snarl, and tore from the room.

Then Des knew he had it.

"UVI."

"UVI. What's that then?"

"Urban Vulpine Influenza," said Des. "You know, the fox flu." The fox flu: popularly referred to as *breakbone* — and also as *fascist fever*, because UVI showed a shameless preference for people of colour. "Can last a month. You get six weeks off. Automatic. Which is scary in itself. Comes in waves."

Lionel smiled and said, "The fox flu. That's old Horace, that is. Sending you his lurgy. You possessed by Horace. Seriously though, Des. You want to watch that with the baby. Her being half black and all."

"Yeah. They say you're only infectious before and after. Not during . . . Jesus."

"Don't worry, Des. You come to the right place."

They were in the Spa Bar at the Pantheon Grand . . . Lionel had spent three nights up in Cape Wrath. From his taxiing aircraft, at City Airport, he summoned his nephew to what he called a *family meet*. He sent a car. Des found Lionel at his ease against a background of bamboo and marble, with his feet up on an embroidered pouffe, scanning the *Financial Times* and drinking a tawny liquid from a fluted glass.

"Uh — uh, Geoffrey? I'll have the same again. Gin and carrot. And give the boy here a treble Bloody Mary. With masses of spice."

"My pleasure, Mr. Asbo."

"No, Des, it's the only answer. We'll get that down you, and then ne'll do some weights. Have a rub and a sauna. Sweat it out. It's the only cure."

. . . Now they lay side by side on black leather benches. Lionel was pressing a hundred kilos. Des was doing what he could with fifty-five.

"Arch you back a bit. Oy! Lock you elbows on the upthrust! . . . She was transformed, Des. Grace. She was sitting up and talking to me. To me. Not the wall. Not the lightbulb. Me. Her lastborn son. And guess what. Just so you know me state of mind when I come in the room . . . Well, I suppose it's only natural. The old niggles just melted away and I felt all — I felt all *sad*, Des. All melancholy. Okay. She had her faults, Grace. But she did her best. Okay. She could be a bit wild. Like *your* mum. But she did her best . . . And she said, she said, *I've got something on me conscience, dear.* And she looked away. And a tear rolled down her cheek. I said, *Come on, Mum. You can tell me, for goodness' sake! Come on, Mum. What is it?* And she says . . ."

Desmond went still.

"She says . . ." Lionel, too, went still. "Oy. Keep you rhythm there. She says . . . Daddy

379

Dom. Daddy Dom. She reckons she should've made a proper go of it with Daddy Dom. Instead of messing around with all them foreign blokes. *A proper family*, she says. *Just me and Dom, and you and you sister. I* humbled *you, Lionel, from the day you was born. With them brothers all shapes and sizes. Can you ever forgive me?* . . . Okay. Two hundred more and then we'll do the squats and the deadlifts."

. . . Now they were chin-deep in the frothing jacuzzi.

"I said, *Ah, love. This is no time for hard feelings! For rancour! The past is past. And, Mum — look at me now! . . . I'm a wealthy businessman. The people of this country have taken me to they hearts. No, you boy's at peace with the world. Rest, Mum, rest. You had it hard too, don't forget. Seven kids.* And I told her something I remembered from Sunday school. I said, *God can't be every-where at once. So he sends us mums . . .* A nice touch, don't you think Des? *Rest, Grace, rest!* Okay. Sauna."

. . . Now they sat on slatted wooden stools with plump white towels round their waists. It seemed to the younger man that the air was not unbreathably hot — it was just unbreathably thick.

"So you were up there three nights, Uncle Li."

"Yeah. At the hotel. Got distracted. With a DILF. Jesus, is that you teeth chattering? Des, look at yer. Sweating and shivering at the same time! Stay clear of the baby, Des . . . Where's she sleep anyway? In the kitchen?"

"Yeah. You've seen her. In her basket on the trestle table."

"You ever have her in with you at all?"

"No. Never." Des effortfully explained. "Dawn's cousin. Marigold. She lost a youth that way. Crushed it by accident."

"What you do for ventilation? In these temperatures."

"There's the fan. And we keep the balcony door back. And sometimes we open the window in your room, Uncle Li. Just for the flow."

". . . You know, Des, I been thinking. When you uh, when you gran passes away, it'll be the end of an era. How about I get a flat — at the Tower. And the baby'll have her own nursery!"

"Well, that'd be massive, Uncle Li."

"And I'll go on uh, defraying you rent."

"Uncle Li . . . You'll still look in on us, I hope?"

"Course I will," said Lionel, slapping his

knees and getting to his feet. "Course."

They then submitted to the expert cruelty of the masseur.

. . . In one of the ground-floor lounges Des looked on with a glass of water (even water tasted foul) as Lionel quietly consumed, in its entirety, the Restoration Tea for Two — crustless egg-and-cress sandwiches, buttermilk scones with strawberry jam and clotted cream, apricot tarts, and sherry trifle, washed down with four or five tankards of Black Velvet . . . Des was not alert that afternoon. Had he been, then certain aspects of the Asbo performance might have struck him. The elevations — of appetite, vocabulary, sentiment. But Des was not alert that afternoon.

"I still keep me penthouse at the South Central," Lionel was saying as he finished up. "But it's getting ridiculous. There's a prank fire alarm almost every fucking night. And we all milling around the foyer in our bathrobes." He glanced over his shoulder. "The Pantheon's got other strengths. Good order, Des. Good order and restraint."

. . . Bouncing his lighter in his palm, Lionel led the way out into the squarelike street or streetlike square that served as the hotel forecourt, with its doormen, its question-mark lamp posts, its dedicated taxi rank. Desmond's courtesy car stood by.

"You know," said Lionel with a rueful compression of his nose, "I couldn't help having a little tease of her before I went. I said, *Remember the schoolboy, Mum? In his purple Squeers' blazer?* But she couldn't remember that of course. Went blank. I said, *You want something on you conscience, Mum? How about the schoolboy?* I was smiling, mind — just having her on. *Yeah, Mum. You sealed his fate as sure as you slung the noose youself. Messing about with a* schoolboy . . . Went blank. Vacant. Started babbling again. In her funny language. So I just tiptoed out the door . . . Mrs. Gibbs says she's clammed up now — turned her face to the wall. You gran's got pneumonia, Des. The sacs of her lungs, they filling with pus. Her whole body's rotting. Here. You car."

Des said, "Pneumonia. The old man's friend."

"They'll treat it. Antibiotics. But when it comes back — nah. Let nature take its course . . . I'll be phoning in. And keep a bag packed. We'll want to be there when she goes. Watch you UVI, Des. Don't be spreading it. Spare a thought for the baby."

Grace was giving up the ghost in the home on Cape Wrath, and Horace was noisily and smellily pegging out in the terminal ward at Diston General (with his daughter confined to the far side of the smeared screen), and Des, in Avalon Tower, was also dying — dying of insanity. His mind was the mind of a London fox: *Vulpes vulpes* in the great world city.

All day, all night (what was the difference?), eyes open, eyes shut (what was the difference?), Des attended the cinema of the insane. In beady pulses and thudding flashes he rehearsed what he supposed were essentially vulpine themes and arguments to do with anxiety, hunger, and shelterlessness, refracted through an urban setting of asphalt and metal, of rubber and cellophane and shattered plexiglass. It was the longest motion picture of all time; and his attention never strayed. The definition was as sharp as a serpent's tooth. The lighting was indecently and lawlessly lurid. The dialogue (sometimes dubbed) and the voiceover and the occasional subtitles were all in the language of Grace.

"That was him again. No news."

". . . Wait. Dawn, wait. Get Cilla. Don't bring her in. Show her to me. You know, I think it's going. I think I'm coming back."

It was Wednesday.

Thursday

Just before ten Lionel entered the flat, immense and telekinetic, like a human chariot. And his steeds, in their spiked collars, were Jak and Jek.

Des stood up with a judder of his chair.

"Something happened. In the night. Her signs are going, Desi." Lionel's face was raw and pleading. "Her vital signs! Come *on*, boy. Where's you bag? God — Christ — *come on*."

Fifteen minutes later Des was up in the control tower of the Venganza — bound, at appalling speed, for Stansted Airport.

"They reckon she had another of her strokes. And in her condition . . . What you grinning at? Today of all days!"

". . . It's just so brilliant to be *out*. You're grinning too, Uncle Li."

"Yeah, well. It's a relief in a way. No more suspense, eh son?"

That morning Des awoke defervesced, fever-free, and astonished by health — health, that mighty power. He had breakfast with the girls, and saw them off, and made more tea and ate on, all the while refamiliarising himself with reality — in a spirit of ponderous gratitude . . . Then came Lionel, a gust, a squall, untethering Jak and Jek and booting them out on to the balcony (*Call Dawn. The dogs stay here. No choice*), unpacking the stiff-sided shopping bag (Michael Gabriel — the Family Butcher), and noisily rootling for the litter tray as Des grabbed his old satchel and threw a few clothes and toiletries into it.

And here they were in a great yellow flower of summer heat on the open road, with the strobe of the sun blatting through the high trees, and Lionel coldly masterful at the wheel, using the three lanes at a velocity that was all his own, like a jogger weaving through a street full of decrepit pedestrians . . . He forwent the use of the potent horn — relying, rather, on the kliegs of the headlights.

"You ever been on a plane?"

"Yeah." Whether speeding up or slowing down, the machine glided through its gradations with seamless surety, as if wired to the road. "Yeah. I did the Cumbria Cannibal. And that torturing nanny in Newcastle. The one with the tongs."

"You should stick to them, Des," said Lionel, using the breakdown lane to overtake a pantechnicon. "Stick to them fucking psychos. And lay off the blokes who're just uh, just trying to earn a . . ." They mounted the ramp to Long Term Parking. "Earn a decent crust."

Des said, "I suppose we don't know how long we'll be gone."

"Back Saturday night. If she's prompt. They got the undertaker lined up. And the vicar or whatever the fuck he is."

They dropped down from the car and assumed the standard modern posture — faces steeply inclined over consoles held at waist height.

Lionel straightened up and said, "Well she's still here. Thready pulse. Hanging on."

Des straightened up and said, "Dawn sends her love. And she'll manage Jak and Jek . . . Cilla's always asking for them. She keeps saying, *Doh. Doh.*"

"I'll be wanting a word with her later," said Lionel, "about Jak and Jek."

They flew to Inverness, and then on to Wick in an open-prop eighteen-seater. As they made their second descent, the tenuous cloud cover was already reintroducing them to the tones of the home — bedding, face powder, antimacassars, spray-thickened mist.

"I was praying. Praying they wouldn't get a point! In they whole campaign! . . . Last day of the season. Upton Park. I'm enjoying me prawn sandwich in the directors' box.

And what happens? They go and hold Liverpool to a goalless draw! It *would* be the fucking Reds, wouldn't it. See, I don't mind the Pool. It's from all that time up in Kenny. Doing me Yoi."

At Wick, in the unserious little airport, there was a liveried chauffeur with a handwritten sign: ASBO. Cape Wrath was still ninety-five miles away. In the limousine Des slept . . . He awoke to the signs for Thurso, Strathy Point, Tongue. On the outskirts of Souness they queued for nearly ten minutes at a roadworks traffic light, and Des saw, through a lattice of saplings to the left, what seemed to be a druidical graveyard. But the tombstones were not tombstones: they were cropped trees, very old, and all caught in different attitudes of huddled infirmity.

"Yeah, Mum," Lionel was muttering to himself. "Yeah, you moving house, woman. Change of address. Yeah, it's the balsa bungalow for you, my girl."

Rob Dunn Lodge stood under the lee of a hillside on the east wing of Lochinvar Strand. They took possession of the Henryson Suite, where they dropped their bags and washed their faces. Then they were driven up on to Clo Mor Bluff.

The first-storey bay-windowed room, with

the sun staring in at it. And seeing what? Seeing the dark screen perched high above the bed, the flashing digits of pulse rate and blood pressure, the metal tree with its fruit of fluid sacs and gadgets that looked like walkie-talkies and adding machines, the plugs and adaptors, the entanglement of wires and tubes. And the wasted woman lying almost flush with the sheets, her face under a mantle of sweat, eyes closed, mouth open. Her son and grandson sat on either side. The first hour was turning into the second.

Breaking a long silence, Lionel said, "You see that uh, architect who topped hisself, Des? Sir John someone. His mum pops off and he tops hisself. And everyone goes, *Ah, he was depressed, see, because his mum popped off.* They always say that — and it's bollocks. It's not that he suddenly *wanted* to. Top hisself. It's that he suddenly *could.*"

"How's that, Uncle Li?"

"See, there's certain things, Des, there's certain things a man can't do till his mum pops off."

Now the second hour was turning into the third. Every twenty minutes or so Lionel sloped out for a smoke. And every twenty minutes or so Mrs. Gibbs, all stern and silent, hurried in and checked the valves and the readings. Finding Des alone (it was now gone five), she said without meeting his eye,

"Your uncle's going to keep his temper today, I hope. Should've heard him the last time. Yelling blue murder. He scared the —"

"Ah, Mrs. G," said Lionel as he strolled back into the room, "what's all this then? Taking her time about it, isn't she? You been slipping her penicillin on the sly?"

Mrs. Gibbs gave him a weary glance as she turned to go.

"How d'you do it, Mrs. G? At your age? That chest! You got the figure of a beauty queen." Lionel grinned as she bustled past. He called out after her, "Yeah, but I bet it's all off as soon as you undo you bra . . . Gaa, Des," he said as the door jerked shut, "remember the GILFs? Horny Hilda. The Bonking Biddies . . . Jesus Christ. *Look*."

Her eyes were open. Her oystery eyes were open, and straining up into the red rinds of the lids, with terror, as if she was falling over backward. Falling over backward and trying to see if there was anyone there to catch her when she fell.

Des had time to hope — to pray — that when Grace fell she would fall like a feather falls, in drifting rockabye. But Lionel was already on his feet, leaning over her with his hands in his trouser pockets and tightly saying,

"Off with yer. Go on. Go and meet you maker. Go and —"

"*Bill!*" screamed Grace.

". . . *Fuck*ing hell."

"*Bill!*"

"What she . . . ? Who's Bill? Another fucking schoolboy?"

"Bill," wept Grace. "Love, love. But it's forbidden!"

"What's this, Des?"

"Chandler reacts badly to predator! Sex, ate!"

And suddenly Des understood: he understood what there was to understand. Not *sex, ate*. Six, eight: 6, 8.

"Crossword clues, Uncle Li. Remember she always did the Cryptic? They're crossword clues."

And Des found he could solve them. *Chandler reacts badly to predator (6, 8)*; anagram: *cradle snatcher . . . Bill, love, love, but it's forbidden (5)*; bill = tab; love, love = nil, nil = zero, zero: *taboo*.

With a desperate wail Grace cried, "Unresisting, even so! Fifteen!"

"What's that?"

"Crossword clue. The answer's *notwithstanding*."

"What's this *fifteen* business?"

"Fifteen letters, Uncle Li. Notwithstanding."

"Predator. Fifteen. Forbidden . . . Ah. Here we go."

This referred to Grace. Who was now engaged in a levitational struggle, with curved back, as if her nerves were being unplucked, a stretching and then a slower unwinding, a sudden retch, a jolt — and the trail of life had frayed.

"How'd he take it?"

"Hard to say. You never know with him." Des sprawled back in his seat and cast his eyes round the Alexander Selkirk Bayview Bar. Seen side on, the waves filed past the leaded window in orderly droves. The lighthouse throbbed above the boulders strewn round its base. In a white tuxedo the beanpole pianist played "O sole mio" with noodly fingers . . . Lionel was over in the corner, his third bottle of champagne propped in its bucket; he was talking to Mr. Firth-Heatherington, and to a Mr. John Man — the funeral director. "He seemed plain angry at first. But when she went, he just stared down at her and said, *Look at that in the bed there . . ."*

"And you, darling?"

"I can't tell, Dawnie. Everything seems to be happening to someone else. As if I'm not here. Or only watching. How's that Horace?"

She said, "I'm being good. I'm not getting my hopes up. But Mum thinks he's wavering."

"Well fingers crossed."

They were about to sign off for the night when Dawn said suddenly,

"Oh, Des — the dogs. They're not the Jak and Jek we knew."

"Yeah, that's right. They're not."

A synchronised tingle in the ears and the armpits made Des realise that this had been in the back of his mind all day — the dogs. Twelve hours ago, when the tearful charioteer swept into 33F, Des's immediate worry was that Jek and Jak would make much of him in a way that Lionel could be expected to resent. But the dogs just brushed by him with stiff shoulders, Jak turning his head for a moment with a rictus of scorn — a kind of canine false smile. And once they were out on the balcony they rolled into a muscular heap, growling, snapping, champing. Clearly, Jek was one thing, and Jak was one thing too, but Jak and Jek, or Jek and Jak, were something else again.

"And guess what. They're queer for each other. And they're brothers. That's incest."

She laughed, so he laughed too, but it came to him like a pang in the brain. Incest. *Insect violation? (6). I scent tangled crime (6). No-no disturbs sin, etc. (6).*

"Jak'll climb on Jek. And Jek'll climb on Jak. With their back legs quivering. Not that I mind that. Much. It's the way they look at the baby."

Des said, "Tell."

"They look right through me. But with Cilla — they stare at her, all panting and drooling. Not friendly. As if she's a *rival*. And of course she wants to pet them. I'm not having them in here, I can tell you that."

"No, keep them out, Dawnie. Sling them their meat, but keep them out."

Something made Des turn. Lionel, leaning over him from behind, opened his palm for the phone.

"Uh, Uncle Li wants a word . . ."

"Dawn? Sorry for the uh, imposition, girl. No alternative." He nodded as he heard her out. "Well. She lived life to the full. Ripe old age and all that . . . Listen. Give the dogs they steak tonight — but no Tabasco . . . That's it. But give them the *lot* tomorrow. The whole bottle . . . Yeah, well, they on a controlled diet. For the hare coursing. All right? And latch that door. Leave it open even a crack and they get they snouts in there and they *worry* away at it. Keep the dogs out, Dawn. Shut it tight."

Before very long Lionel led Des to the Dunbar Dining Room.

"Eat something substantial, son. You've lost weight from you flu. Here, have the duck." *The duc-kuh.* "Or the pork."

". . . Jesus, it's twenty past nine and it's still light out!"

"Mm. Reckon I'll have game. The woodcock . . . Okay. Now tomorrow I'll be doing the necessary with uh, with Mr. Man. While you twiddle you thumbs. Take the car, Des. Go to Cape Wrath on the ferry. We'll plant her first thing Saturday. Be back in London by teatime."

Their shrimp cocktails came, and the first bottle of claret.

"You know, I'm ever so slightly concerned," said Lionel, taking out his phone and briefly and dubiously consulting its screen, "about Gina. See, these days, Des . . . I know it's naughty, but these days I go and pick her up in the Ferrari. With the roof down. And her poor old lord and master, I make him follow along behind.

On a moped . . . So of course now it's all over Town. Bit naughty. See, I fancied giving Marl the extra niggle. But now I'm concerned he'll go and do the obvious."

"What's the obvious?"

"Whoop. Don't look now, son, but there's me DILF . . . Me Dunbar DILF. Bruise healing up nicely," he said, giving a wave and a smile. "Ooh. She doesn't seem best pleased to see me. Dear oh dear. Quick — there. In the red gown and the fishnet stockings. Feast you eyes . . . Yeah, the DILFs've come flocking back, Des. That's down to uh, changing perceptions, that is. That's down to the Chav Chauffeur."

"Oh yeah. The Chav Chauffeur." And Des recalled the much-discussed case of the Chav Chauffeur. In late May a young car-tuner and stunt driver (who was once on the Asbo payroll) broke into the cellars at "Wormwood Scrubs." The next morning he and his two accomplices were found in a heap on the village green, all mauled and maced and tasered. *Mr. Asbo will not be pressing charges*, said Sebastian Drinker in a terse statement to the press. *He believes he has made his position perfectly clear . . .* "That changed things, did it? The Chav Chauffeur?"

"The Chav Chauffeur? Completely turned

396

it around with the DILFs. See, you DILF, Des," said Lionel, as he addressed himself to his main course, "she wants a bit of piss and vinegar. Not all that *Love*child nonsense. Not bleeding West Ham. Not the *mother's* boy. No no. But jamming a cattle prod up a burglar's arse — you DILF can respond to that. Anyway. Fuck me image. No more Goody Two Shoes. It's going to be Lionel Asbo from here on in."

The dessert trolley, the cheeseboard, the third bottle of claret. Then nuts and tangerines. Then coffee and, for Lionel, a selection of the choicest liqueurs. It was gone ten-thirty when Des felt the hum of his phone. He went out into the passage with it.

"We're asphyxiating here," she said. "It's not that hot but I can't get an airflow. I went to open the window in Lionel's room. And it's locked!"

"Locked?" He thought for a moment (this had happened once or twice before). "Well do the usual anyway." Which meant standing with a flapping towel by the open front door for fifteen minutes before bedtime. "That'll move it a bit. Then train the fan on her. And don't open the glass door, okay? . . . I know . . . I know. But not even a hair's breadth. Latch *down*. All right?

How's Cilla?"

"Cilla's Cilla. She's great. Have you noticed, Des, when she smiles, it comes to her eyes first. Before her lips. And her eyes just *beam*."

"Yeah," he said. "Straight to the eyes. Light speed. And they just *beam* at you."

In the interim Lionel's ladyfriend had been prevailed upon to pull up a chair. She was an expressionless, blue-veined, porcelain beauty, with a beige smudge on the orbit of her left eye. A presence from the silent screen (an imperilled heroine, perhaps). Or so it kept on seeming to Des, because nobody spoke. The turbid atmosphere was incomprehensible to him, and he soon pleaded tiredness and said his goodnights.

It was getting on for eleven o'clock.

He took a shower, and then settled on the window seat in the smaller of the two bedrooms. *You know I'm happy*, Dawn had told him, in the dark, not long ago. *But it's as if I can't . . . There's this* waiting *feeling. Waiting for Dad. A waiting feeling. When's the train coming? When's the train going? I've had it for four years. Like a clenched fist in my stomach. You don't know what that's like.* But he did know. He knew the clenched fist

398

of care; and now, within him, these tight fingers were easing free.

That morning on the open road he had felt it — the limitless talent of the world. And here, under a powerful moon (just one size short of full), the restless ocean pitched and yawed, the slow churn of its facets, each of them vying to get a share of creamy light — the motion magma, the rolling mirror-ball of the sea.

Des tensed and listened: the slammed door, an anarchical yawn, the words *Not best pleased*, spoken with dry deliberation. A minute of thickly carpeted silence, and then the crash of the upended minibar . . .

On the far promontory the lighthouse loyally pulsed. And it reminded Des of something. What? It wasn't a visual memory. No, it was auditory (and the tempo was quite different). That throbbing glow reminded him of the most courageous sound he had ever heard: the (amplified) beating of his unborn daughter's heart.

He humbly took delivery of this memory. The thought of Cilla made it clear: it was him, Desmond Pepperdine, that all this was happening to. Him, and not somebody else. Here he was, in health, among the abnormally alive, and looking out over the talented water.

"Hello? . . . Hello?"

Was it a bad line or a wavering signal or a skewed satellite? All he could hear was a howl. A howl, with a tinny edge to it. This resolved itself, after a splutter, into his wife's trembling voice.

"Des. Oh Des. Words can't . . . I'm . . ."

But she talked on, and by now he was out of bed, and drawing the curtains, and plugging in the kettle for his tea. "I'm happy for you, Dawnie," he muttered, nodding his head with a look of inanity in his eyes. He was fielding all his usual thoughts. So the old supremacist (and emeritus traffic warden), in the wisdom of his last hours, had finally yielded. Four years of ostracism: as Horace himself might put it, this was deemed to suffice. "I'm glad for you, Dawn. And I'm glad for me."

"It'll have to be tonight."

". . . You're not taking Cilla to Diston General."

"Of *course* I'm not. But Des, you see what I'm saying. It has to be tonight. He's fading, Desi. And Mum says Saturday's when they go round with the methadone. On Saturdays they go round *killing* them with the methadone!"

Lionel came into the dining room just as the kitchens were closing.

"Uh, Uncle Li. There's been a development. Dawn's dad's —"

"Too right there's been a development. Gina. Yeah, mate, she's been done. Acid. Jupes Lanes." Now Lionel turned to the menu and attentively ordered the Full Caledonian Breakfast. "But none of you Aberdeen blood pudding," he told the grizzled waiter, who took note. "And none of you uh, none of you fucking Orkney kippers Just the English bit . . . Yeah. Jupes Lanes Broad daylight. Seen what it does — acid?"

Des tried to feel sceptical (how true wa this?). But for twenty years he had been fully conscious resident of Diston Town where calamity made its rounds like a post man. Gina, he thought — with that smil those eyes. He took a mouthful of cold co fee and let it drip back into the cup throug his teeth.

"Makes the face look twisted Stretched . . . A Moroccan-type bloke di it. Yeah. Sped past on a bike in his whi robes. *Here. Have that.* Did it J-cloth styl see. See, Gina's jouncing around in her hal

401

top and tutu. *Cover youself up! Whore!* Oh yeah," said Lionel, nodding. "Bollocks. Knickers! It's *Marlon*. Courtesy of Marlon . . . Can't say I blame him, mind. But Gina. Ah, lovely."

Lionel looked down fondly at the shield-like plate and all it contained: farm-fresh poached eggs, Grampian sausages, cured bacon rashers, heirloom tomatoes, Strathclyde field mushrooms, rough-hewn hash browns, artisanal baked beans, and Highland fried bread.

Strenuously chewing, Lionel continued, "But he's gone and shot hisself in the foot, hasn't he. Marlon's gone and killed the goose that laid the golden . . . Because I won't be going near her now, will I," he said, assembling his next mouthful, "with her clock in that state."

"Uh, Uncle Li. Dawn's dad's —"

"Oh yeah. You was saying."

"Dawn's dad's —"

"That's right, Des. You were saying. Speak you mind, Des, speak you mind."

Lionel sauntered out with him to have a smoke while they waited for the car. He had his phone in his palm and was monitoring its screen. He said,

"Ah. She's having second thoughts. Me

DILF's having second thoughts. Look at that. She's taking her two lads to they fencing lesson. Imagine having *her* for a mum. And not some old fuckbag like . . . The first time, Des, the first time she comes up and she goes, *You not the Devil.*" He took the cigar out of his mouth and examined its tip. "*The Devil's a gentleman. Can you remember you room number, you fucking moron?*"

Beyond, under a mixed sky, the sea still basked and sprawled, with smiling foam. Yet the clouds were regretfully rearranging themselves and now held queries of grey.

"Last night she goes, *Boys like you. They never change because they never learn. They never learn . . .*" He flexed his left hand. "You know, Des, sometimes I scare me own self. My own self," he said, stepping back with a bow as the car made its circle in the drive.

Desmond travelled. To Wick, to Inverness, to Stansted, to Liverpool Street, to Diston North. Along the way, in a Christian spirit, he endeavoured to improve his opinion of Horace Sheringham (this was not a success). Later, as he dozed on the second flight, he kept replaying it in his mind: the ancient waiter refilling the water glasses, the two flies playing leapfrog on the window pane, the sunderings of the surf, Lionel's jaws freezing in mid mouthful and then his categorical scowl . . .

Sorry, Uncle Li, but what else can I do? It's her last chance. This whole thing's been killing her for years.

Lionel turned away. He bared his teeth; and his eyes seemed to recalibrate.

Hang on, he said. *Hang on. You go back. Dawn goes to her dad.*

Yeah. She'll spend the night with her mum whatever happens.

So it'll be you and Cilla. Okay. That'll work . . . Here. Call the people. They'll change you flight. Here.

. . . Well. Say a last goodbye to Grace for me.

No, fair enough. Old Horace is still with us. And what's a dead body? It's nothing. It's rubbish. And we don't want Dawn to suffer. Heaven forbid. No, Des. You place is at home. You place is with you daughter in the Tower.

The plane roused him. They were skimming earthward through the cover, and the plane roughly shook him awake. Its wings creaked and see-sawed. Its portholes were dense clots of white. And he had never experienced this — the muscular violence that lies coiled in clouds.

■ ■ ■ ■

At the clinic the doctor had warned him that his UVI, on its way out, would fleetingly refervesce. And Des's skeleton was making itself known to him all over again as he came up from the underworld and into the streets of Diston: the chassis of his shoulders, his pelvic saddle. The effect was not unpleasant — his bones glowed like wire filaments. And this time round you knew that it would quickly pass, it would pass, the final flurry, the swansong of the city fox.

Going a block or two out of his way, he walked by Gran's old flat — Gran's granny flat on the basement floor. Two empty milk bottles gleamed filmily on the doorstep . . . *Put the kettle on, love. Let's pit our wits against the Cryptic.* And she'd light another Silk Cut, to fuel her concentration . . . An ice-cream van gadded by. Des walked on. Diston air — a mist of grit, the texture of gauze, with motes, blind spots, puckerings, like vaccination scars . . .

Up in Avalon Tower the front door was open and he could hear the self-sufficient altos of feminine animation, like a distant radio play. The passage leading to the kitchen seemed novel to him, seemed freshly invented, and a modest success, impressive in its order and lucidity. Now the cat collapsed invitingly at his feet . . . Prunella appeared. The baby was handed over to him — a clean packet containing something even cleaner. He kissed Cilla glancingly and lowered her to the floor. And it wasn't long before the two women were hurrying purposefully away.

"I expressed about a gallon," said Dawn when they had a quick moment. "Guard her with your life."

"I will."

They exchanged three or four of their usual endearments and vows.

He returned to the kitchen and found Cilla trying to crawl towards the dogs. Des had almost forgotten about the dogs. They were out there sleeping through the heat of late afternoon, in the spoons position; Jek had a forepaw up, lightly steadying Jak.

"I met a man," said Des, "called Mr. Man." Cilla thought this was very funny. "He's an undertaker. He undertakes to take people under." She thought this was very funny too. "What's your name, mister? This mister's Mr. Man." So then they had a read of what was still her favourite book: *Mr. Man.*

After putting the kettle on, Des hoisted

the corpulent rubbish bag out of the tank (which, these days, was ajar) — and stared at it. Normally he would wait till Cilla was asleep and then fly down to the dustbin bay. Dawn, when in sole charge, did this too: Cilla never minded being alone. But Des knew at once and for a certainty that he couldn't leave her up here with the dogs. The latch was down, the sliding door was quite secure; but he could never leave her up here with the dogs.

"Let's make a shopping trip out of it. Fancy going to the shops?"

Besides, he wanted to buy something: a surgical mask. He was once again infectious, and he was continually aware of it: when he held the baby he found he was always breathing over his shoulder. So out they went into Town, Cilla strapped into her pushchair, with both hands raised and active, greeting every face with her unqualified smile. Passers-by paused and wondered — wondered what they had done to earn such approval, such delight . . .

They tried three chemists, the household-goods emporium, and, hopelessly, a hardware store. Typical, that. You saw surgical masks, here and there, all over the great world city, but never in Diston. Diston showed no interest in prophylaxis, in preventive care. Diston, with its gravid primary-schoolers and toothless hoodies, its wheezing twenty-year-olds, arthritic thirty-year-olds, crippled forty-year-olds, demented fifty-year-olds, and non-existent sixty-year-olds.

All they bought in the end was a large packet of ibuprofen and a tin of peach mush for Cilla's tea.

As he warmed her milk on the ring, Des flapped his way through the *Evening Standard* and came across a noticeably cordial item in the diary about "Threnody" and her new book of verse. *These are the poems about my time with Lionel*, she said. *So the theme is grief. But loss and heartbreak are the very mainsprings of deep emotion. Look at Bishop King and Lord Tennyson. Poetry thrives on such —*

The dogs were stirring. They awoke as one being; random limbs disentangled and strained outward; with a trembling yawn Jak rolled over; his tongue uncoiled as if from a spindle and writhed probingly over his brother's snout . . . Des stepped forward and gave the lace curtain a tug. He looked round. Installed in her highchair, Cilla was rubbing her eyes with her knuckles — yes, the little creature, this limited operation, this small concern, after sampling its bottle, was breaking up, was closing down, as babies will, every few hours. He prepared a fortress of cushions on the couch, and within seconds she was asleep.

With reluctance Des twitched the curtain and took another look through the glass door. Jek stood in an expectant crouch as Jak climbed up on him with his back legs hideously taut and twanging.

"*Fuckoff!*" said Jak.

"*Fuckoff!*" said Jek.

At six-thirty Lionel made the first of his two calls.

"I've got her down. Grace. She's in bungalow number uh, forty-four aitch, Inver St. Mary's. I gave the vicar a few bob and we did it on the quiet. Packed her down this afternoon."

"Well, rest in peace, Uncle Li."

". . . I'm in the car. Trying to get back. Don't want to stay up here. I'll get depressed. Wick's shut."

"Yeah?"

"Yeah. A mist come in off the sea. Visibility reduced to nil. Reckon we'll drive to Inverness. Hundred and fifty miles. Good road though. Looking into an air taxi. You all right, boy?"

"Yeah, Uncle Li. Dawn rang. Says it's going to be a long night."

"Fed the dogs yet?"

"Just about to, Uncle Li."

"Don't forget they Tabasco. All of it."

He laid out the dripping steaks on two tin dishes. And he readied the chilli-pepper sauce — *matured for several years in oak barrels to develop its unique aroma and flavour. A few drops will give your . . .* He took a driblet on his tongue, and could feel the fire and bite of it; but the aftertaste seemed pharmaceutical — evidence, he suspected, of microbial lingering in his craw. It took nearly five minutes, voiding the whole bottle on the bleeding meat. What were the dogs doing here anyway? Oh yeah. Lionel was taking them to Surrey when he got the call. Hare coursing. Plausible, Des supposed: hare coursing was violent and illegal, and you could gamble on it . . . Michael Gabriel — the Family Butcher. If Lionel got back tonight, would he come for Jak and Jek?

They were lying side by side with their chins on their paws when Des edged out and placed the bowls by the litter tray.

Cilla awoke much refreshed. He washed her, changed her, and then served her puréed vegetables, with many delicate carving gestures round the mouth with the soft plastic spoon . . . *She takes a little bit more milk in her coffee than you do, doesn't she Des?* Dawn had said again at the end of the first month, when Cilla's colour seemed to stabilise. He placed his forearm alongside the baby's, and agreed. *Well, you're the milkmaid, Dawnie,* he said. With your curds and whey . . .

Father and daughter now gorged themselves on *Mr. Man,* plus *Mr. Messy, Mr. Topsy-Turvy, Mr. Grumpy, Mr. Mean, Mr. Wrong,* plus *Little Miss Giggles, Little Miss Star, Little Miss Lucky, Little Miss Curious, Little Miss Magic,* until, almost with disgust, Cilla pushed *Little Miss Late* aside. Suddenly she laughed and pointed with a bent finger.

"Dah," she said. "Doh."

Through the hanging lace you could clearly see their wedgelike outlines, backlit by the brimming moon. He went and with impatient abruptness yanked back the curtain and shaped himself. The dogs didn't blink. Tensely static, but forward-impending, they no longer looked like a pair or a couple — they looked like a team. And in their spiked collars almost laughably malign: two hothouse orchids cultured in hell. And (Christ) the face of a pitbull, a

411

trap of jaws with two eyes tacked on to it, and then the skinhead ears. Just below knee height, four black nostrils with pink innards were steaming up the glass.

Des put Cilla in her wheelie, and re-approached the sliding door. He made shooing gestures with his arms. Nothing happened. They weren't seeing him, he realised; they were seeing past him or through him, they were seeing the baby. He drew the curtain and left the room, and immediately returned with two pillow slips. He located a box of drawing pins and in a couple of minutes he rigged up a second screen over the lower half of the glass panel. While he did this, his daughter made sounds, undemonstratively, but sounds evoking disappointment (he thought) and perhaps even pity. He stepped back: the silhouettes were no longer visible through the layers of white cloth.

"There," said Des soothingly as he reached for the child. "There."

The phone sounded at ten-fifteen.

"Nah, I'm still up here. Fogged up here. It's all fogged up up here."

There now came the foghorn's authenticating groan or yawn. Des heard feminine laughter and, in the background, the grace notes of the floppy-fingered pianist (who must have been doing the slow ones) as he finished "Yesterday" and started "She's Leaving Home." He imagined the heartbeat of the encaged lighthouse.

"So no flights?"

"Yeah . . . That's okay. Patch it up with me DILF. Silly bitch. Get no armament from her. Nice meal. We haggle am. Lamb. Bolla wino two. Silly bitch. Want a word?"

An educated but foolishly and formidably drunken voice was saying,

"Hello. My name's Maud. I'm Lionel's DILF. Who are you then? One of his boyos?"

Des thought the foghorn was sounding again but it was just Lionel's yawn or groan, topped up by two heaving inhalations.

"Guiss it . . . Here, Des, do I sound a bit pissed?"

"Yeah. You do a bit. Not like you, Uncle Li."

". . . Well it isn't every day you park you mum. This is a wake, Des. Mm. Down she went. With all her sins. Way of all flesh . . . You still here, woman?" There was something like a scuffle, then with his voice again slewing (and again becoming equivocal, like Gran with her doubletalk), Lionel said, "Shut you mouth, you stewpy cow. Shunts another shiner, see. Cheers after the match and set. Goff with yer. So . . ." There was a crash of tableware, and you could imagine Lionel rearing up from his seat. A pause — the ambient noise fading. "So, Des. They had they dinner then?"

"Yeah, a while ago."

"Yeah, well they'll calm down in a bit. Nigh-night." A silence — just the seething of the sea. "Seen the moon? Mind that door now. Seen the moon? Nigh-night."

It was already late, far too late, and a manifest truth was asserting itself: it was going to be desperately hot. With Lionel's room sealed off, all they had was the eight-inch gap above Desmond's bed and the electric fan. He went down the passage, turned the three locks, and wagged the door back and forth for ten minutes. But the thermals of the Tower were dense and heavy, the used breath layered and thickened up over the thirty-two floors.

"Are you all right, my darling? Who's that mister? Why, it's Mr. Man!"

He checked the balcony door and raised a pinched hand to the curtain. And it struck him like an aesthetic evil — because the dogs were just as they were, like moulds of metal fixed to the floor. But now they tipped up their heads and moved back beyond the bowls and the tray and seemed to settle. On impulse he freed the latch and slid back the glass panel — just a finger's breadth. In one scurrying propulsive instant Jak and Jek were there with their snouts in the crack; and when he gave the door a retaliatory shove they dug in deeper, as if ready to have their noses pulped or sheared clean off . . .

"Silly doggies," he said, stepping back. "I think, I think the doggies want to cool down."

Quickly and carefully he filled a tall glass with cold water. He watched the door give an inch, give an inch and a half. One long stride and the jerked splash gave him the moment he needed. He secured the latch and tested it with all his strength.

"There. Good*night*, doggies," he said. "And now, miss. Now you go down."

He changed Cilla for the last time. "You can sleep just like that." She lay in her basket on the trestle table — the plump brown figure in the plump white loincloth. He rinsed her drinking cup. "A little *agua* for you." He positioned the fan (it would sweep grandly past her every five seconds) and dimmed the lights. "Now you're going to dreamland."

It was nearly eleven and she wouldn't go

down, she couldn't quite go down. She continued to smile, continued to gaze up at him with tender eyes — but all was not right in her baby cosmos, and she couldn't quite go down.

"Mummy's coming back tomorrow. Your lovely mummy'll be here in the morning."

A subliminal memory told him that what sent small beings to sleep was the discreet assurance that larger beings were still awake (the complacent murmur of the grown-ups, even that rhombus of carlight as it went across the ceiling and slid down the wall). So, humming, he tidied up: he processed the dinner things, and wiped all the surfaces, and stacked the newspapers in the rubbish bag and dropped it in the tank.

"I'll be asleep before you are! If you're not careful . . ."

He kept expecting her eyes to tire and dip, but they declared their helpless roundness. When he smoothed her forehead he found that his fingertips were moist with sweat. He applied a dampened cloth to her face, and slipped the thermometer into the crease of her armpit: ninety-nine point two. As midnight neared, and as he felt his own bearings start to loosen, he capitulated. The infant's opiate — the syrupy suspension of the purple paracetamol. She took the spoonful willingly. In less than a minute her head rolled back, and she was gone.

And Des looked away with burning eyes. He felt that she had been wronged, somehow, had been gravely wronged. At the same time, as he presided over Cilla's sudden sleep, he was presented with a tabulation of everything he loved in her. This had to be assimilated, all in an instant, and he did the work of it with burning eyes.

Friday was over. Des locked up. Seven times he tried the balcony door. He didn't look out. He tried the balcony door for the eighth and last time.

Stripping to his undershorts, he sought out the bare sheet. From the kitchen, her cotside lamp cast a frilly yellow semicircle on Desmond's wooden floor; and his daughter lay almost within his line of sight. His tiredness, he realised, had a smell: the thick-air smell of ozone and the warmed sea. No, not this wave, that one, yes, that one — that one will carry me ashore.

Saturday

In the dead of night he lay dreaming.

He lay dreaming, not of a ladder that rose up to heaven . . . He lay dreaming of a chamber of varnished pine and white marble

417

and boiling mist where he sat with his mother's brother and six or seven ginger dogs and piebald foxes, some of which were stuffed (by the taxidermist, Mr. Man). He and his uncle were engaged in invisible and mysterious exertions, but there was nothing to breathe and nothing to breathe it with. So he awoke.

. . . "Ah. Here we are," he said, and moistened his tongue. His mouth was working (he could hear it click and scrape), and yet his eyes were gummed shut. He raised a reluctant hand and freed his dried lids. The air around him was as black as liquorice.

Someone or something had closed his bedroom door.

Through various thicknesses a muffled but complex sound now chose to present itself for his consideration. A solid thud, followed by two further and fainter impacts, the crackle of basketry and a pneumatic sigh, then the desperate snorting and scrambling of muscular beasts.

Time now slowed. It would in fact take him precisely 2.05 seconds to get from his bed to his destiny. But it seemed longer than that to Desmond Pepperdine.

0.10 seconds. His legs did it. With one arching bicycle kick he was out and upright on the mat. The plywood door had swelled in the heat, as if its glue had wept and oozed, and precious, priceless milliseconds were lost while he tugged on the handle and tugged again.

0.50 seconds. The kitchen door was also shut. He could clearly — and, it seemed, slowly — hear the snuffling, the rootling, the low growling, the slobbering. An entire centisecond passed by as he tried to identify the strange animal in the passage. Was it a porcupine? No. It was the cat. Between one tug and the other on the sticky handle he had time to feel the unearthly size of the quivering deep-sea wave he would now have to pass through. He stepped into it.

1.45 seconds. He threw on the light and in a voice hugely amplified by the chemicals in his brain he shouted out something — an ancient howl. He stared into the rustling, tinkering neon tubes as the deepsea wave swept by him, and he listened to the click of canine nails on the sanded boards.

2.05 seconds. He looked down. The trestle table lay on its side, the empty basket had tumbled to a halt, four feet away, and now leaned, still swaying, against the leg of a kitchen chair. He fell on his hands and knees and scrabbled about like a beast himself.

The electric fan continued to patrol its space.

There was no blood, and no baby.

Tuesday
Kee you, kee you, kee you. Wicky wicky, wicky wicky. Zhe-zhe diddum eet. View-cha view-cha view-cha. Payee, payee. Tuseetz, tuseetz. Kee you, kee you, kee you. Wicky wicky. Wicky wicky . . .

The two great drapes, the two giant strips of bulging black velvet, remained tightly drawn, but you could hear, outside, the multitudinous chaos — the rasps and rico-chets — of enraptured birdsong. In the expanse of the four-poster a contorted figure gasped and stretched.

"Mao!" it seemed to shout. "*Mao! . . .* Jesus Christ. *MAO!*"

Mal MacManaman opened the door a crack. "Yes, boss."

"Go and tell them fucking birds to shut they — *don't shine that bleeding light in me eyes!*"

Mal's shape withdrew for a moment, and then more vaguely reappeared. "You called, boss."

"Mal. Mal, mate. I'm dying."

". . . Should I get Sir Anthony, boss? Put you back on the oxygen. And the dialysis."

"I'll give you fucking dialysis . . . Oh, Mal, heal me, mate. Heal me."

". . . What can I say, boss? All the cures are old wives' tales. I was looking online. The Romans tried owls' eggs. And fried canary."

"Fried canary?"

"In Iceland they eat rotten shark. Keep a rotten shark on the balcony."

"Where'm I going to find a fucking rotten shark? See this pillow? Go on — put me out of me misery. I won't struggle."

"Sorry, boss, but what you need's a drink. You're in withdrawal. It's your only hope, boss. Hair of the dog."

". . . Say that one more time and I'm sacking yer. *Hair of the dog.* Say that one more time and you sacked."

"Some morphine, boss."

"Yeah. Go on then. Just a drop. Like a pub treble . . . You know, Mal, I reckon she poisoned me. That sort up in Scotland — she poisoned me . . . No. No. Bollocks. This is Lionel Asbo, this is. This is down to Lionel Asbo. I don't need a *doc*. I need a priest! A uh, a fucking *exorcist* is what I need . . . Mal. Is he coming?"

"Yeah, boss. He's coming."

Wednesday

His fellow passengers saw nothing unusual about the young man on the train. He was six foot one, and of mixed race; he wore black chinos and a white shirt; he wasn't reading, he wasn't looking out of the window at the streaming, bending, leaning English countryside. His face was without expression. But there was apparently nothing unusual about him.

The shrunken old lady seated at his side was methodically reading the *Sun*. Gunman Nicked by Grappling Grandad. I Murdered Down's Baby — Mum. Duane Went Berserk When Wife Cried "Harder, Chris!" Dear Daphne. I had fling with banker but he lost interest. Trapped in a man's body. Hubby's six-year cybersex with my best pal. *Dear Daphne, I'm having an affair with an older woman. She's a lady of some sophistication, and makes a refreshing change from the . . .*

Wheezing, slowing, the three-carriage train felt its way into the station called Short Crendon. A recorded voice told our young traveller to collect all his belongings and to mind the gap. He got out and walked through the suspended village.

At the house he crossed the deserted picket line, pressed the buzzer, and announced himself. He was told to wait. After three or four minutes, the tuxedoed butler and a plainclothes security man were making their way down the drive. The electrified gates opened up and let him in.

"Mr. Asbo is slightly indisposed," said Carmody as they passed the Bentley "Aurora" and the Venganza and approached the front door. "May I offer you some sustenance, sir, while you wait? The other visitors are enjoying a selection of beverages and a cold collation. Mr. Asbo does know you're here."

Three knights in armour gazed out mournfully at the round table, at the high-winged saddles of the chairs, at the steel chandelier, many-bladed, like a medieval propeller. The dining hall contained eight people, including Desmond Pepperdine.

"I'm owed," "Threnody" was saying. She replenished her glass of white wine. "I'm due. It's only right. I'm owed."

"But surely this won't affect sales," enthused Jack Firth-Heatherington. "To the contrary, I'd have thought . . . I suppose it's too late to relaunch it with a different title?"

"As it is I'll be a laughing stock, won't I." She had a slim paperback in front of her, face down. Two other volumes were on display, standing upright, as on a table in a bookstore: *My Love for Azwat* and *Reaching Out to Fernando*. By "Threnody." She said, "Danube'll be *pissing* herself."

Seeking confirmation, she turned to the youngish man on her left. His colouring was Levantine: this was presumably Raoul. He removed his toothpick and said (pronouncing the *i*-sound as an *ee*),

"*Pissing* herself."

"They all will. I'll be a laughing stock. A mere figure of fun. So I'm due, Jack. Come on. I'm owed."

"Threnody," Raoul, Jack Firth-Heatherington — and who else?

Lord Barcleigh (the famous face, the famous girth) sat in an armchair with a tray on his lap. Facing him was another learned-looking gentleman, in an open shirt (with white cravat). They talked in regretful whispers. Sebastian Drinker, with solemn nods, was writing on a yellow pad.

At the other end of the room, in profile with folded arms, stood a woman in a white veil. She was looking out through the far window.

"I'm owed. I'm due."

Time passed.

"I'm due."

". . . Mr. Asbo will see you now, sir."

■ ■ ■ ■

Carmody gracefully gave way to Mal Mac-Manaman, who was waiting in the hall.

"Desmond," he said, and offered his hand.

At a meditative pace they started up the stairs.

"Your uncle," he said, "your uncle had a bad reaction to the death of his mother. Up in Scotland there. Funny, isn't it? He didn't seem that attached, I thought. But with these things you never know. Anyway, he went and did himself a bit of an injury. To his brain. That's what they reckon. And then there's all this other trouble. I wonder if you'll find him changed. Here." He reached out and dimmed the light. "Go on in. You're expected."

The room was the colour of beetroot, thickly dark but with a shade of mauve in it.

"Wait. Wait till you eyes adapt . . ."

Des could see a slowly glowing throb in the middle distance. It made his body remember the lighthouse on the northern shore; it made his body remember the sound of his daughter's heart.

"See anything yet? Come on, Des. Come

and sit by here."

He felt his way past heavy furnishings, then crossed a spongy expanse of rugs or hides. In the manner of an usherette in an ancient picture house, Lionel used his cigar to illuminate the bedside chair.

". . . I can't eat. Can't drink. Christ, I can't even *smoke*. Tastes horrible. But it's something to do. I can cough. I can retch. I can *scratch*. There's a word for it, Des. Hang on. *Formication*. You feel you flesh is covered in ants." He took a long drag, and the coal swelled and grinned like an evil eye.

"Who let the dogs in?"

"Oh. First things first, is it." Lionel tried and failed to shoulder himself higher on the pillows. He sank back. "*Un.*" In a tranced voice, with a long lull at every period, he said, "I was under the doctors in Scotland. Little bit the worse for wear, Des. On the Monday I come back and shut meself up in here. I could've made a phone call. But I didn't. Decided to wait for Tuesday and me *Diston Gazette*. Superstitious if you like. I went through it with a pencil torch to spare me eyes. And it was just the usual stuff. Knifings and that. Blindings. No report, no report of the uh, the very sad tragedy at Avalon Tower. And you won't believe this, Des, but you know what I thought? I thought, I thought, Maybe I'll live."

"Who let the dogs in?"

"All right," said Lionel, and raised a palm. "Some might say I uh, overreacted. Went a bit over the top. Pass us that tin, Des. And don't come it all innocent with me."

The gold Zippo flared but cast no light.

"So, Des, satisfy me curiosity. Uh, what went wrong?"

He was like a dog himself — down on all fours, the whirring limbs, the famished whimpers. He was under the table, under the couch, behind the basket, beyond the chair. There was no blood, no blood, and no baby. There was no baby.

With jagged effort and difficulty he got himself upright. He strode towards the balcony, he closed and locked the sliding door. The dogs were swiftly circling. And wait. He would now have to rip Jak apart, rip Jek apart — his hands in the wet jaws, forcing, splitting. He turned to face the unfathomable room.

Then his eyes settled on the burnished cube of the tank. The lid was down. Yesterday the lid was up — and now the lid was down. He went to the thing and threw it wide . . .

Cilla lay on the half-filled rubbish bag, in her nappy, her chest rising and falling . . . He pictured it (and again heard it): Jek's first bound, Jak's first bound, the toppled table, the twirling girl, and the tank snapping shut.

He kissed her eyes until they opened. They opened, and her eyes beamed up at him.

"Well well. Huh. So it come in useful, did it. In the end."

Des stood. He took a few steps forward, a few steps back. He sat, he stood, he sat.

"Easy, Des. Easy, son. Gaa, hear them birds? . . . Okay. Cape Wrath. You know, Des, when I woke up Saturday morning. I wasn't in that suite. No. Just in a normal room. And it looked like about *thirty blokes*'d got pissed in there the night before. Bottles everywhere. All empty. And me poor old DILF. Dear oh dear. With two black eyes and lying in her own dinner. And Jesus Christ, Des, the state of you Uncle Li you wouldn't fucking believe. And I'm standing there. I'm standing there thinking about you kitchen floor. And I did *not* feel too clever. I did *not* feel too clever."

"Who let the dogs in?"

"Not *in*," he said, and swiped a raised finger. "You don't let them *in*. You open the door a crack and the dogs do it theyselves. Acting on they own initiative. Not *in*."

"Who?"

"I was elsewhere, you honour. Up in

Scotland with me DILF."

"Who? Who?"

"Marlon," said Lionel in momentary defeat. "The Floater. But that's a uh, a technicality. *Think*, Des. Did Marlon let the dogs in? Did *I* let the dogs in? No. *You* let the dogs in. You let the dogs in . . . You fucked my mum. And you me *nephew*."

"And? And?"

"Well. We'll have to see, won't we. The fact remains. Des, the fact remains. You can't go round giving you uncle's mum one. Giving you own gran one. No."

"All right."

From his back pocket Des took a white envelope and placed it on the quilt.

"There's a sealed copy of that in the safe at the *Mirror*. There's a sealed copy of that in the vault at the bank. There's a sealed copy of that in the editor's desk at the *Diston Gazette*."

"Go on then. What's it say?"

"What's it say? Everything. Gran and me." And at this point Des actually thought that he need go no further. It was enough: *Gran and me* was enough. Lionel was already flapping a limp hand in the air as Des pressed on. "Gran and Rory Nightingale. Rory and you. The envelope at the *Mirror*'s got something else in it."

"Yeah?"

"Rory's lip ring. With the dried blood. Rory's blood."

Lionel positioned a fresh cigar. Again the gold Zippo with its flabby flame. Now you could see the rusty stubble on his chin and cheeks, the wildly mobile eyes in the crimson mouths of their lids.

"So. If anything happens."

"Yeah yeah yeah."

"Anything at all."

"Yeah yeah yeah yeah . . . Nice effort, Des. Typical. *Finking* youself out of it. Anyway. Truth to tell, son — truth to tell, I'll be going away for a bit as it is."

"What you go and do now?"

"Mm. The DILFs're acting up. Not her in Scotland. Not yet. But once one starts, they all . . . These two Mayfair DILFs. Yeah, it's been building for a while, this has, Des. Be all over the papers in a minute." He coughed, scrapingly, scouringly (you could hear the meshing threads of phlegm in his chest). "See, with them other birds, you can bat them around a bit and then settle out of court. But you DILF — she's got some self-respect. Worse, she's got some fucking *money* . . ."

Des stood to go.

"That's what happens when you got a slag for an old lady. Every time you do the other, you find you full of *rage*. And what's you next port of call? Prison. Well. Prison ain't that bad. You know where you are in prison."

"And why's that?"

"All it is is, Des, when you in prison, you have you peace of mind. Because you not worried about getting arrested. That's all it is."

"That's all it is. Well I'm off."

"Yeah go on then. Before I think better of it. Go on, off with yer."

"I loved you, Uncle Li."

Lionel's right hand paused halfway to his mouth. "Mm. Well. I tried being loved. Thought I'd like it. Didn't do a fucking thing for me . . . Give us a hug then. There there, Desi. There there, son."

Des walked to the door, wiping his eyes with his sleeve.

"Oy. Uh, out of interest. D'you give them they Tabasco?"

"Yeah, I did. What you put in it?"

"Oh you know. This and that. To keep them on they toes. That's what I thought when I saw me *Gazette*. I thought, Des never give them they Tabasco! And them two little fairies went and slept right through it . . . Tell you what, Des. Just for a laugh

I'll give you ten million quid . . . No. I didn't think so. Okay, I'll give you this. You peace of mind. Go on, off with yer. On you cheap return. Go on . . . Bye-bye, son. Fare thee well."

He took the child and strapped her to his chest. They left Avalon Tower. For him it had the solidity of an established fact: there was no longer anything to be afraid of. The air was oyster-grey, as night gave way to morning. Cilla drowsed.

At half past ten, when they returned, the dogs were gone. Quickly he washed her and changed her and gave her a warmed bottle, and they went out again. He had to have her on his chest and that seemed to mean that they had to go out again. Oh yes. There was also the irrelevant — the purely procedural — business of finding someone to come and change the locks.

Des knew that it would be very difficult to include the recent event in the world of things that existed. He kept trying; but he couldn't fit it in. Later that day he took Cilla for a rendez- vous with her mother in the staff car park at Diston General (Horace was still up there in death row on the seventh floor), and on the way he kept trying to fit it in.

She's all flopsy. Oh, she's all sleepy!

Yeah, *he said*. She stayed up too late. *And what kept her awake, he now realised, was her sense of the wrongness of the dogs*. She had a bad night. She had a bad dream.

All this existed: the variegated clutch of dressing-gowned smokers by the back entrance, the man crouched on the blue milk crate eating a bar of dark chocolate, the white vans, the coils of Dawn's golden hair, the tawny tail of that hurrying cloud. Des was trying to make room in all this for the recent event, trying to make room in it for the baby's bad dream. It would be very hard to do.

"He went and had another drink in the morning," Mal MacManaman was saying as they approached the stairs. "Rang down for a bottle of Bénédictine. That's what did for him, they reckon. He'd just finished it when he had his seizure in the car. His skin turned blue. They reckon he was an hour from death when they got him to Tongue. His brain was closing down. He was on eight breaths a minute. So they've given him an oxygen mask and a saline flush. And the dialysis for his kidneys. How'd you find him? You think he's changed?"

Des was full of love for Mal MacManaman. But he just smiled and shook his head.

"The bar bill at Rob Dunn Lodge —" said

Mal, round-eyed and slowly nodding, "they waived it. No one could believe it was true . . . You all right, family all right? Family all right? That's the main thing."

"Thanks. Thanks. Mal, I'm so hungry."

"Well then. Now you got to go back in there."

And with an inclination of his shoulders Mal MacManaman withdrew.

But something was finished, people were leaving, Lord Barcleigh and his learned friend were leaving, Sebastian Drinker was leaving, Jack Firth-Heatherington was leaving, and Raoul, too, was cruising from the room with a curved cellphone pressed to his jaw. Only the two women remained — the woman in the black-and-yellow business suit, the woman in the white veil. Des (who would soon be leaving) took a plate from the stack on the sideboard and began to fill it with green salad, tomato salad, ham, cheese, bread.

"When he scragged them MILFs," "Threnody" was saying into space, "he went and fucked my book. See?"

Des saw: her book was called *Gentle Giant: The Lionel Sonnets*. He saw also that the veiled woman had the darkly carbonated eyes of Gina Drago.

"Gentle giant? Gentle giant, my *arse*. I've got to slag him off now, haven't I. Got to say, you know, without my influence the shithead's gone back to his old ways . . . What'll *you* do, girl?"

Gina spoke. Des felt his flesh tremble when he heard her changed voice — the slurping lisp of her changed voice.

"I suppose I'll stay."

"Mm. While he's inside you can get your face patched up. You'll have long enough. Megan reckons he'll be *forty* by the time he comes out . . . What're *you* doing here, Wes? Come sniffing around for another couple of quid before he goes down?"

"His name's Desmond," said Gina as she stepped forward. "And he's not like that."

"Gutsing himself before he sneaks away . . . Gentle giant. I — I made him *loved*. And now? Now? Danube'll be *pissing* herself."

Des knew that he had to leave, and quickly too. Gina's veil had the near-transparency of misted glass, and he could make out the lineaments of her recentred face. It made him picture a tan balloon, roughly knotted by blunt male fingers. As in a dream, this image elided into another image — something far more terrible. He looked at the hunk of ham on his plate, with its pendulous lip of moist fat, and got to his feet.

"I'm so sorry, Gina," he said as he kissed the gauzy tightness of her cheek.

And in the hall his raised voice was competing with the echoes as he cried out for Carmody.

. . . A towering honey-coloured carthorse with fringed hooves clopped soundlessly by on the grass verge, a little boy straddling it at an impossible altitude, as if halfway to the clouds. With spry jingles of the bell on her handlebars, a woman sped by in a crimson smock and a witchy black hat. On the scalloped surface of the millstream a green-headed, white-collared mallard led a flotilla of young, the busy ducklings weaving runic patterns in her wake. The air seemed to ripple with infant voices . . . Des assumed that this feeling would one day subside, this riven feeling, with its equal parts of panic and rapture. Not soon, though. The thing was that he considered it a perfectly logical response to being alive. He stopped at a grocer's and bought three rosy apples. These would be eaten in just a little while.

For now he slipped down a lane and found a hedge to hide behind. For a full minute he stood on tiptoe, trying to elongate himself, trying to stay on top of it. But it was taller than he was, the pillar of poison was taller than he was, and up and out it came.

All right, no need to hurry — sit in the square and eat the apples. Take a later train. Dawn and Cilla were far away. Not long after midnight on Tuesday morning, Horace Sheringham gave his last groan, and they were down there in Cornwall laying him to rest in the family plot at his birthplace on Lizard Point — so there was plenty of time.

The image that had lifted Des from his chair in the dining hall at "Wormwood Scrubs" was just an image, but it was an image of something real, something that existed or had once existed: a lunge pole, with the pink nudity of a plastic doll skewered on its pointed end . . .

Two butterflies whipped past, doubled back, hovered for several seconds as if to check, then whipped away again. And an ancient Labrador, with a glossy copper coat and three different limps (and a patient young mistress in white bobby socks), also assessed the young man on the bench, smiling wisely with liquid eyes.

. . . He awoke from a near-dreamless sleep to find himself already well within the great world city. His train moved with due caution, past white cabins of electric circuitry, past warehouses pitted with glassless windows, past screeds of uniformly corpulent and cryptic graffiti. He stayed on board till the cleaning crew had come and gone. New travellers were taking their seats as he walked down the platform through ladders of evening light.

Thursday
"We're home!"

She had her new keys in one hand and the shaft of the portable rocker in the other — where Cilla sat, curved in sleep. Dawn listened. From the direction of the master bedroom came a mechanical snivel, nagging, grinding. She opened the door: Des was within, innocently shirtless and down on his knees with a power sander. He looked up.

"Don't bring her in here, Dawnie! Put her in the passage!" He flicked a switch. "The dust."

". . . What's all this then?"

"It's our room now. He isn't coming back. I went up there yesterday."

"You didn't tell me."

"Yeah, I sorted it out with him. He isn't coming back."

Lionel's bed was stripped; in the corner there was a gathered heap of sweatsuits and trainers — a buckled can of Cobra, a steel leash, a few greying copies of the *Morning Lark*. Still on his knees, Des said,

"Well *you* don't look like someone who's just been to a funeral."

She stepped lightly forward to the wide-open window; she looked out, and for a moment a shrill breeze lifted her hair from her shoulders. Smiling open-mouthed, she put her hands on the sill and crooked her right leg behind her left, shin against calf. He said,

"More like a wedding. Or a christening . . . I'm sorry he's gone, Dawnie. Horace, he was all right. He was a great man in his way."

"Come on, Des. Don't take the piss."

"I'm not. He relented. That isn't easy. He did relent. Because if he hadn't . . ."

Because if he hadn't, Dawnie, if he hadn't, my love, (such was the depth, and pliancy, of the premeditation) then it would've been you, and not me, who was here on Friday night, when someone let the dogs in . . . *Who* let the dogs in? Was it Marlon Welkway, was it Lionel Asbo, was it Desmond Pepperdine?

"That's not easy," he said. "To relent.

That's hard to do."

"Yes it is . . . You know, I'm sad at the minute, but I'll be happy now. Just wait and see. And how are you my darling?"

"Uh, still fluey. Bit better. Not sure."

"Mm, you've lost a couple, but you look good, Des. You haven't got a build. You've got a tone. You look fit. How was your Uncle Lionel?"

"Same old Uncle Li. Mean Mr. Mustard."

"Did you pick up your bathers?"

"My . . . ? No. No, I didn't pick up my bathers. He's going away, Dawnie."

"Is he? What's he gone and done now?"

"Tell you later. He isn't coming back."

"Huh. So no more Lionel. No more Dad. They're the ones you and I . . . Lionel, Horace. And your gran in a way I suppose. Grace. They're the ones we couldn't help having feeling for." Her chest filled and her eyes freshened. "Well they're gone. And so it's just the three of us."

Des gave no answer. And now Cilla announced that she was awake, awake and of the company. She did this, as always, not with tears but with song. They thought she must be singing in imitation of the birds — the birds you could still sometimes hear, up on the thirty-third floor, so high above Diston Town.

Dawn backed into the passage. "We've got to have a second, Desi."

"Got to. No choice."

"Pro bono publico."

"It might be another Cilla."

"It might be another Cilla. Say hello then!"

"Not yet, Dawnie. I need a shower. I'm . . . I'm covered in grit."

Raising her voice as she went down the passage she said, "I'll change her. Wash her in the basin. She loves that."

"Go on then. I put the kettle on. Just about to make some tea."

"Go on then. Ooh, I'd love a cup. I'll be needing one!"

She paused, and he paused too, and she heard him call out,

". . . I'll wait!"

PERMISSIONS ACKNOWLEDGMENTS